This is the Dream

Short Fiction

Owen Thomas

Text copyright © 2021 OTF Literary, Anchorage, Alaska

Author Website: http://OwenThomasLiterary.com

The story "Everything Stops" was previously published in *Modern Short Stories: 18 Short Stories from Fiction Attic Press*, Copyright 2014, Fiction Attic Press.

ISBN: 9781734630343
LCCN: 2021916337

OTF Literary, Anchorage, Alaska.

For George Clooney. No offense.

TABLE OF CONTENTS

Everything Stops

It's a steep climb, this last bit of road.

John winces a little at the metal whine blending the air into a kind of sonic foam. He does not like the engine to work so hard. That's when the problems always seem to happen. Because when you force something – anything – to perform against its nature, that's when the thing – whatever it is – stops performing at all. That's when everything stops and the thing sits down in the middle of the road and refuses to budge another inch. That's when you are sorry you were so foolish as to think that if you just pushed it hard enough, if you were persistent enough, you could change the nature of the thing. That's when you wish you could do it all over again with a little more respect.

School buses were no different than anything else. School buses were made for the flat open roads. Like an ocean liner was made for the open sea. Buses were not made for steep climbs any more than ocean liners were made for scaling waterfalls.

The road straightens.

John flicks a glance up into the mirror. His eyebrows are a dirty white. He needs a haircut. The skin of his forehead is furrowed. It reminds him of an old roadmap, a pencil sketch of interstates and rural byways, faded from too many years on the dashboard taking the sun.

The children sense arrival. There is no way for them to know. They have never been up here. But they know anyway. They fidget and squirm in their seats. There is a shriek halfway back. Mrs. Clark stands and turns and points in the general direction. It is enough to do the trick. For the moment.

She sits back down next to Mr. Evans and pretends to adjust her purse so that her knee slants sideways just enough to press itself against his. Mr. Evans, looking out the window at the thin, metal, snow-trimmed railing whose role in the world is to immunize a six-ton bus from the laws of momentum and gravity, does not move his hand from the seat. Mrs. Clark looks out over the wide yellow hood sucking up the road. She pays no obvious attention to her own hand, a veined leaf floating earthward to cover the back of a gold-banded tortoise.

"How much longer?" It is a plaintive query from the medusoid-headed girl directly behind the driver's seat.

"Do...not...speak...to...the...bus...dri...ver," says Mrs. Clark sternly, her head turned toward the child but her back and limbs perfectly still so as not to disturb the delicate, clandestine arrangement on the seat beside her. "How many times do I have to ask you? Whitney? We're almost there."

"I have to pee," says Whitney.

"We're almost there."

The observatory squats like a marble toad on a prominence connected to the parking lot by a snowy concrete path. John pulls the bus directly adjacent to the path, stops and opens the doors. Cold air floods in as Mrs.

Clark stands and shouts her instructions about coats and mittens and hats and snack bags and about walking single file behind Mr. Evans.

"And be sure to thank Mr. Singer on your way out for such a fun and safe ride up the mountainside."

They file by, one by one, thanking him.

"Thank you, Mr. Singer."

"Thank you, Mr. Singer."

John nods and smiles. Nods and smiles.

When all of them are out, moving up the path like a fat coral snake, Mrs. Clark zips up her coat and looks down at him. The severity in her eyes is like an animal in a small cage.

"I don't appreciate all the looks, John," she says. "The way you appear to be keeping tabs on me and Mr. Evans. Up there in your mirror. It's really none of your business. You don't know everything. You don't know anything."

John shrugs. He drops his arm down beside the seat and grabs his lunch bag. He opens it and looks inside. He reaches his hand in and moves some things around with his finger, as if to remember what he had packed for himself. The last of the bologna in some foil. A couple of carrots from the garden before the winter came. A bit of cheese. Some stale crackers in a Baggie.

"You're in no position to judge us. You're not married. Are you, John."

It was not a question. John shakes his head anyway, still looking into the depths of the paper bag.

"Right. You're free as a bird. You don't know the things that can happen in a marriage."

6

But, of course, John did know the things that can happen in a marriage. He had been married three times. A serial carnage of matrimony and a colossal waste of ceremony, an emotional wreckage stringing the vows together like a sad sort of garland.

He had tried. They had tried. Bless them. Each of them had tried. Until each had frozen from the effort. And then, in turn, they had stopped trying.

And then he had stopped trying, knowing better than to try again.

And now here he was at the end of a lecture about what he did not know about marriage. Of course, Mrs. Clark had no reason to know. He had always been an unattached loner in the shallowness of her memory. Ten years. Eleven. Beginning on the day he had been saved.

Mrs. Clark had played the organ that first day. *I'd stay in the garden with Him / Though the night around me be falling...*

"You're not going to say anything? Just going to sit there? Judging me."

John looks up at her, saying nothing.

"Fine. Let's go. Bring your lunch. I don't want you sitting out here in the cold, wasting gas. We could use another pair of eyes anyway."

She steps down off the bus out into the cold air, turns and looks back up at him.

"Well?" she intones, her teeth the color of the snow.

John stands, puts the keys in his pocket, and follows her up the path just as the tail of the snake is disappearing into the observatory. He looks back occasionally at the bus, just to make sure the lights are off and that he has not forgotten anything. It sits quietly at the curb, a black-footed salamander with the words "Grace Christian Fellowship" stenciled along its dingy yellow body.

* * *

The small arm grows like a time-lapsed weed.

"Is that the eye of God?"

They are seated on the floor, legs crossed, in a clump before a large screen. John, coat on, sits in a folding chair against the wall in the shadows along the back of the room. Mrs. Clark and Mr. Evans, standing guard over the pile of coats and lunch bags only moments ago, have abandoned their posts for places unknown.

John crosses his legs.

"Well, I don't know. That's an interesting question. I suppose it all depends on who you ask, doesn't it? This is called Andromeda. Say it with me."

She is young. Thirty, maybe. Sleek black hair. Draping magenta blouse. And a little thing, too. A hummingbird poking at the flower of light on the screen.

"The Greeks believed that Andromeda was a beautiful princess rescued by her future husband, Perseus, from a terrible sea monster."

There are giggles at the preposterousness of that explanation.

"But to astronomers, Andromeda is a special kind of galaxy called a spiral galaxy. Does everyone know what a galaxy is? Raise your hand if you know what a galaxy is."

The children knock shoulders in the rush to respond. Blades and shoots stretch upward toward the light. The hummingbird pecks at the flower.

"I want you to look closely at these tiny points of light."

She points to another, and another, repeating herself.

"Tiny points of light. Tiny points of light. Tiny points of light. Each one of those tiny points of light, the smallest that you can see, is actually hundreds or thousands of stars just like our sun."

They are shocked.

"Whoa."

"No way."

"Each ... like... each one of those tiny points of life is a thousand suns?"

"Not life. Light. And yes, sometimes hundreds of thousands of suns. The Andromeda galaxy has a trillion suns. That's a thousand billion different stars."

"Whoa."

"No way."

"But how come ... but... but..."

The poor thing is short-circuiting. Her little mind is melting. The rescued princess now seems more plausible. John unzips his coat.

"You see, it's because they are so very, very far away that we cannot see each of those stars individually."

"So...like...how come they're so close together?"

"Oh, they're not so close as they seem. Each one of those tiny points of light is separated from all the other tiny points of light by trillions of miles."

She watches them. Waits for it to sink in. John uncrosses his legs.

"Sometimes things that seem to be right next to each other are actually so far apart that it would take millions of lifetimes to travel the distance."

Silence.

"In fact, these tiny points of light are so far away from you, that it takes over thirty-thousand human generations just for the light to travel that far to reach your eyeballs."

There is a nervous, uncomfortable giggle at the intimacy of that word – eyeballs – as they contemplate an ocular puncture from an arrow of light loosed from a cosmic bow so long ago. The oldest among them is thirteen. One-hundred-fifty-six months.

"When we look at beautiful Andromeda, we are seeing what she looked like over two-and-a-half-million years in the past. When you look up at the stars, boys and girls, you are time traveling."

"Whoa."

"No way."

John felt something in his heart. As though the arrow, after so many years of travel, had missed its mark.

* * *

"God... it's like... it's like time travel!"

Mick Kelly had been a talker. He never seemed to stop. Which had been more than okay by John, who was uncommonly shy for seventeen and was just as happy for Mick to carry both sides of the conversation.

10

It had been an uncomfortable afternoon for John, an unwilling hostage on his parents' August sojourn to the Georgian countryside. The Kellys were school friends of his parents. John had never been out of New Hampshire. He was a sullen child and liked to be left alone. They thought that perhaps it would be good for him to experience another planet.

So Georgia it was.

Mick was John's age, but of another species. He was athletic, for one thing. He carried a football or a softball wherever he went, tossing it from one hand to another as he walked and talked and watched television. John was not athletic. He liked to read books, ironically enough, about other species from other planets.

Mick was as garrulous as John was taciturn.

Mick smiled and laughed easily. John kept his feelings mostly locked away in the stoic tradition of his father's side, trotting them out at gunpoint only every so often to remind others that he was human.

Mick loved everything about music: playing it, writing it, listening to it, feeling it, philosophizing about it. John did not dislike music. He liked to listen to the radio. But he liked it in the same way he liked to watch fence posts or telephone poles zip past the window at even intervals on long drives. It offered something regular. It reminded him of his own heartbeat. That is to say, it was something he took for granted. Mick Kelly did not.

Mick had been so hospitable, it made John uncomfortable. After dinner, as their parents had reached a crescendo of remembrance that only comes with the fourth highball, Mick had taken John to a spare room in one wing of the spacious Kelly home. Mick had made it into something of a music studio with orange soundproofing sponge on the ceiling. There were three different guitars on stands and a drum set in the corner, arranged around a black stool. The walls were lined with shelving that held every circle of vinyl ever pressed.

They spent an hour or more listening to The Beatles and The Stones and Crosby, Stills and Nash. Mick gushed about the revolution inherent in musical expression. "It shatters all human barriers," he said. "It can't help but bring us together."

John mostly just listened and nodded. Between songs he could hear his parents howling. He wanted desperately to leave, but that was not happening anytime soon. He was human enough to know that simply waiting in the car like a dog was not an option.

When they were done listening to music, Mick asked if John wanted to walk down to the lake. What else could he say?

Outside, the day was dying its glorious death, scorching the cumulous underbellies, and agitating the birds into the secreting trees. The air, quite unlike his northern home, was so warm and thick and fragrant, it was like drinking a kind of nectar. He could not remember ever having been so conscious of the act of breathing.

They had walked across the front lawn, the house blazing yellow light behind them, into the darkening sweet gums, sycamores, and magnolias that surrounded the property like great leafy cliffs. As they walked, Mick tossed his football from one hand to another and talked about how what he really wanted to do was to be a songwriter.

"I want to put words to the music all around us," he said. "And I want to put the things people say to music. I want to be a part of the music revolution, John. I want to break down those barriers, you know? I want to give people the words they want to say. The words they need to say. Know what I mean?"

John had made a kind of noise that might have passed as an affirming word of English and nodded.

"Here." Mick tossed him the ball and ran up the path. "I'm goin' long."

John threw the ball clumsily. It ricocheted off an oak and skittered off in the opposite direction. Mick laughed and ran after it, dodging the trees like they were offensive linebackers.

By the time they had reached a clearing large enough to see anything more than canopy, the sky was deepening out of periwinkle into a mottled purplish bruise. The night was swelling with the sound of crickets. Mick lifted his head and sang out some lyrics about the purple dusk of twilight stealing across heart meadows.

"That's Nat King Cole. You like Nat King Cole, John?" Mick didn't wait for an answer, probably because by then he did not expect to get one. "That cat's got a voice like velvet. But he didn't write the words. That's what I want to do. I want to write something like that someday. 'Purple dusk.' That's beautiful, don't you think? I do."

They crossed a glade and then slipped back beneath the trees, John following the sound of Mick's voice, alternately talking and singing to himself, as the dark closed in around them. Just up ahead – there, then there, then over there – fireflies winked on and off. John thought at first that he was seeing stars.

The trail ended abruptly at the shore of a small, still lake. Mick traced the water's edge to a narrow pier with a square dock at the end. Mick was pulling his shirt off as he reached the end. He kicked off his shoes and shed his pants and his underwear and dropped them all on top of the football.

"Come on, Johnnie Boy!"

In he went, like an arrow, disappearing beneath the dark surface with a sound that the crickets seemed to devour right out of the night air until it was gone.

He resurfaced with a splash and a whoop.

"Come on in, John!" he shouted. "Ain't no snakes in here! Turtle or two, maybe. Salamander. Some fish. It'll be alright. Don't you swim?"

John had walked to the end of the pier and sat down, hanging his legs over the water. It was answer enough.

"Alright then," said Mick. "Don't know what you're missing."

He disappeared again into the depths. The moon was low on the horizon, its reflected light from a sun ninety-three-million miles away whispered through the Virginia pines like a breeze, silvering the surface of the water.

After awhile, Mick hoisted himself out of the lake. He stood for a moment at the edge of the pier, towering over John, as if contemplating whether to dive. John's hand, pressed flat against a plank, grew wet in the runoff.

He did not move it. Did not look up. He kept his eyes fixed on the shimmering water. He breathed in and out.

Mick began slicking the water in silver sheets from his naked body. First one leg, then the other. He pulled on his pants and sat down on the dock next to John, panting a little from the exertion. He lay down and slipped a hand beneath his head.

"God almighty," he said. "Look at those stars."

John turned and looked back down at Mick Kelly, half-dressed, dripping wet, his perfect beatific face washed in moonlight with such an expression of rapturous wonder that for the first time since he had arrived, young John

14

Singer had wanted to say something. Had wanted to shout something. Had wanted to scream something.

Had wanted to sing something.

But the words would not come. He felt as if he might explode. All he could do was look on dumbly as Mick raised a wet, gleaming arm and pointed at the sky.

"There's Venus," he said. "You're not even looking. Lie down."

John had lain down and looked up at the sky, following the length of Mick's arm with his eyes, the universe exploding before him.

"Did you know the light you're looking at is, like, millions of years old? All that out there is like an old movie. Takes the light that long to reach us. Ain't that just a trip? God... it's like... it's like time travel! And see that one there? Looks like one star but there's two of them there, and they're millions of miles apart." Mick sighed a kind of delirium. "Don't have to be asleep to dream, John. And this right here?" Mick had swept his arm to encompass the universe that was packed into that moment, swept his beautiful arm like a god. "This is the dream, John. It is to me. And we're wide awake for it so we can always remember. Almost makes your head hurt."

His head did hurt. Everything hurt. His heart hurt. So much so that he wept in silence there on the dock as Mick sang all the songs he could think of about the stars and waxed about the perfection of nature and about how all music was a kind of prayer to that perfection. Mick counted three shooting stars and gasped at every one.

"You ever had a perfect moment, John?"

John was silent, daring not a single breath in the dark, so close to Mick Kelly that someone only three feet away

15

would swear their bodies were touching. The crickets soared. The shoreline rustled. The world was alive.

"This is one of those moments, John Singer. For me it is. It doesn't get any better than this. When you see something this beautiful. Something perfect beyond words. Something so close but so far away that it almost hurts. You never forget it. You'll always have it and you'll never have it again. It'll be with you forever and it's already gone."

* * *

The children are disappointed about the telescope. The young astronomer says it is still too early to see out into space. Too much light, she says.

"You will just have to come back sometime with your parents for one of our night tours."

"You let people come here at night?"

It is little Whitney. Again. For the past three hours her arm has been up far more than it has been down.

"Oh, yes. We have a group coming in tonight to look at all kinds of celestial objects. It looks like it is going to be nice and clear, too."

"Can we stay? Pleaeaeaeaease..."

Whitney contorts her face up into the rejecting countenance of Mrs. Clark, whose lipstick is fresh and burning.

"Whitney?" says Mrs. Clark. "Now what did she just tell you? I know you heard her. You need to come back with your parents if you want to be here at night. Go get your coat and line up. It's time to go."

16

John watches the line growing at the door. Mr. Evans is inspecting the troops. Small groups of people, adults, are arriving in groups of three and four for the next tour. The night tour.

Mr. Evans is zipping up coats. John thinks of the ride back.

"You didn't touch your lunch, John." Mrs. Clark points accusingly to the bag at his feet. "Kind of silly to pack it if you're not going to eat it."

John looks at her. He sees that she is probably considered attractive in her circles. Or that she could be. The skin. The hair. The white teeth. The unsmiling eyes.

But he sees also that she is not lit from within. She has never known beauty. Perfection. If she has, then she has allowed herself to forget it and it has died within her. Or, worse, she has spent a life pushing it away, forsaking it for a self-loathing that devours her daily like a black hole until she is nothing but skin and hair and teeth and unsmiling eyes, until even her God is but a bit of jewelry swinging from a hollow husk in the mirror.

And in the mirror of her unsmiling eyes, he sees tragedy staring back.

"Don't you think you should have warmed up the bus? We're all going to be cold now. John? Speak, John. You look lost."

He blinks.

"I became lost a long time ago, Margaret," he says. She seems to blanch at the sound of John Singer's voice. As though she is hearing its baritone for the very first time. "Now, I am found. Now... Now, everything stops."

"What? What are you..."

He pulls the keys out of his coat pocket and puts them into her hand. He turns, leaving her with his lunch on the floor, and walks back to the white-domed room with the telescope where others are gathering and waiting to take a good look at the past, and to accept it this time, to hear its forbidden music and sing its exultant, heartbroken melodies.

To finally take all its arrows and remember.

Little Green Men

Wyatt Culpepper looked at Preacher Ben. Tears pooled up in Wyatt's quiet eyes.

"Calm down," said Ben, who sounded like he might just be talking to himself about calming down. As a man of God, Preacher Ben was easily excitable. The Devil and all his many tricks and disguises figured prominently in the weekly sermon. Talking to Ben about something important was not unlike talking to a jittery, sleep-deprived bomb-diffuser.

"What do you mean, she's gone?" he asked. "What're you talking about? What do you mean? What do you mean?"

"Bird's gone," said Wyatt. "One minute she's there. Next minute ... " He shook his head slowly, then held out his hands to show Preacher Ben that she wasn't hiding up his sleeves.

"She run off?"

"Looks that way."

"Wyatt, that ain't like Birdie. You check her sister?"

"Of course I checked her sister. Checked everywhere."

"She been..." Preacher Ben paused. Swallowed. Picked his words. "She been extra friendly with anyone? Anyone been coming around the house?"

Wyatt shook his head. He lowered himself down onto the first pew, where he never liked to sit on Sundays because Preacher Ben always seemed to be talking directly to him and Birdie. And that made him uncomfortable, just as feeling everyone's eyes drilling into the back of his head made him uncomfortable. Wyatt liked to sit in the back of the church and observe the congregation from behind, where he could listen and make up his own mind about things.

"You think she's been taken? Someone come by when you were out and... Wyatt, the Devil lives in these woods. You know that."

"I know," said Wyatt, nodding.

Most of the roads in the preacher's life cut through the Devil's front yard.

"Yeah, I know that. But it probably wasn't the Devil." Wyatt rubbed his face with his big hands, wanting to cry. Wanting to pocket the truth Preacher Ben was offering. That was why he had come.

"Wyatt!" Preacher Ben stomped his foot and the sound slapped its way around the tiny wooden church. "How do you know? Just how do you know? You smelt any sulfur near your place? Had any strange dreams?"

Wyatt took his hands off his face. The two stared in silence at each other. The sun was finally up. The stained glass was setting fire to part of the ceiling. Outside, a pickup with something hard and loose in the bed rattled and bounced down the road, probably on the way to the store. Preacher Ben's expression was frozen, contorted into the shape of his question. "Wyatt?"

"Yeah," said Wyatt. "Had me a doozy of one last night. Got me all upset. It's why I come to see you."

20

"What was it?" Preacher whispered. "Tell me."

"I dreamed ... I dreamed I was out looking for Birdie. Like I've been doing every night for a week. Up and down every road on the hillside. Only in the dream I was walking, not driving. Walking like Birdie used to do."

Wyatt stopped. Listening to that past tense echo in his head. Used to. There was no going back to change it. He pushed on.

"Anyway, it was black as pitch. Couldn't see my own hands. All I could see was shadows of things. I was calling her name but it was like the darkness in the air swallowed up all the sound so it wouldn't carry nowhere. I could barely hear myself. But I kept calling anyway."

Wyatt paused again. He wiped his forehead with the palm of his hand. Preacher Ben sat down on the pew next to him. "Wyatt," he whispered.

"I got up to the end of Backstitch Road, near the pond. The moon was out there. Just there. Nowhere else in the entire county. Just that one spot. Just hanging there above the pond. And that's where I seen her. On the road. Didn't have no clothes on. Dragging her apron in the dirt. Rest of them was naked too."

"The rest of them? The rest of them? Who, Wyatt? Who?"

"She was kind of in the middle of the pack. Must have been a dozen or so. They were small. And green. Like vegetable children. Heads come up to around Birdie's shoulders. They had their little green hands on her... on all her parts. Then they all turned around to look at me standing there on the road. All of them except Birdie."

"Wyatt...?"

"They weren't no children, Preacher. They's all men.

21

The moon behind them was so big and bright it burned my skin. I was burning."

"Oooh, Wyatt," said Preacher Ben, slow and soft and terrified like he was seeing the back legs of a poisonous spider slipping down into the collar of Wyatt's shirt. "Oooh, Wyatt."

Wyatt felt like the pew had come unmoored from the floor and was swinging beneath him. This set his head to spinning and he closed his eyes so as not to be sick. Preacher Ben started in about the Devil.

"Wasn't no bad dream, Wyatt. When the Devil's about, living in the world is the dream. Takes God to wake us up from the nightmare of sin and corrupted flesh. Oooh, Wyatt."

All Wyatt could do was bury his face in his hands and mutter to himself.

"Birdie's gone. Birdie's gone. Birdie's gone."

* * *

Birdie came up the lane a step at a time. She slowed near to a full stop. She squinted in the dark, switching the bag of sugar for the umpteenth time from one hand to the other. A red dot was glowing up the hill inside the screened porch. It inflated and then died away. Like a lightning bug taking an enormous breath and then letting it go from its little lightning-bug lungs.

Wyatt was up there smoking one of his home-rolled like he liked to do. He liked to sit out in the dark and listen to the crickets and the hoot owls when the air was heavy and still. When the moon was new and the night was truly dark. He smoked his cigarettes and drank his beer and listened. If it had rained recently, Swallows Creek would be running high. Wyatt had been known to sleep out on the porch, drifting off to the sound of water. But this had been a hot, dry month and the creek was low. You had to listen for it through the crickets.

"Bird?" Wyatt called out.

"It's me, Wyatt," said Birdie, shuffling forward again. She trudged up the hill toward the dark house, pulling herself up on the smell of Wyatt's tobacco like it was a rope or a railing. She opened the screen door to the porch, stepped inside, and let it slap closed.

"You get the sugar?" he asked.

"I got it," she said.

"What are you gonna make, anyway?"

"Don't know. A cake, maybe. Lemon cake."

"That sounds good," he said after thinking about it. "How's Louise?"

Birdie set the bag of sugar into the house by the front door.

"She's okay. Going to Florida next week."

"Florida?" Wyatt took another drag and blew out the smoke. "Why is she going to Florida?"

"Earl's taking her on vacation. For their anniversary. Going to see the kids. Disney World, too."

Wyatt leaned down for the bottle next to the swing. He took a drink and dangled it between his fingers over the floor. He swallowed and took another drag on the cigarette.

"Well, I'll be," he said. "A vayyy-cation."

"Mmm hmm," said Birdie.

"Earl won't last ten minutes at Disney World. That's for damn sure. Glad you don't go in for such nonsense, Bird."

"Mmm hmm." Birdie smudged a rough spot on the floor with the toe of her shoe, like she was trying to smooth it out. Her legs were tired from walking.

"What's wrong, Bird?" asked Wyatt in his knowing tone.

"Nothing's wrong," she said.

"Oh yes, there is too, my beautiful Birdie. Something's wrong. I can hear it in your voice. Can't see your face, but I don't have to. I can hear your voice. Your sad little bird song."

"No. You can't."

"Hell I can't. Thirty-four years? No sound you can make that I don't know what it means."

Birdie looked at him. That rugged face she could never resist. She could not see his eyes from so far away. But she could feel them trying to find her shape in the dark. And he was right. Just like Wyatt was always right. He did know everything there was to know about Birdie Mae Culpepper. Which maybe wasn't that much. But still.

"Come on, Bird. Come have a seat. Tell me."

Wyatt set down the beer and patted the cushion on the seat of the swing that was to be hers. In the daylight, the two cushions on the swing were a worn, dirty grayish color with darker shapes of tulips here and there. Birdie had made the cushions herself, covering old sofa pillows with material from a town dress that she never used and that no longer fit her anyway. The dress had been a bright butter-yellow with deep purple tulips in a pattern of clusters.

"Come on," he said again.

Birdie walked across the screened porch to the swing and sat down next to Wyatt. The swing creaked and the cushion wheezed a little as she sat. Her shoes scraped against the dirty plywood floor. It needed a good sweeping, she thought.

"Tired?" he asked, pushing off so the swing began to move. Wyatt knew what she liked.

"I guess," Birdie nodded.

"Long way to go for some sugar. I could've taken you over there in the morning."

"I like walking," she said. "Gets me out."

"Yes, you do like walking. You sure enough do, Bird. You walk a curious amount for someone named Birdie."

Birdie smiled a little at that and Wyatt, seeing this, gave her a playful little push on the shoulder.

"You always take the truck anyway," she said.

Wyatt stopped the swing.

"Now, we been through all that. I take you wherever you damn well need to go. I will. But I need the truck. I can't have you driving off to see your sister or Louise or your cousin's pig farm or any other damn thing if I might need the truck. And if you were ever to run that truck off the road ... in these hills..."

"I know. I know. I like my walks."

"I know you do." The swinging motion started again. "Now, are you gonna tell me what's on your mind?"

Birdie took a breath, not quite sure how to answer. There were three pops in the distance.

"Winston Groat," she said matter of factly. "No doubt shooting at a bottle on a stump. This time of night."

"Bird." Wyatt patted her on the knee. Birdie sighed.

"I saw a light, Wyatt. I saw a light. I know I did."

"A light? What kind of light? Where?"

"Up. Up in the sky. Between Digger's Peak and Hounds Tooth."

"Mean like a star?"

"Nope. Weren't no star."

"What then?"

Birdie fell into silence. The din of crickets seemed to hush a little and she could hear Swallows Creek up behind the house. Only tonight it did not sound to Birdie like the sound of water flowing so much as the sound of something emptying. Something trickling away. Another three pops.

"Bird."

"Like a ... like a spaceship. I saw a flying saucer, Wyatt. Only I couldn't see the actual saucer because it was inside a bright, bright light."

Wyatt took another drag. He held this one awhile and then blew the smoke out slowly.

"A spaceship."

"Yes."

"Mmm hmm. Between Digger's Peak and Hounds Tooth."

"Yes."

"What time was it?"

"I don't know, Wyatt. Maybe eight o'clock."

"Tonight?"

"No."

"Didn't think so. What day was it?"

"My birthday night. Eighteenth of the month."

"Mmm hmm. So two weeks ago then."

"Yes."

"Bird?"

"What."

"That was the full moon."

"No."

"Yes."

"No. Wyatt. I know the difference between the moon and a flying saucer. The moon was up there too. This was different. This light was kind of ... kind of shimmery glowing more than shining. And it moved real fast. Zig-zaggy like."

"Mmm hmm."

Wyatt snubbed out his cigarette. He pulled a red and black lozenge tin out of his shirt pocket and opened it up on his lap. On the empty lid of the tin he laid out a rolling paper and then laid some broken tobacco leaves on top. He paused to take a drink of his beer, set the bottle down, and then finished rolling the cigarette. He put the tin back into his shirt pocket and in a single smooth motion extracted his blue lighter. He lit the cigarette, pulling air through the broken leaves until the tip glowed.

Birdie waited in silence, listening to the crickets and the draining creek and Winston Groat off in the distance, plugging a stump from a chair on his front porch. She almost stood up to go inside. She had sugar to make a cake.

But she didn't stand up.

"Bird," Wyatt said. "You remember when Buster got loose and got himself hit by Elmer and Becca Flanders on their way down to the store?"

"Yeah," said Birdie, knowing what was coming. "I recall. You were angry with him because he chewed up your shoes."

"And your shoes too. And your hat and every other damn thing in the house. Told you dogs belong outside. You remember?"

"I remember."

"And he got himself hit. Wasn't nobody's fault except Buster's. Am I wrong?"

"You're right, Wyatt," said Birdie.

"You remember how you swore for days after that you'd seen fairy sprites down near Possum Flats out there in the woods, holding hands and dancing in a circle? You remember that?"

"Yes."

"And you remember that for maybe a week after Buster died, all you could talk about was the fairies until at church, I asked Preacher Ben to talk to you and he told you that there was no such thing as fairy sprites? Remember that?"

"Yes."

"And Preacher Ben told you that those kinds of imaginings was the same as inviting the Devil inside your head to play. Then you got to worry about getting the Devil out. And he talked to you about all the things you needed to do to get the Devil out? And so you decided that you'd been mistaken about the fairy sprites?"

Birdie cleared her throat. "Yes."

"And do you remember when your momma passed and you went on and on about waking up in the middle of the night six feet off the ground?"

"Yes, Wyatt. I re..."

"Said you could float? Said you spent the wee hours every night flying through the house?"

"Said I was floating. Not flying."

Wyatt sighed and leaned forward on the swing so that his elbows were on his knees. He took a big pull and let out the smoke, shaking his head. Birdie waited. Wyatt leaned back again.

"Okay," he said. "Floating through the house. Not flying. You remember that?"

"Yes."

"And what happened, Bird? What happened then?"

"Don't remember."

"Oh, don't give me that, Birdie Mae. You do too remember. I may have been born at night, but I wasn't born last night. You do too remember. What happened was we got into a big old hollering fight because of you carrying on about how I was always trying to keep you and your momma apart or some such nonsense and you said she was paying you visits from the hereafter. Teaching you how to float, is what you said. And then I stayed up all night one night just to prove to you that you were not floating through the house. I sat right there and proved it to you. And then you said you must have dreamed it all. You remember now?"

"Yeah. I remember now."

"And you remember when Billy met himself that girl, Carla?"

"Darla."

"Just making sure you remember. Darla's right. And Billy, all of sixteen, came to you and said, 'Momma, I'm in love and I'm moving to Nashville to race cars'? You remember?"

"Of course I do, Wyatt. Our only child and you just let him go."

"Got to become a man sometime, Bird. No sense putting it off."

"Wyatt, we don't know if he's alive or dead. Hasn't said boo for eight years."

"My point is, Bird, that for a month after Billy left, you claimed that the chickens and the pigs up at your cousin's place were talking a kind of language. You walked all the way up there near everyday – four miles if it's a foot – and when you'd finally come home, usually late like tonight, you'd tell me that you and the chickens and the pigs were telling jokes and talking politics."

"Wasn't politics, Wyatt." Birdie snorted a little and swatted at him with the back of her hand.

"No, not politics," said Wyatt, "but some kinda nonsense for sure. And it wasn't 'til I took you up there myself and asked you to translate that you decided that maybe you had just sorta imagined what they were saying. You remember?"

"Yeah. I do."

"Alright then. You want to know what I think?"

"No."

"I know you don't. I know. But I'm going to tell you anyway. Because this is something you need to hear and because I don't want to keep doing this. Okay? I think,

Birdie Mae, that you don't take so well to bad news. I think you're a sensitive sort. And that's a good thing, mostly. It is. But when something in the world happens that you don't like, your mind runs for the hills. You protect your feelings by hiding in a wet pile of nonsense."

"Oh, Wyatt..."

"No, no. Hear me out, Bird. I think your nerves can't take disappointment, see, and they whisper things up to your brain to create all manner of distractions. And then, when enough time passes and you calm down, you come on back to your senses."

"Wyatt..."

"So when you come up here tonight and tell me that two weeks ago on your birthday you saw a flying saucer ..." Wyatt put the cigarette between his lips and grabbed both of Birdie's hands in his own, looking hard into her eyes, "Bird, I know that just isn't true. That dog won't hunt. Okay?"

Birdie did not respond.

"Now... I know... that that night ... you walked up to your sister's house hoping to find a cake and a present or at least a birthday song... and that instead what you got was a big fight about who your momma loved best."

Birdie looked down at her tiny hands in his.

"How do you know that?"

"Because you aren't married to a dummy, Bird. I saw Buddy the next day. He said you two were fighting. He said you were upset. And what I figure is that you were walking home as that big old full moon was rising up between Digger's Peak and Hounds Tooth and you just had one of your reactions to disappointment. Your imagination looked up and found that moon and decided it was a flying saucer.

Because the moon is of this world and a flying saucer isn't. And now here you are, telling me about a light in the sky."

Birdie was silent. She pushed off on the floor with her feet to get the swing moving again, but Wyatt kept it still. He squeezed her hands but she would not look at him out of shame.

"Bird," he said in a more philosophical tone, "bad news is like a bully. Disappointment is like a bully. You've got to start showing the bad news and the disappointment who's boss. You can't keep them from coming round. You can't always keep them from ruining your day. But you also can't let them run you off from your own life. You've got to learn to stand up to disappointment. Even heartbreak. You've got a damned life to live, Bird. You can't be running off to a pretend land with fairy sprites and talking pigs and flying saucers every time your life disappoints you. You've got one life and you've got to live it in the real world. Can't live in a dream. This here's the real world, honey."

He let her sit there, quiet, for a good minute. Then he set the swing to swinging and let go of her hands. He took out his blue lighter and relit his cigarette and slipped the lighter back into his shirt pocket. He tousled her hair and nudged her gently in the ribs with his elbow.

"Flying saucers," he said. Birdie made a sheepish sound. "You know I'm right, don't you, Bird?"

"Yeah," she mumbled. "I suppose you are. Probably just the moon."

"The birthday moon," he said with another elbow prod.

"Yeah. So pretty, shining on Catfish Pond. On the water it looked just like a flying saucer, Wyatt."

Wyatt slowed the swinging enough to send a message.

"But I know it just looked that way," she said. "I know. It was probably just the moon."

"Atta girl. You keep your feet in the real world. Show the disappointment who's boss. Send that mess packing. You don't need flying saucers and little green men."

"You're right, Wyatt."

"Go make us a cake. Go on. I'll be in."

Birdie stood up and walked over to the door and stooped to pick up the bag of sugar she had borrowed from Louise, who was off to Florida to see her kids on an anniversary vacation. Disney World. Take the whole bag, Louise had said. I got another.

"Hey Bird," Wyatt said, staring out into the dark. She turned. "What the hell were you doing all the way over at Catfish Pond? That's all the way on the other side of the hill from Buddy's place. You must have been some kind of upset."

"Oh," Birdie said, moving the sugar over to her other hand. "I was walking right down Ridge Road and I saw your truck turning off onto Backstitch, so I turned off too. I waved but you didn't see me back there in the dark. Thought maybe you got worried and was out looking for me. I waved. Got all the way out to Catfish Pond and I saw your truck at Tandy Miller's place. I went up to knock, figuring I may as well get you to take me the rest of the way home. You all were upstairs with the windows open. You know..." Birdie paused. Swallowed. "Carrying on. So I left, not knowing what to think and I was upset and I stopped at Catfish Pond and that's when I saw the light. That beautiful spaceship inside a light."

The porch was silent. The swing was still. For a moment the crickets stopped and Swallows Creek ran completely dry. Birdie Mae Culpepper listened to the world around her for an echo of her own heartbeat and heard nothing. Absolutely nothing.

"Bird..."

Her eyes blinked once in the dark.

"I know. You're right, Wyatt. It was just the moon. The birthday moon. I know I've got to stand up to disappointment better than I do. Got to send it packing as you say. Got to look out after myself. Being as I only got one life and it isn't some dream we're living."

"Bird, I..."

"And I never needed a bunch of little green men from another world." Birdie opened the door and took a step. "Just one good one. One good man. That would've done me just fine."

Paper Walls

The walls were made of paper. So she could hear everything.

Everything.

The unbidden movie now playing on the screen of her imagination was as disgusting as it was implausible. She lay awake, staring at her white, waxy ceiling, waiting for it to end.

She wanted to pound on the paper-thin wall behind her bed. She wanted them to know that she was just right there on the other side, held hostage by their angrily amorous feelings for each other.

But she did not.

Ruth never did that kind of thing. She had never been that kind of person. She endured problems, even problems like this one, until they simply went away.

Ruth's sister, Desiree, would have pounded once on the wall and if that didn't do the trick, she would have stomped right out into the hallway in her little underthings and kicked the offending neighbor's door in. Desiree solved problems like their mother did.

Ruth, on the other hand, followed her father's lead. Exceedingly nice. Exceedingly polite. Good things came to those who waited.

And waited.

And waited.

The Cordial family was an odd assortment, to be sure. Ruth's mother never stopped talking and looking for fights. She had a list of enemies as long as her arm. She was the tough-as-nails neighbor with an ironic name.

Ruth's father, a machinist who spent his days listening to conversations between bits of metal, rarely said anything. He was beloved by just about everyone, even those who barely knew him. All her parents' friends were really her father's friends who accepted Ruth's mother as part of the package.

And then there was Ruth's sister. Desiree was a police officer for the Chicago Police Department and mostly took what she wanted from life. As a rookie, Desiree had set her sights on the assignments she wanted and always got them so fast that she was frequently the subject of gossip around the department that maybe she was bartering her way to the top.

When Desiree saw the man she wanted, a young architect named Malcomb, she hauled him off a barstool by the short hairs and married him within six months of learning his name.

Desiree wanted a nice home. So now she lives in a nice four-bedroom, wrap-around deck, two-car garage, two-fireplace pad in Cedar Heights with a nice big lawn. Desiree wanted three children, a boy and two girls, and zip, bang, boom, Praise Jesus, now she's got those too. Desiree was just like that.

But Ruth. Quiet Ruth Cordial. No man. No kids. No real friends. Working as a quality inspector at Sweet Toot's Confection Connection. Trying to sleep in a tiny room with paper walls that shook with the force of her neighbor's conflicted affection for his guest soprano. And yet, Ruth was unwilling to clear her throat about it, let alone pound out an objection on the wall.

She would wait.

The man in 10B was new to the building. Ruth had seen him just yesterday out in the yellowing, half-lit hallway. He was pulling a rolling basket of groceries as he searched every pocket for a key to his door.

He was a crumpled cigarette of a man with a sour expression on his face and a balding white pate. He muttered to himself as he walked, like he was holding down two sides of a whispered argument that no one was winning. The air around him smelled of garlic and smoke. A carton of Marlboros poked out the top of the bag. Ruth had surmised almost instantly that she would not like him.

She had said hello anyway. The man did not respond. Didn't even look at her.

Another nut, Ruth had thought, shaking her head.

She was surrounded by nuts.

The grim woman across the hall in 10C, who laughed uproariously at some program every night between nine and ten, and then argued about money with someone on the phone between ten-thirty and eleven, turning the yellowing hallway blue with profanity.

The man in 10E, who wore the same plaid pants and striped shirt every single day, without exception.

The man next to her in 10F, which, whenever he opened his door, smelled like dying fish and cheap cologne.

And now the nut in 10B.

She did not know any of them beyond a passing nod every now and then, as chance would have it. She couldn't say that she had ever actually met any of them. They all stayed in their separate little spaces. Ruth did too.

The night was long and restless. Morning came early without any regard for the quality of Ruth's sleep. She pushed herself up and sat on the edge of her bed, sturdy brown feet on the floor, staring out the window ten stories above a dingy white carpet of week-old snow.

She listened. All was quiet on the other side of the paper wall. It seemed that the cigarette man and his angry lover were sleeping soundly. She wanted to turn up her clock radio as loud as it would go, or throw shoes at the wall, or sing something by Smokey Robinson at the top of her lungs. Just to see how they liked it.

But she didn't.

When the cobwebs had mostly melted away, Ruth forced herself up and made the bed, carefully fluffing the pillows and tightening the bedspread as though to impress eventual guests, even though she knew that there would be no guests. Not tonight. Probably not ever.

Ruth never had guests. Guests were friends. Guests were lovers. Guests were even one-night mistakes from some poorly lit lounge where the bartender yells out 'last call' and you think, oh what the hell and introduce yourself to the man putting on his coat. Ruth had never made her bed as a child, or all the way through high school. Then, once she graduated, got a job at Sweet Toot's and moved into Apartment 10D, she decided that she was going to be the type of person who had friends and lovers and one-night mistakes. She started making her bed in the mornings on the force of the lie that she just might have company of some sort or another.

She had waited. And waited.

Now the lie she had once told herself in the mornings had become purely habit, a kind of vestigial optimism reduced to a set of rote arm movements over the white, sagging rectangle on which she slept. Or tried to sleep.

She showered and dressed and ate some cereal. She put on her coat and gloves, closed the blinds and headed off to work, locking the door behind her and yawning powerfully, as if in a silent scream. The doors lining the hallway to the elevators were all closed. Her fellow tenants were either already gone or sealed inside their compartments like bees in a honeycomb.

It was cold outside. Ruth muttered her little prayer as she crossed the parking lot to her car, a brownish beat-up second-hand Chevy that liked to cause her problems on cold mornings.

"Please lord, let it start. Just let it turn over."

She opened the car door, looking back across the parking lot to her building. It towered above her, a perfectly square box with one-hundred-and-forty-four holes punched in it. Ruth counted up and sideways until she found her little space in the box. She did this every morning just to make sure she had remembered to close the blinds and turn off the light.

She had. But there was a tiny little itch in the back of her mind anyway. Like she had forgotten something.

"Please, please..."

Ruth climbed in and turned the key. It was close. Too close. For a minute she thought for sure that she would have to take the bus, which would have surely made her late for work. But just at the last second the Chevy backfired and, once again, sputtered to life.

She drove to work, steam coming out of her mouth like she was a cup of dark, bitter coffee, listening to the radio. Had it been up to her, she would have preferred that the heater work and that the radio be on the fritz. But it had not been up to her. So few things were.

The box of business cards was still in the passenger seat where she had forgotten them. Sweet Toot's had decided to reward each of its quality inspectors by having two-hundred business cards printed up for each employee and presenting them as a special Thank You at the last annual review. The cards came packed in a small box. The card stock was barely thicker than ordinary paper. Besides that, the size was all wrong; they were much too large and square to fit any regular wallet.

Worst of all, they misspelled her first name: R-u-t-t. All two hundred of them.

Ruth did not know what she was supposed to do with business cards anyway, even if they had been the right size and had spelled her name correctly. She pictured herself handing them out to people on the bus on mornings when her car wouldn't start. The idea of it almost made her laugh. The little box had been rolling around in her front seat for a month.

A raise would have been much better than a box of unusable cards. She should have said something. She should have spoken her mind. Ruth shook her head slowly in a disappointment that was tinged with anger and self-loathing.

At least it was the morning jazz hour when she drove to work. Ruth liked jazz. They were playing John Coltrane. She liked 'The Train,' as her father called him. "My Favorite Things." She turned it up a little and then turned it up again, trying to buoy her mood so that she could meet her job with the full head of steam that she would need to get through her day.

And it would certainly take a full head of steam to get through the day. Sweet Toot's Confection Connection was still in the Push Zone, or sometimes just The Push or The Zone, which is how Sweet Toot's management chose to refer to that stretch of calendar between January 10 and February 10, when the demand for chocolate candy spiked in anticipation of Valentine's Day. Sweet Toot's shipped out more boxes of chocolate candy in The Push than in the next six months of the year combined. To handle the demand, Toot's always added another shift in all departments, including another shift of quality inspectors, and it never really seemed to make any difference. It was always a mad scramble.

So every day in The Zone took a lot of energy. If you didn't have the energy, then you couldn't keep up. If you didn't keep up, you got written up. Get written up three times in a year and you were O-U-T out. Simple as that.

Many people showed up to work at Sweet Toot's, highly caffeinated from lattes or energy drinks, slipping into their baggy whites – the sterile garb all employees were required to wear inside the production room – nervous and jittery and looking like they wanted to break into a full-out run to their workstations. Ruth could not handle caffeine. Even just a little bit in her system kept her awake at night. Not that it would have made any difference, given those paper walls.

They were now only halfway through Push Zone and Ruth already had two strikes against her. One of them was fair and one of them completely unfair. The unfair strike stemmed from an instruction that she inspect a batch of Nummy Nougat Squares that, it turned out, had already been inspected by a second-shift inspector. The second-shift inspector lacked experience and had put the boxes in the wrong bin. Ruth had inspected sixty-five boxes before she realized the mistake. By that time the second-shift inspector was gone and Ruth was left holding the bag, having wasted a lot of time. Virgil Pearce, her supervisor, had given her a look from the platform above the production floor.

"Strike two," said the look.

Totally unfair, but that hardly mattered now. She had two strikes. She needed to be perfect for The Push. After that, the pace would lighten a bit and keeping up would not be as difficult. But for the next two weeks, there was no room for mistakes.

"Giant Steps" started in after "My Favorite Things." Ruth turned up the radio some more and cut through a neighborhood to avoid the construction that the road signs had been promising for the past mile. The houses were squat, brown little things, each identical to the next except for what might be hiding inside, arranged in decorous rows that were separated by snow berms piled up against thin wooden fences. There was something inexpressibly sad about them. Like they were waiting for something that would never come. Ruth turned up the music, bouncing in her seat a little to stay warm, and hummed all the way to the freeway.

She parked in slot 7J in the North Lot. Slot 7J in the North Lot had been Ruth's assigned parking space since the first year of her employment. The space was exactly dead center of Column J, which itself was almost in the middle of the rows that were lined up like ridges bearing colorfully bruised metal fruit stretching out across the North Lot.

Ruth climbed out, slammed the car door with the requisite authority to keep it closed, and trekked across the North Lot for the Production Building. John Coltrane was

42

still in her head, psyching her up for another day in The Push.

Inside, she put her coat and gloves and purse in her locker, clocked in, checked out her baggys from the supply clerk and suited up, piling her hair on top of her head beneath what resembled a white paper shower cap.

Out on the floor, a small army of people, all in identical white baggys, were busy assembling thousands of boxes of chocolates in thirteen different sizes and assortments. The fruits. The nuts. The crèmes. The nougats. The mallows. The wafers. The milks. The darks. The whites. Small box. Medium box. Large box. Jumbo.

The machinery in the room was uncomfortably loud, even with her earplugs in, and the air smelled so intensely of sugar and cocoa that it gave Ruth a headache just breathing.

She used to love chocolate before this job. Now she couldn't stand the stuff.

Not that Sweet Toot's was supplying the world with a premium chocolate product anyway. Far from it. The ingredients were strictly bottom shelf. Toot's distributed only to the lowest-end box store retailers and sent nearly half of their supply overseas to Africa and Asia. The thing Toot's had on the competition was price, volume, and a longevity that had given it a recognizable name. On every box, no matter the size or the assortment plan inside, was the large pair of lips that had been the Sweet Toot's logo from the very beginning, back when William and Suzanna Tute hung out the Welcome sign in the window of a narrow storefront in Springfield, Illinois. Along the bottom of every box were the words:

Sweet Toot's Confection Connection

Smooth, Creamy, 51% Pure Chocolate
America's Chocolatier since 1956

Ruth walked out to Inspection Station 4, looking up at the platform, a big flat rectangle on a concrete pole with a set of metal stairs sloping down from one end. Virgil Pearce and his big, bald head were on duty. He had his back turned, looking over the railing on the other side, down at the drizzle pads. She was disappointed. Ruth had wanted Virgil to see that she was on time – a little early, in fact.

A figure in baggy whites was bent over the table at Inspection Station 4, counting and making notes on her sheet. The scheduling craziness being what it was during The Push, Ruth had no idea who her alternate was supposed to be this week. When she reached the table, Ruth tapped the person on the shoulder. The baggys made everyone look so much alike from behind that it was almost like tapping herself on the shoulder. The alternate turned. It was LaVonda Roberts.

Ruth and LaVonda knew each other, but not well, having exchanged only maybe two dozen words in passing each other back and forth across the production floor, and then a little chitchat last spring over a lunch break.

"I hate this place," LaVonda had said back then. "I'll be gone before the next Push, you watch and see, Sue. You watch and see."

Ruth had not bothered to correct LaVonda about her name. To this day she supposed that LaVonda, who despite her intentions was obviously still working the Push, still thought Ruth's name was Sue. Ruth marveled at how little the Sweet Toot's employees, sealed away in their baggy whites, really knew one another.

LaVonda hardly registered Ruth's presence before she snatched her count sheets off the table and abandoned

Inspection Station 4, pushing past Ruth and heading off across the production floor toward the exit.

Ruth watched her go. Then she picked up where LaVonda had left off, starting her way through a fifty-stack of medium Lover's.

A Lover was short for Lover's Delight, which corresponded to an Assortment Plan of 30% nuts, 30% crème, 30% nougat, and 10% fruit, each to be half milk chocolate and half dark chocolate. Ruth sat down on the stool, filled out the top of a count sheet with her name, employee number, the time, date, station number, and Lover's Delight as the first APB – which stood for Assortment Plan Batch – inspected on her shift.

One by one, Ruth opened the rectangular boxes from the stack in front of her. All the boxes she inspected in a given shift were to equal one-tenth of the total production of that APB for that shift. At the height of the Push, Toot's was producing ten thousand boxes of Lover's Delight, its most popular assortment plan, every shift. The target inspection ratio, therefore, meant that one fifty-stack at a time, Ruth would look at a thousand boxes of Lover's, plus an equivalent ratio of at least four other Assortment Plans, before she clocked out for the day.

Falling behind was discouraged.

She already had two strikes.

Lid off, she lifted the padded white paper cover. Counting the chocolates – each keeping quietly to themselves in their little paper holes – she then verified that the actual assortment corresponded with the Lover's Delight assortment plan. She made a note on the count sheet, returned the padded paper cover, returned the lid, placed the box on the return cart waiting at the near-end of the inspection station, and then picked the next box off the fifty-stack and started again.

In twenty minutes she was through the entire stack. She rolled the return cart across the floor over to Production Bin 4B and stacked all the boxes onto the shelf for wrapping and sealing. Then she loaded another fifty-stack from Production Bin 4A onto the return cart and rolled the cart back across the floor to Inspection Station 4. She loaded the boxes up onto the station table, started a new count sheet, and pulled the top box of Lover's off the stack.

"Giant Steps" and "My Favorite Things" were playing on a private loop as she worked, Coltrane's notes skittering around her head like undisciplined children on a green field in summer, like her sister Desiree's kids out in the backyard when Ruth sat for them while Desiree and Malcomb spent a week at the beach in South Carolina. Ruth – the kids called her Auntie Ruth – had stayed at Desiree's house for that week, taking time off from her job so that she could have a kind of vacation herself. Desiree's house was so open and spacious that every room – very few of which were truly enclosed – led to an impulse to stand in the center and spin with her arms completely outstretched. The children laughed at this and copied her until they were all dizzy and started falling down onto the furniture, which felt to Ruth like falling into clouds.

A large sunroom off the kitchen looked out over the backyard. Ruth had spent much of her week in that sunroom, sitting on the over-stuffed sofa with lemonade in her hand and watching the children chase each other, giggling and shrieking through the sprinkler. On the coffee table in front of the couch was a large leather book of family photographs. It was like a photo journal of everything Malcomb and Desiree had ever done together and every place they had ever visited.

That week had only been two summers ago. It felt like ten years had passed.

Ruth worked steadily until her lunch break. She looked up to the platform on her way back across the floor. Virgil was up there, leaning against the railing like he liked to do. He was looking down right at her. Their eyes made contact. He nodded, as if to acknowledge that Ruth was there and on pace. Ruth nodded back.

It was important to be on pace when you got to the lunch break. If you were behind the pace at the time you took your lunch, it could be very difficult to make it up before the end of the shift. Ruth had done it before, made up lost time. She had done it more than once. And each of those times she had worried that the third strike was coming. It wasn't easy.

In the summer months, Ruth usually ate her lunch out in her car with the windows rolled down and the radio on, which was infinitely preferable to eating in the din of the cafeteria, where each production zone had assigned tables. She was assigned to Table 9. In the winter, when it was too cold to sit outside in the car, she usually ate a sandwich in one of the chairs lined up along the back of the room and read a book until it was time to get back into her baggys and head back out onto the floor.

Today presented something of a problem, which she did not realize until she had opened up her locker. She had left at home the book she was currently reading. That had been the little itch in the back of Ruth's mind as she stood looking up at the towering rectangle of her apartment building, praying that her car would start. The book. She had forgotten the damned book.

The book was another improbable romance potboiler by Josephine Banks. She had written at least a dozen and Ruth had read most of those. This one, *Overdraft*, was about an accomplished international spy who falls for a bank teller in Long Island. Ruth had gotten up in the middle of the night and fished it out of her purse in hopes of reading

47

herself to sleep. Not only had that strategy failed to overcome the sounds of angry lovemaking that had kept her awake, she had also forgotten the book on the nightstand. Now she had nothing to pass the time over lunch. The prospect of sitting in the back of the cafeteria for an hour was not appealing. Nor was eating off the cafeteria menu.

Ruth grabbed her coat and gloves out of her locker, purchased a sandwich, chips and a soda from the vending machine and headed outside to her car. It wasn't summer, but maybe it would do for today.

The temperature had risen a good ten degrees, which was welcome, but the sky was still an oppressive, cottony white, like someone had laid a paper sheet over the world that diffused the sun into a fine mist that sprayed evenly over everything.

Ruth walked across the North Lot over to Row J and then down to her car in slot 7. She climbed in and closed the door. She ate her lunch with gloves on, alone, surrounded by empty cars.

Ruth turned on the radio.

The interviewer was asking questions of a woman with a low, raw voice – a smoker's voice – with a New York accent. From the sound of it, she was an older woman. They were discussing relationships. She had a sense of humor. She was irascible. She did not suffer fools, most of whom, in her experience, were men.

The interviewer reminded the audience for those just tuning in.

Ruth was astounded. Josephine Banks.

What were the odds of that? Having forgotten the book, she had stumbled upon an interview with the author. What were the odds?

But that was not quite right, was it? It was not so coincidental after all. Coincidence belongs to the realm of unconnected events and chance collisions in time. But Ruth had stumbled upon the interview with the author precisely because she had forgotten the book. It was, she thought, like someone, somewhere, was trying to tell her something.

Ruth turned up the radio.

"You have a new book coming out."

"Yes. *Cutting Paper Hearts.* My publisher says it will be out on Valentine's Day. Which is appropriate, I suppose, since the protagonist is employed by a greeting card company."

"So this character actually writes the messages in the Valentine's Day cards we see in the store."

"Yes. He ends up as a suspect in a series of murders in New York in which his little love ditties somehow end up stenciled onto the bodies of the victims. As the case unwinds, he ends up in a... a, relationship, shall we say, with one of the detectives working the case."

"So then the Valentine's Day release date is hardly a coincidence of timing."

"There is no such thing, Terri, as a coincidence of timing."

"Josephine, it's no secret that you were a very lonely child when you were growing up. You've written about that."

"Yes. As a child and into my early adulthood. I was always alone. Didn't have any real friends. My parents...well, I suppose we've talked enough about them already. I was on my own, emotionally anyway, from an early age."

"You have a fascinating account in your biography about how you met your husband and long-time editor, Moe Asner. Can you share that?"

"Moe. God bless him. Such a good man to put up with this old battle-axe all these years. I met Moe... well, let me tell it this way. When I was a seventeen-year-old girl, I had a job as an assistant librarian in the New York Public Library. My job was to shelve books. I shelved a billion books a day. That's what it felt like, anyway. Very little contact with others. You pick up the books laying around, you put them on the cart, you sort them, you put them on the shelf. It was a pretty good job in the sense that it provided me with some money and I liked being in the company of books. Those were my real friends, those books. On my breaks I had favorite little places where I could curl up and work on my writing. But it was a very lonely time for me. The world beyond that library seemed inhospitable and frightening. I didn't know how to go out into that world and exist. I just didn't. I felt trapped and very isolated."

"And just to set the scene a little, you were seventeen or so, which makes this about, what, nineteen fifty..."

"Oh, 1955. Maybe 1956. And so I'm spending a whole heck of a lot of time cooped up in the New York Public Library and feeling pretty sorry for myself. And one day I'm sitting at this table in front of a big stack of books. I used to kind of build a fortress wall of books on the table to write behind, and I was trying to think of a story to write and nothing was in my head except how miserable and alone I felt. And without really thinking about it, I tore off a piece of paper from my pad and I wrote out a little note."

"What did it say?"

"It said this: I am here. A word. A name, languishing at the bottom of an ocean of tiny, sterile letters, desperate to be spoken. Desperate to be the sound on your lips. I am waiting. Seek me out. Rescue me from this cruel, still oblivion."

"Wow. Okay. Seventeen."

"Seventeen. Yes. And then I put my name and address at the bottom of the note. This was back before any of us were concerned about privacy or personal security to such an extent that you did not want people to know where you lived. I opened up the closest book and I stuck in the note."

"Kind of like putting a rescue me note in a bottle and tossing it into the ocean."

"Exactly. I was on an island. Something about doing that felt so desperate and at the same time strangely liberating."

"Why do you think that was?"

"I was such a timid and shy person that the act of inviting rescue was a kind of self-assertion. It was an affirmation that I wanted to live and that I deserved to be happy even if I seemed to have no ability to achieve those things for myself. And so I kept doing it. Multiple times a day. Every day."

"You wrote notes and put them into the books."

"Yes. The notes weren't all exactly the same. Sometimes I slipped in some poetry or some quote that I thought was particularly profound. But they were all variations on the theme of inviting rescue. And they always included my name and address."

"And did you get any responses?"

"A few, yes. The most immediate response was from the head librarian who found out about it and fired me on the spot. She was outraged that I was abusing my position with the library to actually invite what was certain to be morally depraved men into my life. She was very sensitive to scandal and so out I went. But I also heard from a man who found one of my notes in *A Tale of Two Cities*. He showed up at my home, looking for me, with a bunch of flowers."

"Did you think that was sweet? Were you pleased?"

"Oh, immensely. Yes. But he was a good twenty years older than I was and he had picked the flowers out of my mother's garden, which was not something one did and lived to tell about it. He didn't even make it up the front steps before my father kicked him off the property. There were a couple of other people that made contact. Including a woman who was very nice. Alice Sellers. She was a secretary at an accounting firm. We became friends and were friends for a long time thereafter. Alice became what I thought of as the success story from that silly little experiment. As I grew older, I began to come to terms with the world and took some greater responsibility for my own happiness."

"Did you have any memorable romances?"

"Romance was never really a part of my life except, ironically, it was the thing I wrote about as much as anything else. I am known as a romance writer although I like to think I am offering much more than that to my readers. Anyway, in those years I had sort of resigned myself to be a writer in the purest sense, committed to rendering life more than living it. I did marry once, to an advertising man, when I was in my early thirties. It was a disaster of a union and it ended ugly. We divorced after only a year and it confirmed for me that I would always be alone."

"And then one day..."

"Yes. When I was thirty-nine-years old I was working as a copy editor for Houghton Mifflin. I was sitting at the counter at Woolworth's, eating my lunch and reading a book. A man walked up to me. He was in a nice suit and a smart hat. Are you Josephine Banks, he asked. I said I was. He asked, did you used to live at 1414 Sommerset Way? I said that yes I had. He said that his name was Moe Asner, and he worked as an editor over at Knopf. Very confused at this point, I asked how I could help him. He sat down next to me and pulled out of his pocket a scrap of paper. The paper had my handwriting on it. He said, I believe this belongs to you. I found it in the middle of _Great Expectations_."

"What did you do?"

"Well, I didn't know what to do. I think, to Moe's great amusement, I just sat there sputtering in disbelief. Finally, I found the wherewithal to ask when he had found the note. He told me he'd had it for ten years. That was about the time that my first book of stories was published. Moe had read that book and I think he was sort of impressed, given my age, which was only about six years younger than he was, but still. He was impressed. And when he found the note, well, Moe made the connection, and he thought that it had to be the hand of fate that he found this note just as he was reading my book. He did his research, confirmed the address, and then tucked the note away. He kind of followed me from afar. He purchased everything I published after that."

"Why did he wait ten years?"

"Even though Moe by that time was already a brilliant editor, socially he was very shy. Very reclusive. I learned later just how much courage it took for Moe to approach me like that. It just so happened that two days earlier, he had just finished reading an article that I had written for a regional magazine about Valentine's Day. I'm not sure I can recall what the article was about. Ghastly, I'm sure. But Moe had happened upon the article because it was the only magazine on the table to read in the barbershop where he was waiting to have his hair cut. He decided that there were no coincidences in timing and that he would set out to find me. And he did."

"Find you as a person or as a writer?"

"There is no difference, Terri. Not for me anyway. And not for Moe."

"What did he think about the note? What did he tell you that day in Woolworth's?"

"Criticism I will never forget."

"Criticism?"

"Yes. He said it was much too passive. You laugh, but that's god's honest truth. Too passive. From that moment on, Moe Asner was my editor. Still is. Everything I do still goes through Moe. He proposed a year later. We've been married ever since. Two children. Six grandchildren. Three great-grandchildren."

"Josephine, that is just... That is such an incredible story. And it never would have happened if you hadn't..."

Ruth turned off the radio and wiped her eyes. Her nose was running. She wiped it clean with her napkin. Her fingers and toes were numb from the cold. All the windows were steamed to an opaque frosted white. There was nothing of the world that she could see and no way for any of the world to see her. All she could feel of herself, the only proof of her existence, was the ache in her chest, which was like an altogether different kind of cold, pulling her ribcage inward with frozen chains as her heart fought the good fight of expansion.

She looked at her watch. She had fifteen minutes before she had to be back in her white baggys, walking across the production floor to Inspection Station 4. If she knew what was good for her, she would be early. She could impress Virgil Pearce up there on the platform and stay ahead of the pace. She already had two strikes.

She wadded up her napkin and stuffed it into the empty bag of chips and then closed it up inside the triangular plastic shell that had previously contained her corned beef sandwich. She placed the container in the passenger seat.

She looked at it, sitting there next to the flimsy, oversized business cards she had never used. Ruth opened the box and pulled out a cheap, flimsy card.

Rutt Cordial
Product Quality Inspector
Sweet Toot's Confection Connection

That was all. Not even the famous Toot's lips logo.

Ruth leaned over and opened the glove box and found a pen. She thought for a moment, breathing out steam. Then she turned the card over and wrote:

> I am here. A flavor. A cordial. A lover's delight – brown, creamy and only 80% pure – languishing at the bottom of a tiny box of tiny boxes. Desperate to be free of these paper walls. To taste and be tasted. Rescue me from this cruel, still oblivion. And my name is Ruth, not Rutt.

On the other side, she crossed out Rutt, substituted Ruth. Beneath her name, she wrote her phone number.

She held the card up to the frosted light and looked at it, turning it over and over in her hand. Coltrane's "Giant Steps" was back in her head, refusing to be silent. Ruth looked down at the box of cards. She pulled out half the box and stuffed them in her pocket, along with the pen.

She pushed open the car door, slammed it hard to keep it closed, and walked so fast across the North Lot to the production building that it was almost a jog. The truth was, she needed to hurry. The afternoon shift was going to be much less productive now.

The sky above was still oppressively overcast. But the clouds were definitely thinning. And lifting. To the west, as Ruth darted into the building, a veiled glimmer of sun flashed like a kind of lightning.

Like the eye of God preparing to peak beneath the lid.

FAILURE TO THRIVE

Act I: Flying and Lying

There was a moment, looking up at him, when I thought I wouldn't move. I just sat there. Like I'd died in my seat. I even stopped blinking and held my mouth open a little. Just for effect.

He was patient. I'll give him that. I couldn't help but wonder just how long he'd wait.

From behind him came a collision of carry-ons. He turned to see. I unbuttoned the top of my blouse while he was distracted, exposing more than was seemly. I assumed he'd take it as an oversight, another casualty of the security gauntlet.

He returned his attention. Glanced at the slip of paper in his hand. Glanced at the numbers and letters above the seats. Down at me. He smiled, his eyes never seeming to venture below my orbital bones.

This was all well pre-pandemic, in the halcyon days when the only people wearing surgical masks on airplanes were hopelessly lost surgeons.

So I could see everything.

He had a simple, boyish face and thick, straw-colored hair that made him look ten years younger than what I had assumed to be his real age. He was sturdy. Thick. No stranger to football or hockey, I guessed. Farm work. Construction.

He adjusted the backpack slung over his shoulder. Waited.

He had a book in his hand. A paperback. *Failure to Thrive*, by K.P. Sorenson. I thought that was funny in an ironic way. *K. Sorenson*. What were the odds of that?

His meaty index finger was stuffed into the pages like he was taking its temperature. He substituted the boarding pass for the finger. Waited.

It was not my intention to be rude. Or maybe it was. I had not written a single word in five weeks. I was empty inside. Utterly hollow. The twenty-six letters that I use and abuse to make my living were like a pile of broken sticks at my feet, and me with no imagination left with which to start a fire.

That, and air travel, have a way of making me obstinate.

I used to like to fly. I used to look forward to it.

There was something suspenseful about the prospect of arching over the earth, as if spit from a cannon. Or snapped from a slingshot. With all its preparation and waiting, the process of air travel was inherently anticipatory. Something big was about to happen. That was why we all packed a bag and called a taxi and waited in line and proved our identities. Something fresh and original was about to happen. New food and new people in new, exotic places.

Disneyland.

Hawaii.

New York City.

There was once an innocent time in my life when I conflated the idea of being someplace else with the actual process of getting there. Going somewhere else and being somewhere else were the same thing. The line to the first Disneyland ride started at the Milwaukee airport.

When I was young, my sister Kelly and I used to dress up to get on a plane. Dresses and nice shoes and coiffed hair. Necklaces. Bracelets. And hats. We loved hats.

We were not unlike other identical twins. We did everything alike back then. We watched the same television shows. We ordered the same food. We did our homework together and made the same grades. That kind of twins. The kind that went absolutely everywhere together and dressed identically in every context. Doublemint disgusting.

Air travel was no exception. We had matching carryon luggage, cerulean blue fabric with dirty-pink piping and Hello Kitty luggage tags. Identical purses. We each carried the same *Nancy Drew* mystery on board to read, starting and stopping together so that neither could claim any greater knowledge of the young detective's latest predicament. Reading ahead without the other was a kind of twin sin. We each did it, of course. But it always felt wrong.

When someone asked a question that applied to both of us (Are you girls all buckled in?), we harmonized our responses. (YYeess, MMaa amm. Wwee ssuurree aarree. SSeeee??). We moved in a silent, mirrored choreography that came to us by a combination of instinct, osmosis and a kind of freakish behavioral echolocation. We never had to work at it. It was like breathing.

Looking back, the digital technology analogies are unavoidable. We were continuously uploading data from each other. Actions. Reactions. Emotions. Intentions. We were always syncing ourselves to a common experience. A common existence. To see us coming through an airport, or down the jetway, or threading our way between the rows of seats was like watching Olympic synchronized swimmers who had lost their way to the pool.

The double-takes were constant, a good thing because it was often the reaction of others that kept our unity in focus. The more people stared, the more we knew that we were not Kathy and Kelly, but a perfect combination of Kathy and Kelly. A single, obnoxiously perfect, squeaky-voiced, color-coordinated entity.

A Kekathllyy.

Our mother had very clear ideas about what it meant to be a twin. For she, too, was a twin. The photos were everywhere in our home. My mother celebrated my Aunt Maxine like her Catholic friends celebrated the Pope, garlanded on the walls and the tops of dressers. But, as is probably always true with garlanded photos, the reproduction was wantonly unfaithful to the original.

Poor Aunt Maxine. The whispered family lore is that she was so misguided as to think herself an original, chaffing constantly against the unwelcome likeness of her twin. She died in Kansas City, when she was eighteen, jumping into what she thought was the deep end of a quarry. Maxine, they say, was under the influence of marijuana and a wastrel named Dirk Duzz.

Well, Dirk duzzn't any more, and neither does Maxine. They jumped together. They were in love, a tragically heavy and shallow state of mind for people so young.

My mother was devastated for years after Maxine's death, but emerged believing more than ever that twins were twins for a reason. Originality was unnatural. And dangerous. She worried whenever Kelly and I were apart. And because children adopt the fears of their parents, we worried too. We stayed shoulder to shoulder as much as possible. We slept in the same room in separate twin beds but felt compelled to push the beds together. We brushed our teeth together at the sink. We showered together. We rose together in the middle of the night and padded down the hallway in our matching pink pajamas.

We waited for each other to pee. One flush. We were only trying to be safe.

I am certain there is a clinical term for that kind of dysfunctional self-concept. There must be. Hyperphobic Sympathetic Siamesism. HSS. As children we suffered from chronic HSS. Thanks, Mom.

My father was not a twin. My father was an only child and a disabled vet who left the better part of his left leg in a Southeast Asian rice paddy. He used a prosthetic that made the process of walking look like a barely controlled prelude to a pratfall, a rolling stumble. Every time the leg caught his weight seemed like it would be the last time such a thing was even possible. The next step always promised disaster.

At night, my father stood the leg up in the corner of my parents' bedroom. It was crooked and covered in fake tattoos. Just to give it a little personality, he liked to say. Without the prosthesis, my father used crutches. His good leg – his only leg – seemed lonely without a mate. It was impossible not to imagine the real leg pining for its plastic counterpart, willing to ignore everything that was alien about it for even the slightest semblance of companionability.

My father was a complicated man, haunted and given to bouts of anger and self-loathing. As identical as his daughters were, he always seemed to prefer Kelly's company to my own. I have no explanation for this. She simply connected with him better than I ever could.

Of course, we each felt this way, convinced that my father's affections ran disproportionately toward the other. So in that respect I suppose we were identical even there.

Eventually, with more than a little help from the savage crucible of high school, life warped Kelly and me out of sync. Whereas before we had resisted the voice of the self like it was the whisper of the Devil, suddenly we found ourselves starved for original experience. Original thought. Original expression. Similar, but not identical, was not an option. Originality was suddenly its own value.

Broadcasting our newfound originality was imperative, which meant that by our senior year we were dressing like we had been shat upon by the St. Vincent de Paul Thrift Store fairy. My favorite party ensemble included white pumps, plaid culottes, and a backless, banana-yellow, polyester disco blouse.

And a hat, of course. Go Brewers.

Kelly favored capes and clusters of fabric fruit pinned into her shoulder pads. And high-top basketball shoes. She stopped wearing hats altogether and picked up a fetish for sunglasses instead. Sometimes, in just the right light, she looked like Elton John wearing high-top basketball shoes.

I never wore makeup, even on formal occasions. Kelly always went full kabuki, even if she was just going out to the movies or a ball game.

Our social circles fractured. Kelly's friends hated me. My friends hated Kelly. We never went to the same parties, a kind accommodation to spare the hosts the awkwardness of catering to feuding siblings and their respective cliques.

To be fair, it was less an accommodation to our hosts than a concession to the fact that Kelly and I, once inseparable, could not stand to be in the same room together, let alone share a keg of beer. Inevitably, our exploding self-concepts as unique and original beings required that each of us see an enemy of sorts in the other. Each of us had, somewhere along the way, ceased being a twin and had become an evil doppelganger.

It would be an overstatement to say that Kelly and I hated each other. We didn't. But we did fight a lot. Terrible name-calling, slapping, hair-pulling, property-destroying fights. She once used an iron to melt all my Beatles albums. In retaliation, I drizzled a strand of glue into her mascara.

Spy vs. Spy had nothing on the Penwell twins.

Kelly moved out of the house to live with a friend two months before graduation, leaving me to deal with our overwrought mother and the ghost of Aunt Maxine. Kelly was not into quarry-diving, but she and her wastrel boyfriend loved the high dive at the public pool. The similarities were almost more than my mother could take.

Mom did everything she could to broker a lasting peace. She made our favorite foods. She bought us identical, but different-colored clothing. She even proposed a family trip to Disneyland.

But peace was never in the cards. Nothing worked. Not even the mountain of guilt that finally sloughed off the backend of my mother's angina attack was enough to bring us together. Kelly and I showed up at her hospital bedside ashamed of what we had done and ended up fighting over which of us was the real culprit. My mother eventually saw the hopelessness of the situation when the nurse asked us to keep it down or to leave. My mother asked that only one of us stay with her at a time. We fought viciously over who should leave first. The nurse returned in a huff to make the dispute irrelevant.

Ultimately, Kelly and I tumbled into an emotional, matter-antimatter estrangement that we each knew had to be enforced and reinforced if we were to survive as individuals. Kelly was my kryptonite, and I was hers. As important as it had been to us as children to be the same – to be identical – it was equally important to us in our late adolescence to be different.

To be opposite.

It never occurred to us that one mindset was just as ridiculous as the other. Ridiculous because just as there were actually many things that individuated us when we were inseparable (I loved apples; Kelly did not. Kelly frightened easily; I did not), there were just as many things binding us in similarity when we were estranged. We liked reading. Creative writing. Long-distance running. Old musicals. We tended to bump into each other in the take-out line at the same restaurants, having ordered the same thing. Without consulting each other, we applied to the same six universities and were accepted by the same four.

As adults, we graduated from different schools with the same MFA degree. Kelly graduated thirteenth in her class. I graduated fifteenth. I moved to Minneapolis and married a civil engineer named Stewart. Kelly moved to St. Paul and married an electrical engineer named Stuart. I write fiction for a living and subscribe to the St. Paul Pioneer Press for my news. Kelly reports news for the St. Paul Pioneer Press and writes stage plays in her free time. We both drive 2006 Nissan Sentras. Mine is black. Kelly's is silver.

Neither of us have children but both of us have tried. I lost my son – Elvis, it is important to say his name – when he was two days old. He was born slightly premature. Stewart and I hadn't chosen a name. We had wanted to be surprised about the gender. We assumed that when we first saw our child, the name would come to us. We would be inspired in the moment.

I was big on inspired creativity. I was the writer and mother, so Stewart deferred. Elvis and Angelina were just stand-in names, the names we used until the big day and we, meaning I, was inspired with an actual name.

Inspiration never had a chance.

The doctors did not have any good reasons. They said Elvis suffered from a failure to thrive, a diagnosis that comes with a free shoulder shrug. Eight months later, my sister Kelly had a miscarriage.

No one to blame really. If anything, I'm inclined to blame my own ambivalence about having children. I suspect the same of my sister. Neither of us is in a hurry to try again. I think we're both terrified of having twins.

It wasn't until much later that I learned that my son's namesake had a twin. Jesse Presley died at birth and haunted Elvis to the end. Always makes me wonder if I had some subconscious twin-sense that influenced me to pick Elvis as a name. Makes me wonder who Jesse would have grown up to be. Who Elvis would have been. When I imagine the Presley twins, I tend to conjure roughly parallel trajectories. Army and Navy. Blue Hawaii and Red Daytona Beach. Caesars Palace and Mirage. Or maybe none of that for either of them. Sears and Walmart.

Having matured into our middle-adulthood and grown more secure in our individuality, Kelly and I are on reasonably good terms and visit each other three or four times a year. I no longer see my sister as a threat to the quintessential me. Indeed, our likenesses tend to bring our differences into sharp relief.

So, for example, we both write for a living. But, as a journalist, Kelly collects facts already in existence and then rearranges them on the page for an editor's approval. Not unlike a six-year-old pushing magnets around the face of a refrigerator.

By contrast, as a fiction writer, I conjure my own facts and I answer to no one. I can use obscenities and poor grammar; Kelly cannot do these things. I can play God, bending the fate of my subjects to my own will. Kelly, sadly, cannot.

That makes me freer than she is. It makes me more creative and original. It makes me an all-around better person with a superior claim to happiness.

Not that I'm always deeply creative and original. Far from it. I have my moments, but the truth is that my writing career is marbled with long, fat stretches of doubt; periods in which I feel completely bereft of any lean, original thought. I can stare at a blank screen for hours, waiting for some evidence of intelligence to animate my fingers and to start spelling itself out. The agony can be enough to make me want to trade in my laptop for a ouija board. Spooky maybe, but faster.

I imagine in those empty hours that I must be experiencing what it is like to work for SETI, staring up into open space, watching and waiting for something wholly alien to make its presence known. I am not picky about what this alien intelligence has to say for itself. I just need not to feel alone and powerless in a universe of possibility.

In such languid, unproductive spells, I tend to sit, staring at an empty screen, my single heartbeat sending out a message, waiting for a response. An echo. Anything. This can go on for weeks at a time. Months.

Even casual observers can tell when I am lost in the creative desert, because I seem to suffer from a kind of general IQ leakage. I start sentences with Like. Greetings are punctuated with cries of Dude! and Babe! My conversation is too often structured around banal observations about the weather. I drink cheap box wine and watch a lot of late-night talk shows. My powers of discernment weaken. My political opinions all congeal down into a halfhearted preference for moderation in all things and a wistfully generic longing for the imaginary good old days.

It is a more persistent problem than I like to admit. The interval between my first and second novel was almost exactly a year. The interval between my second and third novel was three years, during which time I did a lot of social media marketing and website designing and book touring, and very little creative writing. I travelled the country accepting invitations to talk to book clubs and writing classes about my creative methodology. Character development. Plot mechanics. The tricks to staying fresh and original.

Which is great. Except that it's all a lie.

There is no "trick" to being a fresh and original writer. You either are, or you are not, a fresh and original writer. There are only tricks by which you might make yourself appear fresh and original. Tricks like traveling the country and lecturing people on the subject of fresh and original writing. Tricks like slandering the up and coming generation of writers by penning essays for industry publications entitled "The Death of Originality" and "Plagiarize This!"

The only trick is in suggesting that there is a trick.

Certainly, there is no way to be an original writer if, in the pink of your marrow, you harbor doubts about the originality of your very existence. You cannot be an original writer if, despite years of stridulous and even violent individuation, you still think of yourself as a copy. As one of two.

My sister likes to visit me in such moments of despair. Not actually, but in my mind. She shows up in dreams and idle moments with that supercilious expression that I hate – made all the more aggravating because it is an expression arranged out of facial features identical to my own. It's like I'm sneering at myself.

Kelly will look at me in my mind's eye and say something outrageous like: Did you see that car accident on the corner? I think I'll write a newspaper article about it. Won't my editor be pleased? Won't tens of thousands of my readers be pleased to read the words that will take me ten minutes to type? ... What? Having trouble being original?

In my deeper slumps, it is impossible not to feel like a complete fraud both as a writer and a person. Drinking can become a problem. I pick fights with Stewart over ridiculous things like remote control monopolization. My libido takes a nosedive and yet I will often dress more provocatively and flirt compulsively with strangers.

And not eyelash-batting flirt, either. Pole-dancing flirt. Tuck some Washingtons into my elastic flirt.

Not that I'd actually do anything with a stranger. I love my husband. But there are times in the depths of a writing slump when I have to convince myself that I really... might... just... do whatever it is I'd never actually do. Something completely unexpected. Something otherwise unthinkable.

Something Kelly would never do.

This behavior is highly dysfunctional, I know, but hardly idiopathic. I know well from whence it comes. I am trying to find that second, telltale heartbeat. The one to which my own heart is calibrated. I need to find it, to hear it, to feel it and then to snuff it out so that I might convince myself all over again of the independence of my own heart.

This is how I remind myself that I am alive. That I am unique. Original.

I think of the trauma of being born, of being summarily expelled from the womb and no longer hearing that other heartbeat – the heartbeat of creation – enveloping my entire body.

I think of Kelly floating next to me. Thump-thump. Thump-thump. The two of us sounding off together, harmonizing like we do. TThhuummpp-tthhuummpp. TThhuummpp-tthhuummpp.

And then, suddenly, it is just me, a crimson, screaming half-truth, alone in the blinding light of the world, my heart like the stump of a one-legged orphan.

Thump.

Thump.

Thump.

It is hard not to feel abandoned and forsaken. Less than whole. The feeling never really goes away. Thus the cloying eccentricities of twindom.

And thus, strangely, the urge to write original prose.

Writing something original – that is, creating – fulfills a circulatory function in my life. It works a kind of pump that moves the lymph and the blood, stimulates the brain, and aerates the viscera, not of the body, but of the soul. When my creative voice leaves me, I cannot write. And when I cannot write, the pump that animates my existence wheezes to a stop. All that is in me, all that is me, all that is not my sister, settles into an eerie stillness that portends an unbearable solitude and leaves only half a self.

Thump.

Thump.

Thump.

So, in the grips of my recurring existential crisis – the one where, staring at a blank screen, I fear I may never be able to write another word – I tend to overcorrect. I tend to overcompensate for the tenacious feeling that my creative life has left me for dead, trying to prove to myself that I am still a vital demiurge. I live to manufacture a kind of extreme spontaneity – the more outlandish the better – as a cheap substitute for originality.

In my writing life, this desperate overcompensation manifests itself in a fairly ridiculous and artificial profusion of language. My prose starts to preen and strut, leaving a trail of ostentatious and sesquipedalian paragraphs collapsing from the weight of their own pretension. All too casually I toss in glittering, distant words like they were alms to the poor. Words like stridulous and whence and demiurge and idiopathic.

And sesquipedalian.

In such fits of self-loathing, it gives me shameless comfort to believe that if my readers do not understand what I am saying, if they cannot intellectually afford my words, then they will acknowledge the bargain of my original genius. I do not pretend here to be honorable, merely veridical.

Conversationally, my penchant for overcompensation comes in the form of what I call unsanctioned fiction. This is more commonly referred to as lying.

Were I to write it down on paper, put it between two pieces of cardboard, and adorn it with encomiums and a vaguely representational drawing, the world would call it a work of fiction. The world would even pay money for it and ask me to read parts of it aloud through a microphone at people trying to shop in local bookstores.

But if I fail to render the fiction on paper, and instead speak it to my neighbor over a hedge of shrubbery, then the world considers my words an intentional misrepresentation and judges me harshly. Nothing about this seems fair or sensible, but it is absolutely true.

And yet, even knowing this, I cannot help myself. The lie – that ugly, reviled, tiny, tiny, tiny stepchild of the novel (which, let's face it, is really just a very long lie) – is an original creation. The lie is invention itself. It is the familiar creative heartbeat for which, in the depths of my alienation, I long. It proves to me that I am still alive.

Stewart knows me well enough to double-check virtually everything I tell him whenever I am in my creative doldrums. Trust but verify, said President Reagan. Stewart can see me coming and always takes precautions against undue reliance.

The same cannot be said for our friends who, knowing and suspecting less than intimates, are at the mercy of my threadbare compassion. And if our friends are at some heightened risk, then strangers, I am sad to say, are sitting ducks.

The man with the backpack and the book and the patient look cleared his throat. His eyes, finally, took in some cleavage.

"I've got the window seat," he said, gesturing. I smiled and bent my legs sideways, implying an invitation to crawl over me. He was nimble for his size. He stuffed his pack in the overhead bin and cleared my knees with room to spare.

I forced myself to leave him alone for much of the flight. Some part of me was conscious enough to be ashamed of how I can behave in those desperate moods.

But it had been a long, dry spell for me. My most recent novel at that time had been on the bookshelves for almost nineteen months. It was posting middling sales, but I had long grown convinced that it was terribly contrived. Worse, in all that time, I had yet to have a single idea for the next novel, the one that would correct what I assumed had to be a growing misimpression among my readers that I was actually a stale and unoriginal writer. Nineteen months was a long time to keep the faith. Too long.

I was certain I would never write another word. I was dead. My epitaph was scrawled across the cover of my new seat mate's book: *Failure to Thrive.*

It usually does not get any worse than dead. But in my case I was dead and flying to San Diego for a writers' conference at which I was to pretend to be very much alive. I was scheduled to address writers and aspiring writers, my colleagues, my agent, and my publisher, on the subject of, of all things, productivity. How to turn out those pages. How to keep the creative momentum without losing that original signature – that certain je ne sais quoi that makes one stand out on a crowded bookshelf. They wanted a positive, encouraging address.

That, by any measure, at least at that time in my life, was worse than dead.

So I lasted until we were somewhere over Utah. The flight attendant advanced, relentlessly swiveling her pinched expression left and right, left and right, left and right, a metronome of implicit rejection. She gave me a look as I thrust my three little empty bottles out into the aisle. She was obviously still miffed about having to tell me four times to turn off my phone. She took the bottles, stretched her lips at me and kept moving.

I looked over at the sturdy farm boy by the window, reading his book. I was wretched. I couldn't help myself.

"Enjoying the book?" I asked. He looked at me, a little surprised.

"Hmm?"

"I said are you enjoying the book?"

He looked at the paperback in his hands. *Failure to Thrive.* It was as if it had taken my question for him to realize that he was even holding a book.

"Yes," he said. "I am."

"Good," I said. "It took me long enough to write it. Glad to know it was worth the effort."

The man-child's jaw went a little slack. A wisp of confusion crossed his brow like a lazy cloud. I jutted my hand across the seat.

"I'm Kathy Sorenson," I said.

He shook my hand, simultaneously glancing at the front of his book.

"K.P. Sorenson," it said.

He flipped it over to the back, confirming what I already knew: no headshot or biography of the author. I held on to his hand longer than necessary.

"Don't worry," I said. "I have a strict policy about imposing myself on the reader's experience. I'm just glad to know you're enjoying it."

"You wrote this?"

"Yes. Not one of my better sellers, but I have a personal fondness for it. I was writing that one when my kids were born."

His face cleared. I could see he was impressed. This, for him, would be one of those you'll-never-guess-what-happened-to-me story-telling moments. I released his hand, smiling.

"You're K.P. Sorenson?" He squinted. It made him smile, softening the incredulity in his eyes.

"Kathleen Penwell Sorenson, at your service." I pulled the boarding pass out of the pocket of my very open blouse. I held it out with my finger on the name: Kathleen Sorenson. "You can call me Kathy."

"Wow." He looked at the boarding pass and then at me. "What are the odds?"

"Better than you'd think, actually." I pointed to the book. "There are a lot of those books out there. And I fly a lot, so..."

"I'm Lance," he said, with a little self-conscious wave, realizing, I think, that he had flubbed that essential, introduction part of the handshake.

"A pleasure. You've got a nice face, Lance. Wonderful eyes. People tell you that, don't they?"

"No," he said as his nice face began to take on color around his wonderful eyes. "Not really." I let the awkwardness hang between us, watching him grope for another subject.

"So you were writing this when your kids were born?" he asked.

"Well, not literally; I was giving birth when my kids were born."

We both laughed.

"I mean, I'm pretty good at blocking out distraction, but..."

We both laughed.

"I mean, maybe if it had been just one, but twins? Give me a break. I can't develop plot lines giving birth to twins."

We both laughed.

"How old are your kids?"

"Seventeen." I rolled my eyes dramatically. Seventeen, the eyes said to him. God deliver me from the world of seventeen-year-old girls. "Fortunately they live with their father now. I raised them while he was busy catting around, so now he can deal with the drama of teenage twins."

I laughed. He watched me laugh.

"Twins. Do they not get along, or...?"

"My girls? Oh, they fight like cats and dogs. They're very close. Clara and Carla. They love each other, but they hate each other a little too, you know what I mean? They're kind of too close, you know?"

"Hmm."

"Mostly it's all the drama with boys."

"Boy trouble," said Lance, nodding.

"Lots of boy trouble. That's probably my fault."

"Why?"

It was a cautious question. Lance squinted as if fearing I would tell him that it was none of his business. I hesitated, as if plotting a course through a field of mines.

"Because I gave them the boy-trouble gene, that's why. My engine has always run a little on the hot side. I could never get enough of the boys. Still can't. Well, men. You know. Probably a good thing I'm divorced."

I laughed. He laughed.

The flight attendant appeared from behind us and slowly receded down the aisle, twisting and untwisting her neck; left, right, left, right, left, right.

"You married?" I asked.

Lance looked away. There was sure a story in there someplace.

"No," he said.

"You're too young to be married. Take it from me. There's a lot to see out in the world. A lot of people to experience. A lot to learn. You can only really take advantage of that as a single person. Marriage slows you down."

"You think?"

"I know. Listen. Since my divorce? I have gotten my body back into better shape than it's ever been, I have better sex than I ever had, and I have traveled to every continent at least twice."

"Twice? Really? I'm impressed."

"Well, not Antarctica. I've never been to Antarctica. But all the others twice. Been to Africa three times. I go to Australia four times every year."

"Australia. Just as a tourist, or..."

"Yes and no. I own a sheep ranch in Queensland so I have to go out there about once every quarter to meet with the managers and make sure everything is, you know, copacetic. I get a lot of writing done when I am out there, too."

"Sheep?"

"And horses. And kangaroos. More sheep than horses and kangaroos. Obviously."

"What do you do with them?"

"Well," I crossed my legs, sending my right unshod foot dangerously close to his leg. "The sheep... we harvest the wool. The horses we breed and sell. The kangaroos we rescue and relocate. They have a serious wild kangaroo problem in Queensland."

"They do?"

"Really bad. Trampling and biting schoolchildren. Blocking traffic..."

"Biting schoolchildren?"

"Oh yeah. Well, they're starving. Queensland is getting so developed that the kangaroos have lost their habitat. It's driven them into the city. They're grazing in neighborhood gardens."

"But children?"

"They're not eating the children for food, Lance." I pushed playfully against his bicep. The top of my foot made contact. "The children look out the kitchen window, see a kangaroo and, being children, their instinct is to go out and pet the pretty kangaroo. That's dangerous."

"I guess it would be."

"We're talking about a wild animal. They can be very aggressive."

"They can?"

"Yes. And fully grown, that's a two-, three-hundred-pound wild animal with razor sharp teeth."

"Really? Three-hundred-pound kangaroos?"

"Fully grown, Lance. You know, adults."

"Oh. Right."

"Right. So people get fed up and they just start opening fire on these poor creatures. It's not their fault. They're just kangaroos. But then you have three-hundred-pound dead kangaroos in the street and slumped over vegetable gardens and playground equipment. Something had to be done. So the government is paying ranchers to capture the kangaroos and relocate them. Problem is there's a relocation backlog due to the tagging requirement, and..."

"Tagging."

"Yeah, Australian law requires tagging all captured wild horses, kangaroos and something else. Badger, I think. Monkey? Is there such a thing as a monkey badger?"

"You mean for scientific ..."

"No, no. It's all politics. Like everything. The Aborigines demanded some sort of reparations for some rather impolitic remarks... well, no need to sugarcoat it, some highly offensive remarks, made by the Australian Secretary of Indigenous Relations."

"What did he say?"

"I don't even know. All I know was that it created this national uproar and the Aborigines demanded satisfaction. The press was with them the whole way. So they won the right to tag and monitor kangaroos and monkey badgers."

"The Aborigines. They tag and monitor the..."

"Yes. Absolutely. Contrary to the stereotype, they are a very tech-savvy people. Not all, obviously, but the Dingclatch Council – that's the Aboriginal communications and public relations ministry – the Council is very tech-savvy."

"Oh."

"Anyway. Tagging backlog. We end up having to hold onto the kangaroos for as long as eight months to a year before we can relocate them and turn them loose."

"That's... that's... hmm."

"Yeah, fortunately the government pays most of our expenses. It's kind of a financial loss, but we make up for it with the sheep and the horses. It's a good cause."

Poor Lance was quiet for a moment. I waited, the plane roaring beneath us. He couldn't resist.

"What got you so interested in... sheep farming in Queensland. Are you from there, or..."

"No, no. I was born in Portugal. My father was in the foreign service. I lived all over as a kid. Portugal. Nairobi. Lisbon. Australia was about the only place I didn't live as a child. I only started going to Australia after the divorce. I sold our place in the Hamptons and six months later, I was the owner of a working sheep ranch on five hundred acres in Queensland."

"Just like that? On impulse? An Australian sheep farm?"

I laughed.

"I can be very impulsive," I said, giving him a wolfish smile and leaning just a little forward so that my blouse might hang just a little lower. "Dangerously impulsive. I see something I want and I simply must have it."

I laughed. Lance swallowed.

"I love your name. Lance. Such a strong name."

"I guess."

"So..." I wagged my eyebrows, "lance much? I'm guessing you lance-a-lot."

I laughed. He did not answer. He looked out his window. I thought it shyness at the time. Retrospection has not been kind.

"So are you working on something now?" he asked finally.

"Oh yeah. I'm always working on something. If I don't write it down, I'll explode."

"Another novel?"

"Yep. Yep. I'm writing a novel. About a journalist."

"What kind of journalist."

"Newspaper reporter. Turns out she's a fraud."

"Oh?"

"She does an award-winning exposé on massive, clandestine investments by the fast-food and cigarette industries in human genome research."

"Because..."

"Because? Lance. Open your eyes. Think of the profits involved if pubescence triggered not only pimples, but a genetically encoded addiction to sugar, fat and nicotine."

"Hmm. Okay. I get that. So she writes an exposé."

"Right. Lots of accolades. Problem is she plagiarized the whole thing. Made it all up."

His lights dimmed. His forehead wrinkled.

"Well... did she plagiarize it or make it up?"

It was a good catch. Well above, frankly, what I assumed of his capabilities. But I recovered quickly.

"Both. She plagiarized it from a short story. Spun it into pretend journalism. No basis in fact whatsoever."

"So she plagiarized fiction for a newspaper story."

"Right. Cheating is cheating, Lance."

"So what happens?"

"Really? You want the spoiler? I'm a novelist! I have my pride, Lance."

Lance smiled. "Now I have to know."

"Okay. They take away her Pulitzer and she kills herself." I lean in, putting my mouth close to his ear and whisper. "Or at least that is what big tobacco would have you believe."

"Wow. Sounds like quite a yarn."

"Oh, it's all based on a true story."

"I thought it was based on a short story."

"No, her journalism was based on a short story. My novel is based on her, which is a true story. Mostly. I embellish a little here and there."

"Wait. So all that is true? The Pulitzer for the genome research newspaper reporting?"

"Absolutely."

"Where was I when all this was happening? I completely missed that. What was her name?"

"Kelly Altenbach. Early nineties. She wrote for the North Brunswick Sentinel in New Jersey. Big scandal. I actually met her just before she was fired. We were at a rollout party for another book of mine. She showed up looking for attention from my publisher, which was Knopf before I switched horses to Little Brown. She was really bragging it up. Coming on pretty strong, if you know what I mean. I don't have a problem with the occasional lesbian tryst, but with a reporter? She had some nerve, I'll give her that."

I laughed. Lance laughed.

It went on like that for nearly an hour, the words pouring out of me into that flying microcosm of the world, and combining into a new, wholly imagined reality. I was

81

creating again. Rebuilding myself from the ground up. Storytelling. Writing.

Lance was the perfect audience. Attentive. Encouragingly curious. Easily surprised. He was just sequacious enough to make it possible, but not so intellectually servile that there was no challenge involved. It was all the more satisfying to have known nothing about him.

He was no one. So he was everyone.

I might have asked something more about him. I might have let him fit a word or two in edgewise. But Lance was too willing to let me have my way with the conversation. He was mesmerized. I could see myself blooming in his expression. I was unlike anyone he had ever met before. I was a singular experience. An original.

I reported nothing; repeated nothing; recalled nothing.

I created everything.

The needle on the seismograph all but seized. The more I spoke, the more my head ticked with new ideas begging to be sculpted into a longer, coherent narrative. Plot lines started to unfold like vast umbrellas opening above my battered esteem. Characters, twirling their leitmotifs like silver batons, started a small parade through story settings, both grand and mundane. Stories that I could not have imagined only two hours earlier.

The aphrodisiacal effect of that airborne conversation was undeniable. I wanted Lance like I wanted oxygen. He seemed too far away, like his words and interest could barely reach me. I needed to be closer.

I was not particularly subtle about it. I invaded his airspace. I invited his scrutiny. Caressed his calf with the top of my naked foot.

I told myself that I would never actually do anything. That I loved my husband. But that self, in that moment, was about as true as the Australian monkey badger. For I would have done something. In the throes of such exuberant invention, I invented a new self. And that new self certainly would have done something with young, sturdy Lance.

But the flight was not long enough and Lance was not so adventuresome. Perhaps all to the better. Aircraft lavatories have become so inconveniently cramped.

In the end, all he asked of me was to autograph his book. Just as the seatbelt and telephone police were making their final passes, I penned an inscription inside the yellowing front cover.

> To Lance, from his friend and seat mate, K.P.
> Sorenson. I hope you enjoy the book as
> much as I enjoyed the flight.

Lance was silent during our approach into San Diego, book closed in his hands, gazing out the window at the sun extinguishing itself in a shimmering paleness of blue.

I left him alone. I was busy brainstorming. Unborn characters were falling over themselves to get my attention. The ideas, coming fast, struck like arrows.

A newspaper reporter is fired for plagiarizing a story about the commercial exploitation of cloning research. She is pregnant. Amid the blooming scandal, the baby is born and then lost in the same week. The doctors shrug, unable to offer a good reason. Unable to offer any reason. The grief is too much. Her husband means well, but he is too reassuring. Too resilient. Too forgiving of scandal. He wants to try again. He has a list of baby names. She feels like a fraud. As a writer. As a mother. She divorces, moves to Australia and hires on at a sheep ranch.

Lance elbowed me gently in the arm and pointed out the window at a flock of white birds. His expression was one of awestruck reverence. I waited for some explanation for his enthusiasm, but there was none. I took a second look, nodded, and then closed my eyes and resumed the birthing of my next book.

That night in my hotel room, lost in my newfound creative fervor, I neglected preparing my remarks for the conference. Instead, I sat crosslegged on the bed with a notepad in my lap and roughed out a story arc, catching details in little ink boxes that I drew compulsively in the margins.

The reporter has offended powerful interests. She has a sister, working as a lobbyist for those very interests, whose motivations are suspect.

It suddenly all came so easily, pouring out of me like a dream. I remember taking a breath and actually thinking that. This is like a dream, a thought as hopeful as it was disappointing. I imagined that I'd wake up to a blank notepad, having merely dreamt this new surge in creative power. But then I looked down at my hands, blue with ink, and my pages of scribble scattered over the tiny desk, and I knew that if this was a dream, then the dream was real.

This is the dream and the dream is real.

I. Am. An original. Again.

The sister sends a man with a crooked leg and a gun to Melbourne to look for her. There are large kangaroos dying in the streets.

84

FAILURE TO THRIVE

Act II: Katja and June

June 28, 1963

K.P. Sorenson
1024 W. 109th Street, Apt. 7C
New York 25, New York

Dearest Katja:

Received your letter of May 3. Sorry for the delay. I
have plenty of excuses, all having to do with my
editor at the London Times and his belief that I am
able to be in six countries at once. But none of
those excuses are worth the ink it would take to
explain them to you. Sorry, love. I'm a terrible
friend. Let's leave it at that.

I am freshly back to London from Berlin. I can now
say that I have seen your dashing President in the
flesh. He is strangely handsome in person in a way
that he is not in two dimensions. He is a confident
man, isn't he? Camelot indeed. But then all you
Americans are confident. Something in the water I

suppose. It makes your teeth gleam and your eyes command that other people get out of your way. No, that is too harsh, isn't it? We British already own the look that says out of our way. American eyes say coming through! And let's be great friends about you getting out of the way! But it means the same thing in my book. America has appropriated our imperialist air and added a dashing smile and a pixie dusting of youthful naiveté.

In any event, quite a speech. Very well received on this side of the pond. I suppose it has made the GDR rather uncomfortable since they are now trying very hard to have us all believe that the infamous wall is an act of love, that it merely seeks to protect its people from anti-socialist inclinations by holding them close. Very close indeed.

Imprisonment is an odd way to show one's love, don't you think? Cruel really. If they would leave you, then you don't deserve them in the first place. Locking them up behind the wall of your own fear only proves the point. The East Germans think they are husbanding their resources, but a society that is not free can never thrive. Not that the GDR is ever amenable to such reason. I should think your President's speech did nothing to alleviate their concerns.

I am assuming that you watched the speech on television. I dare say you had a better prospect than I did, sandwiched between a bunch of smelly reporters all banging elbows as we scribbled the words *Ich bin ein Berliner.* That line was like a lightning bolt aimed right over the bloody wall at the heart of darling Nikita. The air was electric. A fight nearly broke out between German and American correspondents over whether your President had just declared himself a pastry. I thought it all rather silly. I knew what he was saying, and I was more than a little pleased that someone had the starch to reach over the wall and pop the Soviets in the chest. But apparently it was not as silly as I thought. Two days later the German satirists are having a field day with talking donuts.

How are you, my dear Katja? I miss you terribly. It has been too long since I have seen you. How is the new book coming? Do you have a title? Will you send me a chapter? I cannot stand how long it takes a novelist to reach the end of things. I could never be a novelist. You know my impatience. But I admire the reach of your imagination and the little boats that you fashion out of even the most ordinary words. When it is done, you must read it to me. It has been too long since I have heard the sound of your voice reading aloud, like the wind pushing against those little paper sails. You must take me sailing again, Katja.

Sadly, I am not due to visit New York in the near future. I am off to Rome next week to write something about the new Pope. I hope it's a fashion piece, so much to write about in that regard and I do so abhor religion. But then, alas, it's off to South Vietnam where, apparently, people are unhappy that they're locking the monks up in prison. So between the Catholics and the Buddhists, I've no time to see my favorite Atheist. When can you come to London? I've found some wonderful new riding stables. Gorgeous mares. You must come.

I was in a bit of an accident yesterday after my return from Germany. I was riding my bicycle and was struck by a taxi. Not to worry. I am perfectly fine. A scrape on the arm. But the gentleman in the taxi cracked the windshield with his lovely noggin.

It was all entirely my fault. I was not looking where I was pedaling. That taxi driver was very upset and might have lost his temper were it not for the intervention of his injured passenger. So I felt perfectly wretched about it and was strangely disappointed that I did not have more injuries of my own to show for my inattention.

Anyway, I'm afraid the passenger did all the bleeding and all the apologizing. He insisted on a coffee. I am seeing him tomorrow afternoon. I have every intention of paying. He is a very nice-looking man. I suppose if one must crack a man's skull and buy him a coffee, he may as well be handsome.

I adore you. Kisses.

June

July 9, 1963

June Cale
c/o The London Times
Correspondent Mail Service
1 Pennington Street
London E98 1XY

Dear June:

I just received your letter of June 28. I suppose I should
feel flattered that you can so easily speak to me as though I am
a native-born American with a claim to dental superiority and
politely imperialist eyes. You know otherwise. My people are
from Poland and Belarus, where the eyes are much less
confident. I have lived in New York my entire life as a
naturalized citizen and yet I still have a far greater
temperamental kinship with my ancestry than with my adoptive
countrymen. I am proud to be here and I am proud to call Jack
Kennedy my President (yes, I saw the speech and I too was a
Berliner in that moment), but to be perfectly honest, the can-do
brashness of my country is exhausting at times. I often feel as
though I am writing into a cultural headwind that blows too fast
and high off the ground to appreciate detail and nuance and
emotional subtext. My editors are too young and full of
themselves.

Listen to me. I sound as though I am sixty-eight. I am
thirty-three, same as you. And I should be so lucky to write as
well as so many excellent American authors. I am, as usual,
intensely frustrated with this novel. It is not yet what I want it
to be. It fights me with every word. You have asked for a title.

The working title is *Under the Waterberry* but this thing is so stubborn I may yet change the title to *Bastard!* No, I will not send you a draft chapter. I love you too much to bludgeon you with dullness and amateurish foreshadowing.

I read your piece on Pope Paul VI. Brilliant as always, June. For someone who professes to loathe religion, you have remarkable insight into that mindset, and you write about it without a hint of any of the derision or the biting condescension of which I know you are so capable. I was disappointed that you never mentioned the Papal hats and the shoes or the astonishing lack of originality in the name. We Americans could teach the Vatican a thing or two about sobriquets. Pope Jack I has a nice ring to it, I think.

I was alarmed to learn of your accident. Even knowing that you came through it with barely a scratch, I was shaken to think of how close you came. I have seen you at death's door before, June. Never again. I will be interested to learn who pays for coffee. Keep me informed. I must protect you and I don't trust him. (Joking, of course.)

I would love to come to London. Or we could rendezvous in Melbourne to visit your father's ranch. That was such an exquisite trip. I cannot leave anytime soon, but we should plan something.

You ask if I will read to you. I promise that when I am done with this beast of a book, I will read it to you. Of course I will. Everything I write is written for you anyway, June. You know that. Be careful in South Vietnam. I will worry.

Yours,

Katja

July 27, 1963

K.P. Sorenson
1024 W. 109th Street, Apt. 7C
New York 25, New York

Dearest Katja:

Received your letter of July 9. I am now in my third week in Saigon. I think I am to be leaving soon, although the Times has changed my schedule twice already and nothing is certain in this place except for the heat, which is bloody awful. I am writing to you on a small desk in a hotel room only slightly larger than your average loo. I am mostly naked and my feet are in a pan of tepid water that used to float a few cubes of ice. There are no words for this kind of heat. India was never this hot, was it? Have I just forgotten?

I share the room with a young BBC reporter named Lester Moore. As I write, he sleeps on a cot beneath the window, wearing a pair of boxers and an expression of loathing, like his upper lip is trying to protect his sinus passage from some hideous odor. Makes me worry what I look like when I'm asleep. I suppose you would know better than anyone, but you are much too kind to tell me that I look like a buffoon when I am unconscious. I will follow your example and keep his slumbering countenance to myself.

I call him Les rather than Lester because I am incorrigible and because there is something about the name Les Moore that appeals to me. Poor bastard, Les. It's only his second assignment outside England. His first assignment was Toronto. He follows me around Saigon like a lost puppy, tail tucked between his legs, terrified it will be stepped on. Turns out there is some basis for that concern, actually.

A few weeks ago, just after Les and I arrived, a group of American journalists got into a bit of a row with the police. The Buddhist protests have been growing steadily. Apparently, they have decided not to tolerate being shot in the street and having their flag banned while the Vatican flag waves in the hot breeze. July 7 was the ninth anniversary of Diem's inauguration and the Buddhists took the opportunity to stage a massive demonstration at the Chanatareansey Pagoda, in north Saigon. Some of your countrymen, Peter Arnett and Malcolm Brown were taking pictures. Nhu's Secret Police bloodied Arnett's nose, knocked him to the ground and began kicking him viciously. They broke his camera to bits.

Les and I saw the whole thing. I thought Les was going to run all the way back to the airport. I had to hold on to his belt. I even yelled at him once. Told him to "act like a reporter," which I very much regret because he is so sweet, really. He was justly frightened and I would be lying if I said I did not feel panicked myself, wondering whether the events would escalate like they did in 1955 in Patlala. (*You* are the only good thing that came out of that riot, Katja. I suppose I would do it all over again just to meet you, which makes you more important to me than what I lost in that brutal melee. Sorry. I needn't have written that last bit.)

In the end, your David Halberstam (NYT) saved the day when he waded into the thick of the little Vietnamese policemen, swinging his arms and shouting "Get back, get back, you sons of bitches, or I'll beat the shit out of you!" Next to the secret police, David looked at least forty-five meters tall. It was quite like watching Godzilla gather the news.

Enough about me. How are you? Are you done with that bloody book yet? It's been three weeks. Surely that's enough time to write a novel. Scribble "The End" or "happily ever after" and send me the draft. I confess to rather liking the title *Bastard!* for a novel, but perhaps that is only because it sounds like the kind of novel I would write if I had the ability for such an endeavor. *Under the Waterberry* is much more becoming for someone of your talents. In any event, I'm not sure that even the great K.P. Sorenson could get away with writing the words happily ever after at the end of a book called *Bastard!*

I suppose there is one more bit of news about me after all. The gentleman whom I nearly killed by bludgeoning his taxi with my bicycle turned out to be quite lovely. He bought the coffee (he was most persuasive in the way he showed up early and paid before I even arrived) and he followed that trick by taking me to dinner all three nights before I left for the Papal catwalk in Rome. His name is Colin Peters. He's been to Cambridge and he is working in London for a civil engineering firm. We dined together twice upon my return and went to the ballet, which was not nearly as boring as I should have thought. I fear that any man who can convince me to tolerate the ballet could just as ably talk me into marriage. Can you imagine such a thing? I am joking, of course. At least I think I am joking. Good lord. Maybe I'm not joking at all.

In any event, I have promised to take him riding in return and I was pleased that he sounded terrified at the prospect. He has sent me two letters since I have been in South Vietnam, which is one more than I have received from my dearest friend. So do keep up, old girl. He seems quite determined and I should hate to have to make excuses for you.

Write soon. Kisses.

June

August 12, 1963

June Cale
c/o The London Times
Correspondent Mail Service
1 Pennington Street
London E98 1XY

Dear June:

I received your letter of July 27. I worry for you in your job. You take such risks. There are so many ways to die and you seem attracted to every one of them. I cannot protect you from here in New York. You're going to have to exercise some common sense. Avoid steering your bicycle into moving traffic. Stay out of South Vietnam. Let David Halberstam cover Southeast Asia and you can work as a financial reporter covering Wall Street for the London Times. You can stay with me.

While I am dispensing unsolicited advice, I am also concerned for you in regard to Colin Peters. It is all happening suspiciously fast, June. I am worried that you are about to throw yourself into a situation that will leave you just as lost and helpless as young Les Moore in the sweltering turmoil of Saigon. Wouldn't it be better to let a platonic friendship develop at a more natural pace? Nothing good can come from rushing.

Of course, I offer such advice as a slow-writing, long-winded novelist to a quick-witted reporter who is trained to adapt to rapidly changing environments and to commit herself to writing the news at a moment's notice. Nevertheless, my advice is the same. I worry for you, June. I worry for your heart. I remember well our conversation beneath that shocking, full moon in India – that brilliant blue coin above our table on the river – when you told me how your precipitous inclinations have served you well as a reporter but have only hurt you in matters of love. You told me then that romance should be the blossom on the long stem of a great friendship. You told me to remind you if it ever seemed to me that you had forgotten that lesson.

So I am reminding you. Take care, June. There is no sense in rushing. If this Colin of yours is worthy of your affections, then make him earn your trust.

Come see me. Better yet, tell me when you are available to go away to Melbourne. We can do lots of riding there. As you know, I am not the least bit afraid of horses and I find them more noble than most men. You are free to fall precipitously in love with all the horses you want.

Yours,

Katja

September 4, 1963

K.P. Sorenson
1024 W. 109th Street, Apt. 7C
New York 25, New York

Dearest Katja:

Received your letter of August 12. Having been in
London a few weeks, I still say a little prayer for the
cool air coming in my window in the mornings. It
seems selfish that England has all the lovely
mornings and Vietnam has all the wretched ones.
I'm sure the Vietnamese would all very much
disagree with that assessment. At least, that is
what I tell myself when I thank the god in which I
do not believe that the humidity is not boiling in my
lungs before breakfast.

I am surprised, really, that the Times has not sent
me back to Saigon, given the turmoil. You have no
doubt heard of the raid on the Buddhist pagodas
throughout South Vietnam. Hundreds dead. Many
hundreds more injured and imprisoned. All because
the Buddhists had the temerity to want to see their
own flag flapping in the breeze during religious
observances. There is no question in my mind that
it was Diem's brother, Nhu, who was behind that
travesty. The ARVN uniforms were a ruse to put the
blame on the army.

My sources are abuzz with all sorts of intrigue that
I dare not shovel through the post in such a casual
way. Suffice it to say that your dashing Kennedy of
Camelot has some interesting choices ahead of him.
Lester Moore, my BBC mate, is still in Saigon.
Seems he's finally found his courage. He tells me of
concerns that the Diem regime is rather vulnerable
to a coup and that your CIA is right smack in the
middle of it. Destabilizing South Vietnam will not do
much to help the fight against the godless
Communists, now will it? On the other hand,
fighting for a Catholic government that has inspired
monks to light themselves on fire in the middle of
the street cannot seem very satisfying in the greater
cause of freedom. I do not envy your President
Jack. It all must have seemed so much simpler in
Berlin.

This will be a much shorter letter than you deserve.
Colin is due within the hour to take me all the way
up to Grimsby. His parents have a home by the
river he promises will charm me into utter silence.
We'll see about that. I don't like silence. I'm a
reporter. Silence is like starvation. Besides, if his
parents meet me as a quiet person, I should feel
like a complete fraud.

Colin, fortunately, seems to take my incessant
burbling in stride. He even claims to like it, a sweet
claim not to be believed but which I confess I do
believe in my weaker moments. He really is a
wonderful man and I count myself lucky for having
almost killed him. We have seen each other at least
four or five times a week since I have been back. We
are beyond the point of pretending this is not a

romantic attraction. I cannot say who was the last holdout in that silly charade, him or me. It doesn't matter, really. We put that particular pretense out of its misery a week ago and we are both excited for it.

I know you worry for me, Katja. I love you for your concern. I love you for reminding me of my own moonlit declarations in India. That was such an extreme time in my life. It feels like such a long time ago. Another existence really. I was barely an adult. Everything and everyone had abandoned me. As I lay dying, you were there to pull me back into the world. Back into the glory of living. The things I said were true at the time. But they were also influenced by the magnitude of my loss and by my keen appreciation for having almost lost my own life. The world was a wonderful place, but it was also a savage place that seemed to care nothing for me. I was on my guard and wanted nothing more to do with love. I likened love to a kind of wild animal that needed to be fully domesticated before it could be trusted. You were the only one I trusted, Katja.

I am now less suspicious of the world. No. That is very poorly put. I am not less suspicious of the world. I am more accepting of its savagery as unavoidable, and I am more trusting in my own capacity to withstand that savagery. I think I have been testing the waters all these years by putting myself into precarious situations and marveling at how I always manage to wake up the next morning. Like it or not we are, each of us, in a relationship with the world, with the life around us, with life itself. Existence courts us, taunts us, threatens us, every minute of every day. And while we can be coy about it, while we can do our damnedest to hold ourselves apart from it, we cannot deny the relationship itself.

In the end, we must embrace it, Katja. Love. Even when it threatens to end us. That is the nature of the beast. It is not a beast that can be tamed or domesticated to fetch the paper. With all due respect to the younger version of myself whose words you have so dutifully quoted back to me, if we wait until all the savagery has been domesticated out of existence before we dare to live, then we will never live. We will never love.

A taxi collision is as good a reason as any to fall in love, Katja. If that seems recklessly precipitous to you, then I can only tell you that I am in full agreement. I am throwing myself headlong into something I only partly understand and cannot control. You cannot protect me. I do not wish to be protected.

It's all a waste of ink, anyway. Colin's parents are bound to loathe me. I swear like a sailor and I eat like a pig. I had to cut off all my hair to tolerate the heat in Vietnam and I look frightful. They're just as likely to drown their son in the river for making such a horrid choice as they are to serve me tea. Wish me luck.

I do adore you.

June

October 10, 1963

June Cale
c/o The London Times
Correspondent Mail Service
1 Pennington Street
London E98 1XY

Dear June:

I have received your letter of September 4. Sorry for the delay. Evidently your letter was misdirected. I just received it today.

Allow me to be perfectly blunt about it. The chance that Colin's parents will not like you is the least of your concerns. Of course they will like you. What is there about you not to like? They will adore you. As I am sure Colin does. That is not the concern.

The concern, June, is that you will allow yourself to be seduced by the affections of someone who is not worthy of your complexity as a person. Simplicity is attractive. It is beguiling in its promise of a happy shelter from the storms of living. We are reluctant patriots, you and I, and we distrust political dogma of all stripes. We have each renounced all the organized religions on similar grounds. But is love – particularly any romantic love whose flag is so hurriedly hoisted – any less a religion? Are its simple promises any less deceptive? Are its revelations, draped in profundity, any less illusory? I think not.

I thought we were agreed on this point. How many discussions have we had on the siren song of romantic love? About the narcotizing effect of sexual attraction? About the blindness of men in need? I am surprised that a single collision with a man in a taxi was enough to completely reverse the trajectory of your thinking. Perhaps you did more than merely scrape your arm.

It is not my purpose to malign poor Colin Peters, nor cast aspersions as to his motives. I am sure he is delightful and honorable as far as he knows his own mind. I cannot see, however, that you have had a real opportunity to know his true depth. You should never surrender yourself to someone whom you do not know and trust to the core. It takes a very long time to really get to know someone. There is but one person in this world that I know and trust enough to accept my surrender. There is only one person whose flag I would salute as my own.

If I recall correctly from your description of a time before we ever met, your relationship with Rajeev (I can never remember the bastard's last name) lasted three times longer than you have known your Colin. You told me that Rajeev, too, was handsome and considerate and charming. You allowed yourself to be swept away by the newness of his culture and his religion. It was all so intoxicatingly exotic. Had it been possible for you to convert to Hinduism on the spot, you would have done so. And what did that impulsiveness get you? Abandoned and pregnant on a continent you did not know and that nearly killed you. Rajeev did his damage before I knew you. I had assumed that you had learned your lesson. I have never known a June Cale under the spell of a Rajeev. Until now.

I worry for you, June. I am sorry to say it, and I do not mean to hurt you, but I do worry. I wish you happiness, of course, but I fear the opposite. I fear the quiet corruption of your life into something that, in a few years' time, you will not recognize and no longer love. I fear your isolation behind a great wall of connubial commitment that will only alienate you from the freedom of spirit, and freedom from all conventional allegiance, that is at the heart of the person I know so well.

You are better than that, June. I see you racing headlong into distraction, away from all nobility of purpose, without which I believe you will never truly thrive as an autonomous person. Is that not too much to compromise?

I wish we were not separated by an ocean. I suspect that if we could discuss these developments face-to-face, you would better appreciate my perspective, a perspective that once used to be your own.

Do take care, June.

Yours,

Katja

October 20, 1963

K.P. Sorenson
1024 W. 109th Street, Apt. 7C
New York, NY 10025

Katja:

Regarding your letter of October 10, I am
profoundly disappointed in your attitude and your
pessimism for me. A stranger reading your words
would easily conclude that you do not actually wish
to see me happy, that you would rather I be alone
and deny my feelings until I am too old and it is too
late to act on them.

Fortunately, I know you too well, and trust you too
implicitly, to believe such a thing. Which leaves me
to wonder not whether you meant those words, but
why you chose to write them down and shoot them
across the Atlantic like so many poisoned arrows.

We are different beings, Katja. As much as I admire
you, as much as I owe to you, I cannot be you. You
have a novelist's capacity for solitude. You are like
a great blue whale that takes her breath and
disappears into the deep, unseen by another soul
for miles at a time. As far as I can discern, you have
almost no life except to work on your excellent
novels, meet once a week with your writers' group,
and sit alone in Manhattan delicatessens writing

letters to me. You are a young and beautiful woman. I mean that word most particularly. You are brilliant, of course. That is a given. But you are also beautiful to behold. Everybody thinks so. I think so. You should have more in your life, Katja. More diversity. More people. More men.

Yes, Katja, men. They are brutish and dangerous and selfish and shortsighted and endlessly preoccupied with their own anatomy and all the other foibles on which we have agreed over the years, but they are not evil. Not always, anyway. They are not unworthy of the challenge. I know you believe that the romantic life is a distraction, and I know that I have agreed with that sentiment over the years, but I believe it is a distraction worth having.

I wish to be happy. We all do. Our work, noble or not, is insufficient to that end. In order to thrive (I will use your word) in whatever else we attempt in the world, we must find a corner of our lives that offers us unconditional happiness. Wherever we live, whatever we do, we each need a garden.

I am in love, Katja. I cannot deny it. I have no wish to deny it. I have found a wonderful man who seems to tolerate everything about me that I have always assumed is a liability when it comes to relationships. I must say that love changes a person. When I am with Colin, I am not the restless monkey with press credentials that you like to mock. I am calm, content with my circumstances.

You should be glad, Katja, for even if you are suspicious of his motives, you must surely approve of his aim. Colin has convinced me to ask the Times for domestic assignments so that I can stay closer to home. You should be taking comfort that unless London is invaded by the French, I will not be reporting from active war zones.

There, you see? Here I am skirting the news, hesitant to tell you because I know it will not be well received, which breaks my heart, Katja, because it is good news and because my first instinct is always to share my good news with you and to imagine your joy at learning it. Enough then. Here it is: Dateline London. June Cale Warms Bun in Oven, Shops for Miniature Clothing Before Slapdash Wedding.

Try to be happy for me, Katja. Your worry about Colin is entirely unfounded, I promise you. Try to trust the world enough to let it be what it will be. The ceremony will be on Friday the 22nd of November at St. Mary the Immaculate in Lincolnshire, which is near Grimsby where Colin's parents live. It is a beautiful church, abutting a meadow, but with a very stately circle of flags in the front by the fountain that makes it look a bit too much like an embassy. It is unlikely to have been my first choice, but I am much more agreeable now. The wedding will be a very small affair but I would wish for you to attend if you are up to the trip. I know that such could be a tall order for you and I promise not to be offended if you are unable to come. I know, despite it all, you will be there in spirit.

If it is a girl, I am naming her Katja. I mean that. If it is a boy, what do you think of Jack? Or Lancelot?

Camelot indeed! Still waiting on any tidbit you deign to fling my way regarding your latest masterpiece. You are quite cruel to deprive me so.

Kisses, June

November 2, 1963

June Cale
c/o The London Times
Correspondent Mail Service
1 Pennington Street
London E98 1XY

Dear June:

I have received your letter of October 20. I write to you not from a Manhattan delicatessen, but from the privacy of my tiny apartment with a view six floors above a narrow, litter-strewn alley where the winos like to sleep and fight and relieve themselves. Directly across the alley is a man sitting at his window. I have concluded that he too is a writer. He is there every day. He does a lot of staring without seeing. His window is almost always closed, but I can hear the keys strike the carriage in my head. He is working on something. I imagine for the sake of convenience that it is an article for some mechanics magazine.

A novelist likes to believe she is unique; that she is the only one in the world writing a novel. It hurts us somehow if we are forced to acknowledge that others do what we do. Isolation is all part of it. It helps us live in that other, wholly imagined, world. So it is convenient for me to assume that this man across the alley, the one that I see every day in his window and who sees me every day in my window, is writing an article. If not about mechanics, then maybe about politics. A cartoonist would have been even better, but he is clearly typing, not drawing. He's always there. Always staring into space.

Having read your letter, I cannot leave this place. I am a prisoner of my own grief and my own shame. I have cried until my throat is raw and my eyes hurt. I do not know what to say, June. I am a writer with no words.

I should never have sent that last letter. Or, at least, I should have expressed myself differently. You are right. You know me too well to think that I do not wish you every happiness. I do. Wherever you find it and with whomever you choose, I do wish you happiness. My concerns about the suddenness of your romance with Colin Peters were genuine. I stand by them. But it was never my intention to imply some disapproval of Colin himself or of your efforts to find happiness in his company. You deserve to be happy and I have no reason to suspect Colin's motives. I do, however, have every reason to suspect my own.

I am much better at writing about the fictional feelings of fictional people than honestly expressing my own feelings. I am more at home in the relative safety of the make-believe. In all our years since India, that fact cannot have escaped you.

My current disaster of a project, *Under the Waterberry*, concerns the benevolent mayor of a massive, wealthy subterranean city called Underlin. Underlin citizens want for nothing except sunlight, for which evolution and technology have supplied a biochemically effective, but emotionally unsatisfying, substitute. The city is mostly self-contained. There are portals up to the Overlands, but they are carefully guarded to prevent discovery from above, the pillaging of Underlin's many treasures and the corruption of Underlin's strict egalitarian ideals. The primary narrative centers upon the Mayor of Underlin, who falls deeply in love with one of his own subjects (for they are really subjects more than citizens), an elite security operative who conducts dangerous reconnaissance missions up across the Overlands for information about nuclear military concerns, the nature of which I will mercifully spare you.

The salient point is that the Mayor of Underlin is hopelessly in love with his own spy and she, the spy, is utterly oblivious of the Mayor's feelings. The spy is oblivious because the Mayor has never let on. The Mayor has never let on because to divulge his feelings to her would compel him to act on those feelings, which would compromise the strict egalitarian ethic that governs his position and his life. For what is love, June, if not a vote of extraordinary preference for one person over all others?

Well, as you might guess (for this novel is not nearly as clever as I imagined it would be), the security operative finds herself attracted to the Overlander official she has been sent to deceive. Her excursions to the Overlands grow longer and longer and, eventually, the Mayor realizes what is going on in the sunlight above him. While the Mayor could have let her go, choosing her happiness over his own, he opts instead to hold her as a prisoner of Underlin. All sorts of drama and heartbreak ensue.

I will withhold the rest of the plot on the slim chance that this mess of a yarn actually turns into a book that you can read and judge for yourself. It is intended to be a political allegory capturing the international conflict and ideological warfare that surrounds us these days and that you have so capably covered in your career.

Ordinarily, I would not have breathed a word of this to anyone, even you. You know too well my creative hermitages. But I share it with you now because when I read your letter, my hypocrisy lunged at me from between your words. I realized that I am the Mayor of Underlin, willing to sacrifice the happiness of the one I love to keep her close. I am no better than the GDR, June, building a wall around you with my affections. The realization was monstrous, shredding my heart from the inside.

So, why then? It must be asked and it must be answered. For all my pretensions, I am not immune to romantic love. I do my best to deny it. To push those feelings away. It helps me to escape down into my writing. I am not accountable for my feelings in those other imagined worlds. But here, in this world, I am accountable, and I realize now that I am in danger of wounding someone, the only one, ironically, who truly matters.

From the first moment, June, at the hospital, long before you ever opened your eyes, I have loved you. I have spent every day since then trying to parse that word, love, into all its niggling shades of meaning. I have hidden my feelings in words like friendship and collaborator and savior and admirer. Even sister for a time. I honestly do not know whether I have been successful in that deception or whether you have seen my shoes sticking out from beneath the curtain of these inaccurate descriptors.

The ugly, shameful truth is that I have always wanted you for myself. The ardor that you now express for Colin Peters has, in the depths of my childish imagination, always belonged to me, even if only in some unknown future. His gain has become my loss. I know that is not precisely true, and yet my feelings have made it true. It is very difficult for me to see it any other way. I am happy for you and I am devastated. I feel as if I cannot breathe.

I should have told you, of course. I should have been more candid. But that assumes I knew my own mind and had the courage to explain it. I did not know my own mind and I had no courage. It was easy enough to extoll the all-encompassing virtues of friendship as though I was laying everything out on the table. You have forgotten, but the bit about romance blossoming at the end of the long stem of a great friendship was mine, not yours. You repeated it willingly enough, but I was steering you, building my wall around you, even then.

So I did not leave everything on the table. My pockets were full. In retrospect, I told you almost nothing of my feelings for you. You seemed so indifferent to the multitudes of men who crossed your path, I was able to believe what I wanted to believe. You and I were the same, I told myself. I felt safe.

Then along came Colin. You are to be his wife and have his children and live a life of which he is justly the center. It is all so sudden, June. My happiness for you is a thin voice in a raging storm. I am sorry. I cannot attend your wedding. I will not make up some excuse. The sad truth is that I am not strong enough. I will only poison the happy occasion.

Do not worry about me. Please do not call. I do not wish to break our letters-only pact in that regard. I will do my best to resolve these feelings and I promise I will not spend your wedding day cooped up in this tiny hole staring at the man across the alley. I will change my scenery. I will take a trip. I think I will go west. I have never been out west.

It is my practice never to reread a letter before I send it. It only invites doubt and a self-conscious urge to tear up the words and start again that is anathema to the art of letters. Having now violated that rule and reread this particular letter, I am consumed with pity and self-loathing. I am making everything worse. You are right about me, June. I am a blue whale. I can hold my breath a very long time. Your news having brought me to the surface long enough to write this wretched letter, all I crave now, suddenly, is the familiarity of solitude.

So I will dive again. Back to my own personal Underlin. The only question is whether I will take this letter with me into the depths.

You are everything to me, June. When you read this lett --
-

November 2, 1963

June Cale
c/o The London Times
Correspondent Mail Service
1 Pennington Street
London E98 1XY

Dear June:

I have received your letter of October 20. First of all, allow me to apologize profusely for my last letter. I can be so ridiculously over-protective if you let me. But I do trust your instincts and if you say that Colin Peters is the one, then he is the one and I am ecstatic at the news. You must tell him, however, that – notwithstanding his obvious success – I am still of the firm opinion that there is a better way to meet women than running them over with a taxi. I hope Colin will allow me, Aunt Katja, to teach his new child at least that much.

I would love to attend your wedding, if for no other reason than to see you dressed in white chiffon standing in the middle of a church. The sight is almost too incongruous to imagine, and, as you know, there is almost nothing that I cannot imagine.

Unfortunately for me, and perhaps fortunately for you, I have made plans to travel west for two weeks starting on the fifteenth. Mostly a change of scenery; I have never been out west, but I also have plans to see an old friend of my father's in Dallas on the day you are to be married. I hope you are not disappointed, but I suspect you will get on just fine without me.

I do expect a detailed account of the wedding and honeymoon that is worthy of your profession.

You have asked, once again, for details about my book-in-progress. When will you ever learn? Not so much as a single character name until it is done (and it may never be done).

Cheers, June, to you and your Colin. I thrive less on my own dull existence than on your penchant for so fearlessly embracing what, and who, you love in the world.

All my best,

Katja

November 21, 1963

K.P. Sorenson
1024 W. 109th Street, Apt. 7C
New York, NY 10025

Dearest Katja:

It was with such great relief that I received your
letter of November 2. I honestly cannot fathom what
has gotten into me these past few days. I have gone
from calm and happy to a nervous wreck. I have
lost sleep thinking that you have completely written
me off as mentally unstable. I almost broke our
pact and rang you.

My thoughts and feelings are all such a jumble,
Katja. My wedding is tomorrow and just to write
those words on the page is enough to send me
screaming through London like a bloody lunatic. I
know that if you were here, you would tell me that
these are natural feelings, that I am just
overreacting to the impending pageantry of it all.
You would be right, of course.

I do love Colin dearly and to take his hand
tomorrow will be among the happiest days of my
life. I really do not doubt those things. You needn't
ring me up to convince me. It's just the knee-
knocking jitters of standing in a church wearing a

116

white dress. Me, Katja, in a white dress! In a bloody
church! This is utter madness.

There is also very bad news recently that I fear has
made all these otherwise normal jitters more
powerful. My lovely friend from the BBC, Lester
Moore, darling Les, has died. It pains me to think
that I ever joked or rolled my eyes at his lack of
courage. Les died in Saigon at the hands of
unknown assailants. My contacts at the Times and
the BBC do not know many details but they know
that it was ghastly and cruel. I received a letter
from Les only two weeks ago, just after the coup
and the assassination of Diem and Ngo. He said he
had developed some strong army contacts and was
getting some good information about those final
days of the regime. He was writing to thank me for
my help. He said he felt like a real reporter.

Poor Les. He was such a dear. I feel in some way
responsible, Katja. I feel like I abandoned him in
that place. Colin has tried his best to be a comfort,
keeping my attention on happier thoughts. The
wedding. The baby. He reminds me that I could not
possibly have any accountability for Les, that I am
no longer that kind of reporter, and that I should
focus on the future. He is right, of course. I can see
that Colin will be the only one with any common
sense in this marriage.

I must tell you this, Katja – and only you, for you
are the only one who truly understands me – I
dreamed last night that I was back in Vietnam. I
was looking for Les. I dreamed I found him on the
street, broken and bleeding. I was wearing white
and ripped off pieces of my clothing to stanch his

wounds. He regained consciousness and I gave him water. I kissed him and he kissed me back. He accused me of whoring about while he was dying. We laughed. I felt so relieved for him. And for me.

When I awoke, for a moment before Colin stirred next to me in his bed, I felt disappointment. I wanted to crawl back into the dream. I remembered keenly what you have told me about how novelists so often want to curl up inside the make-believe worlds they imagine. Except that I felt as though I had been dreaming of the real world and that the waking world is fantasy. That this is the dream.

I have just reread all this blather. Try not to hate me for such an egregious waste of ink and paper. These feelings will pass and tomorrow it will all seem so silly. If I had any common sense, I would tear it up and wait to write you a glowing, postcoital account of the happy occasion, cigarette hanging from my lips, as poor Colin lies in a snoring heap in some corner of our hotel room having narrowly escaped death-by-shagging. All as God looks on wondering how he could have ever sanctified this union.

When next you hear from me, I will be happy, spending unconscionable amounts of my new husband's money on baby clothes (I think I am addicted to that, by the way), and thriving in matrimony under the name June Peters.

Alas, I no longer have any common sense, which I fear has taken its leave of me forever. Anyway, I know it is a mortal sin in your book to not send a letter once started and I would much sooner offend

God than you, my dear Katja. So I will send you this wretched thing and ask you to forgive me for all the silly drama.

I know that as you read these words, I am a happily married woman and you are freshly back from your holiday out west. I'm sure you enjoyed it immensely. Did you do any riding? Of course you did. Silly me. How does one go to Texas and not at some point ride a horse? I hear that all the taxis are horses and that you will be arrested if you are not wearing a ten-gallon hat. I must visit Texas someday.

I also hear that your President Jack will be passing through Dallas soon. I do hope you will be there to see him. If you happen to bump into him, I hope you will tell him I said hello. Tell him that I am to be married and will no longer be following him around the globe, listening to him stir the geopolitical pot with his Boston accent and his naively idealistic sensibilities.

Tell him that as much as I admire him (and I do), I am now covering the domestic front in London and he will have to do his best without me. Tell him that we will always have Berlin.

Wish me luck, Katja. I adore you. Kisses,

June

FAILURE TO THRIVE

Act III: The Birds

Sleep, late to arrive, had tried to extend its visit. It had pretended not to hear the thin, precise voices of the NPR affiliate tossing vaguely judgmental words at the pillow. Gerrymandered... Marginal... Underrepresented... Deficit... Empty... They piled up over my head like little sticks of sound that smart, politically progressive, dark-beaked birds were arranging into a nest. Or a burial mound.

The radio finally had its way. Sleep stormed off in a huff, leaving me upright and panting in a tangle of sweat-soaked percale. I fell back against the headboard, blinking and swallowing, trying to separate the two inseparable beasts in my head – one fact and the other fiction – locked in what was either deadly combat or a frenzied act of sexual congress.

Blinking and swallowing. In my semi-conscious fog, I groped for feelings.

I was distressed at having to give a lecture. That was the emotion in my chest: distress. I did not know what I was going to say. I did not know what the lecture was even about. Kangaroos? My head was full of them, along with an urgent need to warn people. Enormous, feral kangaroos were hopping through the streets of Sydney, blithely stuffing hapless children down into their pouches as they discussed regressive voting trends in southern American states and urged public radio pledge drive contributions.

This isn't real, I thought through the fog. This is the dream.

Time, place and purpose returned with a flush of fog-clearing adrenaline. I did not shower or primp, leaving that for the cab ride, which was devoted equally to putting on my makeup, eating a bagel, reading over my presentation notes and pretending conversation with the driver. I chewed and nodded and made randomly affirming sounds as I excavated a pen from my purse and circled all my essential points for writers trying to stay creatively productive, something I had not been for years.

Outline (have a road map).

Set production goals.

Write every day.

Kill your television.

A hard, squealing stop prompted by an illicit lane change sent the bagel skidding across my notes onto the floor of the cab. I never skipped a beat, nodding in absentminded agreement at the driver's storm of expletives. I licked the cream cheese from my fingers and kept circling.

Plow new ground.

Hemingway: take breaks only in the middle of a good sentence.

Write first, edit later (just get it down!)

The conference was well underway as I stepped into the quiet ballroom. A lanky, smartly dressed woman sporting temple-length, finger-wave hair-curls stood on the dais behind a podium. The woman, an agent of some repute, had paused in mid-sentence for dramatic effect as she pointed at the audience with her glasses. People cleared their throats and coughed, poking sounds at the uncomfortable silence.

I remember thinking that the woman's anachronistic, flapper hairdo betrayed some hope that the two-hundred-or-so aspiring writers might credit her in some abstruse way for the success of *The Great Gatsby*. I would like to say that any such hope was misplaced, that the attendees at such conventions are not so credulous. But I knew better. We were lecturing to sheep, each of them just desperate enough to believe that the things they needed to be successful writers could actually be taught.

Behind the agent was the long, cloth-draped panel table at which I should have been seated with the five other presenters. My chair sat conspicuously empty behind a glass of water, a yellow notepad and a paper placard that publicly berated me for being late: Kathleen Sorenson. Not wanting to interrupt by crossing the stage to take my seat, I stood quietly in the back of the ballroom and waited for Zelda Fitzgerald to come out of her dramatic pause and continue.

"Because things are moving very fast," she was saying, making a point about trends in publishing. "It is not enough to know what people are interested in reading now. Your agents and publishers are green-lighting the stories that people will be interested in reading a year from now. Stories they do not even know about yet. The now is already too late. If you are not thinking at least one year ahead of the now, then a whole lot of work will go into delivering a product that will completely fail to thrive in the market."

She popped imaginary balloons with the rim of her glasses.

"DOA. Why? Because by the time you bring that book into the world, there will be a dozen others on the shelf just like it. And everyone will be putting their money on the next original story."

She finished forty minutes later to enthusiastic applause. During the Q&A, I made my way to the presenters' table and took my seat, offering my whispered apologies to the panel. Each of them nodded an unconvincing pardon.

Three more presenters would come and go before my turn. I pretended to listen and nod with interest, but I was mostly focused on a last review of my own remarks. When I finally took the dais, the room had a heavy, somnolent air. My audience was in the thick of digesting its lunch. Men crossed their arms over their chests. Women checked their teeth in tiny mirrors.

Words died in my mouth. Those that cleared my lips sank quickly, like bodies hugging blocks of cinder, wrapped in burlap and rolled from the deck of a boat. I made all my points in more or less the order I had hoped, holding myself out to the assembled, sleepy, sated sheep as an expert on maintaining creative productivity.

Set production goals.

Write every day.

Kill your television.

Plow new ground.

If I convinced any of them, I did not convince myself. The previous night's creative frenzy was rapidly receding, slurping out of my head down the pipe of my brainstem, leaving behind a residue of self-delusion. Even as I lectured, my mind grasped for those ill-conceived characters that had sprouted up out of the festival of lies I had told my seat mate on the flight over – the plagiarizing, grieving reporter; the shady, lobbyist sister; the man with the crooked leg and the gun on his way to Melbourne; all those sun-soaped Australian sheep and the dying kangaroos. Those characters and that extravagantly original plot were the only proof I had of my enduring creative fertility. They were the credentials by which I accessed my own self-esteem as a fiction writer. They were what gave me permission to be on that stage.

But, one by one, the characters abandoned me, leaving only shadows and clouds that no longer resembled anything. I ticked through my advice as prepared, but the words were empty vessels carrying no conviction. I spoke to them with almost the same emptiness with which I had spoken to the cab driver. When I paused to wipe a streak of cream cheese from my notes and then absently inserted the tip of my finger in my mouth, pausing unnaturally in the middle of a sentence about creative focus, no one seemed to notice.

In retrospect, I'm not quite sure what I expected. Perhaps that a grateful audience would rise to its feet in ovation. Reflecting. Confirming. Sanctifying my claim to demiurgical greatness. Instead I received a smattering of perfunctory applause and a stifled, spinach-speckled yawn from a fat man in the front row.

There were no questions.

I returned to the presenters' table, sat heavily and poured myself a glass of water, wishing it were gin. The woman next to me, an agent for writers looking for international distribution and screenplay credits, patted me on the forearm and lied politely.

"Well done, dear," she croaked. "Riveting."

She was tan and draped in silk and expensive jewelry. Her honeyed hair was pulled back into a tight bun, no doubt fastened to the same bolt that kept her skin taut. She diddled with a pair of expensive sunglasses on the table. It was all I could do not to empty the pitcher of non-gin into her lap.

The conference coordinator leapt to the podium Peter Panishly, with extra verve. I can only assume he sensed the gathering ennui. A mass, mid-afternoon exodus would have reflected poorly on the conference, so I knew better than to mistake his motive as a favor to me. As he emoted, I drank my water and plotted my escape. It would be lost on no one that the person who showed up late also left early. I did not care.

"Well," gushed the coordinator, "thank you Kathleen Sorenson for such great advice. That was really spectacular. Kathleen is with us every year, all the way from Michigan."

"Minnesota," I said, leaning toward the table microphone.

"Minnesota!" He laughed like I had given the winning answer to a difficult game show question. "My apologies, Kathleen. *Minnesota*. Kathleen's latest book is a thriller entitled *Don't Forget*. I believe it's still out the on the bookshelves so pick up a copy or search for it online. Okay..."

"*Not... Forgotten*," I said in a loud, slow over-enunciation, trying not to spit into the microphone.

"Excuse me?"

"It's titled, *Not Forgotten*."

"Well... I'm zero for two, aren't I? My apologies, Kelly."

"Kath...leeeeen."

125

The audience was laughing. He was laughing. My fellow presenters were laughing. I was scowling like a wet cat. I realized too late that he was having some fun at my expense just to rouse the restless, under-stimulated attendees.

My resurgent smile was far too slow to convey sincerity to anyone in that room. Ms International Movie Star Agent patted my forearm again and beamed enough for the both of us. The coordinator laughed and gestured like we were in on the joke together.

"Well, enough funning around," he said. "Let's move on, shall we? We have a real treat for you this afternoon. As many of you may know, Katja Sorenson..." He broke off. Looked over at me. "Hmmm... Sorenson. No relation, I assume, Kathleen?"

I shook my head, warily. He continued.

"Just checking. Anyway, Katja Sorenson died a year ago in February. If you were a fan of Katja's writing, then I know you have mourned her passing. She was a magnificent writer, all the more so as a Polish-born, Norwegian émigré for whom English was a second language."

There is a feeling I get when something awful is about to happen. A simultaneous buzzing in my gut, my chest, and in the center of my cerebellum. It's like a trip alarm when a circuit breaks, lighting up a network panel in the basement of some heavily armored command-post along my central nervous system.

"Orphaned as a young child, Katja came to New York when she was nine. She arrived in the care of an uncle who died in a traffic accident only a month after setting foot on American soil, leaving Katja in the hands of the State. I will not depress you with the details of her captivity – and there is no other word for it."

126

The buzzing inside me grew. It shifted and then traveled, like an insect searching for exits. The last time I felt this unsettled, I was returning home from college in the summer following my freshman year. I was a week earlier returning than I had told my parents. I had plans that did not include them.

"We remember Katja for the incredible works of fiction, both long-form and short-form, that she gave to us in her sixty-year career. Fifteen published novels, dozens of short stories, countless letters. Katja was alone in the world for most of her life. She was a solitary writer. She was a solitary person."

The buzzing had started just as I passed the regular turnoff for my parents' house – which was still my house too – and kept driving, threading the pre-dawn traffic and imagining my father rolling over in the bed, his tattooed prosthetic leaning up against the nightstand, as my mother put on the coffee.

"But Katja had one good friend. Just one. Those that have followed Katja's life know that it is difficult to not hear her name as one-half of a pair: Katja and June. Those countless letters, to which I earlier referred, when you weed out those sent to editors, agents and publishers, were written almost entirely to June Cale. It was a remarkable friendship that spanned almost the entirety of Katja's professional writing career. June Cale was a British journalist of impressive talent who lived and worked all over the world. The decades of correspondence between these two women, these two writers, these two amazing friends, is truly something to behold."

By the time I had pulled into my boyfriend's neighborhood, the vibration had grown from curious sensation to something more akin to nausea. I tried to convince myself that it was simply nervous sexual energy, pent up from a long night's drive, a lot of coffee and not enough sleep. I should have known better.

"If you have not read it already, I highly commend to you the authorized biography that June Cale wrote of Katja Sorenson's life entitled, *Letters from Katja.* The book, a wonderful tribute to her friend, was published six months before June Cale tragically died in a plane crash in Africa. It is no surprise that Katja was devastated by the loss and lived only another handful of years."

If there is any feeling worse than that premonitory buzz, it is the feeling in its place when the buzzing, without any warning, stops. It is the feeling of absence. Emptiness. It is nonidentity. Nonexistence. My boyfriend's driveway should have been empty. I'd have known my sister's car anywhere. Identical to my own, just a different color.

"Our guest for you today is a tremendous fan of both Katja Sorenson and June Cale. In fact, there may be no greater fan. Please welcome June's son, Lance Peters."

Gone was the somnolent murmuring that had greeted me at the podium. The ballroom was alive with fresh interest. The applause was loud and sustained as a young man in a dark suit rose from a seat in the middle of the room and made his way to the dais. The buzzing in me suddenly stopped.

He was sturdy looking.

With a boyish face.

And thick, straw-colored hair.

I choked on my water. Ms. International Movie Star Agent swatted me smartly on the back.

Lance, I marveled in abject horror. It's... Lance. Lance-a-lot.

My mind defensively rejected everything my eyes and ears were confirming to be true. Rejected that he was here at all. Rejected that he had been in the audience from the beginning. Rejected that any of this could be happening.

He strode confidently to the podium. Cleared his throat.

"Good afternoon."

The voice was the same. Good afternoon. Those two words were like loose boulders, announcing the coming avalanche. I closed my eyes.

"Good afternoon. Thank you. Thank you for having me. Thank you to Bridgette and Steven for inviting me.

"I will not keep you long. I am not a professional writer or a speaker. I own a construction company in Duluth. I do not belong in this distinguished group. Not because I cannot write. Like many of you, I have an MFA certificate on my wall. Sadly, however, I was never strong enough to take the vow of poverty. I have a weakness for comfortable living. That, and I have a problem with rejection."

Laughter burbles over the heads of the audience like slow water over river stones. The agent next to me makes a laughing grunt and swats me in the shoulder with the backs of her bejeweled fingers. There is no room in my head for her existence.

"My only occasion to speak to groups of people is by invitation from organizations, like this one, that represent writers of all stripes – journalists and fiction writers – to talk about my mother, June Cale and her famous friend, Katja Sorenson. I have done it many times since Katja's death. It is something I like to do and that I feel obliged to do. These were truly remarkable people and I think they have left an enduring legacy. So I speak to you now in that connection and as an avid reader of books. I love reading what you people write. You guys keep me alive. You really do. So I thank you for that."

He waited as the group applauded lightly in its self-congratulation.

"I also want to thank Steven for plugging *Letters from Katja.* If you do not already have a copy, I encourage you to get one. You will not regret it. I am here in part because my mother's publisher pays me to help them promote this wonderful book. I would certainly do it for free. But let's keep that just between us. That's not for publication."

As the audience laughed, I still could not believe my eyes. Lance. Lance of the window seat. Lance with the burly bicep beneath my unbidden palm. Lance with the book by K.P. Sorenson.

He had the book with him up at the dais. He pointed with it. He caressed it like a talisman.

K.P. Sorenson. I wanted to slither beneath the presenter table, pull the tablecloth over my body, and die. But I couldn't move. His voice was a neurotoxin that kept my brain from talking to my muscles.

"I was fortunate enough to spend many hours with Katja Sorenson. My parents were both British. They met in London in 1963 when fate steered his taxi into her bicycle. Ironically, as the story goes, he was the one who was injured, cracking his head against the windshield. Within the space of five years, my parents had exchanged names, had their first coffee together, conceived a child, married, separated and divorced. It was a short and frustrating union for both of them. My mother's globetrotting lifestyle meant that full custody went to my father. Happily so for everyone, I think. My father was a civil engineer. Around that time his company got a contract consulting on a series of bridge projects in Michigan. One trip to America and he was hooked. The last time I called London my home, I was six.

"I had a wonderful relationship with my mother. I called her June, not mother or mom. She was not one for labels. She thought they got in the way of things. My father and I lived in Michigan, and then Minnesota, and when she was able to stay in one place, my mother lived in Australia, just outside Melbourne. Her father, my grandfather, had been a cattle rancher. Henry Cale was his name. He died several years after my parents divorced and left June everything he owned, including the Melbourne property. When she was out traveling the globe for a story, she visited my father and me many times in this country, for she was often in either New York or Chicago on her way to someplace else. But when I went to see her, I went to Melbourne. And it so happened that many of those trips coincided with visits from Katja Sorenson.

"June and Katja loved horses, even in their later years. We all went riding as often as possible. We camped out under the stars. We sat around the campfire telling jokes. And I remember reading to each other. That was a tradition. We were each required to bring a book. Any book would do. As long as we liked it. After eating, we took turns reading our favorite passages. It was a wonderful experience.

"I have a good friend in Melbourne and I visit him as often as I can. I still go riding and camping. But I miss the nights with Katja and June. Sitting around the fire, reading by firelight. There is such comfort in those memories. I like remembering Katja and June together, sitting arm to arm on the other side of the fire. Even after having known each other for decades, their mutual affection was always so fresh and palpable. It stayed that way to the very end. It was like they could never get enough of each other's company. They occupied the same thought. They shared something visceral.

"It was difficult to think of one of them without the other. It still is."

I harnessed enough coordination to begin gathering my things, stacking my notes and conference materials and reaching blindly for the bag beneath my chair. My fingers found only shadows.

"June met Katja in 1955 in a hospital room in Sirsa, which is in the state of Haryana, India just south of Punjab. Katja, who was then visiting India researching the book that would become *A Thousand Broken Moons*, had been admitted for an emergency appendectomy.

"June at that time was living in India, working as a stringer for the London Times. She had been admitted to the hospital because she had been nearly beaten to death covering a riot near Patlala. She suffered internal abdominal injuries, a broken jaw, and head injuries so severe that they put her into a coma for nearly two weeks. June was four months pregnant at the time. The baby did not survive her injuries. There was no guarantee that June would survive either.

"The way June tells the story, she woke up one day in a fog of pain to the sound of a woman's voice, speaking at her bedside. June did not know this woman. She thought maybe the hospital had provided her with an English-speaking nurse to make her more comfortable. There was so much pain that even after she was out of her coma, June wafted in and out of consciousness for days. But each time she awoke, it was to the sound of a woman speaking to her in lightly accented English.

"No. Not speaking to her. Reading to her.

"When June was coherent enough to think past the pain and discomfort, she learned that the voice did not belong to a nurse. The voice was that of Katja Sorenson, an American writer in a wheelchair recovering from an appendectomy that had produced some life-threatening complications.

"Katja, it turned out, when she was well enough, was permitted to wander the hospital in her chair at night. She was a very active and independent person and did not take confinement easily, even in her convalescence. One evening, she had happened upon the unconscious June Cale and began asking around about her. Katja learned from the nurses the story of June's injuries and that June was apparently alone in the world, or at least alone in India. She had received no visitors and no calls. Her baby was gone and there was no degree of confidence among the hospital staff that June would ever wake up.

"On every subsequent evening, Katja returned to June's room and read to her. It did not matter to Katja that June was not conscious. It only mattered that June was alone and that if there was even the faintest pulse of a chance that June might hear Katja's voice and follow her words out of the darkness, then Katja wanted to give June that chance.

"So she read. Every night she read, feeding June syllables in the soft spoon of her voice as a kind of nourishment. This went on for days. The Indian doctors, to their credit, were very accommodating. They had done all they could. They let Katja have her chance.

"And then, one day, June fluttered back up toward the light.

"And there sat Katja. Reading. Still reading.

"The book from which Katja was reading was actually the book I have here in my hand."

Lance raised the book in the air. I could feel my own obnoxious inscription calling back at me from inside its covers: "To Lance, from his friend and seat mate, K.P. Sorenson. I hope you enjoy the book as much as I enjoyed the flight."

"This was Katja's very first published book, originally called *The Long Night of Dwindling*, republished many years later under the new title, *Failure to Thrive*. At that time in her life, Katja Sorenson had only published two books and she was in India working on her third, *A Thousand Broken Moons*.

"That makes it sound as though Katja Sorenson was on a winning streak. As though she was holding onto some comet blistering its way toward fame and fortune. Far from it. Katja was going nowhere fast.

"At that point in her life, Katja was engaged in a very rough conversation with herself about whether she had what it took to be a writer. Her first two books, including this one, were not selling well. She despaired that maybe she did not have a voice that anyone would care to hear. Alcohol showed up dangerously early in her life and kept her company far too often. Katja was used to being alone. She had always been alone. A child of orphanages. On that trip to India, she had almost nothing to her name. No friends. No family. Nothing to think of as a real home.

"In those early years, Katja had an undeniable talent, a cautious but willing publisher, and two books to her credit. She had been born into the world of books. But there was still hanging in the air above her the very real question of whether she had what it took to actually thrive as a writer. In the throes of answering that question, India in 1955 was a very dark and desperate time for Katja. As she has said several times over her career, Katja felt lucky to have survived India at all.

"I have read all Katja's books. Objectively speaking, _Failure to Thrive_ is not my favorite. It is an early precursor to Katja at her best, which was still a decade away. But it is my sentimental favorite, because I believe that book saved my mother. I believe that June did follow Katja's words out of darkness. I believe those words saved her and, in so doing, made her life possible.

"This book made my mother's much later collision with a London taxi possible. Which made _me_ possible.

"So I read it again every so often, tracing those words, imagining the sound of them in the quiet of an Indian hospital ward. I found this book on a shelf in the airport bookstore yesterday as I was waiting for my plane. So I bought it. I'm reading it all over again. It is one of those absorbent books that seems to fill itself with the world around you at the time you are reading it.

"I try to stay receptive to the things and to the people I encounter when I read good literature. It helps me see my life and remember it in a way I otherwise would not. The next time I pick up _Failure to Thrive_, maybe several years from now, I will remember this afternoon and speaking to all of you in this beautiful city. I will remember the dinner that I am going to have tonight with the parents of my life-partner, Robert."

The sickening revelation that Lance was gay, that my open blouse, naked foot and playful sexual airplane patter had been aimed at someone who could never have been tempted, felt like a cruel piling-on. I pressed both forearms against the table for support, bowing my face into my palms. I listened in darkness.

"I will remember the ... well, how to describe it ... the remarkable plane ride out here yesterday. I met a woman who I believe was quite desperate to become a professional fiction writer. I suppose mental illness is another possibility. It can be hard to tell sometimes."

I felt him look at me. Impossible, since I was behind him. But I felt it anyway. He knew I was there, listening to him speak, just as he had listened to my presentation. That meant he was actually communicating to me. He was telling me he thought I was mentally ill. I leaned back in my chair, removing my hands from my face but keeping my eyes closed. I concentrated, trying to focus all my mental energy. Spontaneous combustion was not in the cards.

"You laugh," he said when the carbonation around him had settled. "If you doubt me, ask your spouses. They will tell you that, in their experience, the line separating writers from the truly delusional is razor thin. The next time I read this book, I will remember the woman on the plane. I will wonder how she is getting on. I will worry for her. She too is now in these pages. Because when one encounters good writing, it is an experience in and of itself. And like all experience, it comes to you in memory infused with everything and everyone that crossed your path in that moment.

"The paths of Katja Sorenson and June Cale crossed in the pages of the same book – this book – and from that moment, they were in each others' lives forever.

"People have long spoken of Katja and June as sisters, enough so that there has been much confusion on this point over the decades. It did not help that they were each striking women who vaguely resembled each other. Nor did it help that their obvious affection for each other was so easily interpreted as familial. In several of the more circulated photographs, particularly when they were both staying in Australia, they could have passed as sisters. They were not actually sisters, of course. But they thought of themselves as such, if not in a familial way, then in a life-partner sort of way. They reflected the world for each

136

other. They celebrated and grieved for each other. They wrote for each other.

"When I say that they wrote for each other, I mean to include more than the voluminous and eloquent correspondence for which they were known. I mean to include everything they ever wrote after meeting each other. Every one of the hundreds of newspaper articles my mother wrote from nearly every country on the globe. Every novel and every story that Katja published, and all the things she wrote but, for whatever reason, did not publish.

"Katja wrote for June. June wrote for Katja.

"And this is what I want to say to you today. This is what I would say to the woman on the plane and to anyone who aspires to be a professional writer. Literature – the written word – is a binding agent. It is connective tissue that holds together the human family. I like to think this is true of art generally, but it is undeniably true for music and writing. After India, Katja came to believe that the act of written storytelling, if it is done correctly and in the right spirit, is nothing less than a confession by the writer of what he or she has in common with the reader. It is the author's way of reaching out over distances and dimensions great and small to say, simply, I am like you. We care about the same things. We love the same things. We have the same nightmares. We have the same heartbeat in our ears. We are twins in the womb of humanity. Do not forget that I am here. Remember me. I am here.

"I believe that Katja was successful as a writer because she was doing so much more with her talent than simply making things up for attention. She was writing *for* someone. She was throwing a ball, not just anywhere, not just high or fast, but throwing it purposefully, to that person over there, June Cale, standing in the sun with her hands stretched out, waiting to catch it.

"Writing *for* someone – writing *for* June Cale – gave Katja's talent for words purpose and meaning and soul. June saved Katja in that hospital room every bit as much as Katja saved June. It was June, whether she knew it or not, who set Katja on the path as a true writer. Because from the winter of 1955 on, Katja was always writing for someone.

"As writers, you are feeding someone with your words. Nurturing someone. Exciting someone. Wooing someone. Terrifying someone. You are assuring someone that they are not alone in the world, that they have a brother or sister in words, and that your heart beats with theirs.

"My mother died in a twin-engine Cessna outside Webuye, Kenya, right near the Ugandan border. She and a colleague with the London Times were off to cover a story on the Ugandan elections. It was a followup to a story June had written the previous year. It had been another groundbreaking story for June and the follow-up was much anticipated.

"There were no survivors. June was 72 years old. I don't think that anyone could deny that she died doing what she loved.

"As perhaps you already know, Katja Sorenson took that tragic turn of events very hard. She went into isolation for two or three years. We all tried to reach her, and by that I mean emotionally connect with her, but it was no use. She kept everything to herself. She kept herself to herself. The alcohol, which had been waiting fifty years for a promotion, finally found its time to reintroduce itself. I will spare you, and her memory, all that.

"Eventually, Katja pulled herself together enough to come back into her small society of friends. She even published two more books: *Unchaining the Wind* and *The Holcroft Affair*. They were not bad books. Sales were certainly okay. But Katja candidly hated them both.

138

"If you ever read them, you will see that those last two books were not written by the same person that gave us *All Saints Summer, Tomorrow as Ever,* and *Under the Waterberry.* That magnificent author, Katja Sorenson, I believe, died in the wreckage with June. The person who remained in her place wrote books for a living, looked like Katja, signed Katja's name inside the book cover when people asked her for autographs. But it was not the same Katja. She wrote those books, but she did not write them for anyone. She just ... she just wrote them.

"Katja Sorenson died at the age of eighty-three on the tenth anniversary of June Cale's death. On the tenth anniversary to the day.

"She had spent most of those ten intervening years living in June's home in Melbourne. My father and I were both with her when she died. She was eighty-three, but she seemed reasonably healthy for her age. She did not have pneumonia or congestive heart disease or cancer.

"The doctors did not have any good answers for us. Katja simply let go of the world. There was no longer enough to hold her here. She failed to thrive, as they say. Thriving takes a kind of wholeheartedness that Katja no longer possessed. In the end, we are either thriving ... or we are not at all. We cannot, it seems, simply live. Living takes effort. We must thrive to survive, which is to say that just as a writer must be writing for someone, we must live for someone or something. We must have someone or something to wake up to every day as our purpose.

"Every day. Every day. Every day. We must wake up to someone or something every day or we will fail to thrive.

"It is the connections we make in our lives that keep us in the game. We live as a narrative between lonely bookends. We are born alone. We die alone. The length of time between those two events depends on how successful we are in finding reasons to thrive while we are here.

"I am not a writer, but I have taken a lesson from two writers, Katja Sorenson and June Cale, about living. The lesson is this: connect whenever you can. Reach out. Let others reach out to you. Even strangers in airplanes at thirty-five thousand feet. They will do the most outlandish things. They will astonish you with what they say. Let them. Let them. Don't resist. Let them. Let them read to you from the book of their own lives. Let them autograph your book, the one you carry around inside of you. They are only trying to connect. They are only trying to find themselves in you. I'm here, they are telling you. Don't forget me. We are the same.

"Don't resist. Let them.

"If you wish to be a true writer, then you must write purposefully, with enthusiasm, not as an act of distinction, but as an act of communion. You must always write for someone. You must write with the heartbeat of your reader so hot and close in your ears that you are not able to distinguish the reader's pulse from your own.

"If you are lucky enough to see your name on the cover of a book, then I hope you are also wise enough to know that the book is not a testament to you. It is a testament to the relationship that you have forged with another person. A reader. It is a testament to how alike you are, how much you need each other, and how fortunate you are to have found each other."

The applause was warm and robust. Everyone stood. I found my bag and began stuffing my things inside, hoping that the commotion of applause and changing speakers would allow for an undetected exit. It was bad form, I knew. My agent-to-the-stars table mate rotated her rhinoplasty concernedly in my direction and stretched her eyes as best she could. You're not leaving, the eyes asked. I was supposed to stay for the duration of the conference. What about the Q&A?

But I was not about to risk bumping into Lance Peters. I would feign illness. A bursting appendix. Scurvy. Rickets. The Black Death. Anything.

I smiled back vacantly and tightened my thigh muscles. But before I could stand, the room calmed back into quiet.

"I have time for just a couple of questions," Lance said, pointing. "How about you? What's your name and where are you from?" I settled back into my chair as a bearded man in the middle of the ballroom was rising.

"Glen. Kansas City."

"Hi Glen. What's your question?"

"Did you ever think about following in your mother's footsteps, or in Katja's footsteps, and making a living as a writer?"

"No, actually. One of the things I learned early on from these two women is that you are either a writer or you are not a writer. It is either in your bones or it is not a part of you. Building is in my bones. I work with my hands. I have no interest in devoting my life to being someone I am not. And neither should any of you. Writing is not about making a living. God knows that too often writing is about not making a living. Plumbing, now that's a living."

The room boiled over with mirth. Glen from Kansas City sat down. Dozens of hands snaked up into the air as Lance continued.

"Writing is about something altogether different than making a living. Or it should be. Don't waste your time, and as an avid reader I would say, don't waste my time, if you don't feel it in your bones. Yes, you in the blue."

A woman stood in the second-to-last row. Many in the audience looked at her and then swiveled their heads in confusion to the presenter table and back again. They were wondering how I could be in two places at once. I would have liked to help them understand, but I was as shocked as they were. Almost.

"Kelly," said my sister, wearing the exact same blouse in a different color. "From St. Paul, Minnesota."

"Hi Kelly," said Lance, slowly rotating himself to look back at me. My eyes tried to skitter away in different directions like frightened roaches, but in the end I could not help but meet his gaze. I gave him a sickly, apologetic smile.

Yes, the smile said, there are two of us.

"What's your question?"

"I'm a journalist. I write for the St. Paul Pioneer Press. My sister is a novelist and she takes a certain pleasure in lording that over me. She believes that creativity unconstrained by objective fact has a greater claim to truth than does objectivity unconstrained by the need to entertain. So, I ask you, as the son of a great journalist and the friend of great novelist, which do you think has the greatest claim to truth?"

An uncomfortable murmur rippled through the audience like a cold breeze disquieting the surface of a lake. The attendees were each busy answering that question for themselves. Lance crossed his arms and stared down at his shoes, thinking.

* * *

After the conference, Kelly jabbed her arm between the elevator doors just before they closed. She was surprised to see me inside, but she covered it well.

"Nice blouse," she said, poking the already lit Lobby button. "You sure bolted out of there in a hurry."

"Since when do you come to these things?" I asked.

"Since all the time. I didn't come just to hear you speak if that's what you're implying. I didn't even know you were speaking."

"I'm not implying anything," I said. "Just surprised to see you is all."

She smiled a little and we both snickered at the odds of picking the same writers' conference, wearing the same blouse. I looked down. The shoes were also the same. As the elevator doors slid open, I was remembering my sister, my other self, holding hands down the aisle of seats as we sang songs and creeped out our fellow air travelers. It must have been tempting to see each of us as each one-half of a single being. A Kekathllyy.

But that is completely wrong. I am not one-half of a Kekathllyy. I am a whole Kekathllyy. And so is my sister. That is the paradox of twindom. We are simultaneously separate and combined. We each occupy two whole spaces in the world. We are not half anything.

* * *

When Lance had finally looked up at the audience, I was, true to form, already heavily invested in my sister's question. To suggest that the journalist, who simply regurgitates the things that have happened, has a greater claim to truth than a novelist was plainly absurd. I wanted him to put her in her place. Not brutally so. Kindly dismissive would have sufficed.

"What a great question, Kelly. I'm not quite sure how to answer it. I'm not sure there is an answer. But this is what comes to mind.

"When my plane was landing yesterday, as we were coming down out of the clouds, I could see San Diego. The city was a cluster of buildings huddled up against the immense, glimmering Pacific which was then in the process of swallowing the sun whole. And there was this flock of birds. Maybe fifty or so, below and in front of us. I'm not an ornithologist. I can't tell you what they were. They were small and white and beautiful. Sun flashing off their wings. I watched them intently for the brief minute or so that they were in view. They kept changing directions. Fifteen degrees seaward and then, suddenly, thirty degrees back toward land, and then seaward again. They acted as a single organism. No discernible leader. No hierarchy. A single organism.

"And yet it was a single organism comprised of many dozens of individual birds. And while each of those unique, individual feathered beings was looking for the next place to be – to eat, to nest, to do whatever it is they do – every micro-change in each bird's direction had an immediate impact on each of their respective neighbors. The entire flock careened one way and then quite dramatically another. An inefficient route to say the least. Because there was no route, except in the most basic instinctive way. There was only the search.

"Is it fair to ask which of those individual birds had the greatest claim to direction? I don't think it is. We are all looking for the same thing. If you want to call that thing truth, I will not quibble with a room full of writers over semantics. The point is that, whether we know it or not, whether we like it or not, our human flock is searching for it together. All of us. We are adjusting course as a species, traveling in groups, seeking in concert. If it is truth you want, then the truth is that we are never really traveling alone. We adjust our course at the slightest brush of a wingtip. Because that is our nature. And because maybe the truth about our species is not any destination at all, but the search itself. It's not the landing that matters so much as the journey. The flying. The breath of feathers at our sides.

"I cannot tell you what binds a group of individual birds together. But for us, in my opinion, that thing, that connective tissue reaching throughout our single human organism, is simply the innate desire to not be alone in this life. Each of us wants to be able to look into the face of someone else for confirmation that we are alive and that the world around us is miraculous and horrifying and inexplicable.

"Katja and June were dramatically different people. Different sensibilities. Different temperaments. Different professional focus. A fiction writer and a journalist. In some respects it is hard to imagine two people who were less similar. But even separated by half a planet, they were always, in their own way, wingtip to wingtip. The slightest impulse of one was always felt by the other, and almost never without consequence.

"We are all wildly different. And we are all so much the same. From even just a short distance, we are identical."

Put that way, it was difficult for anyone in the audience to disagree, even me.

I remembered Lance pointing to the birds through the plane window and I remember me not caring. His words at the conference had the effect of garnishing my humiliation with a renewed sense of professional inadequacy. I thought about my dizzying electric brainstorm the previous night, scribbling page after page to outline a novel about a pregnant newspaper reporter fired for plagiarizing a story about commercial exploitation of cloning research as kangaroos died in the streets of Melbourne. It seemed, suddenly, a purposeless invention for the sake of invention; an arrow fired out into the void, never aimed with the intention to hit any human target. It seemed pointless and beneath me.

In my humiliated beeline from the ballroom to the elevators, I felt almost queasy at the thought of how willing I have been to write and think and live short of my true potential. I wanted to write with purpose. I wanted to write for someone. I wanted a June Cale of my own. I wanted to throw a ball for someone to catch.

Kelly and I ended up sharing a cab. It turned out we were both staying at the same hotel. Not terribly surprising since we both prefer Marriott. I think it's the logo that appeals to us. We stopped at the front desk to ask about late checkout. The clerk could not stop staring.

"Wow," she said in amazement. "That's just... wow."

Kelly and I rolled our eyes at each other and headed down the hallway, making plans to have a drink and maybe dinner, although I was feeling the simmering of new ideas.

A newspaper reporter is fired for plagiarizing a story about commercial exploitation of cloning research. Her sister is pregnant. Amid the blooming scandal, the baby is born. The baby, little Jesse, survives and is in good health when he is abducted.

I needed to make some notes before I lost them.

The clerk could not stop staring. It was easy for us to shrug off the amazement. We had each experienced a full childhood of those kinds of reactions. There was no way for the clerk to know that I always book the highest floor available and Kelly always likes the ground floor.

Which I tend to think makes me just a little better person.

HATING GEORGE CLOONEY

Noon came and went, a vagabond hour drifting through the day, stale and unshaven, looking for something to pass the time.

Danny paid it no mind. He emptied the last of the cereal into the puddle of sugary pink milk and changed the channel.

It might have been a new experience, weekday-morning television. It might have presented a whole new landscape of entertainment for him while the rest of the world was punching a clock.

It should have been different, at least. Different than what he normally watched after work in the evenings, catching up on the news and then fully reclining for that familiar parade of characters and improbable conundrums, his body letting go, releasing the hard rhythms of the factory floor as the darkness outside thickened and the smell of Janice's pot roast settled like an aromatic dew over the furniture. Monday-morning television might have offered something new – exotic even – as sunlight splashed the Pennsylvanian autumn through the back windows, painting the floor and the walls of the living room with maple and black cherry.

It might have.

But cable television had destroyed the night and the day. There were no morning shows and afternoon shows and evening shows. It was all one thing now. One endless show. One unbroken river of pixilated light gushing from a plastic black rectangle mounted on the wall.

Danny's thumb spasmed through another cycle. He would be canceling his cable subscription now anyway. Maybe for the best.

George Clooney was stepping out of a jetway. Walking through an airport pulling a rolling black carryon. Black suit. Black tie. Smooth as can be. Like he owned the future in the same way that death owned the future. Like he walked on time itself, squishing each second beneath his polished black shoes.

George had a job. He fired people for a living. Not George, George's character. George himself had nothing that even remotely resembled a job. George's character fired people from a list. One city, then on to another, and another. Danny had seen part of the movie before. He didn't care to see any more of it.

Janice loved George. She loved George more than she loved Danny, apparently. Probably for a long time now.

Around him the whole house ached and convulsed like an empty stomach.

At one o'clock Danny turned off the television and went upstairs to the bedroom. He changed out of the flannel robe Janice had given him the Christmas after his father passed, and put on the same clothes he'd worn the day before. Not because he didn't have anything else to wear, but simply because yesterday's clothes were closer to where he stood than the clothes on hangers behind the closet doors. Naked, he bent to retrieve them from their elongated pile – socks, pants with the belt still in the loops, underwear, shirt, undershirt – on the floor by the unmade bed, where he'd left them like a sloughed skin.

He brushed his teeth and thought about shaving. He ran a comb through his hair and then left the house, stepping outside into a deceptively sunny breeze. The air had more of an edge to it than yesterday. A little colder. A little meaner. It rattled the papery red and gold leaves with just a little more menace. Danny locked the front door and climbed up into the truck.

Janice's blue scrunchy hair do-dad was still around the gear shift where she liked to keep it just in case she needed one when they were out. He kept meaning to bring it inside for the box he said he'd mail to her. She'd have a new one by now.

He started the truck to make the drive into town, as much for something to do with himself as for something real to eat. He backed out of the driveway, cranked the wheel and then kept slowly inching backward until he could see in the rearview mirror the long driveway up to the large house on the cul-de-sac at the end of the street. There was no point to this exercise anymore. Like so much of his life, this too had become an empty habit.

He idled for a few seconds at the row of white mailboxes, looking backward, knowing it would look like he was checking his mail. He even opened his window and thrust his hand out to the box that still included Janice's name on the front. He didn't actually open the mailbox. Nothing good would come of that. Not now. Maybe not ever again.

The long driveway behind him lay still beneath a skittering of leaves. Danny rolled up the window, put the truck in gear and drove.

He had never been in McGuinley's at one-thirty in the afternoon. The lunch crowd had come and gone and the smell of solvent was like a sickly sweet film that found the back of his throat. It was too bright. Too quiet. The tables, which in his experience usually disappeared inside overgrown clumps of hunchbacked, happy-hour regulars, now looked bare and forsaken, like defoliated tree stumps.

Danny took a seat at the bar and ordered a cheeseburger. The bartender gave him a beer and then disappeared into the back.

"What the hell's the opposite of happy hour?" Ross clapped Danny on the shoulder and sat down next to him.

Danny had seen Ross coming in the mirror against the back wall of the bar, his hard, thin, black-eyed face seeming to grow out of the neck of a liquor bottle. Before Ross reached the bar, the disembodied idea of Ross had slapped Danny on the back and taken a seat, giving him a second or two to prepare for the company he did not particularly want.

He hadn't seen Ross since the New Year's party. He was wearing the same black coat he always seemed to wear, with its carabiner zipper-pull connected to a miniature bottle opener. Danny took a drink before he answered.

"Place needs a pink-slip discount," Danny said.

"Got that right."

The bartender showed up, putting new batteries in a remote control. He turned on the game but kept the sound off. Ross ordered a shot and a beer. Danny gave him a look.

"Seems between the two of us, Ross, you're the one with a job. What are you doing drinking boilermakers all the way up here in Tionesta?"

"Slumming," said Ross with a smirk as the bartender delivered the order.

"Oh, like Sugar Creek is some kinda heaven. And here you are tying one on at one-thirty in the afternoon."

"Called in sick," Ross said, throwing back the shot. "I hate my job."

"You're just going to make me mad, Ross. Least you got a job."

"I know," he said. "I hate it anyway."

"Well then give it to me."

Ross laughed and started on the beer.

"I just don't see you selling corn chips and batteries and pork and beans and... goddamned... disposable razors, Danny. Although it looks like maybe you could use a razor."

Danny half-turned to look at Ross and ignored the part about the razor.

"Oh? That mean you see me assembling strollers and car seats and cribs and baby gates even though I don't have a kid? That something you see me doing, Ross? Because I did that for a lot of years. So if you don't like your job at Foley's then give it to me and I'll do it."

Ross took a drink and let some of the hardness drain out of his face.

"Can't," he said. "I need the work same as you. Sorry about the plant closing. Figured it was just another rumor. Seemed like Baby Cloud had been folding for a long time."

"Yeah, well." Danny turned back around and didn't finish. He looked up at the game.

"What are you going to do?" Ross asked.

"I don't know."

"How's Janice taking it?"

Danny thought about whether to answer that question, which was really nobody's business. And it was Ross' business least of all.

"She moved out," he said eventually. "Living at her sister's in Philly."

"Because of the plant closing?"

"It's complicated, Ross."

Ross nodded. "That's marriage for you. Always complicated. Once is enough for me." He took a drink and swallowed. "Well, is she coming back?"

"I don't know. Maybe not."

The bartender came out of the kitchen with a cheeseburger and fries on a brownish ceramic plate and placed it on the bar. Danny chewed and they both sat in silence and looked up at the soundless game of football like they were watching images on the surface of a soap bubble. The scoreboard told its story and then the commercials took over. George Clooney walked into view, drinking espresso from a tiny glass cup. He swallowed and gave his little smirk. Danny shook his head.

"Getting really sick of that guy," said Danny. Ross looked up and then over at Danny and then back up at the screen.

"Who? Him? How come?"

"Because people like him," Danny started and then took a bite of his burger to block the rest. He shook his head and chewed.

"You mean fancy coffee drinkers?" asked Ross.

Danny looked sideways at Ross and finished his mouthful.

"No. I mean people that have everything because nothing they do in the world ever turns to shit. And I mean not ever. Not once. Some people hog all the luck for themselves and then walk around looking all..."

Danny didn't finish. He shook his head again and chewed. After another ten seconds or so he started again, pointing up at the screen, which then showed a closeup slow-motion animation of vacuum cleaner bristles pulling up dog hair, but in Danny's head it was still George up there sipping and smirking.

"I mean, this guy's never had a bad day in his entire life. Bullshit movie star. Richer than God. Beautiful women his whole life. One after another, like he grows them in an orchard in his backyard and he just reaches up and plucks a new one whenever he wants. All his bullshit movie star friends with so much money and luck, they don't know what to do with it all, patting themselves on the back and showing all those teeth like everything is always so goddamned wonderful and funny, falling all over themselves to show which one is having a better time."

Danny jabbed his finger back up at the television, which showed a fake insurance agent in front of a pile of soggy timber that used to be somebody's house.

"Then he gets hitched and we all have to look at his wedding photos twenty-four-seven, like he's the only one that's ever gotten married and like his love is more special than anyone else's love. Then it turns out he's always had some wild hair for tequila and that he's invested some money into making his own tequila."

Danny wiggled all ten of his fingers in the air and elongated the sound of the word own – his owwwwnn tequila – stretching it like putty above the bar. It might have been a decent place to stop the tirade and let the rest go. But Danny had Ross' attention and didn't want to let it go. It felt good to get it out.

"Might have been a turn for the better if that's what he wanted to do with his life. Quit farting around in the movies and work hard at making a good tequila. But not this guy. No, no. This guy dabbles, Ross. He pretends at it. So, okay. Other people pretend at business. They dabble. And then they get punished for it because the world is for serious people who know what the hell they're doing. The world doesn't reward dabbling. Dabblers lose their shorts. They go bankrupt and the people they love leave them and they curl up in a ball in an empty house and hurt for awhile, smelling like the tequila they used to make. But not this guy. No, no, no. This guy dabbles; he pretends for three or four years at making tequila, then he sells the tequila company for a billion dollars."

Ross snorted and stifled a laugh into his beer. Danny stopped pointing at the soap bubble television and jabbed his finger at Ross instead.

"You think I'm exaggerating. A billion dollars, Ross. It was all over the E-TV. Billion with a goddamned B. Guys like us? Like you and me? Nothing but hard times and plants closing and women leaving and pianos falling from the sky. But people like him?" Without looking, Danny pointed up to the place he imagined George was still sipping his coffee. An old man was eating a bowl of soup as a woman holding a clipboard asked him questions. "For people like him, it's nothing but fluffy white clouds of money and luck."

"I know," said Ross, suddenly serious. "Reminds me of my boss, Foley. He's got so much money from that store of his, plus the one up in Erie, that he doesn't know what to do with it all."

Danny could feel that the tirade had run its course. He picked up the burger. "Never met the man. I've only ever been in Foley's once for a six-pack. Years ago."

"The store in Franklin is a lot bigger now," said Ross. "You should come by sometime."

Danny shook his head. "Corner Store here in Tionesta's got all I ever need. Not driving all the way out to Franklin."

"Well, you should. Now that you have all this time on your hands. I'll show you Foley's office. He's almost never in anymore. He's off traveling the world with his hot wife."

"Oh?"

Ross whistled. "Like she stepped out of a magazine. Never met her but she is one fine-looking piece, I'll tell you what. And Foley's office bookshelves?"

Danny chewed his burger without looking at Ross, regretting all over again that he had picked this place at this time to eat. Ross repeated the question, both hands suspended in the air, waiting.

"The office bookshelves?"

"I know what bookshelves are, Ross," said Danny, unable or unwilling to keep the irritation out of his tone. "So what?"

"Nothing but framed pictures of all the places Foley's been and all the things he's done. Skiing and boating and riding camels and jumping out of planes and lying on the beach. He's got money and luck to burn." Ross points up at the game. "Just like what's his name."

"George."

"Right. Just like George. And Foley's just asking to get himself robbed, too. Not because he's dumb either. He just don't care. He's got so much, it just don't mean anything to him. He just don't give a shit anymore."

"The store got robbed?"

"No. I'm saying he's asking to get robbed. I'm saying Foley's got so much money, he wouldn't care if he did get robbed."

Danny rolled his eyes and gave a little snort. "Come on. Rich don't mean stupid."

"Didn't say stupid. Said not caring."

"Well."

Ross lowers his voice a little. "Okay, smartass, well then you tell me why he keeps that safe open all day long."

"What safe?"

"The one in his office surrounded by all the pictures of him and his playmate model jumping out of planes and riding camels. He unlocks the safe in the morning and it stays unlocked all day until the store closes."

"Thought you said he's never there."

"He isn't. I haven't seen the man in two months."

"Well then, how's he unlock the safe?"

"It's electronic. He pushes a button from wherever. Vail. Bahamas. Egypt. And click. Open sesame. When we open up in the morning, we get enough money out of the safe for the till, then at the end of the day we do the books and put the money from the till in the safe and close it up and it automatically locks. Stays that way until we're ready to open up in the morning."

"Why doesn't he just give you the combination or whatever? Aren't you like a manager or..."

Ross shrugged. "Doesn't trust me, I guess."

"Sounds like maybe he does care about the money."

"Not enough. Not near enough."

"So it just stays, like, open and unlocked?"

Ross nodded.

"He can't be bothered with it. We used to have to call him every time we needed more cash for the till and one day all we had was large bills and we couldn't make any change and Foley was supposed to be up at the Erie store but no one could find him and it was a mess. From then on, he just unlocks the safe in the morning and lets it stay unlocked so he only has to worry about it once a day."

"He is taking a risk, isn't he?" says Danny.

"A big risk," said Ross. Danny looked.

"How big, exactly?"

"Depends on when he makes a deposit run. He just lets it stack up until he can be bothered to go to the bank. Some odd morning we'll open up the store and see Foley has come by in the night and emptied the safe and left us just enough cash to get started. We always assume it was him, anyway. Could be anybody and he wouldn't know or care. That's how much he doesn't need it. Just sits in there waiting as he's off playing. Like I say, we haven't seen him in a long time. Safe is full."

Ross elbows Danny in the ribs. "Eh? Eh? Little retirement planning, Danny?"

Danny brushes Ross away with the back of his hand, turning back to his plate.

"Come on. Bet there's cameras everywhere, Ross. A man that knows how to unlock his safe from a thousand miles away knows how to set up some cameras. Probably looking at you on his cellphone every time you go in that office."

Ross closed his eyes and slowly shook his head. Danny wanted to punch him in his ugly, hawk-nosed, black-eyed face for what he was saying. For what he was suggesting.

"Nope. No cameras."

"And just how do you know that?"

"Because I've wondered myself and looked. I'm in that office every day and I've looked. And also because he bought a camera system for the whole store last year and it arrived while he was off playing with his centerfold, as usual, off living the high-life with his bombshell playmate, and he's never even bothered to open up the damned box."

"You're sure."

"It's still in the bottom of the office closet where I put it near a year ago. Hell, someone who knew what they were doing could walk back there and haul away three thousand dollars in almost brand new surveillance camera equipment."

"So you're saying the store has no alarms or anything?"

"Of course it has alarms, Danny. Perimeter and motion. We set the system every night and Foley can confirm while he's off skinny-dipping with his own personal mermaid whether or not the system is armed. He can always arm it remotely himself. He's ready for break-ins. But that was mostly an insurance thing. Wasn't really Foley's idea. And he hasn't done squat to protect his money during the daytime. Anyone could just amble back there and load up a bag of money. Stroll right back out easy as you please."

Danny pushed the mostly empty plate away and wiped his mouth. "That is peculiar," he said, shaking his head.

"Only if you assume he gives a shit," said Ross. Then he pointed at Danny's plate. "You don't seem to be interested in the rest of those fries."

"You want them?" Danny slid the plate sideways. "Take them. Just about the last thing I really need."

Ross stuck a fry in his mouth as if it were a cigarette.

"And that's just about exactly my point."

The next morning, after a long and sleepless night in front of the television, Danny sat tucked into the stern of Clayton's aluminum skiff, drinking coffee from a thermos and watching silver beads of water rappel the slant of his fishing line down into Komo Lake. Dark gray clouds had abducted the early light. A stiff breeze worried the water, perforating the stadium of trees and rattling a billion paper leaves into a frenzy of yellows and reds.

It was too cold for comfortable fishing, which might have been okay if the fish were biting. But the fish were not biting, so it was not okay. Danny could not remember the last time Komo Lake had coughed up something he could take home to eat. This morning was no different.

He'd once reeled in a sea-green, size DDD brassiere, which had been good for a few laughs and a photo of Danny proudly holding up his prize catch. He'd taken the photo to the Baby Cloud plant and pinned it on the lunchroom bulletin board just to be a card. But the only thing that particular catch had fed was Danny's imagination. For some time afterward, he had wondered about the circumstances preceding the submergence of a size DDD bra into the lake.

He'd made the mistake of speculating openly to Janice about the bra owner, noting that there were only but so many large-breasted women in the Tionesta area. Janice, whose breasts were the size of tart Pennsylvania apples, had pointedly speculated in return that maybe the woman was dead, tied to a cinderblock at the bottom of the lake. The possibility had never occurred to Danny. Truth was the idea of some poor woman decomposing at the bottom of Komo Lake had made him feel a little sick inside. The following Monday he had gone to work and clocked onto the assembly floor as always but then made an excuse to leave for the bathroom. Diverting to the cafeteria, he'd taken the photo off the bulletin board and dropped it into the trash.

Danny glanced over at Clayton, who shifted his pole to his other hand and pulled his hat down more securely over his head in a way that made it seem like maybe he was trying to keep his body heat from escaping out into the fall air. He did not look any more comfortable or optimistic than Danny.

Clayton was a large man with a boyish haircut framing a quiet, unsmiling face that almost never showed what was going on inside. Years ago, the day Clayton lost his brother in a shootout with the state troopers, he learned the news from a call on his cellphone out on the assembly floor. He and Danny had been pre-assembling the A-Sides for a shipment of Deluxe Baby Cloud Cribs. Clayton had finished his shift without saying a word about it. No one, including Danny, had any idea anything was wrong. Same old Clayton.

The next morning the newspaper told the story of a burglary gone bad. The article had quoted Clayton as saying that his brother had come to the end of a long run of bad luck and felt like he had run out of options. Without hope, Clayton had said, everything looks a little different. All kinds of things become possible that maybe should have been unthinkable.

Danny knew that Clayton was in the boat for the same reason that he himself was in the boat: a promise of sorts had been made as they were each cleaning out their lockers at the Baby Cloud plant. Neither of them had known what the future held, and that had made a few hours of fishing on Komo Lake seem like a great idea. At the very least they could catch some sexy lingerie. It was the only laugh either of them had had that day, which made the idea seem even better. They'd shaken hands on the plan in the parking lot, when the air was warm and the sun had encouraged them both to think better of their fate. Neither of them had wanted to be the one who canceled.

"Any word from Janice?" Clayton asked.

"Oh yeah," said Danny, shifting. "Plenty of words. None of them nice."

"Think she'll come back?"

"I don't know, Clay. Doubt it."

"You okay?"

Danny shrugged. The water slapped up against the skiff like a kind of laugh, mirthless and bitter.

"Screwed up too many times with Janice," he said eventually. "And now there's no money. Going to lose the house. Can't say I blame her. She's better off."

They were quiet for long, windblown moments. Leaves, airborne from all directions, hit the surface of the water and stuck. They accumulated in colorful patches, overlapping and combining like scales over the back of an enormous yellow and red reptile that might eventually stand up and saunter off through the woods, carrying Clayton's silver skiff between its shoulder blades.

"You own your place?" Danny asked. Clayton reeled in his hook and cast it back out over the water.

"Mom took out a second mortgage three years ago for her treatment. Boy," Clayton shook his head. "If I could do that over again. Money lasted eight months. Mom lasted nine. I've had my second cousin twice removed living with me for the past year. He's been paying rent."

"That going to be enough now that you're out of work?"

Clayton made the same laughing sound as the lake water slapping against the skiff. He looked up at Danny from beneath the bill of his cap. He didn't need to answer.

"What's he do for rent?" Danny asked.

"Seth? Grease monkey ex-con working out in Tidoute. Also pretty sure he's stealing cars for the chop shops."

"Keeps your roof over your head though. For a while anyway."

"I guess. Seth's not around much, which is probably good. Spends most of his spare time out at the speedway. He's got a married woman he likes to play with. Candice. Seth calls her Candy. She stays over every now and then; they keep the whole neighborhood awake. Then I don't see her for weeks. She lives out past Sugar Creek somewhere I think."

Danny reeled in his line and pulled the hook out of the water. He cleaned away the lake muck and added fresh bait and then sent it sailing back out into the wind, which took it well east of where he had intended it to land. He watched it plop into the water and adjusted himself in the boat, squaring his shoulders to the line and turning his back a little to Clayton. He hadn't planned it that way; sometimes things just work out. Better that eye contact was not so convenient.

162

"Saw Ross yesterday," Danny said. "Speaking of Sugar Creek."

"Oh? Haven't seen Ross in... hell, I don't remember the last time. New Year's, I think. Two years ago. He was at the party. How's he making out these days?"

"Still working out at Foley's Got it All in Franklin and bitching about it."

"Least it's a job."

"That's what I told him," said Danny.

"What else he say?"

Danny took a slow, extra breath. Into the slate gray sky an army of trees bled yellow and red as the wind steadily rattled them into skeletons.

* * *

"I'm just saying that it's not going to do any of us any good, least of all you, if you get pulled over on the way back for drinking and driving, let alone wrapping your car around a tree."

Clayton kept all the irritation out of his voice, speaking as though he was sharing a casual observation. But Danny could tell that his friend was reaching the limits of his patience. Seth either couldn't tell or didn't care.

"One," said Seth, grabbing the pitcher and pouring another full glass. "I bought this pitcher and I intend to finish it."

163

Seth's hands were permanently stained a shadowy bluish-black from engine oil, with fingernails like little coal shovels. On his fingers, right beneath the knuckles, were letters tattooed in a gothic font: HARD on the right hand and FAST on the left. Beneath the short, dirty-blond hair and the ratty red Pennzoil cap were boyish features that might have cleaned up with some effort and soap and acne cream and a diet of something other than deep-fried meat. Seth's eyes were a watery blue and his teeth were straight and snowy white. Not so long ago, he might have been a different sort of person.

"Two," Seth banged the pitcher back down on the table and took a long drink of beer. "Wasn't my idea to drive all the way up to the goddamned Frog Pond in goddamned Union City to have this goddamned little meeting. Three, wasn't my idea for all of us to take separate cars so I got no choice but to drive myself back. Four, I can drive drunk better than any of you peckerheads can drive sober so that's enough of that shit. Five..."

"Okay," said Danny, looking at Clayton, and then to Ross, and finally back at Seth. "Enough counting. Can we just get back to planning this... this..."

They all looked at him trying to come up with the right word. He knew the word. They all did. He just still had trouble actually saying it.

"Lesson," said Ross, simply, helpfully, like he was nudging a needle into a different groove. "We're planning to teach old man Foley a lesson, plain and simple. We're talking northward of forty-, fifty-thousand pinto beans, boys."

They all sat quietly for a second, calculating.

164

"Why the hell doesn't someone go make a damned deposit?" asked Danny.

"He should," said Ross. "He used to. Every Wednesday and Friday. But, like I say, Foley hasn't been around for awhile."

"Then why not you?"

"Me what? Make the deposit?"

"Yeah."

"Not like I haven't offered. Foley always insists on doing it himself. And he always says it like I'm too stupid to know what's going on."

Clayton and Danny looked at each other uncertainly, concerned that maybe they were stupid.

"What is going on?" asked Danny.

"Foley's skimming," said Ross. "He's screwing Uncle Sam is what in the hell's going on. Just like all rich people. We pay our taxes like we're supposed to, like we need to do to keep this country running. But people like Foley... that deposit is always thirty percent light. He's spending on his girl tax-free. I'd sure as hell like to spend on my girl tax-free. Wouldn't you?"

Danny and Clayton, neither of whom have a girl, slumped a little into their beers. But Danny felt himself nod just a little. He did wish he'd had more to spend on Janice while she was still around. He wished he'd pampered her more. Would he have cheated on his taxes for her? If it would have made her happy, if it would have made a difference in the end, would he have fudged a few numbers on a ledger? Yes, he thinks. He would have.

"My girl spends on me," boasted Seth. "I'm a kept man."

"Your girl," said Clayton, "is married to somebody else. Which means she's stealing from her man to give to you. That make you feel special?"

"So how long has it been since Foley's been in?" asked Danny, not caring to hear Seth's justification.

"Over a month," said Ross. "Near six weeks."

"Maybe he's dead," said Seth. "Heart attack maybe."

Ross shook his head and emptied his glass.

"The only thing that's wrong with Foley is that he can't be bothered to care about his own business. I called him just three days ago because our propane vendor needed a personal authorization to renew a contract. And do you think Foley asked me anything about how things were going?" Ross looked intently around the table. "No. It was all I could do to keep him on the phone for more than thirty seconds and the whole time I could hear his girl moaning in the background. Foley's doing just fine. Trust me. He's halfway around the world, bending a girl young enough to be his daughter over the railing of a yacht. I haven't had a raise in three years. I can barely feed myself. Meanwhile Danny and Clayton get shit-canned by Baby Cloud? Without so much as a thank-you after years of work? And Seth here is busting his ass fixing cars without a home of his own and trying to make it on next to nothing? Are you shitting me? That's no way for any self-respecting man to live. Any one of you work harder in ten minutes than Foley does in ten years, only you don't have shit to show for it and what he's got, he leaves laying around like it's worth nothing."

They all listened, staring into their drinks like it was the beer making the case for robbing the Foley's Got It All and not its general manager. Danny ventured a careful look around the table to see how it was all playing. Clayton was doing the same. When their eyes met they hesitated a beat, confirming that it was all really happening, that it was not just a weird dream, before looking back into their respective glasses. Ross kept at it.

"It'd be one thing, maybe, if Foley cared enough to protect what's his. Or if he needed the money. But you know what? He don't care and he don't need it. People like him never do. And when it's gone? He's just going to ask me to fill out an insurance claim. And the insurance company will send out someone to ask me all the same questions that the troopers will ask after I call it in. And then the case will close and the insurance company'll pay Foley back everything he lost. And then you know what the insurance company is going to say?"

Ross sat upright in his chair and pursed his lips to narrow his face into something effete and prim. He spoke in a high, lilting accent and batted his eyelashes.

"'Well, I declare, Mr. Foley, we gon' have to raise y'all's rates.'"

Ross stayed in character for a second or two as the others chortled into their drinks. Then he relaxed his face, returning his features to their natural proportions as the black, glossy hardness reclaimed his eyes.

"And then Foley is going to take another drink of champagne and turn his model sex-maniac over on the bed and laugh and laugh and laugh."

Ross let the silence settle over the table before continuing. The longer he waited, the heavier the silence became, like a kind of dark snow filling up the spaces between them and burying them all where they sat.

"So I say let's teach Foley a lesson and help ourselves out in the process. A lesson he'll never really learn and that won't hurt him anyway."

Clayton scratched his large head and looked up from his beer.

"Here's what I don't understand, Ross. If this is so easy, why haven't you just done it yourself?"

"I have," said Ross with a shrug. "Here and there. Fifty one day. Hundred another. But I can't clean him out alone. I need to assume I'll be suspect number one. When it's a murder, they start with the spouse. When it's a heist, they start with the GM. I need to assume they'll want a closeup look under my bed and in my bank account. Those boys'll be up my ass. Bet on it."

"So you'll be telling them what, exactly?" asked Danny.

"I'll be telling them all about a lanky black man, mid-thirties about yay tall in a skull cap and Steelers hoodie with a white gal, early twenties with blond dreads and bags under her eyes, wearing a dirty blue coat that was two sizes too big with a tat of a frog on her neck."

168

Seth scrunched up his face like he was wringing out a wet sponge. "What?"

"They were in the store, twice, couple weeks back. Caught them loitering in the hardware section the first time and I chased them out after thirty minutes because they were up to no good. They were casing. I could just tell. They were back two days later and it was the same thing, only this time they were hanging out by the gun case. I took their picture and told them to get the hell out or next time I'd report them. I'd bet anything that kid was high as a kite and that he was packing. They were screwing up their courage to knock us over. I thought it might go down right then. It might have, too. But then girly pulled him by the arm and they left. Everett saw the whole thing."

"Who the hell's Everett?" asked Seth.

"Just a kid. Store employee. Point is he can corroborate."

Ross pulled out his cellphone and turned it on. He swiped and poked at the screen for a few seconds, then turned it around to the others. They all leaned in. The couple were just as Ross had described, looking oddly placid leaning up on either side of the Foley's Got It All gun display case.

"Next week they'll be back, see?" said Ross. "They're going to come in just as I'm closing up after Everett's gone home. The woman will watch the door as the man points a cannon at my head and marches me back and makes me clean out the safe into a plastic garbage bag. He'll take my cellphone on the way out, thinking he's being clever but not realizing that all my photos are backed up in the cloud. It'll give the Troopers something to dig for."

169

"How the hell you know that's going to happen?" Seth was genuinely perplexed, then indignant as he took another drink. "I thought the money's ours?"

The others looked at each other in a silent, uncharitable consensus. Clayton rotated away from Seth to address Ross.

"What'll Foley say when the Troopers come asking?"

"How the hell do I know? And why do I care? He's never around. He'll either say he has no clue about anything or, if he pulls his head out of his girl's ass long enough to remember, he'll tell them that when I called him to ask about the propane contract, I mentioned having to chase off a couple that looked like they were casing the place. Because that's what happened. That's exactly what I did. They'll ask Everett too and he'll say the same thing because he was there."

"And when the Troopers get ahold of those two," Danny pointed to Ross' phone, "and they clearly had nothing to do with it?"

Ross shook his head. "They're long gone, my friend. The day I chased them out, I saw them across the Burger King parking lot hitch a ride on a semi. They were just passing through, looking for an easy score on the way to their next high. They could be anywhere in the country by now."

"I don't understand why we're doing this in broad fucking daylight." Seth interrupted. "Let's just go by at three in the morning and you let us in and we'll get it and be gone."

Ross drew a breath and drank the rest of his beer.

"What?" asked Seth, looking at Danny and then Clayton. "Makes more sense than..."

"That might just be the worst idea I've ever heard," interrupted Ross. "The security log will show an unforced three A.M. entry. That points the finger directly at me. And once the safe is closed at the end of the day, it's locked and I can't open it."

"Okay, then just have the shit ready in a bag and one of us will come by and pick it up. Drive away. Slam Bam. Why are you making this so damn hard?"

"Because there's another employee to worry about. We've got to pull this off under Everett's nose. Can't just hand over a big bag of money to someone who pops in."

"Then we break in. Like normal."

"Alarms."

"You're the inside man," Seth said impatiently. "Disable them bitches."

Ross looked slowly at Danny and Clayton before turning back to Seth and answering the question. "Foley can always see whether the alarm is enabled or not. And there's a record."

"You said there're no cameras. Let's just go for it. Let the alarm make its noise. We'll be long gone. Ain't complicated, man."

Ross leaned in over the table toward Seth.

"You know, it almost seems to me like you want me to go to prison."

That word – prison – is electric. Around the table, muscles quietly convulse. The server, on her way over from the kitchen to check in, thought better of interrupting and changed her course.

"You're lucky you're even in this conversation. Seth. If I didn't think we needed two people in the store and a separate driver in a waiting car, you wouldn't be here. Now, if Clayton here says you're good, then I'm willing to take his word for it. To a point. So, tell me, Seth. You going to let me run this thing or not?"

All of them looked at Seth, who leaned back in his chair, shaking his head. He emptied his beer and refilled his glass.

"Whatever, man. Yeah. Go on and run it. I'm just saying, is all."

"Good."

"What do you want me to do?"

"I want you to wait in the car, like I said. When Danny and Clayton come out with the money, the three of you are going to haul ass to Spartansburg. Like I said. You're going to the barn. Like I said. You're going to divide up the money into four even shares. Like I said. Danny is going to hold my share for safekeeping. Like I said."

Seth's expression hardened, the flesh of his face stretching tautly over his cheek bones. The soft blue of his eyes clouded. "Say like I said one more time and I'm out. Hear me, Ross?"

But Ross continued as though Seth had never said a word.

"Then, after the money is divided up, you're going on your merry way, and Danny is going to get in the piece-of-shit truck that's waiting and he's going to give Clayton a ride to the bus station. And then no one is going to see or talk to any of the rest of us for a month. None of you can call me on any phone that I have access to and I will not be calling any of you. Danny and I will settle up at some point after that."

Ross smiled and his eyes finished the sentence: *Like I said.*

"I don't understand the whole thing about the bags," said Seth.

"You don't need to understand about the bags. The bags don't concern you. The bags are inside the store and you're outside the store. In the car. Motor running. Waiting. Got that?"

Seth ignored the question. "Anybody need a piece? I got plenty."

"No," said Ross in a sharp whisper. "No guns. No guns. No goddamned guns."

"Well, why the hell not?" asked Seth, suddenly like a disappointed child outside an ice cream store.

"First, because if you listened to the plan, you'd know there is no need for guns. Second, if we get caught," Ross made a point of looking quickly at Danny and Clayton, "which we are not, but even assuming we did, armed robbery is a different ballgame entirely than simple theft. Third, this isn't about getting anybody hurt. This is only about helping us all out of a jam and teaching Foley a lesson, which he'll think about for maybe ten minutes as he scuba dives with his girl before passing the lesson on to his insurance company."

Seth scrunched up his face. "What's the lesson again?"

"The lesson is for Foley to take about ten seconds out of his globe-trotting sex party and give a shit for a change. If he don't care about his money, then why should anyone else care? The lesson is to consider other people for once." Ross looked over at Danny. "He can have his orchard of young beautiful women and sip his fancy coffee all he wants, if that's all he cares about. That's fine with me."

* * *

Komo Lake, pocked with early morning rain, slowly disappeared behind a veil of condensation. It coated the inside of the front windshield and the two side windows of the truck with such an even, white translucence that Danny felt like he was sitting inside a Ping-Pong ball. He looked again at his watch, then closed his eyes and put the seat back to wait.

Twenty minutes later, he opened his eyes at the sound of another car pulling up next to his. Danny climbed out, locked the door to the truck and folded himself into the backseat of a blue Chevy Caprice. The vinyl seat had been badly knifed and yellowish foam stuffing was extruding up through the coil springs. Danny slid to the other side of the car.

"Sorry we're late," said Clayton, jerking his thumb toward the driver's seat as the car reversed and then shot forward.

"Oh, shut the hell up, Clay," said Seth. "You know we needed to change the plates."

"Yeah. We needed to change the plates last night. What we didn't need is to start out this morning and then remember that you forgot to change the plates and to then go back and look for the plates and then..."

"Will you just... damn! It's not like we have an appointment or something. Ross said around noon. Guess when we're going to get there? Around noon is when. Meantime, Danny got some extra sleep." Seth looked at Danny in the mirror with a counterfeit smile. "Didn't you, Danny?"

Danny nodded once and looked out the window at the red and yellow smears of wet foliage. He kept mostly to himself on the ride out to Franklin, letting the nervous bickering and joke-telling from the front seat seal him off into a world of his own.

He found himself swimming back to that little island of time – the twenty or thirty minutes he was lying in bed between coming awake and getting dressed. The elephantine reality of all that could go wrong had taken a seat on his chest and kept him from sitting up. He'd stared up at the bedroom ceiling and read the words that someone had written up there as he slept: *It was only talking. Talking*

*is legal. Nothing has happened yet. Just stay in bed. Go back
to sleep.*

And he might have stayed where he was. He'd even
rolled over toward the open field of rumpled sheet next to
him where the smooth planes of Janice's back, the curve of
her right shoulder like the path of a sculptor's thumb, had
usually blocked his view of the stately maple outside the
window. Its vibrant gold was now mostly gone, replaced
with a mud-colored skeleton flapping bits of dead skin in
the breeze.

He might have rolled over and stayed. But eventually a
small plane had flown overhead, somewhere above the
ceiling, sawing through the gray sky with a jagged blade.
The sound had slowly faded away, leaving a quiet
emptiness, a ragged hole in the shape of his life. Danny had
gotten up.

"Something goes wrong, I am *pre*-pared." Seth said the
word like it was two, snapping off the first syllable and
saying it with extra emphasis as he held a black handgun up
toward the ceiling of the car.

"Christ, Seth," said Clayton. "Thought we said no guns.
I'm pretty sure you heard that part."

Danny reached forward, toward the front seat, in an
effort to take the gun from Seth's hand. But Seth was
watching him in the mirror and returned the weapon to the
inside pocket of his coat before Danny could even come
close.

"Oh, I heard that part just fine," said Seth, both hands
back on the steering wheel. "I just don't agree. Maybe Ross
gets to say how all this goes down but he is not going to

have any say on whether I can protect myself. He can be sorry if he wants to. I won't be. If something starts to go bad in the Foley's Got It All, then just head for the car. I've got you covered."

"No guns, Seth," said Clayton. "I'm not dying in a crossfire."

"Suit yourself," said Seth. "I'll come visit you in prison."

"You're the one on parole, man. You looking to go back? Waving that thing around like that?"

"Damn, Clay," Seth said with genuine contempt. "You sound like my mother."

Danny leaned back in the seat and returned his attention to the window as they argued in an effort to boil off nervous energy. An endless line of small commercial buildings squatting on spider-cracked concrete slid past, dropping quietly into the oblivion behind the car.

Gas station.

Mini-mall.

A place that sold nothing but yarn.

Plumbing supply outlet.

A boarded-up diner sitting alone on an empty, wet, gray parking lot.

A Janus Auto Parts Hub rose in the distance, its big red sign like a burning flag. The dingy, blue-and-gray edifice came and went with a swoosh but the Janus sign continued to burn in Danny's mind. He read the word as Janice.

She and her sister, Karen, were likely sitting at Karen's kitchen table in their robes, bent over one cellphone or another, or making circles in the Post-Gazette, looking for R&R job prospects. Retail and Reception. Whenever in her life Janice had had to turn the page and start over, it always seemed to begin with a new job in either retail or reception. She was a people-person. Attractive. Engaging. Danny always told her she had a tractor-beam smile that made you want to know more. She could sell anything.

They'd met at the Mattress Barn in Weigelstown. Danny was newly divorced from Beth and had just moved to Harrisburg from Toledo. Janice and Karen had buried their widowed father six months earlier. Janice had given up on art school and had started over with a job selling mattresses.

She'd sold Danny a queen. He had asked her to a movie.

Eight months later, Janice had upgraded him to a king that he did not really need. Six months after that, they were married and loading that same king mattress into a U-Haul bound for Tionesta – in Forest County on the southwestern tip of the Allegheny National Forest – so that Danny could take a job at the new Baby Cloud plant in nearby Pleasantville.

Practical Janice had thrown caution to the wind and gone all-in for Danny. In rapid succession, they had moved into a small but comfortable house, met the neighbors and turned them into fast friends, rescued a hound puppy they had named Juniper, and settled in for something they both understood to be permanent.

To great community fanfare, Danny had helped to open up the Pleasantville Baby Cloud plant and Janice had found a job selling arts and crafts supplies at a place out in Meadville, where she eventually began teaching an after-hours art class three days a week. The neighbors had taken a liking to Juni and had permission to take her for walks when Danny and Janice were both working.

The seasons had come and gone like grand kingdoms of color and mood that, in a graceful order of succession, had risen up out of the earth around their feet, melted away and risen again. The king mattress had comfortably accommodated them all, human and canine.

It was, ultimately, the neighbors' mattress that had proved to be most accommodating. And now Janice was sleeping on a saggy twin in Philly. Juni was sleeping in an old fleece dog bed on Karen's kitchen floor. Danny, the only one of them now sleeping with too much space, still had the king.

The neighbors, meanwhile, had been quickly and quietly reabsorbed into a secret, snowy world beyond Danny's access or understanding. The possibility of a more volcanic dissolution, one more in keeping with how one normally expects adultery to play out, had loomed ominously and had kept Danny and Janice together for almost a year longer than they might have lasted otherwise.

It was as if the wrong way of dealing with infidelity had been so obvious and expected that it had felt suspiciously like a trapdoor to something worse. They had tried to navigate around it, choosing to deal with infidelity the right way. Talking. Counseling. Long walks with Juni in the woods. Trying to reinvest in old and reliable routines to rebuild trust.

179

And that right way of dealing with things had bought them some time.

But that was all: some time. Ten or eleven extra months, tops. As much as they tried, those old and reliable routines were never quite the same. At its very best, and only once or twice at that, togetherness had taken on a pluckily self-conscious, congratulatory air. *Look at us*, their togetherness had said. *Look at us reinvesting in our old and reliable routines. Look at us not letting the mistakes of the past destroy our future.* Those extra months had lined up and blown through them like a stiff autumn wind. The marriage had shed most of its leaves, until the few that remained were only the stubborn, golden memories of happier, healthier times.

Then, before Danny's laminated assembly floor access badge could reach its tenth anniversary, the Baby Cloud pink slips had also hit the wind. It had proved too much for what little remained. So even those last golden leaves of the relationship had finally let go. It was easier for Danny to let others think the marriage had succumbed to financial shock like so many others.

Not honest, of course, but easier.

About now, Karen would be pouring coffee into large mugs and then, elbows on the kitchen table, pushing her sister toward some sort of professional setting. Doctors, lawyers and accountants. She would probably even be making the effort to sell the dental hygienist idea again. Only now – with Danny on the outs, three hundred miles across Pennsylvania on his way to rob the Foley's Got It All in Franklin – Karen would feel free to tout the fringe benefits of a profession that would bring her sister into contact with eligible dentists and four-day workweeks.

180

But Janice would be holding firm, absently biting the inside of her lower lip like she always did when she was stressed, and shaking her head without looking up so that her fine auburn hair swayed against the side of her face. She would be looking for anything to give her a toehold. R&R. Retail and reception. Once she got settled with a steady paycheck, she would reevaluate her options and take the next step. Janice was practical in times of uncertainty. She had her father's resourcefulness. She did whatever needed to be done.

"If the shit goes down, I will do what needs to be done and you can take that to the bank twice on Sunday, my friend."

Twenty miles had done nothing to soften Seth's cocky defiance.

Clayton wrenched himself backward to look over the top of his seat at Danny and then back over at Seth.

"Bank's not even open on Sunday, man. Which means you're going to try to do what needs to be done twice, and you're going to fail twice. How smart is that?"

"Smart as a bullet between the eyes, Clay."

It was just past eleven-thirty when they rolled into Franklin. Seth made a couple of slow passes through town and then up US-62 almost to Oil City and back again before pulling into the Burger King parking lot as Ross had instructed. They parked in a space close to the highway.

On the other side of the road, sliding quietly beneath the sound of relentless traffic, the Allegheny River moved like a slate-gray snake secreting itself beneath a carpet of leaves.

Seth turned off the engine. It clicked and popped in the cold air as they all looked out over the hood and across the mostly empty sea of concrete at the Foley's Got It All.

Foley's was a large, wooden, single-story building the color of faded rust. Two glass doors met each other at the dead center of the edifice, flanked by three narrow windows on each side. Three cars sat parked along the side of the store next to a half-open green dumpster. Out front, in the middle of the parking lot, a thick, yellow pole hoisted a large, white rectangular sign with black script lettering: Foley's Got It All.

They spent a few quiet minutes taking a measure of the activity in the lot. In the space of fifteen minutes, what had started as six cars swelled to as many as fourteen and shrank to as few as three.

It was not difficult to imagine the kind of business Foley's did in a single day, thanks mostly to its provident location on the shore of US-62. It was near impossible not to imagine the stacks of cash collecting in the back room – day after day, week after week – all because the store owner already had so much money socked away that he no longer cared about it and couldn't be bothered to come by his own store, stick it all in a bag and take it to the bank.

For a moment, it had bothered Danny that the man who cared so little about his own money, so much so that he couldn't be bothered to protect it, was the same man who regularly underreported to the IRS and skimmed the store receipts in order to keep as much money for himself as possible. It seemed odd that Foley would not care about the money that was his, and yet be willing to risk tax fraud to keep the money that belonged to the government.

But that moment had passed. Either because he did not care enough for what was his, or because he was stealing what belonged to US taxpayers, Foley did not deserve to keep what had been quietly accumulating in the office of his store. It seemed fair that he should be deprived, at least for the short period of time before his insurance company reimbursed his losses.

"No cops around," said Clayton. "Guess that's a plus."

"May as well get on in there, Clay," said Seth. "Time's a-wasting."

Clayton sighed and looked over the backseat at Danny, the vinyl groaning under his weight.

"We really going to do this?"

Danny shrugged.

"Give me ten minutes," said Clayton. "Then come on in. I'll make sure Everett leaves you alone."

Clayton got out and closed the door. They watched him make his way across the Burger King lot toward the Foley's lot, pulling his jacket sharply down at the waist and brushing his sleeves. Like he was headed in for a job interview. He stopped for a green minivan sporting a custom-painted logo for Allegheny Brews. The minivan crossed his path on its way to a parking spot near the Foley's sign.

"We should knock over a brewery next," said Seth, nodding at the green minivan. The gun had found its way out of Seth's coat pocket and was now sitting on the front seat.

"We're not knocking anything over. We're not criminals."

"Speak for yourself. I don't mind being a criminal." Seth lifted the gun up over the seat. "Long as it all works out in the end."

"Fine. I'm not a criminal. And put that fucking thing away."

Seth put the gun back in his coat just as Clayton pulled open the door to Foley's Got It All and disappeared inside. Seth found Danny's eyes in the mirror.

"You're sure as hell about to be," said Seth. "But think on this while you wait: Just because it's wrong don't mean you won't love it."

Danny left Seth alone in the mirror and looked out the window. In the space next to them, an empty candy wrapper fluttered beneath a dirty, white paper bag with a bottle inside. The wrapper – bright yellow with a red leaf-shape across the front – brought him a bright autumn day two years earlier.

Juni was on her leash, yanking him every direction but forward, sniffing a carnival of decomposition beneath a thick blanket of red and yellow leaves. She had rolled in something unknown but disgusting.

Juni had been oblivious to Danny's abrupt change in mood. She seemed not to care that the walk had been cut short. She also had no inkling that she was destined for an unpleasant dousing with the garden hose. Not that it mattered; nothing could dampen Juni's pleasure at being out amid the riotous rot and decay of a Pennsylvania fall.

On the final turn for the house, Danny spotted his neighbor, Amanda, up the road, standing at the array of dirty-white mailboxes. She turned and saw them still a hundred yards off. Kneeling, she slapped a handful of mail against her leg, and shouted for Juni, who then found the reason she needed to pull forward in a straight line. Danny might have unleashed her and let her sprint the rest of the way.

But he'd known better.

"Keep your distance," he warned when he was close enough not to shout. "She rolled in something awful. We're headed for the nearest hose."

Amanda had not moved. Setting the mail on the road, she had placed her hands on either side of Juniper's sleek brown face, holding it still, just beyond the reach of the lapping tongue, as the rest of Juniper wriggled and squirmed. Amanda had cooed as if to a toddler.

"Has Juni been naughty? Has Juni been a dirty girl? I know. I know, baby. It's wrong but we love it, don't we? Just because it's wrong doesn't mean we don't love it. Isn't that right, honey? Isn't that right, Juni baby?"

Towering above them, Danny had looked down at the top of Amanda's head. Her hair was yellow-blond, falling to just below her shoulders in long, relaxed curls. She wrapped her pale, slender fingers around Juni's snout and scratched her floppy brown ears. Whereas Janice was almost never without nail polish of some color, Danny had never seen Amanda wearing polish of any color. Amanda either did not feel undressed, as Janice did, without dots of color on the tips of her fingers and toes, or she did not mind the feeling of being undressed.

Amanda gave Juni a kiss between her eyes, regathered the mail and stood.

"Afternoon, Mr. Danny," she said with a smile.

She was in her early thirties, easily ten years younger than Matt, the man she lived with, who was a good five years older than Danny and Janice. Matt alternately referred to her as either Amanda or Mandy, depending on the occasion, leading Danny to a familiar, momentary hesitation whenever he was called upon to speak her name. He'd tried Mandy once, thanking her for taking his plate after a New Year's Eve dinner, but it had seemed wrong somehow. Presumptuous. Intimate.

"Afternoon, Ms Amanda," he said, bowing his head in mock formality.

Juniper, stinking powerfully from below, had resented the sudden lack of attention. She made a leap in Amanda's direction before Danny could take the slack out of the leash and pull her back. Her front paws left two trails of muddy grime down the front of Amanda's blouse and along her denim thighs. Danny had channeled his embarrassment into scolding Juni and commanding her to sit, which was next to impossible when she was excited. Amanda had looked herself over and laughed, pulling her shirt away from her body.

"Sorry," said Danny, still hunched over Juni.

Amanda cupped him on the shoulder with her hand and its undressed fingers, bringing him to attention.

"Guess now you're going to have to hose us both down."

Janice and Amanda had hit it off almost immediately, bonding first over Juni and then, at Amanda's encouragement, over the plight of sheltered animals throughout northwestern Pennsylvania. Within the first six months of the move to Tionesta, Amanda had deputized Janice to help with a community campaign to spay and neuter pets and to raise money for animal shelter expansions in Franklin and Stoneboro.

In the course of this work, Janice had made other connections. Amanda introduced Janice to Kendra, the owner of the art supply store in Meadville. Amanda had recommended Janice for a job as if they'd been best friends for life. Kendra had hired Janice within the week.

Amanda herself was not employed. Matt owned a furniture manufacturing business just outside Titusville that, along with the Hepplewhite tables and chairs and the Chippendale credenzas, also seemed to manufacture a great deal of money. Matt and Amanda – or Matt-n-Mandy as Danny referred to them with an almost playful derision whenever he was inclined to make fun of their perfect-couple persona – lived in a home three times the size of Danny's. It was set much farther back in the woods than the other houses, connected to a cul-de-sac and the main road by an extra-long driveway. They could easily have lived in some well-to-do suburb of Pittsburg, but Matt liked his privacy, preferring the remove of nature. As Amanda had playfully put it more than once, the idea of living on the cusp of a national forest appealed to them on a *soulular* level.

And it may have. Forest County Pennsylvania was not lacking those who drew inspiration and vital energy from nature. But Matt exuded an urbane, metropolitan essence. Always well groomed and closely shaved, he wore expensive clothing, even when he wasn't headed off to a place he called work where, were it not a western Pennsylvanian furniture factory, one might be able to imagine the need for business attire. Matt favored blazers pulled over white, open-collared shirts, nubby trousers and expensive shoes.

Not that he was at all effete. Far from it. Matt always split his own wood, stacking it by the cord along the wall of a large shed he had built himself on the edge of his property. When the shed wall would not accommodate another log, Matt loaded the remainder into his truck and drove it three hundred yards up the main road to Danny and Janice's house, where he piled it into a neat, pyramidal structure in the backyard next to Juni's doghouse.

Matt had also built the doghouse. Danny had noticed it after returning from a night of drinking and poker with some of his Baby Cloud coworkers.

"What in the hell is that?"

He had pointed through the kitchen window at the pitched roof structure sitting in the dim wash of the back porch light. Janice had joined him at the sink, momentarily setting aside her irritation that Danny had neglected to tell her about the poker game and that, since his cellphone was off, she had been this close to calling hospitals.

"Matt," she said with a shrug. "He said Amanda had been lobbying for a doghouse for Juni. Said it only took him an hour."

"Bullshit."

"Well, that's what he said."

"Jesus. It's even got a little... a little..."

"A porch."

"A porch. Juni has her own porch. Jesus."

"Stop with the Jesus. You always say Jesus when you're drunk."

Danny had not taken the bait, nor looked at his wife. He couldn't stop looking at Juni's new home.

"We've got to do something to thank him," he said. Janice had turned and left him at the sink, putting away the dinner she had never actually served.

"Matt said we should thank Amanda," said Janice. "He said Mandy'll do anything for dogs and that he'll do anything for Mandy."

A former building contractor, Matt kept his own home in good repair with plumbing, electrical and carpentry skills far exceeding anything Danny could ever claim. When Janice found a leak in the kitchen ceiling one wet spring, she had called Matt for a roofing service referral. Matt had come by the next morning with a ladder to diagnose the problem and then proceeded to repair a strip of flashing that had been damaged by an ice dam the previous winter.

But Matt's masculine qualities, even including his sincere and passionate devotion to the Reds and the Bengals, exhibited themselves with a relaxed refinement that was not believably a part of the forest in which he lived. He was a gregarious, ridiculously attractive man, fit, with short, salt-and-pepper hair, a square jaw and dark eyebrows that conspired with an orbital bone structure to perfectly frame his soft, brown eyes. He spoke in a textured baritone made for radio. Genuine leather and silk and wool were always close at hand. His pulse aerated white bergamot, orange and Antilles lime. He smelled expensive. And Matt knew his wine, which he kept in a well organized cellar beneath his house, although in the early evenings he was just as likely to be found nursing a bourbon highball.

In the lit hours of the day, he loved espresso.

Matt's relationship with Amanda was, at least to Danny, bewildering, like an Escher drawing in which up and down, in and out, light and dark, battled in the mind for a dominant claim to perception. From a certain perspective, the one that Danny had frequently called the Matt-n-Mandy Show, or the M&M Lovefest, Matt and Amanda were not merely romantically devoted, but so completely enamored with each other as to make their dinner guests feel invisible. The passing of asparagus came with lingering looks and enigmatic smiles. They touched each other incessantly: palm to nape was a favorite, as was the brush of fingertips across the brow, as if removing something not actually there. They draped arms over shoulders. They enveloped from behind. Every topic of discussion offered limitless opportunity for remember-the-time-when anecdotal escapes into their own romance. In a thousand different ways, both obvious and clandestine, Matt and Amanda were always coming home to each other.

It was disconcerting, then, that they were not married. And that they seemed to have no interest in marriage. Even as the neighborly relationship matured and as Amanda and Janice had developed a friendship that allowed some measure of personal disclosure, the reason they had never married remained elusive beyond Amanda's less than illuminating explanation that they just didn't think it was

190

necessary, and the equally useless flourish that love always belongs only wherever it wants to be.

Matt and Amanda spoke of each other's romantic histories with disarming ease, referencing old lovers like mutual friends or siblings with whom they remained interactively and emotionally involved.

"Clint called again," Matt said to Amanda once as he was reaching between Danny and Janice to freshen up the Bordeaux.

"Yeah? How does he sound?" Amanda was removing the last of the plates and retaking her seat.

"Like he's been dumped. Like he needs some company. I tried to boost his spirits. You know," he had added with a mock contemplativeness, "I really don't think Clint cares enough about the Bengals' win on Sunday."

Amanda and Matt had laughed at each other across the table.

"The Bengals." Amanda snorted. "Matt, Clint hates the whole sport. He's an artist. He's a curl-up-with-a-good-book or an old-movie-on-a-rainy-day kind of guy. Clint doesn't care about a bunch of big galoots bumping into each other."

Matt had mocked shock and surprise. "Oh, I think Clint cares plenty about bumping."

Smirking, Amanda had pulled one bare foot up onto the chair and hugged her knee with one arm as she extended her empty glass with the other. As Matt poured, she had looked across the table at Danny.

"My last boyfriend. When Clint falls in love, he never really gets over it. He's a great painter and an absolutely hopeless romantic. For two years he's been with this woman who I think is totally beneath him."

"Bryn," said Matt.

"Bryn." Amanda shook her head. "I warned him about Bryn when they first started up."

"I did too," said Matt, returning to his seat. "This is not a surprise."

"No, it's not. Bryn was like... like..." Amanda had set down her glass and pulled her golden tresses behind her head, staring at the ceiling as if the words she needed might be full of helium. "Bryn was this corporate-ladder climber working in the digital services subscription business. A middle manager at best but she had that whole dog-eat-dog vibe. She's exactly the opposite of Clint, who's this very sensual, emotional being. He's a wonderful guy. So in touch with himself."

"Well, he's sure in touch with himself now," said Matt.

Amanda continued as if she had not heard him. "Bryn was just wrong on so many levels. And now she's taken off with some loser she works with – and Clint is lost and wallowing in loneliness."

"Yeah, but it's not really her, Mandy," said Matt. "It's you. Clint's never gotten over you. I mean, you have to see that. Bryn was just a distraction. She kept his mind off you. Now Bryn's gone and, well, here you are again. Keeping Clint awake at night."

Danny had thought the remark another bit of softly sarcastic, slightly sexual levity, anticipating Amanda's retort in kind. But Amanda had only nodded, sincerely, and with a muted concern on her face. She took a drink of wine and said nothing.

"You should go see him," said Matt. "Stay with him a week or so. Get him back on his feet."

Amanda had nodded again, swallowing. "I should. I'll call him tomorrow." Then, as if in the wash of an afterthought, "Good thing I renewed my passport."

She must have seen the confusion on the faces across from her.

"Clint lives in Montreal."

That dinner had been nothing unusual in the relationship between the two couples. Amanda frequently called Janice and invited them over to help them out with some extra food they needed to eat before it had to be tossed in the composter, or to celebrate Friday, or test drive Matt's new barbecue sauce. The occasions were so frequent that Danny had taken to expecting what he wryly dubbed Happy Hour at Matt-n-Mandy's.

But the dinner of the Clint discussion had popped its head up above the others, standing out in Danny's mind. It was at that dinner that Danny had allowed himself to acknowledge his attraction to Amanda, and, relatedly, just how much he resented Matt's good fortune for having her.

This quiet revelation did not occur at the dinner table, but later in the evening, after they had moved to the well appointed, fawn- and chocolate-colored den, where another bottle of wine had softened them all into overstuffed love seats arranged around a lively fire. Amanda, ever the flaxen-haired, seventies earth-muffin in her light blue peasant blouse, bell-bottoms and bare feet, had curled herself onto the space of a single love seat cushion with Matt at the other end.

As they all told stories and laughed at things that might never have been funny in any other setting, Danny had found a strange fixation on the way in which Matt – so refined and sophisticated, every hair in place, every muscle in his face under perfect control, seemingly immune to intoxicants, cradling the curve of his wine glass in the fingers of his right hand – comfortably palmed the top of Amanda's bare, delicate foot with his left.

There was no mistaking this calm and assured claim to the affection of another, this casual display of possession. And yet, Danny could not reconcile what he saw on the love seat with what he had heard at the dinner table. The man whose hand played so proprietarily upon Amanda's ankle and foot was the same man who, not thirty minutes earlier, had all but insisted that Amanda, a woman he had chosen not to marry, spend two weeks alone in Montreal with a heartbroken, former lover.

The incongruity had plagued him for the rest of the evening. As that incongruity was still unresolved by the time they were saying their goodbyes, it had congealed from something merely inexplicable down into something unpleasant. Something resentful.

Amanda, soft and warm and pliant in her drunkenness, had kissed Danny lightly on the lips in the foyer as Matt and Janice were in the kitchen, loading the last of the dishes. Amanda had run the tips of her naked fingers through the hair at his temples.

"And thank you, Mr. Danny," she said in a quiet breath that he could feel on his face, "for keeping Matt honest."

He knew the remark was merely a reference to what had been the greatest joke of the evening: Danny calling out Matt for surreptitiously eating from Amanda's bowl of ice cream as he simultaneously exalted his own self-restraint and refused any for himself.

Nevertheless, careful to keep his hands on the slopes of Amanda's shoulders, Danny had found himself flirting with an altogether different, deeper meaning to those words: someone needed to keep Matt honest. Someone needed to remind Matt that it should take more than merely a casual hand on the foot to keep someone like Amanda; that if he left her unwed and unguarded to the lovelorn Clints of the world – if Matt took his own good fortune so for granted as to assume either that Amanda would never leave him or that he would be able to replace her with someone equally special – then one day Matt would wake up sorely mistaken.

One day Matt would wake up as Clint.

"Why, Ms. Amanda," he had replied in a bad southern drawl, taking her left hand from his temple and kissing it, "it was, and will forever be, my great honor."

It had been snowing heavily all afternoon, evening and very early morning. Endless white sheets rippled in the night breeze, covering the forest with a heavy, suffocating quiet. As Amanda and Matt bade them one final goodnight and closed the door behind them, Janice had pulled Danny's arm around her and clung to his thick wrist with both hands, stepping carefully into a drift almost up to her knees.

Danny might have appreciated the trust and intimacy inherent in the act of clinging to him for support. The marriage had, over the years, tended to economize on expressions of tenderness and affection that at one time had flowed with profligate abandon and without the prompting of snowdrifts. Marital familiarity had bred, not contempt so much as a claustrophobic yearning for some modicum of independence; just a little relief from the presumptions of companionability woven into their vows. Competing interests had found their way into the widening breach, snagging the fibers, loosening the weave. Danny had developed friendships with a group from work. Designated poker and bowling nights had followed in due course, expanding his sphere of autonomy along with his tolerance for stout beer.

The change in the relationship had been gradual enough at first to avoid arguments about the relationship itself. The early arguments, instead, had tended to be microcosmic snits over all the smaller things serving as petty proxies for the relationship. Unthinking, unintended slights. Careless, semantic missteps. Unobserved courtesies.

Danny not calling to apprise Janice of his after-work plans. "Stay out as late as you want, Dan, I really don't care. It's just basic respect to let me know what the hell you're doing."

Janice repeatedly resurrecting offenses for which Danny believed he had already apologized. "Jesus, Janice. What else do you want from me? How many times do I need to tell you I'm sorry before it counts?"

But those early, microcosmic snits were like baby wildlings adopted from the forest. They grew. They took in great lungsful of oxygen, becoming larger and stronger on a diet of sublimated hurt and wounded pride. Eventually it was no longer fair to call them snits.

It took shouting to be heard. It took breaking things to be felt.

They made up, of course. Each time, often passionately or with welcome tenderness, they returned to each other in ways meant to erase time, resurrecting the irrepressible lovers who, having consummated a commercial mattress transaction in a manner not condoned by management, were then ready to devote their lives to each other.

These emotional reunions made them feel stronger, closer, even a little self-satisfied at the durability of a marriage that had been battle-tested and that had endured, despite it all.

And yet, usually in the quiet morning that followed a night of reconciliation, with the first breath of sunlight streaming through the kitchen smelling of scrambled eggs and ground arabica, Danny finished his breakfast, kissed his wife, and then headed off to the Baby Cloud plant with a nagging disquiet. The feelings had always started small but they grew and became more agitating with every new mile he laid down between his rear bumper and his home. He tried to push them down, covering them with the radio news or the classic country station.

But such efforts were pointless. The feelings rose from the depths like bubbles up from the bottom of a gassy lake, popping at the surface of conscious understanding in a predictable sequence: Peace would never have returned to his marriage without a Herculean effort on his part; most of that effort had involved him selling a tearful concession to Janice's point of view that, for days after, would leave a residue of debasement; such emotional upheaval should not be necessary; marriage should not produce a toxic buildup; marriage should not require cyclical lustrations to keep it clean; and, ultimately, the final bubble usually surfacing and popping just as he pulled into the Baby Cloud parking lot: Not all relationships were this way because not all women were this way.

The cycle time between each reconciliation and the next emotional upheaval had lengthened mercifully when Janice began spending more evenings in Meadville teaching her after-hours art class. On those nights, Danny had felt much freer to indulge his own social life without risk of offending the rules of common marital courtesy. It helped to know that Janice was not waiting for him at home, tending a dinner he would not likely want, waiting in the remains of the day for him to prove himself.

But if separate diversions and greater personal autonomy had lessened the conflict in the marriage, it had also changed the prevailing climate. A steady dusting of languor had fallen over the top of the relationship, dampening not just the feelings of frustration that might otherwise have flared into conflict, but everything. Dampening everything. Quieting everything.

Until, at last, it seemed to each of them that they only ever came alive as a couple when they were in the presence of other couples who exuded the kind of youthful, irrepressible ardor that they remembered feeling. It was not unlike hearing the song that decades earlier had made you swoon for its ability to, in some indefinable way, set your own life story to music and convince your non-rational self that the lyrics and melody were written especially for you.

That was the feeling – the old but unforgotten song echoing in an empty hallway – that usually washed over Danny whenever they had dinner with Matt and Amanda, whose easy romantic charm was, time and again, utterly beguiling. Danny usually found himself feeling just a little closer to Janice for those few wine-soaked hours – demonstrating his affections, taking her side, humbling himself in comparison, making her laugh, touching her – in a way that had become increasingly unlikely whenever it was just the two of them in their own home.

So many times either Matt or Amanda had commented on what a great relationship Danny and Janice had, compliments bashfully received and never corrected. For both of them had secretly longed for those compliments to be true, even if for just a little longer until it was time to help with the dishes and go home, where the truth of their marriage waited patiently in the snowy quiet for the sound of their footsteps on the front porch.

On the walk home the night of the discussion about poor, lovelorn Clint, Janice had kept Danny's arm pulled tight around her shoulders, less for support in the snow than to prolong the glow of the evening and the cozy, romantic, warmly intoxicated buzz that always seem to carry her out of a Matt-n-Mandy's Happy Hour.

Janice spoke about the story Matt had been telling her in the kitchen – a rabbit riding a horse that had become a viral video and that somehow had ended up nudging a nine-year-old cancer patient into remission.

"Just before she was admitted," said Janice, "the girl had a dream about a horse, standing alone on a hill along the side of the road."

Danny counterfeited sounds of interest, unable to follow her words. He had cocooned himself inside thoughts of Amanda. The sensation of her lips on his. Her breath on his face. The way she had moved through the evening, sinking her naked fingers into the golden river of her own hair. Her relaxed, uncomplicated sexual presence in the room, as she drank her wine and smiled with her eyes and laughed from deep within her throat. The way she curled her body into a chair or a love seat like a cat in the sun. The purity of her snowy bare foot beneath the palm of Matt's hand.

Matt's hand.

Danny's feelings for Amanda had had more than just a little to do with Matt. The way he looked and walked and smelled and sounded and acted and said things with his handsome face. Danny's conscious awareness of these various resentments changed like the weather. Sometimes he could conjure Amanda in his mind and see only her, re-experiencing her in a vacuum as though they had only ever been together alone. Having dinner. Drinking wine by the fire. Alone.

Other times he could not help but imagining Matt, intruding, strolling into Danny's mind in his fine shoes and one of his nubby, bullshit sweaters with the sleeves pushed just ever-so-much up the forearms as he carried that insufferable air of invincibility, so confident in his face and his hair and his voice and his money and his wood-chopping, home-fixing, doghouse-building handiness that, even as he invaded Danny's own private fantasy and found

199

Amanda undressed by the fire drinking wine from Danny's glass, all it took was the palm of Matt's hand on her naked foot and she was his.

And why? Why was she his?

Because the Matts of the world have greedily harvested all the luck for themselves. They get more because they have more and they have more of everything, simply because they have utterly convinced themselves that they are entitled to more. And, seeing the monstrous self-confidence that comes from such self-indulgence, and from the proven knowledge that they can never ever, ever fail in life, the world cannot help but give itself over to men like Matt. Such certainty in the eyes of a man is not to be resisted. A palm to the foot is all it ever takes.

In the days and weeks and months that followed, Danny had found reasons, of varying degrees of authenticity, to go by Amanda's house when Matt was not home. On the weekend mornings, when Danny sat in his living room drinking coffee and reading the paper as Janice buzzed about in the kitchen, he sat facing the window that offered a clear view of the road. On the occasions that he noticed Matt's truck pass by, either headed into town for supplies or out to the county recycling center, Danny found himself calling out for Juniper, asking if she wanted to go for a walk. It could not have been a more ridiculous question.

Juni only ever had one answer.

None of the various scenarios that Danny had conjured on these walks were even remotely realistic: Amanda spotting them from the upstairs bedroom window, half-dressed, hair wet, inviting him inside. Or, after they had passed the house and were working their way into the body of the forest, Amanda surprising him from behind, holding her hands over his eyes, turning him around and kissing him on the lips, breathing on his face so that he could take in her scent, before leading him back to the house.

The reality was that he had never once encountered Amanda on any of these walks, nor even seen her, until the day that Juni serendipitously rolled in something disgusting and he had encountered Amanda at the mailboxes.

Guess now you're going to have to hose us both down.

The exchange had ended there. Regrettably, Juni's bath had not involved Amanda, whose breezy flirtation had followed her up the road into her house behind a closed door, leaving Danny and his malodorous hound at the mailboxes, which were arranged all in a row like a subdivision of tiny, floating Quonset huts jutting out over the road.

That encounter had pushed his sexual agitation to near obsessive levels. The line between fantasy and reality had not been entirely erased, but it had become so obscured by desire and the frustrations of his marriage and everyday living, that Danny began pursuing the fantasy as though it was realistically attainable. His life – from the moment he came to consciousness in the mornings until the long, still hours of the night, lying in bed next to Janice and waiting for sleep to take him – was a single, nearly continuous sexual machination. His intellectualized goal was not so much to cheat on his wife as to prove that Matt's air of entitlement was unfounded; to prove that by taking the world for granted, Matt and his ilk could easily lose the world to those who did not take it for granted.

Danny's effort to arrange a serviceable encounter with Amanda suffered some practical limitations. There were only so many times he could take Juni for a walk in the mornings before work, in the evenings after work, or on the weekends. There were only so many times he could call up

Amanda when Matt was not at home and ask if he could come by and borrow one of Matt's tools.

Once, as a heavy, gray, early October rain pelted windows throughout western Pennsylvania, Danny put on his coat as soon as he heard Janice turn on the shower and went outside, up the road to the mailboxes. He collected his own mail and then gathered the mail out of Matt and Amanda's mailbox. Danny had walked up to the end of the road to the house in which he and Janice had enjoyed dinner only twelve hours earlier.

Gripping a collection of letters and magazines close to his chest to keep them dry, Danny prepared to explain that he had been standing just right there at the mailboxes when the mail truck arrived and that he thought he would save her the trip in the rain.

He had been reasonably confident Amanda would be alone. Matt had mentioned over dessert that he needed to go into work first thing in the morning. Unusual for a Saturday, but unavoidable for reasons he had not made clear.

Amanda had answered the door in a long, pale blue bathrobe.

"Sweetie, you need someone to bring you in out of the rain and slather you with some heavy affection."

Pulse at a full gallop, Danny had been momentarily confused about how, exactly, he should respond, concluding that Amanda must have seen him approach from an upstairs window and that somehow, in that magical way of hers, known his heart.

Amanda had smiled and pointed to the earbuds he could not see. She had mouthed the word *phone* as he held out the handful of mail. She took it from him sweetly, beaming gratitude. Then, hand on his wet shoulder, she had mouthed the word *thank* and then, separately, the word *you*.

They had waved at each other just as Amanda's eyes absented themselves into the abstracted conversation that claimed her attention.

"Clint, honey, I know. But I was just there. I'll be back. I will. But probably not until..."

Amanda had closed the door as Danny was turning away. Her pale, naked feet, appearing and disappearing in his mind's eye beneath the swish of a blue robe, had followed him all the way home.

Once, one Saturday afternoon in November, when the snow was falling in fat, heavy, pancake-sized flakes and Janice was ensconced in the spare room painting a seascape, Danny had come upon the idea of simply showing up at Amanda's house and shoveling the driveway. She would hear the scraping and look out her window and there he'd be, laboring. No reason. Just because. Sure, Matt had built Juni a doghouse, and he had kept them well supplied with chopped firewood winter after winter. True. But had Matt ever just appeared with a shovel and cleared their driveway? No, he had not. Matt did not have the corner on sexy, selfless magnanimity, any more than he could lay claim to all women.

As Danny was stepping out of his own garage, Matt's truck had glided past, Amanda in the passenger seat. They honked and waved. Danny had raised his blue shovel in the air like a protester looking for a picket line. He had watched them until the truck finally disappeared in its own billowing white fantails. Disappointed but undaunted, Danny had walked up the street to shovel his neighbors' driveway, twice as long and as wide as his own. Amanda would not be home to discover him in mid-heroism, but his labors would not go unnoticed.

It had taken most of an hour. When he was done, hot and exhausted, he had dragged the shovel back to his own driveway. Janice found him in the garage, stomping the snow off his boots.

"When you're done shoveling the driveway, will you go down in the crawlspace and just take a look at the pipes? The plumbing is making that awful sound again. I called Matt. They must be out."

Danny had sighed, closed his eyes and nodded. Janice, her hands streaked with the colors of Cape Cod in the spring, had no reason to understand. So she hadn't.

"Or, hey, whatever, Dan. I was just asking for a little help. I don't need the attitude. I'll have Matt come look at it. Never mind."

Danny had shoveled his own driveway. Then he had descended beneath the house to pretend to diagnose the familiar but utterly confounding gastrointestinal sounds of his home.

Within three hours, after a series of weekend tasks and a reading of the paper that would normally have started his day, he had paused at the living room window to note that the driveway was no longer a clean trapezoid, but a fuzzy, indistinct half-pipe shape. By the end of the day, when he saw Matt and Amanda returning from wherever they had been, rooster tails of snow fanning up behind the truck, it was impossible to tell that his driveway – and, presumably, their driveway – had been shoveled at all.

And still, Danny's preoccupation did not abate.

On New Year's Eve, Danny and Janice had been pulled in different directions. A contingent of the Baby Cloud assembly crew, including all Danny's usual social group and a lot of others, gathered at the Elks Lodge in Brookville. It was an annual fête and normally Janice would have gone with him. But on this occasion Janice had been invited to a party at the home of the owner of the art supply store where she worked. The argument had started a month ahead of time, just after Thanksgiving.

"Why should I decline my invite?" she had asked in the bathroom doorway, waiting for him to brush his teeth. "I always go to your party. Maybe you should skip your party this year and meet some new people. Better people."

Danny had spit and rinsed.

"What's that supposed to mean?"

"Nothing. Just… some of those guys… especially when they get to drinking…" She had let the suggestion hang, draped over her rising intonation like an old shirt she had pulled out of his closet as a candidate for the trash.

"Oh, they're okay. Just blowing off some steam and ringing in the new year. You always seem to have a good enough time."

"Oh, is that what it seemed to you? That I was having a good enough time? Getting felt up by your drunk work buddies?"

"What? Who?"

"I don't know his stupid name. Longish hair, tiny nose."

"I have no idea… it's just dancing, Janice. Just don't dance with them and you'll be fine."

"Why not just come to Kendra and Bob's? They don't bite, Danny. She's my boss. They're friends of Matt and Amanda. Try them out just this year. I mean… why not?"

"Because I won't know anybody there."

"So? By the end of the night you'll know everybody there. And then next year you won't have that excuse."

"Jesus, Janice. It's not an excuse. It's a preference. I'd just prefer to... you know... be with my own friends."

"And you think I don't?"

That question, sharply delivered as Janice pursued him down the hall to the bedroom, had kicked the exchange into a higher gear, broadening its scope to pull in every occasion over the previous five years in which either of them had capitulated to the preference of the other and regretted it. The fight had rolled through the better part of a week, stopping and re-starting whenever the circumstances and energy level allowed, until Danny had had enough.

"Look. Janice. I'm tired of this. If my friends are not good enough for you, then I suggest you go be with your own friends. Have a good goddamned time."

It had actually helped to put the argument out of its misery. By the time the thirty-first arrived, they had each grown comfortable with the idea of ringing in the new year separately. They kissed each other sweetly in the kitchen in the morning before Danny headed off to Baby Cloud, wishing each other a Happy New Year and exchanging mutual admonitions about not drinking and driving and being wary of others on the road.

Since Danny would not need to return home to pick up Janice for the party, his plan was to leave work and drive directly to the Elks Lodge in Brookville. Janice was to spend the day at home – her employer having sensibly closed for New Year's Eve – and then make the drive to Edinboro in the late afternoon.

For most of his shift, Danny had felt strangely lighthearted and relaxed. Given the day and the coming party, the Baby Cloud plant had a post-game locker room energy that made the assembly crew twice as lively and half as productive. Danny, too, had been more animated than normal, looking for opportunities to laugh and indulge in the camaraderie of his workmates. He felt himself enjoying the prospect of going to the party alone and not being half of a couple. Being less encumbered and accountable. Freer.

But at the end of the day, as Danny clocked out and walked across the snowy lot to the truck, he'd felt his spirit sag a little and take on weight. He was conscious of not going back home for Janice. He found himself wrestling with the discomfiting, anxious feeling of having accidentally left something behind, something vital, like a cellphone or a wallet, or his pen of epinephrine whenever he walks Juni on summer days, things represented by pangs of alarm when not within immediate reach.

He'd felt strangely vulnerable.

He had been somewhat successful in shaking the feeling for the first hour of the party. He'd felt better helping Clayton and others load in cases of beer and champagne and other provisions, including pallet after pallet of deli meats and cheeses, microwave pizza bites, cut vegetables that no one would eat, and single-serving frozen strawberry desserts that people would eat two and three at a time, leaving none for others. Then he'd found some satisfying purpose in figuring out why the sound system and the rented karaoke machine only seemed to work out of the left speaker channel.

But, eventually, once the setup was done and the actual party took over, the distractions of music and booze and the antics of the same people he'd already spent all day with were not enough to beat back Janice's pressing absence. As the celebration had ramped up, Danny had gradually withdrawn.

"Danny boy!" Ross had slapped him on the back, finding him alone at a back table, nursing a glass of warm, flat champagne. He had to shout over the music. "Life of the party, I see."

"Not into it this year, I guess," said Danny, then adding, "How is it you always show up at our New Year's party anyway? What's your secret Baby Cloud connection?"

"Phil and I go way back," Ross had said, pointing to a wiry, longish-haired, button-nosed man flailing to "Rock the Casbah" with a drink in each hand. "He just lets me know the date and I show up and slam-bang, it's a party. So where's the little lady?" Ross' eyes were glassy and unfocused and he swayed on his feet. He broke up his euphemism for Janice into little bits of word-kindling: lit-tle lay-dee.

"Had her own party tonight. Out in Edinboro."

Ross had wagged his finger and his head in a counter-synchronous rhythm.

"Tsk, tsk, my friend. My compadre, daddy-o Danny boy, homeboy. Alone on New Year's Eve. Maybe this is a blessing in disguise. I count no fewer than seven un-a-tended lay-dees here. They're all going somewhere with someone tonight and I can't take all of them so you should go get you some before the year runs out." Ross had pointed. "Got my eye on Bridgette. Little Miss Grand Tetons."

"You're dreaming, Ross."

"Maybe. Maybe not."

"You're also married."

Ross looked down at Danny, irritation focusing his glazed eyes for the first time. "Goddamned but you're a buzz-kill tonight, Danny. Yeah, I'm married. So what about it?"

"Forget I said anything."

"The wife and me got something deeper than whatever goes on... one freaking night a year at the goddamned Brookville Elks Lodge. She knows who she married. She wants me to be happy. And she won't ask any questions about it either. And I know what you're thinking but it isn't like that because the rules are the same for her too. If it makes her feel good, then I want it for her and I don't ask her any questions. She's probably out someplace right now with her legs in the air."

Ross had taken a moment and looked a little harder down at Danny as something close to anger had uncoiled behind his glassy, unaccountable eyes.

"And so what of it, man? What the hell of it? Tomorrow's a new year and me and the missus will slap our resolutions down on the table and be as good as gold. But tonight..." Ross had panned the room before looking back down, "toooo-night, Danny boy, is a night for getting it all out of our system so we can start clean in the morning. You got something you want to do one last time, then you best goddamned get it done."

Danny had lasted another two hours, unable to improve his mood and increasingly drunk with the effort. He had been pulled out onto a raucous dance floor for three songs playing in his head almost continuously since high school. Unable to take a fourth, he had excused himself for the restroom.

It was as he washed his hands, looking at the solitary man in the mirror, that he realized he could not bear another minute. The idea of being in the Brookville Elks Lodge, alone, as people counted backward toward the popping liberation of warm champagne, turned his stomach.

He had escaped to his truck through a side door. He was too drunk to drive, so he sat in the dim parking lot with the window down, alone, listening to the darkness and the still patience of winter absorb the dull thudding from inside the Lodge. Every now and then the side door would open in a reddish-orange burst of sound, closing again behind illicit-minded couples headed out to get high or to get low in the backseat of a cold car.

He had been too alone for too long, sitting out in his truck. He'd thought idly about driving to Edinboro. Thought about walking in the front door of Kendra and Bob's house, people he did not know and did not care anything about, but who were ringing in the new year with his wife and who, for that reason, and because they had invited him to come, would not deny him entry.

He imagined the look on Janice's face. He imagined joy. Even tears. His imagination had turned cinematic. He thought of all those *When-Harry-Met-Sally*-race-through-the-city-to-celebrate-New-Year's-with-the-one-you-love rom-coms that he pretended to hate and that Janice could never get enough of and wanted to watch over and over.

He imagined Janice, tears on her cheeks, melt into some semblance of Renee Zellweger looking over a crowded living room at Tom Cruise: "You had me at hello". Renee had melted back into Janice, who then became Michelle Pfeiffer, defenseless at George Clooney's plaid-clad swagger: "What would you do if I kissed you right now?"

And then, quite unexpectedly, Michelle Pfeiffer had morphed seamlessly into Amanda, standing in the foyer of her home, naked fingers at his temples, her lips on his, her breath on his face: "Thank you, Mr. Danny, for keeping Matt honest."

The memory had lingered, playing over the truck's steam-coated windshield as if it were a movie screen, until Ross had intruded, sticking his hard, thin, black-eyed face between theirs: "You got something you want to do one last time, then you best goddamned get it done."

He had driven home slowly, window down to keep the cold, fresh air in his face and to clear the beer-and-champagne fog still billowing in his head. Traffic was light and to the northeast, the sky had cleared neatly around a shivering, metal moon. Lower down, just above the tree line, Danny could see glittered firework tendrils, red and blue and silver, arching out of existence. He had wondered what Janice was doing in that moment. Who she had looked at or touched or hugged or kissed when three had become two, and two had become one, and the corks had popped.

And Amanda. He had imagined her, too, curled into the back of her fireside love seat, cradling a crystal flute of bubbling gold, Matt's hand atop her foot.

When he reached his neighborhood, Danny had slowed to a crawl but had not pulled into his own driveway. On the approach, he had seen his home waiting with its dark, empty windows. Eyes of a ghost. Sockets. Their emptiness bored into him, preparing to welcome him with abject nothingness, as he pulled even to the front yard. He'd felt a cold ache in his chest of such loneliness and desolation that he could not bear to turn the wheel. He'd let the car keep rolling. He drove past the row of mailboxes to the end of the street, turning into the only remaining driveway, twice as long and wide as his own.

He'd sat there for several minutes, engine off, listening to his own breath and imagining that Amanda would, at any second, appear in the upper bedroom window as a shapely silhouette against a soft-gold glow. He imagined her cupping her hand against the glass as Matt's shadow passed unknowingly along the walls behind her. Imagined her seeing him, looking furtively over her shoulder, beckoning him to the front door below. Imagined her opening the door with a question on her face and him giving her a wry smile. *What would you do if I kissed you right now?*

The fantasy had played from there, several times on a loop, starting all over again with Amanda's silhouette at the window.

And then, incredibly, inexplicably, magically, Amanda had been there in the window. Not her imagined silhouette, her actual silhouette. A moving shade in the light. Left to right and gone. Right to left and gone. Then Amanda had cupped her hand against the window. She had looked down at him, sitting in his truck looking up at her. Just as he had imagined.

Alcohol has nothing to do with it. It is our nature to see what we want to see in the world, even the faces we want to see, when and where we want to see them, reflecting back the golden light of our own self-serving appraisals. We take familiar, welcome refuge in our own kind delusions.

So, even leaning forward over the steering wheel – bringing his face as close to the windshield as he could, clearing the steam with his fingers and staring intently up through the dark, winter air – it had taken Danny several seconds to figure it out.

* * *

The empty candy wrapper fluttered, struggling to free itself from the weight of the bottle inside the dirty, white paper bag. Danny looked at his watch.

"Not yet," said Seth in the rearview mirror, reading his mind. "Few more minutes."

When enough time had elapsed to obscure any association with Clayton, Danny climbed out of the backseat. He looked back once, hand on the door.

"Got your back, bud," said Seth, patting his coat pocket. "Motor..." Danny straightened, turned away, and closed the car door in a single movement, severing whatever next word had hit the window and never made it out of the car.

"Running," he assumed.

A small silver bell announced his arrival, then faded away beneath the spray of fluorescent lights and a thin, tinny blanket of country-pop noise.

Including himself, nine people were inside the Foley's Got It All. At the back of the store, Ross was pretending to compare and contrast various rifles for the benefit of Clayton, who, leaning up against the gun counter, looked up and caught Danny's eye.

Four customers, two of whom seemed to be shopping together as a unit, traversed the shoulder-high aisles, pulling items off the shelves and putting them into black plastic baskets. At the front of the store, right next to the double doors, a kid who looked to be not a day older than twenty was at the counter, coding a stack of blue Foley's sweatshirts into a register.

"Welcome," said Everett, refolding one of the sweatshirts. "Let me know if I can help you find something."

Danny nodded, intending to say something appreciative, but found that swallowing was the best he could do.

"All the fishing gear's half off," said Everett, pointing to a far corner of the store beneath a brightly-stenciled cardboard sign that hung from the drop ceiling by fishing twine: The Fishin' Hole. A lanky man in a green cap was bending a rod like he was testing it for marlin.

Adjacent to The Fishin' Hole was a hallway that disappeared beneath another sign that read The Waterin' Holes (Restrooms). Ross' cocktail-napkin map glowed to life in Danny's head. Women's room first. Men's room next. Foley's office at the end of the hall on the right.

"Might want to stock up on rods and reels for next season," said Everett.

213

"Thanks," Danny managed without looking.

He made a slow beeline for the canvas duffle bags which, true to Ross' description, were on the third shelf along the south wall, just past the Electrical Light Hardware Ropes/Twine sign. On the way, he heard Ross explaining to Clayton how Foley's only carried a very limited stock of hunting rifles in the store but that they had a catalogue and could order whatever he wanted. Over-enunciating his enthusiasm, Clayton asked if he could look through the catalogue.

Danny's duffel bag choices were green and black. Black was much too small and the green was probably a little too large. Ross had been correct about that, too. Danny pulled a green bag off the top shelf, unzipped it and opened it up. The lettering was the same as on Everett's stack of sweatshirts. Foley's Got It All.

He did his best to look both purposeful and casual, meandering the aisles under the direction of an imagined shopping list, using the duffle bag as a useful substitute for the shopping basket that, it would be presumed, he had forgotten to grab on his way in. It did not particularly matter what he put into the bag as long as it was loosely distributed, filled roughly three-quarters of the available volume, and weighed in the neighborhood of twenty pounds.

He tossed items in as he walked, pretending to consider options and read labels. A package of rope. A roll of paper towels. By the time he reached the personal care aisle, the bag in his hand pulled toward the floor with a collection of items – a lock, a set of door hinges, a travel hairdryer – that were too dense and too small, leaving far too much empty space. He considered the soft, airy twelve-pack of extra-absorbent incontinence pads to balance the load.

214

At the front of the store, the silver bell over the doors tinkled for attention. The would-be marlin-fisher was on his way out. As if to take his place, another man entered.

"Hey, Everett," said the man.

"Hey there, Mr. Foley," said Everett. "Long time no see."

Danny turned in the direction of the gun counter. Clayton was already looking back at him. They both pivoted in unison to Ross, who glared back angrily and spoke to Clayton with just a little more force, emphasizing words seemingly at random and flashing his eyes in Danny's direction every couple of seconds.

"We never know from one minute to the next what model they're going to send us. But it don't matter because whatever they send us to put behind the counter, the catalogue is the same. Understand? It's all the same. No difference in the end. You can still get everything you want. So let's just get to picking out what... you... want."

Ross pushed the gun catalogue across the glass, just a little closer to Clayton. Clayton looked back at Danny and shrugged. Danny looked back at the front counter.

"Need you to run an errand for me," Mr. Foley was saying to Everett. "Need you to drive the truck out to the Erie store. Load up a dozen of the new propane tanks. Bring them back here. Can you do that for me on short notice?"

"You got it, boss," said Everett, leaving the stack of sweatshirts. "You closing up then?"

"No, no. Ross'll close up. I'm here a couple hours, and then I'm off. On a plane tonight back to Phoenix."

"Alright then. I'm gone. Have a good trip."

"Good man. No detours, now. Randy knows you're coming."

Everett put on a coat, took a set of keys from Foley and disappeared through the front doors. Foley took Everett's place behind the counter, put on a pair of reading glasses and began poking a finger at the register. Danny looked back at Clayton and Ross. They both nodded.

By the time Danny reached the register, the bag was almost completely full and heavier than it should have been. His hands had acted as free agents, stuffing the duffel without specific consent from his brain, which was wholly preoccupied with regulating his adrenal gland. He looked at the duffel bag on the counter in front of him, having no recollection of putting it there.

"We have baskets," Foley was saying. "And carts outside."

"I wasn't thinking," said Danny. "Next time."

"No harm, no harm. Builds those biceps. Let's see what we've got."

Foley adjusted the bag, pulling it open, and began unloading everything into a pile next to the register. Then he grabbed a hand scanner like a gun. He picked up the 24-pack of AA batteries and blasted it in the barcode with a beep. Danny's mind felt the contours of the gun in Seth's coat pocket. *Got your back, bud.*

"Should I just put it all back in the duffel or do you want shopping bags?"

Danny looked up. Foley was older than he imagined. Thinning dark hair and wire-rim glasses that did nothing to obscure the darkening skin that sagged beneath his yellowing, bloodshot eyes. He smelled strongly of aftershave, but the sallow skin that so loosely wrapped his expressions was unshaven. He exuded a kind of exhaustion, as if it was only the strength of the aftershave that was keeping him upright. He wore a gold band that slid loosely, back and forth, along a shank of finger bone as he held up each item, the knuckle just barely wide enough to keep it from falling off.

"Yeah," said Danny. "Just pile it all back in there."

Foley stuffed in the sailboat shower curtain and then counted out eight pink packages of extra-absorbent incontinence pads.

"These are good," Foley said, tapping one of the pads. "These help."

Danny didn't know what to say. Foley kept talking, as if to himself.

"Damned chemo. Sometimes it's all a person can do to lie there and breathe in and out. Bathroom may as well be at the top of Mount Everest."

Danny nodded, as if this was something everybody everywhere knew to be undeniably true and worth acknowledging.

"Got that right," Danny said.

"Never know who's out there wearing these things," Foley said. He paused long enough to look at Danny over his glasses and chuckled. "I'm just joking. I don't figure these are for you and even if they are, it isn't any of my damned business. Don't mind me, son, just the lack of sleep talking."

Danny laughed with sloppy enthusiasm as a line of three people formed behind him. "No, no, I... Not for me... I just... Ha... no, no..."

When the bag was full again, Foley recited the total and Danny extracted his credit card, stopping himself just in time. He slipped the card back in his wallet and pulled out his cash, counting it out on top of the green bag.

"You have a good day now," said Foley, handing Danny his change and a receipt and directing his attention to the woman behind him. The bell above the door tinkled and four more people filed in. Danny pulled the bag off the counter and then stopped, pretending to notice the Fishin' Hole sign for the first time.

"Half off?" he asked, nodding at the far corner.

"Half off," said Foley to the bag of flour in his hands. "Go take a look."

As casually as he could manage, Danny wandered off to the back of the store to look at the fishing rods standing at attention in the rack on the wall. The bell tinkled again. And again. Six new shoppers. Danny turned back to look at Foley, who was now multitasking with a phone to his ear and a finger to the register. At the other end of the store, Clayton and Ross were motionless. Watching.

Danny left the Fishin' Hole and walked slowly beneath the sign to the Waterin' Holes. He casually turned the corner and disappeared.

The men's room was single occupancy and empty. Danny locked the door and set down the bag. Standing on the toilet, he pushed aside the ceiling tile and felt around blindly to find the empty green duffel bag that Ross had left for him. He then stuffed the full bag up through the square hole, holding his breath, half expecting its weight to bring down the entire ceiling. But it held. He exhaled, replaced the ceiling tile, and tucked the empty green duffel bag under his coat.

He stepped down from the toilet and flushed it for good measure. He even ran the water in the sink for a few seconds. He could feel his own eyes in the mirror. He did not look up to meet them.

218

The hallway was dim and empty and echoed the tinkling and beeping and country-pop busyness of the store beyond. He moved quickly, out and to the left, headed for the blade of light slicing across the end of the hallway from beneath the office door. As he moved, pulling cotton gloves from his pockets, the possibility of discovery lunged savagely at his back like a chained junkyard dog. At any moment someone – anyone – could enter the hallway for the restroom. If that happened, he told himself, he would feign disorientation, double back and head toward the store. He would roll his eyes and shake his head in self-mockery, muttering "wrong way" as he passed the would-be witness for the prosecution.

But the hallway remained empty. He pulled on the gloves. The office door was unlocked, just as Ross had promised. Danny stepped in quickly and closed the door behind him.

The first thing that caught his attention, oddly, was Ross' black coat, hanging askew on a flimsy wire hanger in an open closet just inside the door. The coat, with its telltale carabiner bottle-opener zipper-pull, partly obscured the top of a tower of office supplies, mostly paper towels and coffee filters and dozens of rolls of double-ply toilet paper. At the bottom of the tower was an unopened box of security cameras, just as Ross had said. Disappearing up behind the coat the way it did, thrusting its saggy chest out into the room a little, the tower of supplies almost seemed to give the coat a body, a headless guard to watch over the office. It lent an uneasy presence that registered in the pit of Danny's stomach.

The centerpiece of the windowless office was a large, cluttered desk separated from a wall of shelving by an old, toffee-colored leather chair. A darkened lamp on the left side of the desk arched over stacks of papers, unopened mail and a pyramid of newspapers, each still tightly rolled in a rubber band. Just as Ross had represented, this was the office of a man who had not been around for some time. A man neglecting his responsibilities. A man who had enough going on elsewhere to no longer care.

Behind, and on each side of the desk, floor-to-ceiling bookcases made of varnished walnut lent a dusty but polished wooden glow, mocking the cluttered shabbiness below. It was a sadly judgmental contrast, like that of a portrait of a proud, young man – chin raised, gazing at some distant horizon, the entire world before him – hung on the wall of the tenement where reality had finally chosen to lay its head. If the desk suggested that Foley no longer cared, the shelving suggested that had not always been true.

The photos seemed to leap from the shelves. They were, as Ross had described, testament to a full, exciting and expensive lifestyle.

Foley on a camel.

Foley on a steep, sun-washed ski slope, arms wide, skewering the snow with a ski pole in each hand like he was planting flags in some newly conquered country.

Foley in the open door of an airplane, green lushness below, one thumb enthusiastically up.

Foley from below, in the basket of a yellow balloon, bulbous and solar against an ocean of cerulean sky.

Foley up against the brass-railed prow of a yacht, face tan in the reddening glow of a setting sun.

Foley in a black tuxedo, holding a flute of champagne in an elaborately appointed holiday ballroom, the gold of the tinsel finding itself in the bubbles and in the band on his finger.

In each and every photo was also a woman. Younger than Foley, to be sure, but not grotesquely so. She was indeed attractive. Sleek, corvine hair. Olive skin. Almond eyes. Full lips that, in every photograph, curved into an infectious and inviting smile. She exuded a sensual athleticism. She radiated immortality.

Ross had been right about the extravagance in these photos. The celebration of relative fortune. The lushness of experience they depicted.

But the obscenity, the Gatsbian moral spoilage and rot of character that Danny had expected, was entirely missing. From Ross' description, he had expected to see the glazed eyes of a bankrupt soul.

But, in fact, there was not a single photograph in which Foley was even looking at the camera. In every shot, without exception, Foley was remembered only in profile, his face turned to her. Even standing in the open door of an airplane in the moments before stepping out into open space, Foley's attention was not directed to the photographer, who might have been the last person to see him alive and to capture his image for posterity, nor toward the green earth laid out below, ready to receive him should the parachute fail. No, he was looking at her. Always at her. As if she was the green ground to receive him. As if she was the open sky into which he stepped.

The safe was not the armored vault he had imagined. Between two of the bookcases was a door that might have easily been mistaken for the entrance to an ordinary coat closet except for the slate-black electronic keypad and, in place of a doorknob, a black cylindrical bar-handle large enough to be gripped by two hands.

As Ross had promised, the door was ajar, breaking the plane of the bookcases. Removing the empty green duffel from beneath his coat, Danny pulled the door open.

The interior of the safe was divided unevenly by four shelves, each of which held a jumbled collection of loose papers, shoeboxes full of computer disks and fat weathered envelopes, and gray metal boxes stacked with rolled coins. The largest space was on the bottom, beneath the lowest shelf, accounting for fully one-third of the interior. Danny knew to focus his attention only there, on the floor, on the same dark blue, two-by-two-by-three Tupperware with a snap-on lid that could also be found just down the hallway on Aisle 7 of Foley's Got it All.

Danny knelt, pulled the container toward him, and opened the lid.

The cash, almost filling the container, was neatly stacked and rubber-banded by denomination. The sight of all of it, unguarded and neglected, there for the taking, as if waiting for him, filled him with a sudden panic. Seconds suddenly seemed like minutes. Discovery was imminent. He looked back only to be startled by Ross' black coat against the tower of supplies. Danny yanked open the duffel and began indiscriminately stuffing in the cash with both hands.

As he worked, he could not help but imagine Foley walking through the office door behind him. He imagined seeing through Foley's eyes, seeing the curve of his own back as he crouched on the floor frantically jamming his hands into the bag.

Then it was Foley's face that filled his imagination. Behind the shock and surprise, behind the wire-rimmed glasses, was the baggy-eyed look of exhaustion Danny had seen behind the counter. But not just exhaustion. Worry. And a kind of bottomless, cascading grief that belongs to inevitability. Foley's voice came next.

Sometimes it's all a person can do to lie there and breathe in and out.

Then the image of that loose gold band, sliding down Foley's bony ring finger and catching, just barely, on a protuberance of knuckle.

Then, finally, a younger, happier, healthier Foley, standing in front of a distant, verdant blur in the open door of an airplane.

Looking at her.

Danny forced himself to walk in a slow, casual gait as he exited the hallway and stepped back out into the store proper. He felt the laser-focused attention of Ross and Clayton, still at the gun counter, but he kept his vision forward in order to be mindful of Foley's attention, ready to nod and to lift the green duffel bag in his hand in a goodbye gesture. He realized, too late, that he was still wearing the thin cotton gloves that had no purpose other than preventing fingerprints.

Foley was still at the front counter, head down, squinting over the top of his glasses at a tag attached to a pocket flashlight. A line of six people shifting their weight from one foot to the other, stretched out into the main aisle, forcing Danny to detour around the last of them – a man with a basket of light bulbs – and then angle back in toward the counter and the exit.

As he pushed open the door, the chill of early winter air rushed in around him. Danny gave one last look at Foley, his head bent, his two hands clutching the tiny tag he could not read. As if in prayer.

Seth popped the trunk as Danny crossed the lot and approached the car. Danny dropped in the green duffel, which landed with an uneasy clatter on top of a ratty brown blanket. He lifted a corner of the blanket with two fingers. A semi-automatic rifle and a sawed-off shotgun lay quietly, as if sleeping. He tucked them back in and closed the trunk.

Danny climbed into the front seat and slammed the door.

"Jesus, Seth," he said, taking off the gloves and stuffing them in his coat pocket.

"How'd it go?" Seth asked. "Took you long enough."

"Think you brought enough goddamned guns?"

"Oh. Those."

"Yeah. Those."

"Better safe than sorry, bro," Seth said in a tone that sounded a little wounded in a just-doing-my-best-to-help sort of way.

Across the parking lot, a woman in a red coat opened the door of the Foley's Got It All and held it open for three people coming out. The last of these was Clayton, who zipped up his coat and pulled the collar around his ears and walked in the other direction across the parking lot, toward the highway and the Allegheny River beyond.

"Just go get him," said Danny. "This part is stupid."

"Nope," said Seth calmly. "I'm the driver and that wasn't the plan. We pick him up on the highway like he's hitching. If someone's watching him, we don't want it looking like he came from this car."

"Why would anyone be watching him? I'm the one coming out of the store with the big green bag."

"I'm the driver," said Seth stubbornly.

"Yeah. You're the driver."

They waited until Clayton reached US-62 and had almost disappeared around the bend. Seth put the car in gear, swung it in a long, slow arc away from Foley's Got It All, through the Burger King parking lot and back onto the highway. Clayton was walking backward with his thumb stuck up out over the road.

"Damn! Is it just me or is the temperature dropping like a rock?" Clayton slid into the backseat and slammed the door. He rubbed his hands together vigorously. "Give me some heat."

Seth turned on the blower and eased back onto the road. Clayton leaned forward and patted Danny on the shoulder.

"You are one cool cucumber, brother. I was ready to call it a day when Foley showed up."

Seth snapped his head around, eyes wide.

"Foley was in the store?"

Clayton told him the story of how everything had looked from the vantage point of the gun counter.

"I think Ross actually wanted me to buy a damned rifle. I kept looking at him like he was crazy and he kept pushing. I'm looking through this stupid catalogue waiting for Danny to come out of that hallway and Ross is like, _you need to make up your damned mind and pick one so I can write up the order_. And I'm looking back at him like, this is all pretend, Ross. I'm not buying a goddamned thing. Like, you know, wake the fuck up, man."

Danny felt himself sinking, wanting to be alone. Wanting to be away. He looked out the window, down at the blur of pavement.

"You need to wake the fuck up, Danny," Matt had said, standing in the threshold of his large comfortable house. The words were defensively angry. It was the first thing Matt had said in response to Danny's threatening tirade about how Matt had better stay away from him, and Janice, if he did not want to end up in the hospital.

New Year's Day had been mostly cold and quiet in his house, punctuated by intermittent screaming and accusing and door slamming and muffled sobbing. Having said what his hurt and anger had told him to say to his wife, he'd had time to sit in his chair by the window and stoke the coals in his heart and to work on exactly the words he wanted to throw at Matt's face.

By January second, Danny was ready for anything, including violence, and had pulled on his coat and marched through the snow down to the same house in which he and Janice had enjoyed so many intimate evenings with their friends. He had pounded on the front door for a solid minute. Eventually it had opened, revealing Matt in one of his expensive, nubby Italian wool sweaters, holding a cup of coffee.

All Danny's words had come out as roughly as he had intended. As always, Matt had kept rigorous control of his expression. And then, when Danny had taken a breath, Matt had pushed back.

"You need to wake the fuck up, Danny. You don't even know what you have over there, do you? You think she's just going to wait around for you to pay attention? You think you can just go off and do whatever it is you do? Fucking bowling? Think you can just take her for granted day in and day out and she's just going to hang around forever? You pay more attention to your fucking dog, Danny. If you said a single kind word to your wife for every time you took Juni for a walk past my house, you wouldn't have a problem. But you do have a problem, Danny. Most guys would kill for what you have. And Janice? She's on the way out. Now, maybe you don't really want her, in which case you should stay out of my face and go have your head examined. Or maybe you just don't know how to be a real man in a real relationship, in which case you should fucking practice, Danny. Leave the spares and strikes and poker games to your friends and pay some fucking attention. Because that woman over there is worth the practice."

Danny's mental script had not contemplated this response. His anger had suddenly needed reinforcement. His next words were unplanned.

"Where's Mandy?" he had demanded, using Matt's name for her. "Let's get her down here. I want to hear you give me that speech again with Mandy listening."

Matt had looked at him quietly for a moment. It was possible for Danny to convince himself that the demand had set Matt back on his heels. And maybe it had. But there had been something else in Matt's look that had been just as difficult to name as it was to ignore.

"Amanda's in Montreal for the week. She's back day after tomorrow. Feel free to say whatever you want to her." Matt, back in control of himself, had sipped his coffee and paused before closing the door in Danny's face with a click. "But use the phone."

Danny had not made any effort to contact Amanda. He did not know what to say. Worse, he no longer knew what he felt. About her or about anyone else. He had not seen or spoken to Matt or Amanda again.

Danny's and Janice's mutual and regular need to be out of the house and away from each other had redounded entirely to the benefit of Juniper, who found herself leashed up and headed out into the weather three or four times a day. Her walks with Danny were usually in directions away from the big house tucked into the edge of the forest at the end of the road. Danny wanted no chance of running into either Matt or Amanda by happenstance.

He had made sporadic efforts to glimpse the front of their house when he was headed to work, backing his truck slowly in that direction until the long driveway was visible

227

through the back window. He had tried to imagine Matt outside, pounding on his own front door, shivering and wailing, begging to be let in. But he couldn't conjure the image. The doorway in his mind always opened with Matt comfortably on the inside, sipping his coffee.

The house itself had not shown any signs of life for a full month. Heavy snowfall remained untracked. The postman had placed an orange card inside Matt and Amanda's mailbox. Weeks later, Danny had looked up from the weekend paper once or twice to catch Matt's truck zooming up the road. But that was all. Any semblance of any kind of relationship, even simply between neighbors who did not particularly like each other but who were forced to observe the empty gestures of civility, ceased to exist.

The effort to regain control of his marriage had been excruciating. Every conversation, every word, every look was an open portal to a hellscape of anger and hurt and separate, secret histories of emotional anguish that they had withheld from each other.

The conflict was not, as the traditional metaphors would have it, a battlefield. Holding the high ground was not an advantage. Contrary to what Danny had imagined in the initial flush of his outrage, the clarity of Janice's guilt had not conferred on him any right to dictate the terms of her surrender. Her guilt – its undeniability and her willingness to offer it up uncontested – had somehow made her more formidable.

Janice had not wasted any energy on denying her transgression, nor on suggesting that she was not guilty of a betrayal of the first order. She had, instead, devoted everything she had left within her to explaining the betrayal so that he might understand what had motivated it. It was, of course, an argumentative sleight of hand: To do a thing for reasons that another might understand is to do a

228

thing that another might, from a certain perspective, find justifiable, provided that such a person was reasonable and willing to consider other points of view.

Danny himself, Janice was at pains to prove, was at the heart of her infidelity. He had changed. He had drifted to a place – cold and remote and uncaring – that she could not reach. She had insisted that, day by day, bit by bit, her husband had taken a step further away, abandoning her in a shell of a marriage, a fate far worse than if he had smashed the shell to pieces and left her free to find emotional shelter and support elsewhere. She wished, Janice had screamed at him one evening in the kitchen, that he had been the one to have an affair. She wished she had been set free so clearly and unequivocally by his infidelity. She had drawn a righteous and powerful anger from the resentment she felt at having been left alone in the marriage to cling to the lies of her own hope.

All of which had had the effect of reducing Janice's New Year's Eve perfidy – the white-hot coal burning at the center of Danny's outrage – to something that, while relevant, was made to seem relatively inconsequential in the grander context of the marriage. Danny had kept returning to the moment of discovery – his face up against the windshield and Janice's face up against Matt's bedroom window – so as to relive it for both of them and to keep the shock and shame from fading away. But that had taken more and more effort to less and less effect.

The salience of Janice's adultery had seemed to dwindle with her willingness to concede every detail of that fateful evening. A distressed call from Clint in Montreal had sent Amanda off to Canada for New Year's Eve, leaving Matt to attend the Kendra-and-Bob New Year's party alone. Janice had had no particular knowledge that Matt and Amanda had even been invited to the party until Matt had encountered Janice at the mailboxes on the afternoon of

229

New Year's Eve, hours after Danny had left for work and his own party.

Janice had not been clear on whose notion it had been for them to ride out to Edinboro together, recalling that the idea seemed to occur to both her and Matt simultaneously. Why wouldn't they go to the party together? They were neighbors. They were good friends. Was there some reason they should have taken separate cars?

The ride out to the party had featured a conversation that focused disproportionately on the two people who were not in the car with them. Janice had allowed as how she was still upset over Danny's unwillingness to compromise for the evening. Matt, in turn, had confessed his disappointment at Amanda's decision to go to Montreal. Those confessions, it turned out, had been but marker buoys attached to deeper feelings. By the time they arrived at the party in Edinboro, the windows of the modest Kendra-and-Bob abode glowing warmly through the snow-flecked darkness, neither had wanted to go inside. Neither had been interested in anything except further revealing themselves to the other. For almost an hour, they'd sat in Matt's truck, idling up the road from the party, taking turns. Opening up. Trusting.

Eventually, Matt had put the truck in gear and headed back to Tionesta. They had taken turns extracting cellphones and calling the hostess with their excuses: Matt with the flu, Janice with car trouble that had sapped her resolve. They had laughed at what must have been Kendra's reaction. Then, headlights parting ever thicker curtains of snow, they had resumed talking.

And then, as Matt's garage door had separated from the downy driveway, opening to his empty, luxurious home, they had stopped talking altogether.

"You think Matt is so… so… impervious," Janice had said, wiping her eyes. "So above everything. But he isn't. He isn't, Danny. He's so desperately lonely. He loves her so much, but she refuses to commit. He's in the only relationship Amanda will tolerate. She has to keep proving to him that she's free. And he accepts it. He does. He has to. He loves her. You think he loves me? Me? He doesn't. He loves her."

She had declared this not to vent some emotional pain on her part but as further evidence that her act of infidelity had not, at least for Matt, been about consummating a secret love.

"He loves Amanda. But it really hurts him. The guy's hanging on for dear life. Behind that personae of his – the one that you now, suddenly, claim to have always hated – he's a wreck. He looks at us with such envy, Danny, if you can swallow that irony. We were like this thing he could never have. This? The thing he thinks we have together in this marriage? This is a dream to Matt. This is the dream he can never have. And that night he was just so… I don't know… heartbroken."

"Oh, poor, perfect, heartbroken Matt!" Danny had shouted. "I'm so goddamned glad you were there to kiss it and make it all better!"

Marriage counseling, eventually, had been Janice's idea.

"We can save this, Danny. We can stop this spiral. None of this has to be real. We can make it stop. We have to try."

So they had tried talk therapy. Ultimately they learned that talking was only making it all worse. The counselor in Erie was partly effective in patching up the damage they had done to each other on the rides out to these meetings, but she was never available to patch up the damage done

231

on the trips back home. Each revelation was a new snag in the sweater. They'd each taken turns pulling.

"If you're going to rebuild trust," the therapist had said, "then you need to allow yourself to be vulnerable. I want you to confess something, right here, right now, that you have never revealed before, and in that confession, I want you to imagine yourself falling backward into the arms of your spouse."

She had looked at Janice first.

"I was interested in Matt the first time I met him," she said. "I wondered what it would be like. I wondered it a lot."

"Good. We'll come back to that. Danny?"

The therapist and Janice had watched him take in that bit of news. He'd swallowed and cleared his throat like he had swallowed a large, chalky pill.

He had actually considered the most obvious thing to confess. The thing that would have dovetailed nicely with Janice's confession. The thing that would have put them on something close to the same moral footing and that might have paved a way forward. Somehow lost in the marital maelstrom had been the reason he had been in the neighbors' driveway, looking up at the bedroom window, in the first place, not to mention months of staging convenient opportunities for precisely the same caliber of transgression that Janice had managed to accomplish on the first try.

But Janice's confession, the ease of it, had made him angry all over again and the thing to which he might have confessed, the thing he knew he should have confessed, had slipped away in the fog. The quiet pressure of them looking at him and waiting for an answer had forced out into the open an exceedingly poor substitute.

"I was arrested... convicted of a crime."

232

"What?"

"Janice. Stop. Let him finish."

"I was fifteen. Attempted burglary. Me and some friends. I didn't take anything, but one of my friends did, stupidly, so we all went down for it. It wasn't even about stealing anything. It was supposed to be kind of a stupid prank on this stuck-up preppy guy at school we all really hated. I got a suspended sentence. Suspended from school. Three hundred hours of community service. My parents made me see a counselor. He said I was self-destructive. He said I had low self-esteem. That I run away from good things before they can turn bad and embrace the bad things just because they... you know, just because they're certain."

"Good," the therapist had said.

"Good?" spat Janice. "Did you also cheat on a fucking spelling test? I just dug my hole deeper and you're going to lay down some stupid teenage bullshit?"

"No, no, Janice," said the therapist. "This is good. Let's work with that. Let's show some trust. This is good."

Except that it wasn't good. Janice had looked at him, for the first time, like a traitor. There is more than one kind of perfidy, more than one sort of betrayal, in a marriage. If Janice had, for her own reasons, chosen one of them, he had cowardly, for his own reasons, chosen another.

The ride home after that session had marked the final change. Janice was no longer a study in penitence. No longer a contrite transgressor, desperate to save the marriage. She had no longer cared to stop the spiral. She had occupied the passenger seat just as still and solid and unmoving as a stone. Driving in silence on the way back to a house that was no longer a home, Danny had sensed that she was suddenly gone from him. He'd felt the desperation steadily coalescing in his heart, sinking like a distressed vessel taking on water.

And behind the wet flare of every oncoming headlight had been Matt's face. Calm. Composed. Sipping his coffee. Disappearing behind the darkness of a closing door.

"You need to wake the fuck up, Danny."

Danny looked up as the car pulled over to the side of the road and rolled slowly to a stop. Somewhere between Oil City and Tidoute, they'd left the highway for a quick errand that Seth had playfully refused to disclose. Clayton had given up and Danny hadn't cared in the first place. Now he had no idea where they were.

Seth held his gun to Danny's temple. He looked into the backseat and spoke calmly to Clayton.

"Drop your cellphone in the front seat, cuz."

"Seth... what in..."

"Isn't personal. But it's time we part ways. No reason for anyone to get hurt." Seth pulled back the hammer. "Now..."

"Okay, okay. Jesus." Clayton pulled out his phone and dropped it over the seat.

"You too," Seth said to Danny.

"Or you'll shoot me in the front seat of your car and go up for murder?"

"Guess you'll never know, friend," Seth said with a sad smile. "Funny though that you think this is my car."

Danny shook his head and did as he was told.

"Good. Now, Clay, ease on out. Once he's out then, Danny, you can go, too."

Clayton opened the back door and let in a gust of early winter air.

"Are you really dumb enough to think Ross isn't going to find out and report your ass?" he asked.

"Ross?" Seth laughed. "Are you really dumb enough to think me and Ross didn't set this whole thing up ages ago? Well, yeah, you probably are that dumb. Let's see if you're dumb enough to call the police about the money you stole and conspired to steal."

"Oh, and you think Ross doesn't have his own plan to cut you loose?" Danny asked, having no idea whether it was true but hoping it would rattle Seth's confidence.

"Oh, I'm very sure he does have such a plan. I am very sure about that. I'd trust you boys any day over that low-life piece-a-shit Ross. Now get out of the car."

They watched Seth roll away up the road. They'd left both passenger-side doors wide open, rigging them so they would not close. It was the only act of defiance they felt they could muster with any safety. Five hundred yards away, Seth pulled over again, got out, unhooked the seat belts from the door latches, closed both doors, waved, and then took off sharply into a tight U-turn that sent the car fishtailing forward. He roared past them, headed back toward the highway, window down, middle finger extended, and was soon gone, leaving a thin sooty cloud hanging over the road.

They walked in silence, mostly. Neither of them were dressed for the cold. They kept their hands stuffed deep into their pockets and hunched their shoulders forward into the steel breeze.

"Goddamned Baby Cloud," muttered Clayton.

"I know," said Danny.

"And in what world is it right that Seth keeps all that money?"

"In what world is it right that any of us keeps that money?" Danny asked.

"I know," said Clayton. "Shit. I know. I know. Goddamned Baby Cloud."

"I know," Danny said. "Anyway, there is no money."

Clayton stopped. Danny took another few steps and then he stopped too, turning his back to the hellish breeze and looking at his friend.

"Couldn't do it," he said. "It was all in the bag and then I just couldn't do it. I put it all back and closed up the safe."

"Are you serious?"

"What the hell do I know about Foley? What the hell do any of us know about anybody, Clay? Did you see his face? Those eyes? Foley's going through some kind of hell right now. I don't know but I think maybe he's losing his woman to cancer. I think he's barely hanging on and that Ross was right when he said Foley doesn't care anymore about his own money. But it's not because he has so much of it. It's because the money has about as much meaning as a tiny flashlight up next to the sun."

"Jesus," said Clay.

"Yeah. I know."

"What's in the bag?"

"Paper towels. And a whole lot of double-ply toilet paper."

"Really?"

"And Ross' coat."

"Jesus."

"I know."

When they reached Highway 62, they each pulled a hand out into the frigid air and stuck their thumbs up. It took fifteen minutes to catch a break. A bearded man in a black Toyota thought about it for the length of a couple of football fields, then pulled over. When they were rolling again, Danny asked to borrow the man's cellphone.

"Yeah, I'd like to report a dark blue Chevy Caprice, Pennsylvania plate number Hilo-Hilo-India five six three, HHI563, headed north on Highway 62, just south of Tidoute, driving erratically. I saw him at the truck stop in Oil City putting what looked like an automatic rifle in the trunk. I'm several miles behind him now so he might be coming up on Spartansburg soon. No, my turnoff is coming up here, so... No, I'm sorry, I'm sorry, I don't want any kind of trouble like that. Just wanted to let someone know about it. Thank you."

Danny ended the call with a twitch of his thumb and handed the phone back to the confused and suddenly worried-looking man behind the wheel who looked to Clayton for some kind of explanation.

"Long story," Clayton offered.

The man dropped them within walking distance of Danny's truck, still parked at Komo Lake. Then Danny drove Clayton to within walking distance of his house. They said little upon parting except "good luck" and "see you around."

By the time Danny turned the lock and opened the front door to his own home, the sun was just above the western tree line, no doubt lining itself up with a slot in the thin sheet of ice that covered the lake.

His house was alien in the way he had come to expect, not so much from the still and quiet as from the certainty that it would stay that way. All we ever require to maintain our hope and sanity is the smallest possibility that our circumstances might change. That's enough.

Danny sat down on the couch with his coat still on and stared for several long minutes in the general direction of the dark television screen. When he moved, it was for the landline telephone on the end table. He called information and wrote the number on his hand with a pen from the coffee table.

He called the Foley's Got It All store in Erie and asked for Mr. Foley, saying he had already called the store in Franklin and that they told him Mr. Foley had left so he was calling the other number he had in the hospital records. The young, thin voice of someone that Danny imagined looked like the Erie store's equivalent of Everett explained that Mr. Foley was not there. Danny asked if he had a mobile number that he could call. He did. Danny added the number to his palm. He hung up and dialed.

"Hello?"

"Is this Mr. Foley?"

"Who's this?"

"A concerned citizen."

"What? I'm in line to board a plane and I can't hear a damn thing."

"Your store manager is going to call you tonight. He's going to tell you that you've been robbed. He's going to describe a tall black guy in a skull cap and a white woman with blond dreadlocks. He's going to remind you that they've been casing the store in Franklin. He's going to promise to email you a photo he has sent you before. He'll explain that they stole his cellphone but that all his photos have been backed-up in the cloud. He's going to need you to open the safe. Are you still listening?"

"Yes."

"Tell him you want the police in the room before you do that."

That should be enough, Danny thought. He pulled the receiver from his ear as someone in the background bellowed about carryons. Then he stopped. He leaned forward on the couch, pressing his elbows to his knees and returned the receiver to his ear.

"My wife left me," he said. "It was my fault. I took her for granted. That, and I wanted to be blameless. I betrayed my marriage. I made her carry everything that happened. The whole rotten load. I made her carry it all. I want her to know how sorry I am. I want her to know that I was wrong and that I would do anything for her. I want to be the man who's always there, the man who never stops trying, no matter how much it hurts. The man worthy of her patience. Worthy of her sacrifice. And forgiveness. Time is always too damned short. I know that. And I know you know that too, Mr. Foley. At the end of it all, whether I'm the one in the hospital bed or she is, I want to be next to my wife, laughing our way through a box full of photographs."

Another blur of sound, an irritated, amplified pleading for order and patience. Then a kind of faraway silence.

"Why are you telling me this?"

"I guess because I envy you, Mr. Foley. And because I hate that feeling, like I'm going to die outside the life I want. And I'm telling this to you... I'm telling you this because I need to get the next phone call right. I'm telling you because you answered your phone and because she's worth the practice."

239

ISLAND SANTA

"Katie."

My father speaks my sister's name with the same desperate patience with which he is known to re-enter a computer password he knows is wrong but hopes that, somehow, it will do the job anyway.

"Can I, Dad?"

"Katie."

"Because you said I could. Remember, Dad?"

"Katie."

"What."

"You have your own cookie."

"I ate it already."

"Well, then, I guess that's that."

"But, Dad, you're not eating yours."

"I'm going to eat it later. I'm saving it."

"Dad? Dad."

"What, Katie."

"You owe me."

My father twists his neck another three-quarters of a degree so that he can see my sister. Katie is on the aisle, directly behind my mother. Dad and I have the windows. He tries to see through the crack between the seats, but he has to hunch forward and peer at his only daughter from beneath his own armpit.

He's just not that limber. So he gives up.

My sister reaches out and pokes him again with an electric pink fingernail. I can see the top of my father's head jerk reactively toward the shaded window.

"Dad, you owe it to me," she says. "Because of the bird. You were wrong about the bird, Dad. You just were. So, so ... wrong."

He inches himself up over the top of his seat, growing taller in halting, inelegant spurts, a time-lapse video of a chrysanthemum stretching up over our neighbor's fence.

But this chrysanthemum is wearing headphones. It has male-pattern baldness and is dressed in a sky-blue aloha shirt emblazoned with mango-colored hibiscus.

"What?" My father tries to whisper over the roar of the plane so as not to wake my mother. His expression shows irritation, twisted with the strain of trying to look his daughter in the eyes.

Those eyes dilate in sync with her little nostrils.

"Fact: You said the bird was dead," shouts Katie over the dull thundering that is everywhere around us. People across the aisle turn and look. "Fact: You were wrong. Fact: You owe me that cookie."

They look at each other for a second or two over the top of the seat. I can see enough of my father's face to know how this is going to end.

He is going to lose.

It does not matter that Katie is twelve and that he is fifty-two. He's still going to lose. It doesn't even matter that Katie is wrong about the dead bird. She's getting that cookie. It's only a matter of time.

My sister's relentlessness is not for a lack of other things to hold her interest.

Like, for starters, the fact that we are forty-thousand feet above the Pacific Ocean, traveling nearly five hundred miles an hour.

Or that we are probably only three hours from Oahu.

Or that Christmas is only three days away.

Or that the tow-headed tyrant across the aisle keeps kicking the seat of the elderly man in front of him. Over the past two hours, the man has been turning a muddy shade of purple, having asked the kid's mother no fewer than six times to control her child. He's like a little soccer player over there. He's not stopping.

Any minute now, the old man is going to push the little button next to the overhead light and get the flight attendant involved. Then she will get the captain involved. Then he will get the air marshals involved. And then the little plastic handcuffs will make an appearance. And then someone, either very old or very young, is going to go berserk. And then the in-flight entertainment will really begin.

But none of that matters. Katie is focused. She wants the cookie.

The irony is that Katie doesn't even like this kind of cookie. Macadamia nut shortbread with a hint of lilikoi. Whatever shortbread is. A kind of tropical sawdust from as much as I can tell. Katie sent back half of her own cookie, uneaten, along with the little square of lasagna that she

242

picked at and pulled apart and reconstructed into a kind of
shanty to shelter her two broccoli florets and an ice cube.

Don't play with your food, Katie.

Mind your own beeswax, Peter.

What she likes about the cookie is not the cookie at all,
but its crisp metallic blue wrapper. She likes how it scatters
the beam of reading light around our seats. While we were
waiting for our meal to be cleared, she opened her wrapper
up into a single square of foil, folded it into different shapes
and pushed it around her tray. She pecked a little hole in
the center of it with her fork and then stuck it on her pinky
like a finger hat, cocking her head one way and then the
other in curious admiration. I tried to read my book. I
couldn't help but watch her out of the corner of my eye.

Moments like these have persuaded me over the years
that we have all misunderstood my sister as human. I think
she might actually be a subspecies of raven.

"You owe me, Dad."

My father wrenches his head backward a little more to
look at me. He wants advice. All I can do is shrug. Your call, I
say with my eyes and shoulders. What I want to say is just
give her the stupid wrapper. But I'm staying out of it.

Denying Katie her second dessert would require that
he shatter her illusions about the songbird – its neck
snapped against our sky-tinted living room window. After
Katie pled tearfully with my father to not throw the cadaver
in the trash and to give miracles a chance, the neighbor's
cat quietly removed the bird's broken body from its clump
of grass, leaving Katie to believe that it had opened its little
eyes, shaken its head and flown off.

It's not that my father is incapable of shattering
childhood illusions. He has done it before and he will do it
again, whether he means to or not. He was the one who

broke the news that sea monkeys were really just little brine shrimp and that x-ray glasses were nothing of the kind. He said he was only trying to keep me from being taken in by charlatans who use the comic book industry to harness credulous children into bilking their parents. More likely, he suspected that the Wonder Glide Personal Hovercraft was next on my birthday list.

I think his frugality was just nipping things in the bud.

So it certainly was not beyond my father to shatter Katie's illusions about life and hope and miracles just so he can keep a few ounces of lilikoi-glazed, compressed tropical sawdust for himself.

But suffocating innocence does not normally come easily or lightly to my parents. It's not something they actually want to do. More to the point, where Katie is concerned, my father's willingness to shatter illusions may be irrelevant. My sister's illusions tend to be shatterproof. Her innocence is unsuffocatable.

See, Dad? See? I told you miracles happen! I told you!

The neighbor's cat had made off with the dead bird in the three minutes that Katie had paused her vigil for a potty break. After returning to the window, her excitement had quickly given way to scolding and retribution.

You shouldn't be so quick to just throw life away, Dad! You owe me a free dessert when we get to Hawaii. An EXTRA dessert. After I've already had dessert, I get ANOTHER dessert and Peter doesn't get one, only I get one. That's your punishment for not giving miracles a chance. You have to choose to believe, Dad. You have to choose!

So, theoretically, my father could try to keep the cookie for later as he always likes to do. He could explain about the bird and the cat, puncture Katie's backyard idealism, and assert his inalienable right to his own airline snacks.

But shattering Katie's illusions is never easy. My parents never quite seem to have the stomach for it. None of us do.

At twelve years old, Katie has only recently, grudgingly, conceded the impossibility of unicorns. Not because they never existed, but because they are now, quite recently, extinct. Fairies really exist in her world. Two years ago, my parents eventually agreed that they could not actually disprove Katie's theory that the Tooth Fairy had been manipulating them through mind control (fairy magic) to slip cash under her pillow. They may think it is always their idea, but they would be wrong.

Putting money under the pillow was never _your_ idea! Sillies.

It wasn't about the money for Katie; it was about the existence of fairy magic. She simply wore them down.

She also still believes in Santa Claus. These are not beliefs she is interested in giving up without a fight. Katie's innocence has a fierce survival instinct and razor-sharp claws. No one really has the energy to challenge her.

So my father can see the future. He pulls the complimentary aloha cookie out of his shirt pocket and tosses it into her lap.

"We're even," he says, turning and shrinking back down out of view.

"No. Dad. You still owe me a dessert when we get to Hawaii. We're not in Hawaii yet, Dad. Hey, Dad?"

Katie jabs her hand through the seats and pokes him in the ribs with the cookie. Just to make sure he heard her.

The flight attendant with the big brown eyes and the dark ponytail and the swishy walk stops by. She stoops over us to see if we want anything. I just shake my head. Katie asks for another cookie.

The attendant gives me a knowing smile.

Little sisters, says the smile.

Little sisters, my eyes say back to her, rolling in their sockets.

She winks.

The wink is sly and slow and meaningful in a way I cannot fully comprehend or express. It's a kind of kiss, this wink. It is the color of her lips. I want to wink right back at her. I want to build the momentum of this strange intimacy between us. I want her to know just how much I am not my little sister. I want her to know I am willing and able to prove my almost-sixteen-years-old, non-little-sister credentials. Right here. Right now.

But none of the muscles in my face work anymore. I can only stare back at her, slack-jawed and blushing. She smiles and moves on up the aisle behind us.

Or at least, most of her moves on up the aisle. Not the wink. The wink stays with me for the entire rest of the flight, as if she has tucked a photograph of herself into my front pocket with two of her fingers. Eyes open, eyes closed: doesn't matter. The image of her face is a kind of retinal tattoo that I could not erase even if I tried. I have no interest in trying.

When she delivers Katie's cookie, she is moving much too quickly for any sort of eye contact. She never even breaks stride.

I wink at her anyway, satisfied that I am *putting it right back out there*, tucking my photograph into her pocket.

I try to catch her glance each time she passes, surprised she cannot sense the single-minded intensity coming from seat 22A. I start popping my eyes as she approaches, in the hope of snagging her subliminal attention. But she is always moving too fast, always carrying something for somebody else.

I'm hoping her training will kick in. Her instinct. Her intuition. That little voice that warns her about things out of the ordinary.

Seat 22A. Seat 22A. Seat 22A.

The guy in 18C keeps turning around and looking back in my direction like he has been hit in the back of the neck with a small blow dart, the kind Amazonian Indians use to kill unwanted treasure hunters.

So maybe it's just my aim. I stop popping my eyes. I don't want to hurt anybody.

The flight attendant – my flight attendant – is at the front of the plane when we land on Oahu, buckled into her own seat facing all of us as we jostle and jerk our way into paradise. If I crane my neck, I can just see the top of her head. I stretch my torso over and up, lengthening my neck like a giraffe going for that top leaf, and gently throb my eyes in her direction a couple of times. The plane jolts sideways again, knocking me into my sister.

Katie, who had been trying to apply her fourth post-meal coating of cocoa-banana lip balm, looks at me with withering irritation. She drags the back of her hand over the glistening, sticky tread mark up her cheek. Then she bodychecks me back into my space.

We taxi to a stop and someone turns on the hula music. The effect on my fellow passengers is electric. That first pluck of ukulele is like a starting pistol. People leap from their seats, hands in the air, ripping luggage out of the overhead bins, adjusting hats and glasses. They stand in the aisle, anxious and fidgety, shifting their weight restlessly from leg to leg. I lean out sideways in both directions for a better view. There is no view. Just more people.

The woman five rows up strips off her pants to reveal green Bermuda shorts underneath. She stuffs shoes and socks in her carryon, extracting a pair of flip-flops in exchange. She shakes out her hair and unbuttons her blouse down to the sternum.

She's not the only one. All around, people are shedding clothes and inhibitions. It feels a little like we're all backstage at a Las Vegas musical waiting for the curtain to go up.

I can't see my flight attendant girlfriend. She has disappeared in the sea of bodies. In the pit of my stomach, I know the truth. Now that the plane has stopped, reality has reasserted itself. Our relationship was never meant to progress past that exquisite wink to the next level. Whatever that might have been.

***

There is a breeze. *Inside* the Honolulu airport... there is a breeze. More like a tide. It is something you drink, more than breathe. I am gulping color. Gulping the scent of flowers. I've never experienced anything like it.

Where I come from, airports are concrete bunkers full of tired, souring travelers the color of paste. The airport we left ten hours ago did not smell like flowers. It smelled of Midwestern angst, an aroma less floral and more in the family of processed meats.

The travelers of our departure were all wearing pants. And shoes. Every last one of them. Even the women.

248

Especially the women. No one in the Honolulu airport seems to be wearing pants or shoes. Even the women.

Especially the women.

Bare arms, legs and shoulders are everywhere. And few of them are the color of paste. I pull my carryon behind me, falling further and further behind my family. Sensory overload takes hold. I want to stand still and turn in slow circles, mouth agape, so that I can take it all in. There are trees. In the airport. Inside the airport there are trees. And birds. I am in danger of being trampled.

"Peter!"

My sister is two hundred feet ahead of me, hand on her hip like the pre-pubescent disappointed diva that she is. She points at me with her tube of cocoa-banana lip balm. My parents stop and turn.

"Let's go, Peter," she commands as the flow of travelers collectively takes note and gives her a wide berth. "Let's move it!"

It is our first trip to the Islands. Six months ago my father received a call from Howard Steincamp, an old college buddy of my parents. My father reported that Howard, his wife Gloria, and their son Kip were making plans for Christmas on Oahu. Howard invited us to join them. I think that would be a real hoot, my father had said approvingly. A real hoot!

Katie and I know Dr. Steincamp only through dinner table lore, regaled by my father as he smiles over a glass of wine at my mother.

"Remember that time when you and I and Howard and Gloria Steincamp all snuck into that movie? What was it... _Wait Until Dark?_ Was it _Wait Until Dark?_ It was. Remember?

The fire escape door had been propped open and Howard was still wearing his werewolf mask from that party at whatshername's house? And Howard takes a seat next to this poor guy who is so engrossed in the movie he doesn't pay any attention until Howard bumps his elbow? And when he turns, he sees a werewolf sitting next to him and then literally jumps up – I mean jumps! – and screams in horror as... who was that? Who played the blind woman? Audrey Hepburn. Just as Audrey Hepburn walks right past Alan Arkin standing in the corner with a knife. Half the audience screamed. Popcorn everywhere!"

There must be a dozen different Howard Steincamp stories. The mechanical bull. The wasp inside the football mascot costume. The golf shot into the outhouse. The backward drag race. The chickens in the church.

Most of those stories involve some sort of inappropriate hijinks, conduct that clearly violates my father's favorite finger-wagging advice: Use your head, Peter. Think before you act.

The story about the werewolf going to the movies is one of only a couple in the Howard Steincamp series that involve my mother as a witness who can verify the facts. My father and Howard have known each other longer than they have known their wives.

The Christmas-in-Hawaii idea was a strangely difficult sell for everyone in my family except my father. Strange because all of us except my father had talked longingly about going to Hawaii someday.

I am kind of friends with a kid who moved to Iowa from California. Cody Simms. Cody is two years older than I am, his parents having delayed his schooling just to give his self-esteem a shot in the arm. I always thought that was at least a kind of cheating, if not outright illegal.

You can't just flout the rules like that and expect to get away with it.

Except that apparently you can. Cody is in the ninth grade just like I am. He sits next to me in social studies so that he can borrow my notes. He also borrows a lot of my lunch money. Cody is the most developed sixteen-year-old I've ever seen. He can unbutton the top button on his shirt by expanding his chest. I can't do that. I don't know anybody who can do that.

My uncle Moe can unbutton his lower buttons with no hands. The button on his pants too. But that is hardly the same.

Given his parents' strategy, it is more than just a little ironic that Cody has turned out to be so insecure about his intellect. People think he's eighteen. They wonder, sometimes out loud, why an eighteen-year-old doesn't know anything.

Having given him an unfair leg up, Cody's parents divorced and his dad moved to Honolulu. Whenever Cody returns from a visit, he brings stories of topless women. He says they are everywhere you turn in Hawaii. He has photos to prove it.

Cody is always deeply tanned and wears his shirts open down to the third button. He smokes Pall Malls and says his favorite drink is dark rum. His dad even got him a tattoo of a hula dancer on his arm. Her hips move when he flexes his muscle. It's like being friends with a teenaged pirate.

Hawaii has been on my radar ever since.

My mother has friends that go to Hawaii every single year, like it was some sort of religious pilgrimage or a migratory instinct. She was not shy about declaring at some point every winter that she felt a little deprived.

A lot of money to blow for a one-week vacation, my father would observe. Sometimes, as they were busy pondering the financial considerations, he would toss a follow-up comment out on the table: been awhile since we took the trip out to Milwaukee to see your parents.

No one can be sure of why he was so disinterested in Hawaii except that frugality for my father is something of a sixth sense. It's part of his survival instinct. If my father is ever mauled by a bear in our backyard when no one else is around, he will find a way to drive himself to the hospital just to avoid the ambulance fees.

And he'll bring his own gauze.

But the idea of three nights and four days in Hawaii with the Steincamps had somehow managed to slip past the financial barricades. This time my father was eager to go.

It was the rest of us that had to be sold on the idea.

Hawaii itself wasn't the problem. Christmas was the problem. The holiday season and all its contextually dependent ritual was the problem. What about the snow? What about the gaiety of firelight in the dark of December? What about shopping for a sacrificial tree? What about holding a leash of colored bulbs as my father clings to the corner of our roofline and my mother leans nervously out the window talking to him in tense whispers like she is trying to talk a suicidal man off a ledge? A little to the left, Stuart, that's it, easy now, easy, I can't raise these two kids by myself.

Or what about the Christmas Eve party over at the Hansons' house with the pool table and the first-person shooter video games I am not allowed to own but for which there is some strange seasonal amnesty in honor of the baby Jesus? What about opening presents on Christmas morning beneath a dead and rapidly drying fire hazard?

252

Presents are actually at the very center of the concern. How could abandoning the holidays for Hawaii not have a devastating impact on the volume of wrapped loot that Katie and I have come to expect? Will my parents actually take the time to come in off the beach and go shopping? And even if they do, who knows if Hawaii even sells the right kind of stuff? How will we bring it all back? Our suitcases are only but so big. Why should Samsonite have such a disproportionate say on the size and volume of our Christmas cheer?

Instinctively, Hawaii seemed to be the opposite of all the things that have come to identify the Christmas season. My father, it seemed to us, was proposing a kind of anti-Christmas.

We always attend the Christmas service at the Presbyterian church in our neighborhood, even though ours is not a particularly religious family. Can we really just up and go to Hawaii for Christmas? What would Jesus think?

My mother obviously had her own reservations, although I have no idea what they were. I assume they had nothing to do with my opportunity to blow ragged holes through the heads of advancing zombies on the Hansons' bigscreen television. Whatever my mother's concerns, they were strong enough that our eyes had met across the dinner table, reacting in understated alarm to my father's mid-August proposal.

"What do you say, gang? Christmas in Hawaii! With the Steincamps!"

It was Katie who had actually voiced objection.

"What? Are you kidding? Dad! You can't do that! You can't do that!"

"Really," he said. "Why not?"

I was prepared to calmly speak my mind. Perhaps my mother was too. We had our concerns. But Katie had taken the conversation firmly in her jaws and was sprinting for the border that separates reality from fantasy.

"Why not? Why not? Dad! What about Santa?"

My father stared at her, dumbfounded. If he had anticipated any objections to his proposal, he certainly had not considered that one.

Katie looked at my mother and then at me, hoping for reinforcement. I didn't know what to say. None of us did. She was twelve. It wasn't natural for her to still be a believer. Preserving childhood fictions in a world this cynical shouldn't be possible for that long. Some of Katie's friends were just heading into their hunky vampire fixation phase. Katie was still resisting. In her head, teenaged vampires were silly kid stuff. Santa was real.

Katie looked back at my father, pumping her arms in the air, palms open, like an Old Country Italian grandmother demonically possessing a twelve-year-old girl. "What... about... Santa?"

My parents had a silent conversation with their eyes. I could not fully decipher the exchange, but I know it had something to do with the recent Tooth-Fairy wars. No one wanted that again.

I could see what my father was thinking. He wanted to tell Katie that she was a big girl and that big girls didn't believe in Santa. Or the Tooth Fairy. Or unicorns. Of course, he had actively encouraged all that nonsense in the first place and that would easily be the first salvo across the table.

"Oh, yeah? Well if Santa doesn't exist then why... did... you... LIE... to me?"

He just didn't have the energy. So my father had picked the other road.

"I'm sure Santa will be able to find us, sweetie," he had said with a chuckle.

"Oh, really," said Katie, like he had lost all common sense. Like it was reasonable to believe that Santa could circumnavigate the globe in a single night, delivering presents to every man, woman and child, eating cookies, drinking milk, slipping down chimneys, mushing flying reindeer and all the rest of it, but that it was dangerously naïve to think he could incorporate a change-of-address request four-and-a-half months in advance.

"Christmas is only nineteen Thursdays from now, Dad. Nineteen. His plans are set. You can't switch it up on him at the last minute. He's going to show up here! We have to be here!"

Her eyes had betrayed genuine desperation. It was impossible not to empathize. I hated feeling sorry for my sister. But I did.

"Sweetheart," said my mother softly, touching her on the shoulder. But my father had cleared his throat sharply. His eyes were wide with warning and more than just a little panic. My mother had sighed and stepped back from the precipice of reality. "Your father is right, " she said. "Santa will know. Santa always knows."

"Hey," said my father with a new and hopeful energy in his voice. "Kip Steincamp is just a year younger than you are. You kids are going to have a great time together. A great time. This is the dream vacation, kiddo."

Katie looked at him like he had taken away her shiny red apple and in its place was offering her a napkin full of poodle excrement.

"This is not the dream, Dad. Is. Not. The. Dream. This is a Christmas nightmare!"

She pushed her chair back and stomped off to her room, slamming the door.

We all sat there looking at each other as the dinner grew cold.

"That's going to be a problem," I said as nonchalantly as the door-slamming drama would permit. "Maybe we should just stay home."

But my father was determined. His proposal had already hardened into reality. He convinced my mother behind closed doors. They made the reservations without any further discussion. Katie and I never even got to vote on it.

Family votes are a farce anyway. Believing in the Tooth Fairy is, all things considered, less crazy than counting on dinner-table democracy in our house. Put enough cash under my pillow and I'll pretend to believe in just about anything. But ask me whether I stand a snowball's chance on a beach of voting to stay home for Christmas. Consulting us was just window dressing. We were going to Hawaii.

I clung to the consolation that, according to Cody Simms, topless women are like freaking everywhere in Hawaii, dude. He made it sound like a run-of-the-mill trip to a Hawaiian grocery store was roughly the same as pushing a shopping cart through a women's locker room. If there was even a sliver of a possibility that that was true, then I was willing to sacrifice my Christmas.

My sister was less willing. Katie tried to change the inevitable by sulking and barricading herself in her room whenever possible. When that failed to do the trick, she came up with a list of adult friends of my parents who she thought would probably be delighted to come by the house and check on her every so often. Like she was a fern that would only need a little watering.

But Katie had no more choice in the matter than I did. As I reconciled myself to the prospect of four days of nonstop nudity, there was nothing for Katie to do except cling to the fervent hope that Santa was sophisticated enough to adapt to rapidly changing circumstances. Or, at least, that he was sophisticated enough to consult my mother's Facebook page, which Katie hoped to use as a modern-day, emergency-locator beacon.

***

Our island hotel is not a single, tower-shaped building like I had expected, but a series of fake-bamboo bungalows arranged in clusters of four or five. Each cluster of bungalows forms a tidy semicircle around a small parking lot, a convenience that detracts somewhat from the middle-of-the-jungle illusion that the owners of the Coconut Palms Resort have tried to create. That illusion, after all, is the whole selling point of this place. *Come live with us in the jungle. You might see a monkey.* I can only assume that the more you pay, the more you want that illusion to be true. The greater your investment, the more you want to believe.

The bungalows and parking lots are connected by narrow concrete pathways that serpentine beneath tall palms and around wide, rubbery-leaved tropical foliage that just doesn't seem real. But it is real. In some places we actually have to push the fat lily-padded leaves out of our way.

"Isn't this place something?" asks my father to no one in particular as we follow fake-wooden signs in the shape of arrows to the Jungle Lobby. "I mean did I pick the right place or did I pick the right place? Listen. You can hear the ocean. It's right over there! I mean... just... right... over... there!"

He points off into the trees. I listen. Mostly I hear traffic, which is just... right... there. And there. And there. I don't doubt that he can hear the surf. He's taller than I am. His ears can clear the wall of foliage that mine cannot.

A horn bleats somewhere in the soundscape behind us. I do my best to imagine that it was a macaw.

My sister runs the trails ahead of us, pulling her overstuffed Hello Kitty carryon behind her and ignoring my father's warning to slow down.

"Katie, you're going to kill someone," he says.

But she has disappeared around the next bend in the path. She's already seen one gecko darting across a leaf and there's no stopping her from finding another.

We finally catch up with her outside the Jungle Lobby, where she has abandoned Hello Kitty to crawl on her hands and knees between a row of recycling containers and a large air-conditioning unit. The recycling bins are nearly full. Diet Pepsi and Red Bull would appear to be the beverages of choice in the jungle.

Just ask the hyper-caffeinated ants.

"Katie!" My mother knows how to whisper-scold like no other. "Get... out... of... there!"

"I saw one go under here, Mom. It was a baby, too!"

Inside, my mother takes Katie to the bathroom to wash her hands and knees. My father gets in line at the check-in desk to take care of business.

I decide to pass the time by touring the lobby, which has been decked out for Christmas. Little white lights have been strung everywhere that will support them, including up the trunks of a central trio of palms that ascend through a hole in the ceiling. Instead of pine garlands, they have used long green vines to trim the doorways and drape through the airspace above the central seating area. Where you might otherwise expect bells, they have hung large, bulbous white flowers.

On either end of the reception counter are small fake pine trees wrapped in large colored lights and capped with a silver star. The branches of each tree are dusted generously with white styrofoam powder. There are even little fake pinecones scattered over identical, red felt tree skirts. I can't decide if the trees are just a hospitable effort on the part of the Coconut Palms to accommodate mainstream holiday decor, or a deliberate act of condescension aimed at people with limited imagination.

You want Christmas? Here's your Christmas.

I follow a pathway to an indoor-outdoor café called the Aloha Grill. It has bamboo chairs and tables that hold bright pink penis flowers. Two servers are busying about with trays of sandwiches and ice-frosted glasses. They are both disappointingly men.

There is a separate path to a flower-shaped swimming pool. Several men are drinking while sitting in lounge chairs and talking loudly to two middle-aged women submerged in the water. Both of the women have their hair up. And their tops on.

I know better than to believe everything Cody Simms tells me. I really do. But that doesn't stop me from wanting to believe or from hoping that he is right. Katie has seen a wild gecko before we have even checked into our hotel room. Is a little casual jungle nudity really so much to ask?

I work my way back to the lobby. My father is still at the front desk. I find a chair next to a burbling dolphin fountain and wait.

"Aloha."

The voice comes from behind. Sweet and soft and strangely fragrant. I am not accustomed to smelling voices. But I can smell this one.

I turn to find a woman. Silky black hair falling over light brown shoulders. She is wearing a full-length, white cotton dress. No shoes. Her arms are hung with flowered garlands, some white and some pink like the kind she wears in her hair. She is smiling, bowed slightly at the waist.

"What's your name?" she asks.

"Peter," I say, swallowing.

"Aloha, Peter. My name is Lolana. Welcome to Coconut Palms. May I give you a lei?"

I don't know what to say to this. She may as well have asked me if I needed a fresh penguin for a hat. All I can hear is the voice of Cody Simms shouting incomprehensible things in my head.

I can't take my eyes off her face. I blink at her.

"Oh," I say. It's all I can manage.

She smiles, lowering herself so that her face is level with my own. She extends her arms, one on each side of my head, placing the lei around the back of my neck with delicate fingers. The petals are soft and cool against my hot skin.

I am drunk on the fragrance of her presence. I know it's from the flowers. I know that. And yet I believe in my heart that this is simply how she smells. I have an impulse to kiss her arm. Or lick it or bite it or bump it with my nose. Anything.

But I am frozen in place. I might be drooling.

I should be grateful for this paralysis. Who knows how she would have reacted. But I am not grateful. I regret my timidity. I choose to believe that Lolana would have been charmed to have been kissed, licked, bitten or bumped on the arm. I choose to believe that is the very response she is expecting. I choose to believe that is how sexual opportunity presents itself to virgins vacationing in Hawaii.

So I am not grateful for my paralysis. I am ashamed.

"Aloha and enjoy your stay, Peter," says Lolana, rising again with a smile and then swishing away in the direction of the café. I watch her go, lost in the scent of her, as if her arms are still encircling my neck.

Katie is suddenly next to my chair. She is all over me about the lei.

"Where did you get that? I want one. I want one. Mom, Peter got a flower scarf. I want a flower scarf."

"It's called a lei, dummy," I say, my eyes glued to the path to the café, waiting for Lolana to reemerge.

"How much did it cost? Mom, can I borrow some money?"

"It was free."

"Free? Free? O...M...G. Mom, it was free! Mom. Mom. Did you hear what Peter said? Mom."

But my mother has joined my father near the check-in counter. He is in an animated conversation with a man and a woman standing in front of a tower of rolling luggage.

Howard and Gloria Steincamp, I'm guessing.

The four of them are hugging and laughing as the line to the front counter snakes around them. Howard Steincamp is tall, with broad shoulders and a loud voice. He talks with his hands on his hips, bent over my parents like they are children. Gloria is petite and busty with honey-blond hair tucked behind her ears. She's wearing yellow capri pants and high heels on her feet that bring her forehead up to her husband's shoulders. She touches my father's arm when she laughs, nodding conspiratorially at my mother who steps forward and grips Gloria's forearm in return. Howard grabs my father's shoulder. You'd think they were playing a strange game of hotel-lobby Twister.

A boy appears from behind the tower of luggage. He adjusts a pair of round wire-rim glasses and leans up against the bags.

He is close to Katie's age. Very pale and more than just a little pudgy in cowboy boots, geranium-colored shorts, a flowered button down and a straw hat. It's like Pillsbury Madison has rolled out a tropical, gay, rodeo-action figure.

"That must be Kip," I say. Katie turns and looks.

"Ick," she says, her little nostrils flaring outward from a darkly blooming expression of revulsion. It's the same look she uses to communicate her opinion of virtually anything in the gourd family. Spaghetti squash reliably sends Katie into dramatic fits of gagging and choking, her eyes watering and rolling back into her head as she clutches her throat and kicks at the leg of the dinner table in a nonverbal plea for rescue. It's hard to watch without believing that death is a very real possibility. Vomit, at least, is a very real possibility. We learned that the hard way, hollowing out a pumpkin for Halloween.

Kip Steincamp, fortunately, does not appear to inspire squash-grade revulsion, although his distance across the lobby might have diluted the impact.

Katie pulls the cocoa-banana balm from her pocket and re-goops her lips. "I'm going out to look for lizards."

"Geckos," I correct.

"Lizards."

"Geckos."

"Lizards."

"Geckos."

"Lizzzzz....aaaards."

"Whatever."

I let her have the last word. Katie can keep this up forever. She has kept our "am not" "are so" dispute alive for almost two years, so long now that I've forgotten what started it in the first place. I don't think Katie remembers either, although that doesn't stop her from randomly sticking her finger in my face, in the middle of a conversation or a movie or across the dinner table, and saying to me accusingly, "are so, Peter. Are... so!"

I've stopped responding altogether, hoping that she will just get tired of it. So far there is no end in sight. It's not much different with jinx and shotgun. She thinks the words have magical properties, that they actually confer privilege. She thinks that by saying them over and over, month after month, year after year, she can stockpile them to use however she pleases. By Katie's count, I owe her eleven hundred Cokes, and I'm never allowed to ride in the front seat of a car for the rest of my natural life. She absolutely believes this. She's not playing games.

I don't need another war of attrition with my sister. She can call the geckos whatever she wants to call them. I wander off toward the men's room, which is halfway down the long blue tile walkway leading out to the Aloha Grill. I have no interest in the bathroom. I walk as slowly as I can without attracting attention, looking intently for Lolana.

She is not to be found in the hallway. But I can smell her, of this I am certain.

There is nothing much to be gained in the men's room, certainly not Lolana, and I wonder why I stopped in at all. I wash my hands twice and then dry them with a rolled up washcloth that I take from the pyramid of rolled up washcloths stacked in a woven basket by the sink.

At the base of the pyramid are more freshly cut pink and red penis flowers. They're huge and exotic. They have a waxy, plastic look to them. They belong in a *King Kong* movie. I've never seen anything like them. I can't tell if they are mocking me or encouraging me, but it is definitely one or the other.

I look at myself in the mirror, cringing at the person looking back. He is much younger-looking than I imagine. Too white. Too Midwestern. Hair too spongy.

I unbutton my shirt one button, exposing more of my hairless, undeveloped chest. I give myself a crooked little smile like the one I imagine men give when a woman asks a question that reveals her interest.

Questions like, so where have you been all my life? And, would you like to come up to my room for a cocktail?

I toss the washcloth in the direction of the trashcan without looking. It's a clean three-pointer that goes perfectly with the crooked smile. The attractive, predictable woman of my imagination is clearly impressed, turning to lead me to the elevators. I lean in toward the mirror, expanding my crooked smile to look at my teeth. People always say I have great teeth.

I do have great teeth. Just look at them.

My hand grips the edge of a hole cut into the stone sink counter. Beneath the hole is a basket of dirty washcloths. I realize my mistake.

It is my father who enters the men's room in time to see me rummaging through the garbage.

"Peter, what on earth…"

"I just… I threw the washcloth…"

"Where is Katie?"

"She went to look for lizards."

"Geckos."

"Geckos."

"Come on out and meet the Steincamps," he says.

I find the washcloth, drop it into the proper basket and follow him to the door.

"Nope." He stops me with a finger. "You've been digging in the trash. Wash your hands. Think before you act, Peter."

***

The Steincamps are staying in a different part of the Coconut Palms jungle, about a two-minute walk from where we are staying. The pathway twists and curves unnecessarily around clusters of palm trees and even crosses a tiny wooden bridge that arches over a make-believe creek. Katie has named it Lizard Bridge. She is beneath Lizard Bridge, lying on her stomach like a little, blond homeless troll, as the rest of us pass over her.

My mother has to tell her twice to get out of the dirt.

265

Katie scrambles out, brushes off and climbs back up onto the pathway. She scampers up the path past the others. For the moment, she seems to have forgotten her concern that Santa will soon be visiting our dark and empty home. None of us have any illusions that this concern is gone, but for now the novelty of our surroundings has managed to keep her distracted.

Around the next corner, my parents and the Steincamps suddenly part, stepping off on either side of the path to make way for Katie, who is now racing back in the other direction. Kip holds on to his straw hat as she blows past. She skids to a stop in front me, smiling.

"I forgot," she says.

"What?" I ask.

"Are so, Peter. Are...so!"

"Am not."

"Are so."

"Yeah, whatever, Katie."

"Shotgun! Jinx! Lizard!"

She turns and is gone again in a cloud of dust, roadrunner style.

Beep, beep.

The Steincamps' bungalow is an exact replica of ours, right down to the vinyl plank flooring, the plastic bamboo trim around the countertops and the nylon mosquito netting gathered at the ready above each bed. The bathroom sinks are made to look like enormous clamshells, the kind you always find littering a jungle floor. Even the low-hanging banana chandeliers over the kitchen tables are the same. The Coconut Palms people have made the

266

bungalows look exactly like something the Swiss Family Robinson might have built had the Swiss Family Robinson been made to survive by their wits, a bit of luck, and the thin profit margin of an overextended Tampa-based hotel franchise.

I lean against the open door, breathing the strange tropical air and looking out at a rope hammock stretched between two palms. Behind me, my parents and the Steincamps stand in a semicircle in the living room, talking over each other. My father and Howard Steincamp catch each other up on business matters, my father's accounting practice and Dr. Steincamp's dentistry mill.

My mother and Gloria Steincamp talk about their children. From the sound of things, Kip shows every sign of being a child prodigy in mathematics and the harpsichord.

My mother brags that I might just turn into a writer.

Her only evidence for such optimism is a recent A-minus grade for my English essay on the two books we read this year in school: *To Kill a Mockingbird* and *The Crucible.* It was a compare-and-contrast assignment that kept me stumped for days. In truth, my teacher seemed less impressed with my writing ability than my take on the character of Boo Radley. I wrote that Boo was the personification of a truth that keeps the town of Maycomb, Alabama from believing the fairy tales they tell themselves about other people. Fairy tales about race and gender and justice. My teacher, Mrs. McCaw, thought this was insightful and wrote as much in the margin beneath the grade. She was less enthusiastic about my insight that Arthur Miller's childhood crucible had likely been an over-empowered, bratty little sister, to which Mrs. McCaw assigned a frowny face with the word unnecessary.

My mother makes as much of my scattered accomplishments as she can, embellishing the ordinary into the remarkable. I feel sorry that I have not given her more to work with. I don't have a sport or a musical instrument to call my own. I'm terrible at math. But she manages anyway, bringing enough raw enthusiasm to the discussion to convince herself of my potential and to elicit sounds of respect from Gloria Steincamp.

"Well!" says Gloria. "A writer! How wonderful."

I can tell they are both looking at me from across the room, waiting for me to turn around. I pretend that I have not heard anything of their conversation, focusing instead on the sudden, heaving presence of young Kip Steincamp. He looks like he might be ready to throw up onto a cluster of wide, fat Jurassic leaves arching over the path that leads up to the front door.

"You okay?" I ask. Kip nods but can't answer.

"I'm way faster than you, Kip," Katie calls out, throwing herself onto the hammock. "Way, way, way faster."

Katie has demonstrated twice now that she can make the trek from our door to the Steincamps' door in just under twenty-five seconds. Kip's best time is just over forty seconds. He takes her athletic dominance in stride. He does not point out the obvious difficulty of running in cowboy boots with one hand holding a straw hat on your head.

"You're a fast one alright," pants Kip finally, bent in half and still breathing hard enough to dislodge a lung. He fans himself with his hat as his entire body expands and contracts. "That's okay," he says pushing his glasses up his nose. "I like them fast."

Kip winks at me as he says this, like we share an inside joke. I squint down at his doughy little face, now pink enough with exertion to match his shorts. I try to make sense of what I have just heard.

He likes them fast? He can't know what he is saying.

"The faster the better," he says. "Right, my man? Am I right?"

Kip winks again and makes a clicking sound with his mouth like he is calling a horse. He does know what he is saying. All I can do is shrug.

The faster the better? I have no idea.

***

It is another thirty minutes before the adults part company, agreeing to meet up later for dinner. We return to our own bungalow and unpack. Katie and I change into swimming suits and the four of us head out for a late afternoon walk on the beach.

"So what do you think of Kip?" my father asks Katie, as the ocean finally emerges through the trees. "Pretty smart kid, don't you think?"

Katie turns back and looks up at my father with a version of her spaghetti-squash-gagging-reflex expression. She has on so much sun lotion, her skin cannot absorb all of it. There is an oily white sheen on her face that disappears into her hair. She looks a like a little-girl version of the slick white hatchling creature that burst through the chest cavity of the guy in *Alien*.

"Oh, Katie," he says. "Give him a break. He's a good kid. He wants to be friends. He told me he thinks you're pretty."

"I don't want to be friends with boys," she says. "I don't like boys."

We watch her scramble across the powdery sand toward the water. My mother yells after her to stay close and swats me on the arm, her signal that I have been deputized to help keep my sister from drowning.

Which is funny because neither of us can swim.

As I trot across the sand after her, Katie's words are still in my head. It hits me for the first time that her aversion to Kip has nothing at all to do with the way he looks, or his manner, or his tropical, gay, rodeo, action-figure ensemble, or his poor showing in the bungalow-to-bungalow time trials.

Kip is a boy. That's all. Katie's a girl and Kip is a boy.

The beach is full of people. Many of these people are women. All the women are wearing clothes. It does not take me long to conclude that I've been royally duped. Cody Simms is full of hot air. If you cannot find a topless woman on a beach, of all places, then the odds of finding one anywhere else – grocery stores, restaurants, gas stations – were not very promising.

We walk the length of the beach and back. Nothing.

Cody said they were everywhere. He had pictures. I should have known better. The truth is that I did know better. But I had wanted to believe. Really wanted.

Cody Simms had also claimed that he has a girlfriend in California who is twenty-six. Jessica Something. I don't know her last name. He showed me a picture once on the bus. Cody and Jessica lying on a beach. He was wearing shorts and the same surfing t-shirt I'd seen him wear to school at least once a week.

She was wearing almost nothing.

She really could have been twenty-six. She had one of those smoldering looks that punched right through the picture, like the photo was not something for you to look at but a window in space and time that she used to look at you. Sixteen-year-olds can't do that sort of thing. Not even eighteen-year-olds can pull that off. You have to be at least twenty-four.

Sometimes Cody likes to refer to Jessica as his *old lady*, as in: My old lady's refusing to have any more sex until I graduate so she won't get arrested. He said this kind of thing so matter of factly and with such an understated nothing-to-be-done-about-it-believe-me-I've-tried sort of disappointment that it was hard not to believe he was actually in a long-distance relationship with a twenty-six-year-old woman.

"She's always worried about Johnny Law sticking his nose into our bedroom," he said once. Not her bedroom. Our bedroom. He was so convincing.

But now, as I scour the beach for any sign of public indecency, I have to question everything that Cody has ever told me.

The Pacific spits Katie out of the water and up onto the shore. She lands at my feet, splayed out face down in the sand like a young turtle that has traded its shell for a stringy blond wig.

"You okay?" I ask.

She rolls over, panting, spitting water and sand.

"Jinx. Shotgun. Lizard."

***

We have dinner with the Steincamps at a place just up the road called Hatti's Hula Hut. Hatti's takes up a lot of jungle space with a lot of steel and concrete. It's as much a hut as our two-bedroom, one-and-a-half-bath shoebox at the Coconut Palms is a bungalow.

Just outside the front door of Hatti's Hula Hut is a naked hula dancer.

She is not actually naked. She is not even actually a hula dancer. Or a person. She's eight feet tall and made of something like flesh-colored plastic. And not Hawaiian flesh, either. Mainland flesh. Des Moines flesh. Her left hand is extended in greeting toward the parking lot, while her right hand is pressing down toward her naked, featureless feet. She is an hourglass of nudity interrupted only by a painted grass skirt, a painted coconut bra, and a painted flower lei showing from beneath a real flower lei that the management of Hatti's Hula Hut must change every night.

Her lips are full and red and her eyes are a pale, watery blue, almost exactly the shade of Jesus' eyes in the portrait hanging in the lobby of the First Presbyterian Ministry back home; the eyes that normally greet us this time of year and wonder just a little accusingly where we have been for the last three-hundred-and-sixty-four days. The same eyes that will not find us coming through the front door this year.

"Is that Hatti?" Katie asks as she and Kip sprint from the minivan across the parking lot. They stop abruptly in front of her, too close to take her all in. Kip immediately begins slapping Hatti on her plastic grass skirt.

"Ride, cowboy! Ride!" Kip commands, stomping his right boot in time with the spanking.

"No!" Katie admonishes him sternly. "That's wrong, Kip! That is wrong!" Kip stops, wide-eyed and ready to defer to my sister as the dominant authority in their new relationship. "She's not a cowboy, she's a cowgirl!"

"Oh."

"And you have to use both hands!"

272

By the time the rest of us reach the front door, Kip and Katie are each using both hands to beat poor Hatti on her plastic backside, shouting Ride, Cowgirl! Ride! I cannot help but wonder whether this is among the reasons that First Presbyterian Ministry passed on a Jesus statue for its lobby and went with just a standard portrait instead.

My mother and Mrs. Steincamp simultaneously call Kip and Katie down with stern tones of morally rooted disapproval. As though they are being unconscionably rude to a real person.

But Hula Hut Hatti doesn't seem to mind in the least. Her expression and pose are unchanged. She seems content to represent whatever we want her to represent. Hawaiian culture. Restaurant stripper culture. Rodeo culture. It's all the same to her. As I walk beneath her extended arm, I force myself to not notice the smoothness of her legs or to look up at the painted coconut shells cupping her plastic breasts.

The hostess of Hatti's Hula Hut does not look at all like Hatti. She is at least sixty-eight and, in both appearance and attitude, less hula dancer than a crumpled cigarette in a dress. She checks the reservation and counts out seven oversized menus, each of which is made to look like three slabs of driftwood joined together with little rusty hinges. I do the math as we wait: That's twenty-one slabs of wood in her arms. No wonder she is so stooped and ill-tempered. She needs a wheelbarrow.

Or a donkey.

She trudges off across the floor past the bar toward a distant staircase without so much as a follow me.

We all follow her anyway, single file, like Himalayan hikers behind their Sherpa. She leads us to a large table out on a second-floor balcony overlooking the parking lot. Kip and Katie argue over which of the cars below is ours.

"Don't be difficult, Kip," says Katie. "You're really starting to test my limits."

A tan man in a yellow Hawaiian shirt, a Santa hat, and a shark's tooth necklace sits on a stool singing "Tiny Bubbles" and playing a guitar. Somehow he can sing and chew gum at the same time. He nods and smiles as we pass. I nod back.

The song ends and he takes off the Santa hat, draping it over the back of a speaker. He wipes the sweat off his head and does the thing with his hand that I have come to understand is the sign for hang loose.

I do not know what the hang loose thing actually means. I only know how it is supposed to feel, which maybe is enough.

Cody Simms insists the hang loose hand signal is really Hawaiian code for would you like to get naked and have some sex? Cody gives the hang loose to all the girls in my school. Even some of the teachers.

If I'd ever been inclined to believe Cody's explanation, it has now lost all credibility in my exchange with the bald, gum-chewing guitar player at Hatti's Hula Hut. I really don't think that's what he's trying to tell me.

Even so, I cannot bring myself to return the gesture without feeling like a complete fraud. So instead, I give him an uncertain smile and an enthusiastic two thumbs up.

Although, I really don't know what that – two thumbs up – is supposed to mean either. I worry that I have just inadvertently upped the ante on the man's original unknown proposition. An enthusiastic yes! Twice the nakedness! Twice the sex!

Most of dinner leaves me in no-man's land, neither an adult nor a child and without any natural companion. My parents and the Steincamps order cocktails. Kip and Katie order Cokes. I order a virgin pineapple daiquiri. The drink is actually served in the husk of a huge plastic pineapple with an enormous straw and a spear of purple flowers. It takes two hands to manage and is so tall that it's difficult to get the straw in my mouth with the drink sitting on the table.

It helps to hold the pineapple husk down to my lap.

Katie instantly wants a virgin pineapple daiquiri of her own. Kip, too, raising his hand urgently like he might have to go to the bathroom. What had initially seemed to me like a mature drink for world-weary recovering alcoholics on vacation now just seems childish.

I don't want to be one of the children. I want to be one of the adults.

I scour the fake driftwood menu for a virgin vodka tonic. No such luck.

I try to take an interest in the conversations crisscrossing the table between my parents and the Steincamps, avoiding any involvement in the escalating argument between Katie and Kip over who has the largest thumbs.

"Longer-larger, Kip, not fatter-larger! Tell him, Peter."

My parents and the Steincamps spend most of their time on issues of business and politics. Dr. Steincamp is convinced that America will be an openly Socialist state within twenty-five years. I can tell my father thinks this is a crazy thing for someone to actually believe. He laughs like the comment was just playful provocation.

"I'm dead serious," Howard Steincamp booms. "Twenty-five years. Democracy as we know it today will be dead in America. The government will tell us what we can say, what we can do, what we can think."

Gloria Steincamp places her delicate hand on top of her husband's and pats it sharply. "Now, Howard," she says. "Let's not get into politics."

She looks across the table at my father, leans forward and rolls her eyes, smiling in the conspiratorial way that adults communicate about the children who are sitting next to them. My father smiles back at her.

I can see that my mother takes all this in, too. She is not smiling.

The server comes to take our orders. All the adults ask for some version of the catch of the day. I order a cheeseburger and fries.

"I want a cheeseburger and fries," says Katie.

"Me too," says Kip. "I'll take the burger bloody. And see to it that my fries are hot and crisp."

"I want my fries hot and crisp too," says Katie. "Peter, do you want your fries hot and crisp? You have to tell him or they won't see to it."

"Yeah," says Kip with authority, adjusting his straw hat. "You have to tell him."

The server looks at me like I am a child for whom this might be an actual concern. He stands poised to write a number 3 next to the hot and crisp instruction. I clear my throat and try to keep my voice low. He has to lean down to hear.

"I'd like to trade the fries for oysters on the half shell," I say. "And a virgin martini, hold the olive."

The server looks over at my mother. She shakes her head.

I spend most of dinner looking out at the shadowy trees across the parking lot, dark fronds rattling in the warm tropical breeze. My attention alternates between eavesdropping on the adults, eavesdropping on the children, and listening to the musical talent masticate his way through the highs and lows of the seventies. He rounds out the set with a Caribbean take on "Muskrat Love" and a medley tribute to Tony Orlando and Dawn.

"Howard," my father's voice is suddenly louder and an octave higher than it has been all evening. The guitar player looks over in our direction just as "Tie a Yellow Ribbon" is picking up steam. "I don't suppose you happened to see that dartboard downstairs in the bar."

Howard and Gloria look at each other, mouths open, eyes wide.

"Oh, ho, ho, my friend," says Howard. "I'm not going to let you cheat me again!"

My father holds up his hands.

"Now, now. I know you have some concern, Howard, about that famous game of darts, so long ago. A game I won fair and square, but..."

"It doesn't count if the dart doesn't stick," interrupts Howard, pointing.

"It stuck for more than fifteen seconds. That's the rule."

"Oh, that's a bunch a buckshot, Stuart. Says who?"

My father shrugs, gesturing with both hands across the table at Gloria. "Hey. She went home with me, Howard. Gloria enforced the rules. I just thought you might want a chance to prove yourself."

"Oh, ho, ho, ho!" bellows Howard again. He squints at my father, pointing at him. My dad leans back in his chair with a self-satisfied look. Gloria rolls her eyes at my mother in a boys-will-be-boys sort of way.

"Have you heard this one?" Gloria asks.

My mother smiles. Blinks. She shakes her head.

"First time I met either of them. We were all down in the Commons. Way too much to drink. I needed a ride home. They played a game of darts to decide. They were tied, dead even, and Stuart had the last throw. He hit the bull's eye, but then the dart fell out of the board. They had the whole Commons arguing. It went on for an hour. I almost walked home."

"You are on, my friend," says Howard, rising out of his chair, still pointing. "You are on. Right. Now."

The guitar player is plainly irritated at the competition. Tying a yellow ribbon is now less of a hopeful, love-struck request and more of an urgent and angry command intended to do irreparable harm to a defenseless oak tree.

Howard Steincamp and my father disappear downstairs to the bar. Gloria finishes her last forkful of fish and pushes her chair back.

"I'll go make sure they behave themselves," Gloria says.

My mother laughs in a way I have never heard before. "Good. You keep them out of trouble. I'll watch the kids."

I push my chair back to follow Gloria downstairs. My mother's hand is suddenly on my wrist.

"Nope," she says.

It's the only syllable she needs.

By the time they return, the table has been cleared and the four of us are finishing dessert. We can all tell by the looks on their faces that my father won again.

"Sorry," he says a little too loudly, patting my mother on the shoulder. "Howard kept losing. We had to go seven out of nine just to establish that I am unbeatable."

"Your husband's a cheater," says Howard, sitting heavily. "But you know what? You... know... what? I don't even care. Cheat all you want, pal, because she married me. Stick that in your pipe and smoke it."

Our server comes by and asks if he can bring the bill. My sister, ever vigilant, is not about to let that happen.

"No. Dad. Dad? Dad!"

"Yes, Katie. No shouting please."

"I want another chocolate volcano."

"You've had quite enough."

"No, Dad," says Katie, her chin sporting a velvety brown goatee. "You owe me two desserts. Remember? That bird was alive, Dad. It was dead and then it was alive. I was right and you were wrong. You weren't a believer. You wouldn't give miracles a chance in your own backyard but I was right so you owe me a second dessert."

"No, Katie," starts my father, sternly. He is foolishly ready to remind her about the cookie on the plane. Failing that, he will no doubt assert his authority as the man of the family.

My mother cuts him off, looking up at the server.

"She'll have another chocolate volcano, please."

My father opens his mouth but there are no words inside.

Kip holds out the plate with the remnants of his first chocolate magmatic disaster, pushing up the brim of his hat with a knuckle so he can look his table slave in the eyes.

"Double down, my man. Heavy on the lava and make it snappy."

"Yeah, snappy," says Katie.

The server sighs audibly, taking their plates. Kip and Katie give each other a high-five, followed by a fist bump and something Katie calls a pinky-shake.

"You're not doing it right, Kip," she says. "What am I going to do with you?"

***

Most of the next day, Christmas Eve, is spent further inland. The original plan was to devote a full half-day to the Honolulu Zoo. A must-see, insisted my father. The Steincamps had seemed just as enthusiastic.

But I am the only one who seems to be halfway enjoying the experience. Not coincidentally, I am the only one who either did not spend the night violently erupting – lava in, lava out – or tending to someone who was busy violently erupting.

Exhaustion and dehydration have left both Katie and Kip uncharacteristically subdued. They lean into their respective mothers like they might fall off the open-air tram into the dirt without a protective arm around their shoulders.

It does not help the mood of the visit that when Katie chooses to communicate any enthusiasm at all, it is only an enthusiasm for taking a moral stand against zoos in general.

"You do understand that these animals are all prisoners?" she asks. It is not really a question. "Right? And you still gave them our money. You paid to keep these poor animals in prison, Dad. That's against animal rights. You like to pretend they're free, but they're not. We're touring a maximum-security prison for animals, Dad." She points to the guy in khaki at the controls of our little bus. "And he's no ranger. He's just a prison guard. If this was a movie, he'd be called a bull or a screw."

The ranger looks up in his mirror. His eyes find mine, looking for an explanation. I can only shrug.

"Yeah," mumbles Kip, pulling his hat down over his eyes. "Let's go find us a good old fashioned rodeo. They've got clowns."

"Probably why the unicorns are extinct. People kept trying to lock them up. But they die in captivity. They were made to be free."

"I'd like to ride a unicorn," says Kip.

"Don't be an idiot. They'd never let you."

"Who? The prison guards?"

"The unicorns."

"Why not?"

"Because your legs would hold their wings down. They need the wings to fly."

"Oh."

"But they're all dead now." Katie looks across my mother over at my father. "Because of the_zoos."

After a brief caucus, my parents and the Steincamps agree to abandon the zoo for lunch at a place called the Alamoana Shopping Mall. By the time we arrive and pile out of the Steincamps' minivan, the collective mood has upgraded to something more genuinely enthusiastic.

Where we come from, shopping malls are close structural cousins to bowling alleys and casinos. Fluorescence serves as a poor substitute for natural daylight, which, like fresh air, is often in short supply. Visitors tend to wander in purposeless loops around a dirty tile track, looking in windows at people pacing their brightly colored, curiously appointed concrete cells, or slouching behind counters as the weight of hour upon hour of unbroken monotony slowly crushes them, extruding every last drop of human spirit. The malls in Iowa are zoos of a different kind.

But here. Wow. Alamoana, is it? It's all open to the blue Hawaiian sky. There is sunlight and fresh air. Tall palm trees and lava ponds stocked with large golden koi. There's a stage with live drumming and beautiful grass-skirted hula dancers and men twirling fire on sticks. All of it is surrounded by more stores than I have ever seen in one place in my entire life.

Some of the stores are the same ones we have back home. But even they look somehow fresh and exotic. It's like I've never been in a Brookstone before. Amazing what a little daylight and some tan, partly naked customers can do for a place.

We all start off as a single group, waiting for each other to explore this store or that store, before moving on. The other shoppers flow around us like river water around a slowly growing clump of bramble that eventually becomes large enough to dislodge and float a little further downstream before getting snagged on something else.

The floating cohesion eventually weakens. First we lose Howard to the Big & Tall eddy. Then my father slips into the Apple Store undertow. Then Gloria disappears over the falls of Victoria's Secret.

The rest of us keep floating, my mother making sure we all stay together. None of us can go anywhere without the others. She makes Katie and Kip sit on a bench so they can't wander off. She lends Katie her cellphone, counting on "Candy Crush" to do the babysitting as she darts in and out of adjacent stores.

"Don't let them out of your sight, Peter," she says more than once. I think that since my mother is already in trouble for passive-aggressively overdosing the children on chocolate lava, she is mostly looking to avoid any extra blame for encouraging child abduction in a crowded shopping mall.

I suppose it was inevitable that the four of us would eventually come upon a line of children waiting to have a lap-sitting conversation with a fat man in a Santa hat. He sits on a high-posted throne-like chair that is not unlike any of the other garland-strung Santa chairs I have seen in my life, except that this Santa chair sits in front of two crisscrossing surfboards.

Santa is in a pair of green Christmas Bermudas and a "Hang Ten" muscle-tee. The "Hang Ten" slogan arcs above a pair of decorated palm trees. The word Ten has been crossed out and has been edited to read Tinsel.

The bushy white beard and the red hat with its white trim and snowball are strictly in keeping with Christmas tradition. Same with the alcoholic's nose and the morbid obesity.

But the fireman's boots are not so traditional. I suppose those were all that the Alamoana Shopping Mall Christmas people could find on the Island that might pass as snow boots.

Kip makes a beeline for one of the pointy-eared elves directing traffic. The three of us watch them exchange words and then Kip steps into line.

"Oh, brother," says Katie. Mom and I look warily at each other, not quite sure what to expect. "What... a... fool."

"What? Why?" My mother is genuinely baffled.

"Everyone knows that's not the real Santa. Shopping mall Santas are almost never real. Just how stupid do these people think we are? Santa doesn't surf."

"How... How do you know Santa doesn't surf, sweetie?"

I look warily over at my mother. She shrugs.

"Please, Mom. Santa snowboards. He doesn't surf."

"Oh. Right. I guess I didn't think of that."

"Uh, North Pole? Hello?"

"Well, nevertheless, Katie, don't you ruin this for Kip. You just let him believe whatever he wants to believe. Sometimes you just have to let people figure these things out for themselves."

My sister looks up at my mother, considering her words. It's anybody's guess what she's thinking. She turns abruptly and crosses the stream of people, taking a place in line behind Kip. She drapes an arm casually over his shoulder, a gesture suggesting the generous indulgence of a parent. Katie looks back at us. She winks, throwing in a reassuring nod.

My mother looks over at me and I can tell the irony of the moment is not lost. She has somehow managed to both perpetuate my sister's unnatural belief in the myth of Santa Claus and, simultaneously, encourage a little holiday condescension of Kip Steincamp for, of all things, believing in Santa Claus.

In thirty minutes, Kip is back standing with us as we all watch Katie perch herself precariously atop Santa's knee.

"How'd it go?" I ask Kip.

"I haven't believed in Santa for a long time," he says with a laugh. "I did it for the candy canes." He holds up his hand to show three of them hooked over his pudgy little fingers.

"You waited in line for a half hour for free candy canes?"

"Heck yeah. These things are boss! But don't tell Katie. I pretended to believe so it wouldn't spoil things for her."

"Oh..."

"Yeah, she'll figure it out eventually. She's a smart cookie. Smarter than most I've dated. That's for darn sure."

I look down at him, speechless.

"Girls," he adds with humorous resignation in his tone and a little head shake. He scoots his glasses up his nose. "Am I right, my man, or am I right?"

I look up in time to see my sister showing Santa my mother's cellphone. He gives a few hearty ho-ho-ho's and she leans in to whisper in his ear. Someone in line takes a picture. It couldn't be more iconic.

"I think she just asked him for a cellphone," I hear my mother say, a little incredulous. "She's not getting a cellphone."

When she is done, the four of us walk over to the fishpond and have a seat on the lava wall to wait for the others. When Kip is safely on the other side of the pond harassing the fish, I ask Katie what she told Santa. Her face tells me it's the dumbest question she has ever heard.

"That he's a fraud," she says.

"What?"

She closes her eyes and takes a breath. Like she is about to explain something to a five-year-old-old for the sixth time.

"He started asking me what I wanted for Christmas... and so I pulled out mom's phone... and I showed him the Santa-tracker app... which proves that the real Santa is somewhere over Scotland right now and not in some stupid shopping mall in Honolulu and he tried to tell me that he was Island Santa and I said he could just save his breath because there is no Island Santa and that Island Santa is just some stupid fairy tale that people make up in their heads so that they can pretend to believe something that isn't even true because they are probably bored with their lives and too impatient to wait for the real Santa and they will do anything to make another lousy trip to the mall more exciting, like pretending they can actually meet Santa and sit in his lap and tell him what they want for Christmas when the truth is that you can never meet Santa or sit in his lap because he is way too busy to meet people and waste time all day talking in shopping malls and because Santa doesn't need to meet anybody anyway because he already knows all about everyone and whether they have been naughty or nice and then he said that Island Santa just likes to talk to all the children and so I whispered in his ear that so do pedophiles and kidnappers and that if I ever woke up one day and found myself in a shopping mall Santa suit, I'd go get some help from a head doctor so that I could figure out why I was pretending the world was one way when it really isn't that way and why I was pretending to be someone fake and he said that I sure had a lot of opinions for a pretty little girl and so I told him that Island Santa had better fork over a few extra candy canes or I would tell the rest of the kids in line that they were all lying to themselves if they believed that the fat man in the fireman's boots was the real Kris Kringle, even though I probably would never do that because that would really have been kind of mean and because the real Santa would then just move my name over onto the naughty list on Christmas Eve and save himself the trip to our hotel room, which would suck, but I wanted Island Santa to think I would rat him out because I really wanted those extra candy canes so that I would have more than Kip."

Her eyes have been closed the whole time. She opens them slowly to see me staring down at her in some combination of horror and awe.

"You shook down Island Santa," I say.

She fans out her five candy canes, centering the array over her smiling face.

"He's not Santa, but he's also not stupid. Kip asked him for a jet airplane and a wild stallion. Can you believe that kid?"

I look across the pond at Kip, now embroiled in a make-believe shoot-'em-up with half a dozen carp. He disappears beneath the lava wall with every third or fourth sound-effect-enhanced shot from his candy cane pistols only to pop up again shouting die varmint! at the top of his lungs. I want to tell Katie that, all things considered, the idea of Kip asking Island Santa for a jet airplane and a wild stallion was really not so unbelievable, but I can see she is already on to something else.

"Want to know what Island Santa said when I told him I have a brother?"

"What?"

"Jinx, shotgun, lizard."

"Katie..."

287

"Are so, Peter. Are... so."

Howard Steincamp comes down the escalator and scoops up Kip in one arm.

"Where are the others?" he asks my mother. She shrugs. "Stuart's phone must be off."

"Well, hell's bells, let me call Gloria," says Howard, dropping Kip and pulling out his phone. "Let's blast her blankety-blank out of whatever dressing room she's in. Time to get this show on the road so we can hit the beach."

"There they are!" exclaims Kip, one boot propped dramatically upon the lava rock wall and pointing with a sharpened white candy cane. "Ride them cowgirl, Mom!"

Gloria Steincamp is actually riding my father.

Piggyback.

Her naked thighs are pressed against his ears and he has one hand wrapped around each of her knees. He careens recklessly in one direction, then another, threatening to collide with benches and palm trees and clusters of people who abort their conversations and move quickly to either side of the mall.

This man is not my father. It just can't be. This is clearly someone else inhabiting his body.

Gloria is laughing and shrieking uncontrollably, one hand gripping his neck and the other swinging three different shopping bags. As her balance shifts, her hand slips up over part of his face. He bites down on one of her fingers. Gloria yowls.

"Holy..." My mother doesn't finish.

I don't think cow is the word she is looking for.

A Japanese woman, reacting to Gloria's shrieks and probably sensing the rapid approach of something large and ungainly in her peripheral vision, grabs her toddler's arm and yanks so sharply that the poor kid plunges face first into her torso. He starts crying and she kneels, gathering him up in her arms. There is a slowly receding fear on her face as she watches my father and Gloria Steincamp zig and zag, closing the last hundred feet to the fishpond.

And how could anyone blame the poor woman? How is she to know that the shopping mall piggyback attack isn't the newest thing in domestic terrorism? There is always that first time when no one has heard of it before. There was a first shoe bomber. A first underwear bomber. Why not this? Whatever this was.

When they reach the fishpond, my father turns, lowers himself slowly until Gloria is sitting on the wall.

"Told you I'd get you home safely," he says.

"You nearly killed me! You ... you... maniac!"

They both laugh wildly.

Like the word maniac is the funniest word in the English language.

My mother and Dr. Steincamp, whose index finger is still hovering in anticipation above his cellphone waiting for dialing instructions, stare at them in silent disbelief.

And I do too. Not just because the funniest word in the English language is so obviously monkey, and not maniac, but because my father and Gloria Steincamp seem completely lost inside their own world: a world in which there are different rules, or maybe no rules at all, and in which they are free to pretend to be completely different people.

It's like we can see them, but they can't see us.

"What the hell are you two doing?" bellows Howard. The smile is forced. He looks like maybe he is trying to find his way into their world. Like he has been unfairly excluded from one of those remember-the-time-when stories of the kind that he and my father have been trading ever since meeting in the lobby of the Coconut Palms.

But Howard can't break into that world. None of us can.

Gloria and my father look up at us, as if for the first time, taking in their surroundings. They are gasping and wiping tears from their eyes.

"I twisted my stupid ankle," sputters Gloria. "Stuart offered me a ride home... I mean here. It would have been safer to walk," she adds, swatting him on the leg. They both tumble back into hysterics.

Kip has lost interest. He walks along the rim of the fishpond, a ruthless assassin leveling his candy canes with deadly aim.

"See what we got here is an old-fashioned turkey shoot," he informs no one in particular. "Time to die, varmints. Die. Die. Die. Die."

The poor carp are stuck believing they are merely fish in a shopping mall pond. The idea that they might be evil turkeys, or varmints, never actually occurs to them. They don't stand a chance.

***

We spend the rest of the day at the beach. Katie and Kip and I are out there first, splashing around in the ocean. The sun is still bright and hot and there are people everywhere, all disappointingly clothed.

The regularity of the surf leaves me a little awestruck. One wave about every six seconds. It's been doing this, every six seconds, every day and every night, for millions and millions of years. Since before any humans existed. And if people ever stop existing, these waves will still be here. Washing up on this empty shoreline.

It's a humbling thought. All human existence is really just four quick days at the beach. An economy vacation that we do our best to pretend will go on forever.

Every chance she gets, Katie throws fistfuls of wet sand at Kip's head. For all Kip's capacity for self-delusion, and for all the moments in which Katie has dropped her guard and shown some affection for him, Kip seems to have accurately sized up his role with my sister, which is to absorb her dislike for boys. All of them. Along with his father's big bones and bravado, and along with the baby fat he has yet to shed and the sopping straw hat he never takes off, Kip Steincamp must carry the weight of his gender in my sister's eyes.

On the beach, that means Kip must die a dramatic death over and over and over. He is the hapless cowpoke on the rooftop of the saloon, shot through the heart by the sheriff's bullet, clutching at his chest, staggering from one end of the roofline to the other, looking for the best place to plummet to his death.

The fact that Katie is throwing sand rather than shooting bullets, and that Kip is falling into the Pacific Ocean and not head first into a rain barrel, does not seem to bother either of them in the least. They have reached tacit agreement on the rules in their pretend world. She is shooting bullets and he must die. She hates him because he is a varmint boy and he is okay with that. Those are the rules.

Eventually, Dr. Steincamp is out here watching over us from the safety of a beach chair, drinking a beer. He balances the bottle on the shelf of his belly. There is no way he is going to save anybody from drowning. But maybe there is some sense of security in knowing that he has a watch and will be able to accurately declare the time of death.

My parents are back in the room. When we left, my father was saying things like "I just don't understand what the big deal is," and my mother was reminding him that he is no longer twenty-two.

Like she was trying to re-educate an amnesia victim.

The last anyone saw Mrs. Steincamp, she was limping off alone to the Coconut Palms lobby in search of an ankle bandage. To me, the limp seemed much worse after the ride back to the hotel than it had walking across the parking lot at the mall. But if her injury was actually getting worse, no one else seemed particularly concerned.

With Dr. Steincamp sitting guard, I feel relieved of my responsibility to keep Katie and Kip from drowning. I wander off up the beach toward a point on the shoreline that seems less crowded, where the water is a little bluer and the sand is a little whiter.

It is an odd place to be on Christmas Eve. I think of the holiday normalcy unfolding back home. Tree lights are flickering on all over town. Last-minute shoppers are skidding into their driveways, credit cards on fire. The Hansons are setting out the bowls of party snacks and racking up the pool balls and queuing up the brain-hungry Christmas zombies. At our house, a plate of cookies is growing stale atop an apologetic, explanatory note that ends with the address of the Coconut Palms.

There is no sign of Christmas on the beach. It could be any day of the year. Easter. Halloween. Presidents' Day. There's no way to tell. And yet no one really seems to mind. Whether they are swimming or jogging or playing Frisbee or just sunning themselves, the people here are all having the time of their lives.

I cannot help but wonder whether they have all convinced themselves that tomorrow is not actually Christmas or if they have convinced themselves that this is what Christmas Eve is actually supposed to look like and feel like. Either way, there is a kind of mass delusion at work on the beach, a secret understanding among vacationers that is not much more ridiculous than the pretend shoot-'em-up carnage raging between Kip and Katie a hundred yards behind me.

I round the point of sand jutting out into the ocean. The beach is much less populated here. A few joggers pass me from both directions but there is only one person who has spread out a beach towel. She is a light-brown woman with silky black hair, in a bright white bikini. She sits on her pink towel, looking up and down the beach as she rubs lotion on her legs.

She sees me seeing her. She nods and I look away guiltily, walking faster.

But I hold her image in my head where I can examine it in private. It is inside that privacy that I finally recognize her.

Lolana.

Lolana. Lolana. Lolana. Lolana. Lolana.

Her name comes to me with every step forward. It is not my voice that speaks her name. And it is not her voice. It is Cody Simms' voice, nearly screaming in excitement.

Dude? Lo-lan-a! It's a freaking Christmas miracle!

At the end of the beach, I sit in the sand and stare out at the waves. I look back at Lolana every few minutes just to make sure she is still there. I play my only memory of her on an endless loop inside my head. I can feel the smooth skin of her arms on either side of my face as she lowers the lei down over my shoulders. I can smell her all over again. I can hear my name on her lips. I reach the only conclusions that are reasonable under the circumstances. They come to me one at a time, about every six seconds.

She secretly wants me.

She has been thinking about me ever since that first day.

She is watching me and thinking about me right now.

She wants to kiss me right here on this beach.

She wants to take her top off.

She wants me to take her top off.

I don't really believe these things. I'm not an idiot.

Except that I do believe these things. I actually do. Because my intelligence has absolutely nothing to do with it.

I am seized by the sudden concern that Katie, Kip and Howard Steincamp have already set off down the beach to find me. Whatever I am about to do, if I am going to do anything, I am rapidly running out of time to do it.

I stand, brush the sand off my blinding-white legs, and chart a direct path across the beach to the large pink rectangle that holds my erotic destiny. My entire body is tingling.

And not evenly.

Lolana is on her back when I stop abruptly at the edge of her towel. She raises herself, propping her weight on one elbow, shading her eyes. Her hair sweeps off her shoulders like a curtain of black silk. She cocks her head. Waiting.

I may have forgotten my own name and how to speak. I have to grasp for the most basic elements of who I am. I think of my mother back at our hotel room, trying to re-educate my father on his true age and identity.

"Would you happen to know what time it is?" I ask eventually. I have enough presence of mind to put one hand on my hip and to give her a crooked smile that is open enough to show a few of my teeth.

Lolana smiles a little. She rolls over to grab her little pink beach bag. It matches her towel perfectly. And her toenails. The bottom of her feet arch and wrinkle. They're the color of the sand. Rummaging for a second, she extracts a cellphone and looks at the screen.

"Almost 4:30," she says. And then, "You're Peter, aren't you?"

I nod, feeling a full-body blush light me up like a solar flare.

"Thought so," she says. "I have a good memory for handsome faces. Are you having a good Christmas, Peter?"

I nod again, swallowing. Handsome? The word ricochets around my head. Yes. Of course, I think. Handsome.

"Yes." Desperate for more words, I keep talking. "It's the best Christmas I've ever had. I want to come here every year."

"Christmas in Hawaii is always special."

"You're so lucky to live here! How long have you lived in Hawaii?"

"I was born here," she says.

"Born? Wow!" Like she has told me she emerged from an ostrich egg. "I can't even imagine being born, like," I spread my arms at the surrounding tropical grandeur, here.

She smiles, lifting her beautiful dark eyebrows. Her teeth are perfect. "Well, not right here on the beach, Peter."

I laugh much too hard, more at the sound of her voice uttering my name than at the idea of baby Lolana being delivered on a beach towel. I can't stop myself. Laughter is the only sound I know how to make. It is the only feeling in my fifteen-year-old heart.

"Well, it was nice to see you again, Peter," she says, lying back down on her towel. "Enjoy the rest of your vacation."

My laughter trails off over a cliff and down into the dark, dank realization that I have been dismissed. We are done. That is all there is to be. Reality has reasserted itself with a vengeance. I can feel everything inside me constrict like a python around a balloon.

"Okay," I say, turning. "Well... Merry Christmas, Lolana."

It is the first time I have spoken her name out loud. The sound of it is like some colorfully exotic bird spreading its wings out over the waves.

"Peter?"

I stop and turn. She is sitting up again. I am unable to do anything but stare.

"Will you do me a favor?"

"Sure," I whisper. There is no way she can hear me. Somehow she does anyway. She holds out her phone.

"Will you take a picture of us? So I can recognize you next year? If you give me your email address, I can send it to you."

When I return to the part of the beach that my family has claimed as its own, my parents and Gloria Steincamp have joined Howard. They all sit in beach chairs, drinking out of green bottles and watching the water. The Hawaiian sun is setting in the reflection of their glasses. No one is smiling. No one is speaking.

Closer to the waterline, Katie is busy burying Kip alive in a shallow grave.

"Don't help him, Peter," she warns. "He's got it coming."

"Save yourself, my man," says Kip, spitting sand. "She's a femme fatale. She's a deadly dame."

Katie kicks the mound of sand about where Kip's ribs should be.

"Better shut your hole, Kip, or I'm going to fill it with ocean dirt."

"Hurt me, baby," says Kip. "Hurt me good."

I sit in the sand and let the ocean wash over my feet. A wave every six seconds. Always the same. Always the same. Always the same. For an eternity of lifetimes. And here I am, a slightly different person than I was only an hour ago.

***

I listen to Katie sleeping across the room. It is one-thirty in the morning and I am no closer to sleeping now than I was at one-thirty in the afternoon when Kip and his candy canes were protecting the free world from gangs of shopping mall carp.

It is no mystery that I am still awake. Lolana has almost completely taken over my senses. I feel weightless. There is a strange brightness inside of me. It wants to lift me off the bed and float me around the room. I replay our five minutes on the beach over and over again, spooling it out into infinity.

My parents are out in the living room, arguing in whispers as they wrap presents. My father thinks my mother is over-reacting. My mother thinks my father is not being honest about his motivations. She thinks the whole reason he wanted to come to Hawaii in the first place was so that he could spend some time with Gloria Steincamp, proving to her that he was the one that got away.

"You think you can just pretend like we're all still in college? Like you're not married with two kids? Did you enjoy your little fantasy?"

"I'm pretending? I'm pretending? Why are you pretending that I screwed Gloria in a shopping mall?"

"She rode you like a pony, Stuart. A sex pony."

"What the hell is a sex pony? We were just joking around."

"Oh, who are you kidding? Her thighs were over your ears, Stuart. Hand me the tape."

Katie rolls over. I wonder if she is dreaming. I wonder how much energy it takes for her to still believe in Santa Claus at twelve-years-old. It is willful self-deception, plain and simple.

And yet, how different is that self-deception than her belief that she doesn't like boys? Or that she doesn't like Kip Steincamp in particular? Or that the words jinx and shotgun have special powers? How different is it than believing that a bird with a broken neck somehow just got better and flew away?

For that matter, how different is it than my father thinking he can time travel back to his college years? Or than Kip thinking his candy canes fire real bullets? Or than my mother thinking that sugar interacts with the human body differently on vacation and that Katie could eat two chocolate volcanoes without actually becoming a chocolate volcano? How different is Katie's self-delusion than my hope of finding an island of naked women, or of making out with Lolana on the beach, or that a crooked smile would suddenly make me a man or that I might lose my virginity to the flight attendant on top of the beverage cart? How different was it than any of us believing that the Coconut Palms Resort was actually a hamlet of jungle bungalows?

We all believe what we want to believe. It's that simple. We will pay good money for it. We will stake our dignity on it. We will believe until, like the Tooth Fairy and unicorns, those beliefs suffer a kind of extinction. Until they are crushed beneath the boot of a different, less tolerant reality.

In a few hours, Katie and I will pad out into the living room and see a stack of presents with our names on them, some of which will bear Santa's signature. I will know better, of course. But Katie will choose to believe that a fat man in a red snowsuit with cookie crumbs in his beard somehow navigated a team of reindeer along the narrow path to our jungle hideaway. It will not bother her that we don't have a chimney and that Santa doesn't have a room key. Santa will have paid her a visit.

The real Santa, she will insist, pointing at us each in turn. Not the fake Island Santa hanging out at shopping

299

malls. She will repeat for the umpteenth time that she doesn't care whether Kip believes in Island Santa or not; somebody should lock that fraud up and throw away the key.

And she will say all this – defending the real Kris Kringle; she will insist on it – knowing somewhere inside of her little blond head that Santa Claus does not actually exist at all. Knowing that Island Santa is not a fraud but just a regular guy doing the best he can under the circumstances, selflessly assisting parents to delude local children. Knowing that he probably has kids of his own.

It occurs to me that my sister belongs on a spectrum of charismatic young girls somewhere between Scout Finch and Abigail Williams, one choosing to believe in the goodness of Boo Radley when no one else in Maycomb, Alabama did, and the other with enough ginned-up conviction to convince the good people of Salem, Massachusetts that their friends and neighbors were actually witches who should be put to death before sun-up.

Soon enough my sister's Santa Claus will go the way of the Tooth Fairy and unicorns. Katie will change her opinion about boys. She will embrace the hunky vampire phase that every girl passes through on the path to womanhood. We will all look back fondly on the Santa years.

Until then, all we can do is stay out of her way and let her believe what she wants to believe. We will let her figure it out on her own. We don't really have much choice.

I pull the covers over my head so that I can block out the angry whispers and look at the photos that Lolana took of us together on the beach. Her arms encircle my shoulders, fingers clasped, hair like inky seaweed, her bare skin against mine. My right arm disappears out of the frame so that I can take the picture.

There are five photos like this. I like the ones with the ocean in the background the best. I can hear the waves breaking in my head, one every six seconds out into infinity.

I've almost emailed the pictures to Cody Simms about a dozen times. I think of the stories I will tell him. I think of the look on his face.

I almost send them. Almost.

But then I can't bring myself to do it. I know that as soon as I send the photos, the clock will start ticking down on the truth behind the image glowing out at me from my phone. Cody will bring reality to my doorstep with a lot of inconvenient questions and disbelieving looks.

He will want to rein me in. Pull me back. Tell me how things really are. Looking to pop that bubble.

I brush Lolana's little electronic face with my finger. I can smell her floral presence like she is lying next to me. Whatever is inside those wrapped boxes in the living room, and however they got there, I know that I met my Island Santa on the shores of a jungle island in the middle of the Pacific.

And I wonder what our children will look like.

RANDOM MAN

Ten bubbles, full of lead.

Twice a week makes one-thousand-forty bubbles a year.

She fills each of them slowly, perfectly, at the same gas station, a block from the bus stop. Every Monday. Every Friday. Something about the continuity is reassuring.

The kiosk in the back of the Gas-n-Go is often out of the stubby red pencils. She always brings her own. She does not like leaving things to chance.

The grizzled, potbellied, potato-faced man is behind the counter where he belongs. He gives her his usual sideways smile. She has never known his name. Most of the people we know are nameless.

He receives the ticket from the machine, using two hands, like it's extruding a wide, thin strip of pasta. He puts it on the counter and slides it across with a dirty finger. Like always. He shakes his head in amusement.

"Same numbers," he says. He's phlegmy from smoking. "Every time with the same numbers. Good luck, kid. Maybe this is the one, yeah?"

Zoe smiles a little and shrugs. She folds the paper slip in the same old way and puts it in her right, front pants pocket where it belongs. The sun is low and red. No more bouncing off the pavement. It just comes right on in through the windows and paints everything with its dying syrup. Potbelly potato-face is garrulous today.

"I mean, look," he says, "odds are one day these numbers are going to match. Yeah? Has to happen eventually. Has to."

It's the same motley assortment at the bus stop. Nothing in common except the scoliotic posture of cellphone addiction; standing, heads bowed, as the light drains out of the Los Angeles basin and the darker, heavier dusk rises up over the tops of their shoes and then past their ankles. The bus will arrive when the rooftop shadow line is between the knee and the hip. Never fails.

She gets a window seat today, which almost never happens. She takes it as an auspicious sign. Seems fitting that she'd get a window on the day she picks winning lottery numbers. Seems fitting that when a day breaks your way, the whole thing breaks your way, right down to the seat on the bus.

She fishes the headphones out of her backpack. Ayaan Patel, PhD, will carry her the rest of the way home, trying his best to convince her that all experience is the product of choice, however unconscious. Happenstance is a disguise. Happiness is Erwin Schrödinger's cat, waiting in a dark box. Same with despair. Same with fortune and destitution and loneliness and love and life and death.

Hell of a pet, this cat. Always in a dark box.

Dr. Patel is Bangladeshi. His words are light, rubbery sounds. They bounce off the oncoming traffic like small rubber balls. Even when he talks about death.

Especially when he talks about death.

She did some research. Dr. Patel's first name, Ayaan, means good luck.

Her apartment has been holding its breath for thirteen hours. She drops her shoulder, sliding her pack down her arm into the chair, and then makes the rounds, opening all three windows. The traffic below pushes in new air.

These first few moments home, wading through the same medium of stillness, always provoke momentary longings for a cat. Just for some continuity of purpose. Someone to wait patiently for her to arrive and to fill a need. Food. Milk. Affection. Someone whose anticipation has a name: Zoe.

Someone to stir the air while she is gone.

But the air is unstirred. She wants to ask Dr. Patel what it means when Erwin Schrödinger opens the box and it's empty.

Not that she seriously considers it. She does not want another pet.

When she was nine, her parents crumbled under relentless pressure from her twin sister, Moira, whose very life at that age seemed to hang on whether she, like two of her best friends, owned a cat. They had all gone to the San Luis Obispo Animal Shelter together. Lucky, a black tom with two white paws and a notch in his ear, was waiting at calm attention in his cage. Like he knew they were coming.

They called him Lucky. He lasted exactly one year and one month in the Alexakis family. He was affectionate but restless, always eying the exits. The third time he got loose, Moira had chased him out into the street. And that was that.

Lucky, presumably, had lived up to his name for years to come.

But that was sure the end of Moira.

Zoe's young subconscious had tried to insulate her, warping her dreams to experience the loss. Experience it not just as a twin but as Gloria, the woman driving the black Volvo. To poor Gloria, mother of three, Moira had been more than a strange, loose child. Moira was a rogue double-agent, loyal to a cruel master of randomness. Moira, to Gloria, had been on an inexplicable mission to occupy a precise square-foot of pavement, at a specific, whisper-thin moment in time, subsumed within an infinite stream of centuries. Had Gloria spent just three more seconds at the grocery store. Or three fewer seconds at the dry cleaners.

Zoe's father had been big on names in a proud, Greek heritage sort of way. So Zoe had always known that the name Moira meant fate in the old language. What she had never stopped to consider, until Lucky anyway, was whose fate?

After the windows come the lights. Five of them. Three are wholly dissimilar torchiere floor lamps from St. Vincent de Paul's. They are fit with high-wattage fluorescents that spray light off the ceiling like a radioactive sea foam. The fourth light, incandescent, is in its dingy-white metal box. It glows yellow, barely strong enough to push past the top-shelf orange juice down to the nether stories of softening apples and the feta and the last of the olives. Its twin is next door, ebbing dully into frozen space like a distant, dying sun.

She is now fully addicted to frozen macaroni and cheese. It no longer has to pair appropriately with something else she is eating. Spaghetti. Scrambled eggs. Pizza. The main course is irrelevant as long as the mac-n-cheese is on the plate. She suspects this need has less to do with the taste itself than biochemical expectation and the heartbeat rhythm of habit.

She is just as drawn to pattern and recurrence as the rest of her species. The more we do something, the more we need to do it again. Behavioral patterns form the infrastructure of our cocoons, locking in comfort. Repetition brings a dummied-up predictability to an existence that otherwise defies prediction. Some people have to watch the six o'clock news. Others have to metabolize durum wheat semolina coated in processed cheese spread and Yellow Dye No. 5. Zoe is one of those.

Not that she likes herself much for it. All addictions are inherently demoralizing for the disempowerment they bring. We do a thing. And then we do it again. And again. Patterns harden into a pulsing molecular structure. Like a crystal of kryptonite. Or a rock of cocaine. Expectation, born of repetition, is the crack cocaine of experience. There's no shaking it.

She likes to think she is in control of herself. She isn't. None of us are. And that fact is gnawing away at the concept of free will like a rat in a cellar, chewing on the wires.

Inattention and a flimsy sheet of tinfoil have long since conspired to kill her microwave, which is now a square, dimly lit coffin for stale bread products. So she has to use the oven. To thaw and cook an orange brick of macaroni and cheese, the oven will take roughly forever. The microwave's dying legacy was to permanently redefine forever to mean anything longer than four minutes.

She turns on the oven and tosses the frozen brick into a pan on the counter to wait for the sound of 350 degrees: a long, piercingly loud clarion beep that will falsely signal something penultimate. Arrival. Completion. Redemption. Something more than the start of another period of waiting.

But she will wait. She will endure the length of forever. She has no choice.

The telephone is less patient.

"Hello?"

"Hello, Zoe. Zoe Alexakis. Is that Greek? That sounds Greek to me."

"Dexter. Is that even your real name?"

"No."

"I told you to stop calling me."

"I know. You tell me that every time. And then we talk. How was work today? Tell me about the new job."

"You're a criminal. I'm hanging up."

"Yes and no."

"What do you mean?"

"Yes, I'm a criminal and no, you're not hanging up."

"Oh?"

"Never have before."

"Well, today's a new day, Dexter."

"Is it? Good. So then the new job must be... what? Exciting? Fulfilling? Challenging?"

"Yes. It's all those things. Goodbye."

"Zoe?"

"What."

"I think that's excellent."

"What's excellent, Dexter?"

"That you're getting such instant satisfaction from script wrangling."

"Yeah, well that's not what I do, so…"

"I guess I still don't really understand the new job."

"No. You don't. And do you know why? Dexter? You know why you don't understand? I'll tell you. Because the only things you understand about me? The only things? Came from my luggage. Which you stole off the hotel sidewalk."

"Well. Zoe. Two points. First, I didn't know the bag was yours. It looked abandoned. Who leaves a bag sitting on a Las Vegas sidewalk?"

"It did not look abandoned. I was talking to the bus driver. That was my bag. Mine. Waiting to be loaded with all the others. It was not abandoned."

"Well, now I know. And second, the only reason I know anything about the new job is because you told me."

"Because you pried it out of me."

"I just asked you. It was hardly prying."

"You said you'd mail me my things back if I told you."

"Zoe. Come on. You didn't really believe that. You never believed that."

"Doesn't make it right."

"No. You're right. It doesn't."

"You're a criminal."

"Yes. Yes I am."

"Your area code is Georgia. Are you really in Georgia?"

"No. I'm calling over the internet. I could be anywhere. All of us criminals do it this way now."

"Great. There were at least eight other bags on that sidewalk. Why mine?"

"Like I said. I didn't know it was yours. I just picked one."

"Like, just, totally at random."

"Well. Anonymous, maybe. Wouldn't call it random. I don't really believe in random crime."

"How can you not believe in the existence of random crime, I mean you... you... you..."

"Maybe it exists. I'm not saying random crime doesn't ever happen. But I spent most of my career in the subprime mortgage loan business. I like to think that victim and perpetrator find each other."

"How romantic. And so you think we found each other."

"Yeah. Why not?"

"Because you don't know me and I don't know you."

"And yet, here we are. I meet all kinds of people this way."

"You steal luggage and then just call the person up and... and... strike up a conversation? This is how you meet people?"

"Hey, I don't have a glitzy Hollywood job like yours."

"I don't have a glitzy Hollywood job."

"Yes you do. It's not easy for regular folk to meet interesting people."

"That's really pathetic. You must be lonely, Dexter."

"We're all lonely, Zoe. Even you, I suspect."

"I'm not lonely."

"Oh, yes you are. Who takes a five-hour bus ride to Vegas by herself?"

"I needed a change of scenery."

"Something new."

"Yes."

"I get that. But you do it every year. Same time. Same hotel. The same casinos. Such meticulous notes you keep. Your penmanship is incredible."

"I like to track my expenses."

"And your winnings. You do like those games of chance. Playing the odds."

"Yeah, so?"

"I did the math. Over the past five years, you are sixty-seven percent shy of breaking even. Give or take."

"That's not the point."

"Right. Change of scenery. You need a man."

"What? No I don't."

"A woman then. Someone."

"I'm hanging up."

"Look, I believe you. I do. Your love life or lack thereof is none of my business. That's not why I called."

"Yes, exactly why did you call, Dexter?"

"Like I said, I'm dying to find out how the first day went."

"My first day was two days ago. But that, too, is none of your business. I'm hanging up."

"What's it like being a constancy girl?"

"I'm not a constancy girl."

"You said you were."

"No. You weren't listening. I said I was a continuity girl."

"Oh, right. That's like the weirdest job title I have ever..."

"They don't call it that anymore. That's a term from the thirties. That's not, like, the official job title."

"What's the official..."

"Script supervisor."

"Script..."

"Script. Supervisor."

"You're a supervisor. Wow."

"No, Dexter. I'm an intern. I work for a script supervisor so I can learn the job."

"Oh. Your boss is the script supervisor."

"Right."

"But they like to call you the continuity girl, don't they?"

"... Maybe."

"They do. Secretly they like the way it used to be. They like the old title. More personality. continuity girl. More color than just a script supervisor."

"Really? What color is sexism, Dexter."

"Sexism. It's retro chic. It's got moxie."

"I guess."

"It does. And your boss is a guy with great hair named Rick who sometimes likes to wear a fedora with his tailored pinstripe and who lights up a Lucky Strike at the end of every day just when you're headed home and you say Goodnight and he winks and says Sweet dreams, continuity girl and you want to roll your eyes out of some compulsive feminist bullshit but secretly... secretly you want him to take you someplace quiet to share a splash of bourbon on the rocks, someplace where he stops calling you continuity girl and starts calling you Doll. I'm right, aren't I, Zoe? I know I am."

"My boss is a woman twice my age named Charlene."

"Oh. Well. Can't win them all."

"Or any."

"So you're, like, in charge of proofing the dialogue."

"No. You're completely wrong. Again."

"That's what you said before."

"No. It isn't."

"Mmmm... I don't know. I think you said..."

"Dexter, listen. Are you listening?"

"I'm listening, Zoe. Speak to me. I'm here to listen."

"You have no idea what you're talking about. Okay? First, I'm not in charge of anything. I'm an intern. Got that? Second, my job is not proofing the dialogue. My job is to help the script supervisor, Charlene, whose job is to track the production against the script to make sure that there's, you know, like a continuity of detail from one scene to the next. Got it?"

"Uh... no. Still don't understand. Give me an example."

"Really? You don't..."

"Sorry. I don't get it."

"Okay. Well this is clearly why you steal luggage for a living. Say you're making a movie about a superhero. And the script says that a knife tears open his shirt and cuts his left shoulder. In every scene after that his shirt has to have that same cut, in the exact..."

"Doesn't he have a suit?"

"What?"

"A super suit. If some guy with a knife can just walk up and..."

"Not the point. The point is..."

"Are you actually working on a superhero movie?"

"..."

"Zoe? You are, aren't you? You're working on a superhero movie."

"Yes. As a matter of fact."

"Oh, now that's awesome. What's his name? Her? Is it a man or a woman?"

"I'm not telling you anything. Nothing. This is where I hang up. Bye."

"What's the superpower? You can tell me the superpower."

"No."

"Oh, come on. Who am I going to tell?"

"Depends on whose luggage you end up stealing, Dexter. Or whatever your name is."

"Well, does a continuity girl have any responsibility for making the script believable? Because, you know, a vulnerability to sharp things is really going to make for a tragic superhero. This movie is going to be a downer. And short."

"He's not vulnerable to sharp things. Well, no more than the rest of us."

"Okay, which means he is vulnerable to sharp things. But he's a superhero. He needs to be relatively invulnerable to ordinary hazards. That's the whole point of a... what the hell is that? Is that a fire alarm, or..."

"That's just my stupid oven. Hold on a sec."

A foamy tide of humanity pushes up against the three, low-budget food service tables. They align against a back wall of the studio like a shelf of white limestone attacked by the sea.

Zoe is not hungry. But Charlene is hungry and that's what matters. They wait for an opening between shoulders. A fat man in a headset pushes his way past, between where they are standing and the crowded tables. He nods at Zoe and then at Charlene with an appraising smile.

"Morning, Charley," he says. "Fighting for scraps? Got to get aggressive, ladies. Swing those elbows. Bloody some noses. You'll starve."

He passes in a heavy, rolling motion. As if his forward momentum has been hard-won and it is now difficult to stop. Charley watches him go. Her expression implies some clarity on precisely the nose she would like to bloody.

"Early bird, kiddo," says Charley, refocusing her attention on the table. "You need to be here an hour earlier. Never go by the schedule."

Zoe's mouth is a secret box. Inside is either an apology or a defense, she does not know which. She parts her lips to speak. But Charley is suddenly moving away, lunging toward the tables, jackknifing her sharp, angular body into a rapidly collapsing hole. She emerges seconds later holding two large yellow bananas and a plastic cup of yogurt. She hands Zoe one of the bananas as she passes.

"Let's go, champ."

She is a fast walker, Charley. Hers is a stride proving that certainty of direction conveys certainty of purpose. Garnering respect. Encouraging deference. Make a hole, it says to people in the way. And they do.

Zoe drafts behind in a cloud of Chanel, finding the rhythm of Charley's authoritative heels. They knock against the concrete floor of the studio, only occasionally emerging from beneath a swishy flair of suit pant leg made of gray pinstripe silk. Above the waist, she wears a tailored white blouse, billowing at the cuffs, beneath a half-open, black and gray silk vest. She has long, chestnut hair rolled up into a loose bun and held in place with a brightly painted, ornamental chopstick. Rogue tendrils escape here and there, bouncing in the air behind Charley's neck, suggesting that the chopstick is but a pin in a grenade of follicular chaos.

Charley swings her arms as she walks. In the hand that does not hold a banana and a yogurt, she clutches a cellphone and an unopened pack of cigarillos.

The back parking lot is a lake of early sunlight, calm and yellow, lapping at the tires. Against the building is a collection of director's chairs for people without names.

Charley sits and drapes one leg over the knee of the other. Peels her banana. Pulls back the lid of her yogurt. Dips the one into the other and chews. She is mid-fifties with a face of genetic windfall. The almond eyes, the high cheekbones, the skin without fault, the symmetry, the full lips and white teeth. Features willfully ignorant of time.

Zoe thinks of her annual excursion, taking refuge from reality in clock-less casinos. Charlene Landry has always had a winning hand.

Zoe sits in the next chair and crosses her legs in a way that feels too imitative. She cannot help but compare her denim to Charley's silk, her bobbing tennis shoe to Charley's pointed pump. She uncrosses her legs.

A bald, bearded man in a red golf cart speeds past. He raises a black plastic Kalashnikov in mock rebellion and beeps. Charley looks. Then she finishes chewing.

"Gary in Props," she says. "Good enough guy if you don't mind survivalists."

"He's a survivalist?"

Charley nods. "Turns out I'm approved on Gary's underground bunker list. I never asked, but," she shrugs, "you know, if the nukes start flying or the Glendale latte zombies rise up, I guess I'll have a place to go. But I think that makes me Gary's apocalypse girlfriend."

Zoe laughs at this, less at the prospect of the Glendale undead than the idea that someone like Charley would ever be caught dating Gary the prop guy. Even underground in a concrete box.

"What about you?" asks Charley. "Got yourself a good date for the apocalypse?"

"Not at the moment," says Zoe, by which she means not since the wife of her philosophy professor had inherited the family fortune. Marriage, he had decided one fall afternoon between three-thirty and four, was not an abyss after all. Marriage was a lamp in the darkness.

"Plenty of time," says Charley with exaggerated unconcern. "Apocalypse is still weeks off. Live a little. Be single. No company like your own company, is what I always say."

"I guess," says Zoe, doubting that Charley is speaking from much experience with solitude. She thinks about the cat that is not in her apartment waiting for her, not stirring the stale air in anticipation of her return. She thinks of the man who stole her luggage. Dexter, he calls himself. She wonders if he will be phoning to find out about her day. She wonders what Dexter is doing for the apocalypse.

"So tell me," says Charley, "day four in the movie business. Is it everything you thought it'd be?"

"Not sure what I thought it would be," says Zoe. "Guess I didn't expect so much sitting around doing nothing."

A door in the wall behind them opens. A bearded face emerges, craning in all directions, then disappears again. Charley nods.

"Moviemaking business is like war, kid. Eighty percent waiting, twenty percent shooting. What's your take on the script?"

"Also not what I expected. It's kind of... I mean..." Zoe peels her own banana. "He's got superpowers, but he's not in control of them."

"That's the whole hook. The lab experiment gave him superhuman powers, but it also scrambled all his DNA switches. Different triggers for different traits. That'll teach a guy to monkey with a molecular randomizer."

Charley arches her perfect eyebrows for emphasis. Zoe nods as if to take note of lifesaving advice. Charley points her banana.

"Should've called him *Firefly*, winking on and off like that. *Random Man* is too prosaic. But that's the thing about this biz, kid. They couldn't give two figs for your creative input, no matter what they tell you. It's their product. Their world. Your job is to make sure that their world is internally consistent. You're not an agent of change. You're an agent of history. You're the guardian of cause and effect. The thing that comes next has to grow out of the thing that just happened. You have to keep reminding them of their own origins. Their own rules."

Charley finishes the yogurt and the banana, draping its empty yellow suit over the arm of the chair. She opens the pack of cigarillos and extracts one with her teeth. She holds the pack out to Zoe, who shakes her head and chews contemplatively. Charley blows out a sweet, fecund plume as she checks her phone.

"They're in there trying to get the top of the building to look right. Moonlight on a rainy night is what they're going for. But the problem isn't the lighting. It's the acting. That kid can't sell this role, plain and simple. Too short. Wrong face. I warned Danny and the boys from the beginning. But they don't want my two cents. Not on that they don't. Only reason Paul has the job is that his uncle is on the Board."

Zoe looks. "Really?"

"His audition was in the bag the day his father knocked up his mother. Nepotism deals a helluva hand, kid. Paul Rotella was born to be Random Man. But, hey, this is not a merit-based business. Never has been."

"What about you?" Zoe asks. "You seem to know what you're doing."

"I do," says Charley. "I'm the greatest script supervisor that ever lived. You think that's why Danny-Q chose me over everyone else? Don't you bet on it. He chose me because he's a sucker for nice gams. And that weakness for a shapely calf makes Danny Quirk a lucky man."

"It does?"

"Yeah. Had Danny been one of those directors looking for well-rounded resumes rather than well-turned ankles, he'd have gotten second-best. He landed me instead. Merit? I don't think so. I'd call that plain lucky. Like you."

The tone is unsettling; Zoe swallows the last of the banana.

"Me?"

Another stream of pungent South American smoke. Charley closes her lips into an apologetic smile.

"Think I picked you on merit? Because of all the continuity girl candidates, you were the best?"

Zoe shrugs. "No?"

Charley shakes her head.

"I narrowed the field to five and then started flipping coins. You kept coming up heads. So far you're just lucky. We'll see if you're good."

Charley takes another drag and exhales without looking away. Zoe nods simply, as though selecting interns by coin flip is not in the least bit surprising. As though airborne quarters have always determined everything for her. She looks down at her lap to find that her fingers have been busy separating her empty banana peel into thirds and rolling each third into its own rubbery yellow wheel.

"I'm not saying you had nothing do with it," Charley says. "You had the good sense to enroll in the Victor Massey Film Academy. That old man's got an eye for talent. Vic sends me a name; then I'm ready to roll the dice. Wouldn't have considered you otherwise. Besides," she winks one beautiful eye, knocking Zoe's leg with the point of her shoe, "you've got a good vibe about you, continuity girl. No one else turned up ten heads in a row."

It is, for Zoe and Charley and everyone else, a long afternoon of mis-starts and failed attempts. For that is the plight of Random Man. He does not know from one moment to the next whether he can fly, or bend metal, or deflect bullets, or incinerate objects with a concentrated beam of laser-vision. His is an adrenaline-soaked life of trial and error, fighting crime in a world that makes no promises, as the roulette wheel of his molecular identity spins in one direction and the little white ball of circumstance rolls in the other.

Flying, for instance, is a particular hazard. Random Man cannot, fingers crossed, simply leap from a rooftop. He does not know in that moment whether he can fly or not. He must first throw himself onto the rooftop, arms forward to protect his face. Just like any of us. The effort to launch himself skyward from a crowded street corner is thus either heroic or bizarrely humiliating. If he had a super suit, he would never dare to put it on. The public spectacle of trial and error is bad enough without the cape and mask. And even when he actually can fly, he must take care to keep his speed down and stay very low to the ground, for it is not a superpower that he can count on lasting for any particular period of time. Maybe for days. Maybe just a few minutes.

Unreliable impenetrability poses its own unique risks. Random Man cannot shoot himself in the leg to test whether he can deflect bullets, just as he cannot rush headlong into a spray of gunfire hoping for the best. Survival has required adaptation. So he is never without his signature titanium ring, emblazoned with a bold *RM* and from which unfolds a thick conical spike. Whenever the situation demands, he can test his own momentary constitution by ramming the spike into the flesh of his left shoulder. He is either impenetrable, or he is not.

The vagaries of super speed and super strength are usually less dire, but just as frustrating. He may or may not be able to catch that speeding bus and, even if he can, he may or may not be able to lift it off the road, or even force open the folding doors. At worst, an effort to bend gun barrels with the ease of balloon animals is less life-threatening than it is a perplexing waste of valuable time.

When it works – when all these genetic cards flip over to show a full house – then Random Man is a hero to behold. He is the man America needs. And when it doesn't work – when the dealer looks mild-mannered Randall Moss in the eyes and shakes his head – then evil lives to fight another day.

Building a story around a capricious superhumanity, a story that perpetually straddles life-and-death suspense with a comedic flourish, is no small trick. Credibly rendering that story through a motion picture only adds another layer of complexity. Nail-biting suspense fights gut-busting humor in every scene. Success is when they fight to a draw. Whenever that fight ends in the death of one or the other, then the scene is a failure and must be reworked from the script up. There is never any shortage of opinions about what went wrong.

Zoe watches Charley work, tagging along behind to listen to argument after argument in which the stylish script supervisor lobbies the temperamental director for ordinary continuity in a film premised on superhuman randomness and predictable discontinuity. Every so often, Charley punctuates her pitch with an Isn't that right, Zoe? or, worse, Let's ask our continuity girl; she'll tell you.

But Zoe is not yet in a position to tell anybody anything. She nods and repeats after Charley. It suffices for the time being but heightens a latent anxiety over the future. On some random day, she will be forced to hold her own against the irascible, leg-appreciating Director Danny

321

Quirk. She will have to demonstrate her grasp of events and defend life's logical order.

Multiple rigging failures push the shoot later than expected into the afternoon. Twice, Random Man is stuck swinging helplessly from a crane between glistening plastic buildings. Charley takes her leave for a prescheduled poker game with a pat on the back and the discomfiting instruction that Zoe "make sure the bastard doesn't cut any continuity corners."

Zoe's expression must not inspire confidence. Charley, smelling exotically masculine, bends herself closer so that her eyes and her lips and her timeless skin are all part of the same opening carnivorous flower. She braces Zoe's shoulder.

"Agent of history. Guardian of cause and effect. Don't let me down, kid."

Zoe watches her go, then sits uncomfortably in the chair named for Charlene Landry. The crew is finally lowering poor Paul Rotella back to earth in jerky fits and starts.

She keeps a watchful eye on Danny Quirk, looking for any warning that he might be plotting to cheat the universal laws of consistency. Absent fiendishly rubbing his hands together, Zoe has no idea what such a warning might look like. She is left to hope that Danny-Q has filmed his last take of the day and returns to observing the lead actor's humbling rescue.

He is lowered, at last, to the floor of the set beneath a pile of rigging. Four crew members descend upon him from the shadows, wrestling with the faulty harness. It resembles a scene from an urban safari, the men finally having darted and netted an endangered denizen for relocation, a job made much easier by Paul's fatigue than had they attempted his capture first thing in the morning, fully caffeinated.

Freedom from constraint opens into another sea of mindless waiting. Zoe passes the time in the company of her cellphone as the bouncing, rubbery voice of Ayaan Patel, PhD, tries to demystify coincidence. "You," Ayaan Patel says, "choose your fate. Reality," he reminds, "pulls from a leash of intention."

She is too distracted at first to perceive the murmuring presence behind her. But then, twisting around suddenly, she does. Random Man.

He is in the middle of saying how she must be working with Charley. She yanks out her earbuds and extends a hand.

"Zoe," she says as he takes hold.

"Paul. A pleasure."

He steps forward, lowers himself into a neighboring chair and sighs, shaking his head. He takes off his titanium *RM* ring and fidgets with it absently, pushing on the collapsible spike like he is ringing a doorbell. He is lean but solidly built with precise, boyish features and medium-brown hair, calculatedly tousled so as to convey a lack of calculation. They have him in a cheap suit and a loosened, striped tie, because the character of Randall Moss is a mild-mannered insurance salesman for Sentinel Life and Casualty. His day job is convincing people that they live in an uncertain world. Anything could happen at any time. He is here to help.

"Good that's over," she says, trying not to laugh.

"Feel more like a netted dolphin than a superhero."

She does laugh at this but chokes it off prematurely, fearing the impact of too much enthusiasm on her credibility.

"I think we're probably done for the day," he says, casting a glance toward Danny Quirk. Zoe follows his gaze.

The director is managing two animated conversations at the same time, a conductor simultaneously wrestling with Brahms on the left and Beethoven on the right. She is secretly relieved at Paul's assessment that the day is over. Her vigilance at having to fill Charley's shoes begins to deflate.

"So how are we doing out there?" he asks.

"What do you mean?"

Paul looks at her with a disarming earnestness.

"I mean... as the script supervisor... how is everything holding together? I assume you have an opinion."

A bubble of adrenaline releases itself into the circulatory current. She wants to state the obvious. This is her fourth day on the job as an intern. She knows nothing. She wants to laugh at herself by laughing at his question.

But she can still feel Charley's hands on her shoulders. And she can hear Dr. Patel's bouncing rubber voice, asking her to imagine what sits within the dark box of experience in the nanosecond before opening. This is the moment of accountability she knew would be coming sooner or later. It has chosen to present itself on the early side of sooner.

"I do," she says, nodding with an air of authority. "I do. Think." Her hands, quite on their own, tightly pack an imaginary snowball. "I think it is very much, actually, holding all together. As it should."

She hazards a look. Paul's expression has not changed, teetering between invisible impressions of her worth.

"Anything I'm doing that, you know, is not really working for you?"

"You? No, no, no. No." Her brain cringes. Too many no's. "You're great. This is going to be big. Huge. This is the next big franchise. I think it is. Will be, I mean."

"I can take criticism, you know," says Paul. "You don't have to be gentle."

It is the softness of his tone, the genuine mild-manneredness of it, that pulls her face around. Their eyes connect again but for the first time. His are slightly different colors, one more bluish than green and the other more greenish than blue.

"There is one thing," she starts, shocked at the sound of herself.

"Good. Tell me."

"Your eyebrows."

"My eyebrows."

She falters in the moment, looking down at her hands. Paul shifts in his seat, waiting. Zoe clears her throat.

"Yes. Every time you try to use your x-ray vision, you arch your right eyebrow. And every time you try to use your laser vision, you arch your left eyebrow."

"I do?"

She nods. "Except in this rooftop scene today. You arched your right eyebrow for the laser vision and both eyebrows for the x-ray vision."

"And that's... bad?"

She has done it, she thinks. Left alone once and she has already gone too far. She has given offense. She winces.

"No, no, no. Not, like *bad,* bad. But more like, unrealistic."

"I don't, really..."

"We do things a certain way. So like," Zoe pivots bodily in her chair, squaring her shoulders to his, her hands now pulling apart the imaginary snowball they had just made. "Each of us is defined by a unique collection of habits... which are, like, patterns that form a kind of combination code to our identity. Every time we repeat the pattern, it's like reaffirming who we are. And every time we break the pattern, it's like a first step into becoming someone else. A superhero needs to be, you know, dependable. That left eyebrow has to mean something particular. Every time. The right one too."

Paul's expression abandons the conversation, retreating into memory. His eyebrows – one, then the other, then both – cycle through unspoken scenarios. Zoe, too, retreats inward, astonished at what she has said. Her bewilderment is less at having ventured something critical about the lead actor on her fourth day on the job than at having been unaware of her own opinion until hearing the words leaving her mouth.

Where did that come from?

It makes her wonder what else is inside, waiting down in the depths for a crack of light. Waiting for that random opportunity to bolt for freedom.

"That's an amazing catch," says Paul. He is only halfway back in the moment, blinking slowly into the middle distance over her shoulder. "I mean... you're the only one who's noticed that." He leans away from her in his chair, like he needs some distance to take her all in. "Damn, Zoe. I'm impressed."

She shrugs and pivots away, a tide of blush rising into her face. She shakes her head. "You don't have to be nice."

"I'm not. Charley said you'd be good. She wasn't kidding."

Zoe's head suddenly has a mind of its own. She turns back.

"She wasn't? I mean, she did?"

"Well, yeah. I mean, she said you came over from VMFA?"

Zoe nods.

"No surprise then," says Paul. "Vic Massey's the gold standard. I applied there once when I was just getting into acting. Halfway through the interview, Vic just started shaking his head. That was that. No way I was getting in."

"You had to interview?"

Her unguarded surprise is as dangerous as it is garish. There is now no preventing Paul from thinking that she means to invoke his well-connected uncle. "Nepotism deals a helluva hand, kid," Charley had said. "Paul Rotella was born to be Random Man," by which Charley had meant that Paul had the part of Random Man not because he was good but simply because he had been born into the right family.

She kicks herself. He is no doubt sensitive to the perception that he has only passed through those doors that his last name could unlock. She had not intended to express shock that the Victor Massey Film Academy had insisted on interviewing even the nephew of the Studio Board Chairman.

That is not at all what she had meant. And yet, Zoe allows Paul to think that this is precisely what she had meant.

For what she had actually meant was *you mean the Victor Massey Film Academy requires interviews?* It was a question intimately connected with another: *Why did you have to interview for the Victor Massey Film Academy and I did not have to interview?* These are subversive questions, little hook-shaped thorns in her psyche, and so revealing of her own sublimated insecurity as to be profoundly unsettling.

Paul smiles at her just a little. It is a sad, softly apologetic expression that makes her cringe deep inside, where not even his x-ray vision can reach.

"Vic Massey doesn't care about family connections," Paul says. "He's one of the few purists in this game. It's all about the talent with Vic. So, hey," he opens his hands to her and rises, "you clearly have what it takes. Good meeting you, Zoe. Keep up the good work. I think I need to go talk to Danny about my eyebrows. We've got to reshoot that rooftop scene."

It is not easy to feel sympathy for Danny Quirk. His is not a temperament that encourages commiseration. And yet Zoe is sympathetic.

It is not until she reaches the fourth of the five blocks between the studio and the bus stop that she is able to finally snuff out the image of the embattled director, like a guttering, agitated flame, angrily struggling for fuel. Even with all five blocks behind her, as she stands in the reddening tide of sunlight washing over the sidewalk, she must work to keep Danny-Q out of her head. She must work to keep from resurrecting the memory of the loud reaction that had silenced the entire studio. "What?"

It had never been her expectation that Paul would plant his flag of professional integrity on the battlefield of eyebrow consistency. She had only been sharing her observations. And yet Paul had planted that flag. With gusto. He had refused to move to the next page of the script until the immensely complicated rooftop battle scene had been remade from the beginning.

It must have seemed so capricious to Danny. It was, she understood from the whispers of nearby technicians watching the fireworks, so unlike Paul Rotella to take a stand on anything. He was normally the most compliant person on the set. And yet, there he was, shouting Zoe's words at the director. "A superhero needs to be dependable! My left eyebrow has to mean something, Danny! Every time! And the right eyebrow, too!"

Poor Danny.

To Paul's credit, he had not once glanced back at Zoe or mentioned her name. He had presented the eyebrow concern as his own and had not suggested that anyone else in particular would agree with him, except perhaps his uncle who, Paul had intimated, would be of a similar mind.

But Paul's discretion would not save her for long. Danny-Q was not one to be pushed around on his own set. He would show who was boss. He would fight. Danny would suspect a script supervisor's influence and would grill Charley mercilessly about why Paul was suddenly so particular about consistency. He would repeat Paul's argument word for word.

Charley was no dummy either. She'd know.

The bus does not arrive until she is one of a dozen fares, six standing on either side of the sign. Metro No. 183 swishes by and scoops them up off the sidewalk like twelve dots on a pair of dice, rolling them the length of Magnolia Boulevard toward the Woodman Avenue intersection. The driver and a fare in the front row are nearly shouting in conversation as she steps past.

"... So my supervisor, who was sitting in row five, landed head first in row three," the driver is saying, gesturing behind him. "Two weeks in a neck brace." They both laugh at the spectacle.

"So only four days on the job and the rookie driver is out?"

The driver nods, laughing. "Out. Done. Gone. She maybe should have thought that one through a little better."

"You mean, not even swerve?"

"She'd still have a job."

"Least the cat lived," says the fare, shrugging.

"One lucky cat." The driver shakes his head in a kind of admiration. "One lucky cat."

She alights from the No. 183 into the path of a fat breeze carrying the smell of warm rubber and exhaust. She walks to a nearby bench where she will spend the next fifteen minutes waiting to catch the No. 158 to the corner of Devonshire and Sepulveda. She is not alone. Eleven other adults and one child stand scattered around her, swaying in the breeze like a sparse copse of pale, exotic firs.

She tries not to ruminate over Paul as she waits, taking familiar refuge in the mystery of simple math, selecting numbers at random and then shaking them up. The difference between No. 183 and No. 158 is 25, the exact number of minutes until the bus is due to arrive and exactly double the twelve-and-a-half people waiting. The sum of 183 plus 158 plus 25 minutes plus the 12.5 adults waiting is 378.5. She lives at 378 Memory Park Avenue. Fifth floor.

This kind of thing happens to her all the time. The agony of deciding whether the numbers are agents of randomness or agents of some unseen purpose usually makes for a reliable distraction from whatever may be bothering her.

Usually. But not today.

When the No. 158 arrives, Zoe gets in line and boards with a queue of questions that refuse to go away. Why had Paul done it? What had convinced him to do the thing he never does? The thing that wasn't him. If her words had been the impetus, then toward what purpose did Paul think she had spoken? Was it reason? Truth? Or had the sound of her voice triggered a random neural firing in Paul's brain that had sent him, against his better judgment and normal inclinations, bolting across the busy studio? Was Paul Rotella now someone just a little different than he used to be?

The same questions are behind her as she disembarks, pushing her off the bus and out onto the sidewalk. She walks up the block toward the final bus stop of her commute. She nearly passes by the Gas-n-Go. It is not a need for something inside that stops her. And being neither Monday nor Friday, it is not routine.

It is inexplicable impulse that makes her turn and pull open the door.

Mr. potbelly potato-face seems surprised to see her. He looks up over the bowed head of a woman poking at numbers on a credit card keypad, watching as Zoe heads to the back of the store for the blue-and-white kiosk. Muscle memory takes over. As she reaches the candy aisle, she shrugs herself free of one shoulder strap and searches a pocket of her backpack for the No. 2 stubby. Just like always.

It takes her a quarter of the time. She walks back past the candy, reaching with blind precision to return the pencil to its pouch. She detours down the neighboring aisle before heading to the counter.

"This isn't like you, kid," Potbelly says as she hands him the form. Zoe shrugs and digs for her wallet. He rubs dirty fingers across his stubble. His brow furrows. He is no longer a convenience store clerk. He is now a discerning border security guard, scrutinizing her passport.

"And where are your numbers?" he asks, looking up. "All Quick Picks? You?"

Zoe shrugs back at him and hands over a twenty. He takes it with his free hand, never looking away. The last of the sun is like something spilled, something wet and sticky and sanguineous escaping its containment and gushing over the table of the world, staining the dirty Gas-n-Go windows.

"You're going full random," he declares, as much to himself as to her. "You're shaking everything up, aren't you?"

Zoe places the can of cat food on the counter. She pushes it forward with a finger.

She arrives at the last bus stop six minutes early. Six minutes, multiplied by five people waiting, multiplied by a ten-minute ride, plus the one hundred in the *100% Awesome* emblazoned on the back of the skateboard dangling from the arm of the lanky red-haired boarder leaning against the bus stop sign, equals a total of four hundred, the exact temperature to which she must set her ancient oven in order to heat a frozen brick of mac-n-cheese.

None of this helps. Questions.

Shadows slowly push the last red glow of light into the earth, freeing the darkness to rise up off the pavement, swelling like groundwater up over the ankles, then the knees, then up to the hips of her fellow commuters. Zoe looks up the street for the No. 30-A. They all do.

The No. 30-A is never late. Except that it is. Today the No. 30-A is ten minutes behind schedule. Four hundred minus the No. 30, minus ten minutes, equals three hundred and sixty, the exact number of minutes past midnight before her alarm clock announces another day in the life of Zoe Alexakis.

When the No. 30-A arrives, it is already full. Mr. 100% Awesome gets the last seat. Zoe stands in the back, positioning her earbuds so that Ayaan Patel, PhD and his rubbery profundity might shorten the trip.

"Is it a coincidence that you are listening to these words?" he asks. "No. I am telling you no, my friend. I am telling you that we have arranged to be together, you and I. One tiny decision at a time, we have been working toward this moment our entire lives. That we have not been conscious of our intention may make this moment mysterious, but it does not reduce our time together to a meaningless coincidence."

Five flights of stairs make for a slow walk down a long hall to the east end of an old building made of boxes. She passes them, left and right, hearing the muffled sounds inside. The box assigned to Zoe is number 517. Box 517 has always been quiet. She has never opened that box to find it anything but empty and perfectly still.

Five plus one plus seven equals thirteen.

She searches for her key, musing that some building elevators pretend to skip the thirteenth floor altogether, jumping from twelve directly to fourteen. She wonders if renaming thirteen to fourteen really changes the fundamental properties of the thirteenth thing, or if the thirteenth thing only ever has the properties we give it. Properties like lucky or unlucky. Existing or non-existing.

She inserts the key and turns, listening to the bolt scrape against its metal casing, listening not only with her own ears but with the soft, twitching ears of the cat – black with three white paws and leaf-green eyes – that has been waiting all day for that sound.

"Wishing," says Dr. Patel, "confirms absence. Expecting invites satisfaction."

She twists her hand and pushes, trying to expect.

There is no cat. Not that she can see.

But the air is… different. Moving. Freshly stirred. Enlivened by sounds and smells of the street, five flights below. A white curtain flaps in the dusky breeze from the window she had neglected to close. A ragged sheet of paper towel, smudged with Yellow Dye No. 5, is on the floor beside the assemble-yourself sling-back rocker she had purchased the previous spring at the Goodwill Store. She sees that there is a straight, vertical tear in the dingy white fabric of the back cushion.

Zoe closes the door and lowers her pack to the floor. She crosses the room and cantilevers her shoulders over the chair for a closer look.

It is not a tear, after all, but a long drip of a dark purple stain.

There is a sudden and urgent panic in the ill-lit air somewhere behind her head, terrifying and lethal in the way that anything inexplicable is terrifying and lethal in that first moment. She turns and cowers simultaneously, wanting both to avoid death and, just for the record, to know what is going to kill her.

The bird – for it must be a bird – comes so quickly that it is past her, out the window and gone, through the tree branches and beyond her sight into the darkening sky before she has any idea of what is happening. She feels the ridge of feather across her cheek only after there is nothing there to touch her.

She straightens herself and stands for several long moments at the window, watching the sky release the last of its color into space. She touches her cheek and marvels after the thing she never saw. A bird!

She heats a can of chicken soup for dinner and eats it sitting in the newly stained chair in front of the television as the oven slowly goes to work on another orange brick of frozen macaroni. Next to her sits the telephone she wishes would ring.

Not wishes, *expects*. She openly expects to be harassed and annoyed by the man who stole her luggage. She expects him to ask about her day. She expects him to care about the mystery of Paul Rotella and about the outrage of Danny-Q and about her avian intruder. She expects him to not want her to hang up. She expects all that to happen before the oven issues its piercing notice.

But the phone does not ring. Even after the television is off and the shower has ended its slow, slurping drain, and darkness has cocooned her in bed, the phone does not ring. It waits until she, too, has released the colors of day into space and has followed the unseen bird out the window, soaring above dreamscapes of unrealized intention.

"Hello?"

"Continuity girl's awake."

"Who is this?"

"Who do you think?"

She blinks. The world is slow to return.

"Zoe?"

She glances at the bedside clock.

"It's almost three in the morning."

"Not here it's not."

"I'm hanging up."

"No you're not. How was your day?"

"Weird. I'm going back to sleep."

"Weird how?"

After a long minute of listening to him wait, Zoe pushes herself up against the wall, rubbing her face.

"I made trouble."

"What kind of trouble?"

"They might be reshooting a whole scene because I said something about a guy's eyebrows."

"Eyebrows?"

"Yeah."

"I don't understand."

"Me neither, really."

"So he's mad? This guy with the eyebrows?"

"No. He thinks I'm brilliant. Director's mad. My boss will probably be mad."

"Maybe you are brilliant."

"I'm not."

"I get that you don't think you're brilliant but maybe to other people…"

"I'm not. I'm a fraud. I'm not who any of them think I am."

"Because…"

"Because I never had to interview."

"For the job? Did you sleep with the director, Zoe?"

"Not funny, Dexter."

"Who cares about the job interview? You got the job."

"I'm not talking about the job. I'm talking about the Academy."

"You're in the Air Force, or…"

"I'm hanging up."

"No you're not. You're awake now. Why would you hang up? Listen. Zoe?"

"What."

"Sometimes it takes someone else to tell you who you really are before you believe it yourself. You should listen to Mr. eyebrows. I think he's got you pegged. You're a continuity girl savant."

"You don't know the first thing about me, Dexter."

"Not true."

"Except from rummaging through my bag. Which I want back."

"You're not a victim of random crime."

"Right."

"I didn't pick your bag randomly, Zoe. It's time I confessed."

She is in the process of swinging her legs off the edge of the bed. Her bare feet, dangling in the dark air, are suddenly still.

"What? What are you saying?"

"I'm saying..."

"Dexter?"

"I'm saying we've met."

"We've met? You mean I know you?"

"Not exactly. We had a drink. At the Desert Inn. I bought you a seven-dollar appletini."

"You're him? That was you?"

"One and the same."

"Oh my god. Kevin?"

"Random victimization is way better, right?"

"Oh my god. Oh my god. Why... I mean..."

"A little anger, a little obsession. You led me on and then cut me loose."

"I did not..."

"Yes you did. You said I was your lucky number seven. You said your room was up on the seventh floor."

"Oh my god. I didn't mean it like that."

"How else is one supposed to take that, Zoe?"

"You put up three sevens on Slot Machine Seven at seven o'clock in the evening on July 7. You won seven hundred dollars."

"It was closer to five hundred."

"You lied about how much you won?"

338

"I was trying to get somewhere with you, Zoe. It seemed right at the time. I also never drink seven-and-sevens. And my name was never Kevin. Man, it feels good to get all this off my chest."

"You made up a name?"

"It rhymed with seven. I was going to tell you but you kind of ended things before..."

"You stole my luggage because I wouldn't sleep with you?"

"Of course not. I stole your luggage because I wanted to talk to you again. I thought that might lead to seeing you again."

"Oh... My... God."

"Maybe. Maybe it is God. If you believe in that sort of thing. But it's not random is all I'm saying. Nothing is random. We're meant to be where we are, Zoe, wherever that is. Meet who we meet. Want what we want. Love who we love. We may not understand it but that doesn't make it random. We tend to think of reality as random and disconnected. We tend to think that interconnectedness is the stuff of dreams. But that's nonsense. Reality is the dream. This, Zoe, you and me right now, together on the phone, connected in space and time, this is the dream."

"It is?"

"Yes. It is. Those three sevens brought us together. That didn't happen to two other people; that happened to us. You and me. Because it was supposed to happen. That's why you got on the bus to Vegas alone and that's why I chose that precise moment to pick the slot machine next to yours even though I never, ever waste my time on the slots. I was on my way out after losing big at the baccarat table. I only had seven bucks left on my ticket and the idea of zeroing out on the slots came over me like an irresistible impulse. Except it wasn't an impulse. That kind of thing just feels like an impulse because we don't have a sophisticated enough psycho-emotional vocabulary to identify what is actually going on in the synaptic thunderstorm. I never play slots. Ever. But then I did. And then I won. And there you were next to me to watch those three sevens flip into place and to link them up with all the other sevens in your head and to make me your lucky number seven. There's a reason for everything, Zoe. There is a coherence – a purpose made up of a trillion constituent purposes, each of which is made up of a trillion smaller purposes and so on all the way down to two strangers sitting next to each other at a slot machine going berserk over three sevens – and all that sticky purpose is what holds the universe together. Without it, everything would just fly apart and nothing would ever be connected to anything else. And I'm not selling some bullshit gospel of fate here, either. Fate is just the flip-side of the counterfeit coin of randomness. Fate suggests a master plan carved into the face of eternity, some fixed blueprint we follow like mindless characters in a play that we did not write and probably would never read if we had the choice. But we do have the choice; we always have the choice. So I'm not talking about fate. No, no, no. I'm talking about daisy-chained cause and effect; multidimensional dominoes radiating out in all directions, backward and forward in time, far beyond the reaches of our imagination, let alone our perception. We are here, you and I, having this conversation, because one thing has led to another over millennia of human experience, over a hundred thousand lifetimes. We are having this conversation because we are part of the math, Zoe. We are fractions of the whole. We are adjoining tiles in the grand mosaic of existence. But I don't really need to tell you any of this."

"You don't?"

"No, because you already believe it. You're a numbers person. You're a gambler. You're a sleuth. You look for meaning and continuity connecting disparate elements. You lay wagers on hidden patterns. It's in your blood, Zoe, which is nothing but a red river of coded DNA that connects you to all the rest of existence: past, present and future. Sure, you like to flirt with randomness. You swoon at the idea of sheer luck. You like the romance of it. The magic. You like the idea of plucking something from nothing. Who doesn't want to feel lucky? It makes us feel god-like. Light, suddenly, inexplicably, pulled from darkness. Except that it's all a parlor trick, Zoe, and you know it. Lightning doesn't strike randomly. It's a brilliant exchange of energy between separate bodies carrying electrical charges whose very existence predestines all the flash-bang drama. Every bolt is a scripted connection between two points. Cloud to cloud. Cloud to earth. Slot-machine jockey to slot-machine jockey. Nothing about me is random, Zoe. Nothing about you is random. We connected for a reason we still don't understand. We are part of that sticky coherence that holds everything together. You could have fought against the pattern. You have that power. We all do. You could have sent the dominoes tumbling in a different direction. But you didn't, not at first. You smiled at me with your bottomless brown eyes and called me your lucky number seven and bought me a drink and revealed the floor of your hotel room. And then you did fight the pattern."

"I did?"

"Yes. You did. You got up and left me sitting there with a glass in one hand and my heart in the other. Not because the moment felt wrong to you but because it felt right. It all clicked into place and for a brief, alcohol-enhanced second, the entire universal equation lit up in your head and there we were, right in the middle of it, together, a pair of sevens, twins throbbing with a bonded significance, like a lighthouse or a traffic light, showing a meaningful point of intersection along a vast, hidden, underlying structure. The place where the reef juts above the sea. The place where your north-south road crosses my east-west train tracks. But instead of feeling like an answer, instead of feeling like a revelation in the blink of an eye, it felt to you like a trap. Rather than something liberating, the pattern that explained why you were sitting on the barstool next to mine revealed itself as some kind of confinement, like oceans upon oceans of chicken wire extending out in all directions, all lit up in a frightening flash of lightning. And that scared you, Zoe. That sent you up to the seventh floor alone. And as you walked away, you changed the underlying causal structure of creation. Instead of playing another seven, you put down a three and the entire universe recalculated itself accordingly, spooling out new causal roadmaps with new flashing intersections for you and for me and for the bartender who would have poured us each another drink and for all the people we have yet to meet and all the people they have yet to meet and so on until the number-of-grains-of-sand-on-a-beach comparison becomes too quaint to be of much use and our feeble brains surrender the effort to comprehend what is happening as I watched you reach the elevator and push the button. But you're not the only one who can fight the implicative order, Zoe. Nothing said I had to sit there alone to play a shitty hand. So I didn't."

"You didn't?"

"No. I didn't. I plotted a new course of my own, over to a table at the café where I could keep an eye on the elevator. I stayed there all night, drinking coffee and waiting for you to re-emerge. And when you did, I followed you out to the bus stop. I didn't have any kind of a plan. I didn't know what came next. But I knew enough to understand that something came next. Because something always comes next whether we know what that thing is or not. And when you put your bag next to all the others on the sidewalk and started talking to the bus driver, the thing that came next lit up in my exhausted over-caffeinated head. It felt like an impulse. But I knew better. Our paths crossed again. The universe recalculated. And now here we are. My voice to your ear and your voice to my ear, the opportunity to share consciousness, came with a unique combination of numbers, like the combination to a door lock that I found in your suitcase. We call it a phone number, but it's so much more than that, Zoe. It's so much more."

The sudden silence finds her standing in the dark, leaning against the window behind the newly stained chair. She does not remember getting here. The street below is as still as a photograph.

But in the distance, over the stubbled rooftop of the apartment building across the street, there is a river of light burbling south along the 405 to Santa Monica. Beyond the far shore of that river is field upon field of what seem like fireflies winking on and off in the dark, electric airborne motes refusing to be counted.

"Zoe?"

"You didn't win seven hundred dollars?"

"Five something. Five-fifty."

"I'm hanging up."

"No you aren't. When can I see y..."

Zoe places the phone on the sill and uses both hands to pull up on the window. It opens like the lid to a glass box, dark inside, flecked with mysterious light. She turns the chair around and sits, propping her bare feet against the opening.

A bird, she marvels as the sleep of memory takes her. She grazes her cheek with the feather touch of a finger. *A bird.*

She is earlier to work, just as Charley had instructed. Not that it really matters. The studio set is like a bus stop. People sit and lean and fidget in place, looking with weary expectance for some change on the horizon to signal the promise of movement. The mood is inexplicably anxious and unsettled. Zoe casts glances here and there, looking for Charley but not finding her. At the food service tables, Zoe is prying free a banana when the fat production assistant, headphone cord dragging over the food, reaches over her for a Danish.

"Get it while you can," he says. "My guess is you won't be here tomorrow."

She is prepared to take his words as personally as they sound, to believe that she had been right to be concerned and that she had overstepped her authority as an intern. Dominoes had been falling all night. Today would be her last day.

The man keeps talking as he reaches in varying directions across the table – mini-cereal boxes, donut holes, poppy-seed muffins – as though a hurricane has been assigned a name and is finally on its way to cut the power and close the stores.

"Me neither," he adds. "None of us will be here."

"What do you mean?"

He looks at her for a second and then chuckles.

"You missed all the drama. You really need to get here earlier."

"What drama?"

"Oh, Paul got a wild hair and wanted to reshoot everything we've been doing for the past week. And then Danny-Q got into it with Paul's uncle, which didn't go so well. So Danny stormed off the set, going on and on about how life is too short for this and saying he has twenty other projects to choose from. Then Charley went chasing after him to try to bring him back. Then the Board called an emergency meeting to try to get Paul and Danny in a room to compromise. They both refused to go to the meeting. So the Board Chair, Paul's uncle, had a screaming meltdown, which triggered a heart thing and so now he's in a room down at Saint Joseph's Medical. It's a mess."

The man jabs a thick finger through the hole in a pumpernickel bagel. Zoe looks dumbfoundedly at her watch.

"It's quarter past eight in the morning," she says.

"Got to get here early," he says, shrugging. Then he shuffles away, headphone cord swinging free.

Zoe takes her backpack and her banana to a nearby nameless chair and sits. She peels and chews and looks expectantly at the door and waits. Just like all the others. It is not until nine twenty-five, as Dr. Ayaan Patel is bubbling on about the miracle of manifestation, that Charley enters the studio in a shaft of sunlight. People holding breakfast carbohydrates stick to her as she makes her way forward, talking, shaking her head. By the time she reaches the corner of the fake skyscraper, the accumulated weight of people needing information becomes so great as to stop all forward progress. After a series of conversations that Zoe cannot hear, the group disperses, leaving Charley alone and turning in a slow, fashionable circle until she finds her intern.

"Well, that was a short ride," says Charley, sitting. She is an aromatic storm of bangles and silk.

"Really? It's done? Like, _done_-done?"

"Like an overcooked Thanksgiving turkey."

"What happened?"

345

"What didn't happen? Jesus Christ. Monster egos and stubbornness and temper tantrums all in a teacup. Welcome to the movie business. I gave it my best shot but Danny-Q is not a rational man when he's angry." She looks at herself appraisingly and comes away disappointed. "Should've worn my sundress and a push-up today, I guess."

"Maybe he'll cool off," says Zoe, hazarding hope.

"No way. Danny's gone. And then there's Paul." Charley whistles through a smile. "Who knew he had all that assertiveness locked up inside? You sure did a number on him."

"Me?"

Charley wags a perfectly manicured, red-tipped index finger.

"Don't bullshit a bullshitter, kid. The eyebrow thing? Come on. That's not something Paul Rotella figures out on his own. Takes a whip-smart continuity girl to pick up on something like that. Gotta say, I'm impressed. I looked at the dailies and you were right on the money. Eyebrows every which way."

"You're not mad?"

"Mad? Screw these guys, Zoe. And screw me too if I'm mad. You did your job. But don't let it go to your head. None of us is all-important. You're just one of a billion different factors. Danny-Q's been looking to give the studio suits what-for ever since I've known him. You just kicked over the right domino." Charley stands suddenly, looking at her watch and then back down at Zoe. "I had a feeling about you. Vic Massey has never steered me wrong."

"What now?"

"There's always something next," she says. "I've got your number."

Outside, the morning sunlight is foaming up out of the street, over the concrete curbs, and washing across the sidewalks. An automotive juggernaut splashes the light up against the steel and glass of nearby office buildings, which deflect it back out into the air above the city so finely that it hangs there as a golden, luminous mist immune to gravity.

The studio security gate rolls closed behind her, locking with a clink and a tightening whir. Zoe does not quite know what to do with herself so early in the day. Given the paucity of sleep the previous night, she decides to walk to the bus stop and begin the commute back home for a nap. She follows the sidewalk to the corner and stops, waiting for the white, walking stick-figure to replace the red hand.

A bird, a common pigeon with wings of graying, speckled suede and a dark cap, alights on the signal box as if perched upon the tips of the flashing red fingers. Before the walking stick-figure appears, it is off again in a burst of energy, flapping over the intersection toward a stone fountain outside an office park.

She does not cross the street for the bus stop. Instead, she turns and follows the bird, stepping into the roadway that is not yet ready for her. There is no explanation for why she does this. It is purely an impulsive act.

As the screech of tires and the blaring horns devour everything else of that moment, Zoe Alexakis can hear the voice of the man who is neither Dexter nor Kevin: "We don't have a sophisticated enough psycho-emotional vocabulary to identify what is actually going on in the synaptic thunderstorm."

Maybe so. But the woman at the wheel of the gleaming cinnabar SUV does not care about why. Her eyes are lunar with shock. Her mouth hangs agape over bloodless knuckles that form a ridge of white, bony knobs along the top of the steering wheel. All this woman cares about is the single fraction of a second – a temporal molecule in the infinite ocean of time – in which she had fumbled for her keys before starting the engine and heading off to her morning Pilates class. Not twenty minutes earlier, sitting in the dim sanctum of her garage, the keys had slipped from the woman's fingers, down into the depths of her purse. It had taken less than a second to reacquire them. Less than a second.

Lucky.

Horns hack angrily at the smell of burning rubber. Zoe presses the palm of her hand against the hot, cinnabar hood. Inside, terror loosens its grip. The woman is screaming now, both middle fingers jabbing at the windshield, helping to bleed off the adrenaline. Zoe mouths her apology and finishes crossing the street.

She must traverse a sidewalk and a narrow, sloping sward of grass to reach the fountain. She sits on a stone bench, listening to the traffic on the street behind her flow past the tragic alternate reality that never happened.

On the other side of the fountain, a man is seated on an identical stone bench, eating a sandwich. Not just any man.

Random Man.

Paul Rotella looks up in surprise as Zoe's shadow crosses over his face. He makes a sound that might have been her name had there been more room in his mouth. There wasn't.

"Pretty early for lunch," she says, filling time until he has chewed and swallowed and is able to speak.

"Never too early for lunch," says Paul. He gestures over his shoulder with his thumb to one of the buildings. "Great deli in there. I come here all the time. Going to miss these Reubens. Hey, have a seat if you want."

Beside him is a large, straw-skewered paper cup next to a pile of napkins, an open bag of chips, an empty styrofoam tray losing its cellophane wrap, and one-quarter of a dill pickle, all sitting atop a flattened, white paper bag. Between the bag and the end of the bench, Paul's wallet, car keys and cellphone bask in the sun. Zoe swings free of her backpack and sits.

"Why?"

"Why what?"

"Why are you going to miss the Reubens?"

Paul looks at her like he must have misunderstood something in the question.

"Because they're, like, really good, is why," he says, holding the sandwich in her direction. Zoe shakes her head. Paul retracts and takes another bite. "And because I won't be able to eat them for a long time."

"How come?"

"Getting out of LA."

"Yeah?"

Paul nods. "Finally leaving this city. This ridiculous profession. Going to find something better."

Zoe slides the backpack off her lap onto the bench. "Like what?"

"Hell if I know." He chews and, with the Reuben, gestures vaguely in the direction of the road. "Just going to get in my car and drive. Turn when I feel like turning. Stop when I feel like stopping. Not answerable to anyone. Be my own man. Just, you know, live on impulse until something better presents itself."

"Because of what happened this morning? Back at the studio?"

Paul chews like it is an act essential to the task of considering her question.

"Yes and no," he says finally. "Been coming on for years, I think. I'm not really made out for this business. Makes you feel like a puppet after awhile. Tired of feeling like a puppet."

"You're just going to flush your whole career?"

"Career. My uncle is Sal Rotella. He chairs the Studio Board. But you already knew that. I've had parts in three movies and four television shows and a load of commercials. Uncle Sal pulled the strings for every one of them. My career is more his than mine. So he can have it."

"Hey," she says, remembering, "how is your uncle?"

"Feeling lucky to be alive at the moment, I think. That'll pass. He has these episodes every couple of years. Something sets him off, usually me, and he ends up in the hospital."

"Usually you?"

"Oh." Paul shakes his head and breaks off, considering the last of his sandwich. "I'm a square peg, I guess. I frustrate him. My brother was always the actor in the family. School plays, drama club, then the Juilliard scholarship. You could just tell. He was made for this business. My uncle adopted us both when my parents died. I'm not saying Sal's not a good man. He is. But it was Kevin that Sal really had big plans for, not me."

Paul looks up from the Reuben to see Zoe in a kind of suspension. She is not breathing or blinking.

"His name is Kevin?" she asks. Paul winces.

"Was. Riding his bike across a four-lane intersection. Not as fast as he thought. He was seventeen and, like, absolutely perfect at everything he put his hand to. Smart. Confident. Outgoing. Athletic. Kevin was invincible. Almost."

Zoe covers her mouth.

"I know," says Paul. "Horrible. That's what started Uncle Sal's trips to the hospital. He's never really recovered. None of us have. Not really. Not sure that's even possible. We've all sort of limped along. I was always kind of playing the part of Kevin's understudy anyway, but when he died Sal permanently cast me in the role. I just stepped into those shoes and kept walking. And here I am. It hasn't all been horrible or anything. But at some point I have to stop living the life of my dead twin. You know?"

Paul drops the last bit of Reuben on the bag and brushes his hands with a forced laugh.

"Man!" he says, shaking his head. He looks at her with a smile. "I'm so sorry, Zoe. How did we get off into all that depressing nonsense? Tell me what you have planned now that our little movie blew up."

But Zoe is no longer with him. She is frozen at the intersection of this conversation, at the spot where his road crosses her train track, where the bodies beneath the twisted-metal pile-up of cause and effect have forced detours. New direction. Different destinations.

"You were twins," she says. It is not a question so much as the statement of quiet revelation.

Paul nods, watching her as one watches a bird on a ledge. Waiting.

"Can I tell you something?" she asks.

"Anything to stop hearing myself talk."

351

"You said yesterday that you once interviewed at the Victor Massey Film Academy and were declined. I should have told you something. I should have told you that I never had to interview at all. I should have told you but I didn't. I liked that you seemed impressed with me. So I didn't say anything."

"One, I was impressed... I am impressed with you. And two, I have no earthly idea what you're talking about."

"I got into the VMFA without an interview because I know Victor Massey. That's how I got in. I would never have been there otherwise. And I never would have gotten the internship with Charley or worked on the *Random Man* picture. It's not because I'm good at... at anything. It's because... it's all because of Victor. If it weren't for Victor Massey..."

"So what? If it weren't for Victor Massey, Zoe, you'd never have been there to convince me that my whole life needed to change. I'm sitting on this bench, out of a job, eating my last Reuben from my favorite deli, and preparing to surrender to the winds of fate, all because of you."

"But the only thing I did was tell you..."

"Yeah. The eyebrows. I know. Sounds silly but you basically showed me that Random Man – this character I was asked to become – was an impossibility. You were right: a superhero needs to be, above all else, dependable. Predictable. Right down to his eyebrows. But as a superhero, Random Man is nothing but a super heroic self-contradiction. He doesn't know from one moment to the next who he really is. He's in a constant state of identity flux. Any suggestion of constancy or dependability, even in his eyebrow expression, is... is... well, it's necessarily fraudulent."

As he speaks, Paul Rotella rotates, so that most of his upper body is now facing hers. He pauses, both eyebrows raised into earnest arches, like twin umbrellas offering a shelter of intimacy.

"And it's just like you said, Zoe, every time we repeat the pattern, it's like reaffirming who we are, and every time we break the pattern, it's like a first step into becoming someone else. Random Man's problem is that he cannot possibly be the person he pretends, the person everyone requires him to be. Random Man needs to be able to repeat himself into dependability. Except, thanks to the molecular randomizer, he can never do that. And I need... I need... I..."

He rotates back against the bench, not finishing and choosing instead to shake his head to himself. He begins cleaning up his mess, stuffing the remains of his lunch into the bag and collecting his things.

"You need what, Paul?" Zoe asks, wanting to touch his shoulder.

Paul stands, looking up at the sun like a lost hiker getting his bearings. He looks down at Zoe and shrugs.

"Randomness," he says. "I need randomness."

"So, then... you're just... you're not coming back?" she asks, shading her eyes with a hand.

"No predicting," he says. "That's the point."

Paul digs a hand into his front pocket, then holds it down to her. He places the large *RM* ring into her palm.

"Great knowing you, Zoe. Thanks for opening my eyes. Good luck to you."

She watches him walk off into the cascading sun, toward the parking lot, his last words in her head like one of Dr. Patel's bouncing rubber balls.

Good luck. Good luck. Good luck.

No such thing, she thinks, wishing Paul was still sitting next to her. Not even Lucky had been lucky. Lucky had been a cat with a predictable urge to escape. It had not been luck that young Zoe, empathizing with Lucky's confinement, had propped the front door open just enough. It had not been luck that had allowed escape from Moira's outstretched arms. It was not luck that had avoided the front tires of the car that carried Gloria Massey and a stack of newly dry-cleaned shirts for her husband.

Her husband, Victor.

Luck, assures Dr. Patel, is but a figment of fate. And fate is but a figment of existential despair, a false beacon in a meaningless void for those who do not understand the truth: The darkness in the box of experience is simply the meaning we have yet to assign. We only live the lives we intend.

Zoe releases the black, plastic spike in the Random Man ring. It telescopes out past the bold initials with a tiny click. She resets and releases it in absent repetition, each click an invitation to the next, into a rhythm. All the while she looks at the place in the parking lot she had last seen Paul Rotella. She sits for another fifteen minutes listening to the fountain and the rush of traffic until hunger asserts itself above the fray.

She stands, stuffs the ring in her pocket and shoulders the backpack, uncovering the wallet beneath. She picks it up and extracts the California driver's license: Paul Dexter Rotella. DL. Z0377733.

A pigeon lands on the lip of the fountain for a drink. Zoe zips the wallet into a pouch and saunters off for a Reuben. And she wonders.

She wonders at the impulse that had repositioned the pack off her lap.

She wonders at a license number that, for all the world, looks like her own first name followed by a full house.

She wonders at the window she had opened before setting off to work, and at the bowl of cat food on the floor beneath the chair.

THIS IS THE DREAM

This is the dream. I'm in the science lab. I sit hunched on one of those tall, metal stools in the back of the room. I'm at a long, heavy black table that seems like maybe it was built to hold a full-sized dead person and not a few tiny frogs in their little plastic trays. I'm wearing the Van Halen t-shirt my mother hates, and my denim skirt and my black Converse sneakers.

I don't know where my purse is. You don't need purses in dreams. I'm barelegged and am not wearing underwear.

I was usually in my tights when I wore that denim skirt because it rides up when I sit. I had two classes in the science lab – biology and chemistry – and so twice a day I had to sit up on one of those stools. I was wise to some of the guys pretending to drop their pens, trying to get a glance up at my privates.

I call my privates, *privates*, because that's what they're supposed to be: private. I call the guys, *guys*, because they aren't women and they aren't men and they aren't boys. They're guys.

I've never been able to stand guys. I never dated. I never really tried. You're thinking I'm some lesbian or whatever. Or that I'm too ugly to ever have a boyfriend. It just seemed like such a waste of time. Like this painful and

356

humiliating game that nobody really knows how to play but where everyone has to pretend they're experts. I just kind of stayed out of it. People playing that game only see the other players. Everyone else is invisible. I was one of those.

Anyway, in the dream, I'm barelegged and not wearing underwear. The metal edge of the stool is cold against my skin. My legs are embarrassingly white and covered in gooseflesh. I can see little light-blue veins like the way rivers and streams look on a bleached-out roadmap.

I'm sitting at the table in the back of the room. Just like always. Only it's not really like always because the room looks and feels totally different in the dream. Someone has removed the middle partition wall, so the room is twice as wide as normal, as if God decided to unfold the world and suddenly everything is double, like an inkblot on an unfolded page. Two sinks. Two blackboards. Two sets of equipment cupboards for the Bunsen burners and scalpels and microscopes. Identical periodic charts on each side of the room. Two long tables that could've held two dead bodies.

I half-expect identical Mr. McKenzies to walk in the room from opposite doors wearing identical black plastic glasses and putty-colored sweater vests and offering a reminder in stereo about something having to do with isotopes.

I say I half-expect it. I don't really expect to see Mr. McKenzie at all. Everyone around me is either from American Government or English Lit and I don't see anyone who actually belongs in a science lab. Everyone has their head bent down, taking a standardized test, like the SATs or whatever, filling in the little bubbles with pencils. The test form in front of me is mostly blank. My pencil doesn't work. It's not broken; it just won't make any marks on the page. Like the lead tip is fake.

So, I raise my hand to complain. That's when I feel a hand on my arm.

I put my arm down and look up to see Mr. McKenzie, just one of him, looking back down at me with disappointment all over his face. I don't really register his expression at first. I'm hostage to my view from beneath his chin, like I'm being forced to climb Mount Rushmore or whatever. His nose seems kind of loose and baggy and asymmetrical. His nostrils are like the undersides of two exotic mushrooms. And it's not just the nose. It's like the skin of his entire face needs to be power-washed and re-stretched over the frame.

Eventually, I do make the climb up to Mr. McKenzie's hazel eyes and I can appreciate the entirety of his disappointed expression. Even though he never breaks eye contact, I can sense the restraint he is bringing to the goal of not looking at my mostly naked lap on the high metal stool. I try to tell him that my pencil does not work. All he does is shake his head and point to the front of the room.

I don't walk to the front of the room in the dream. Walking is unnecessary in dreams, like purses. I'm just suddenly up there with my empty test form and worthless pencil in my hand, standing at a long row of tables that have been connected end-to-end so that they block the exit. I'm pulling at my skirt because it keeps riding up and I look around self-consciously. None of the other students are paying attention. They're all completely absorbed in finishing the test I have yet to start.

Over at the far end of the tables, my mother is building an elaborate five-story structure out of popsicle sticks or tongue depressors.

"Mom?" I ask, and she speaks to me without looking up from her tongue depressor hotel, saying something like "If you don't complete the next level, Cali, then you're nobody.

358

You don't get a car and you forfeit everything you've worked for."

"Leave her alone," says my father.

I turn my head. He's sitting at the other end of the row of tables, silently weeping and beating russet potatoes with a silver meat tenderizer. The hammer hits the potatoes, exploding them across the table but without making any sound. "You're wasting your time, kiddo," he sniffs. "There is no future. Go get high. Go get laid."

"Bill, that is the most irresponsible thing...," says Mom.

"I'm pretty sure I never asked for your opinion, Karen."

I'm looking from my mother to my father and back again, failing to see the person standing across the table in front of me until she says my name.

"Cali."

My head stops ping-ponging, suddenly in the grip of the ridiculously blue eyes of Taylor Boss. Taylor shares my species, my age and my gender. Those are the only things we have in common. I'm actually fudging on the species, which is technically the same but not really, in the way that a Great Dane and a Chinese Crested are technically both canines, but come on.

I once overheard two teachers telling a joke about Taylor Boss. The joke had Taylor's mother in the stirrups giving birth and her father asking the doctor whether she was crowning. The doctor looks up at Taylor's father and says, yep, it's a tiara. At the time I heard that joke, I didn't really know what crowning was and I thought a tiara was a kind of Italian pastry. To know Taylor Boss is to get the joke anyway.

So, in the dream, all I can do is stare at Taylor like I'm a farm animal. She repeats my name, this time in its full ridiculous pretension, expecting the sound of it to break the spell. It does.

"Calico Watts."

Her eyes are so clear, like looking over an ocean on a brilliant sunny morning. Her hair is glowing gold. I feel too tall and skinny and drab. My eyes too brown. My hair too flat and shapeless. I ache for makeup and lots of it. I hate makeup.

"Yes?" I ask in a whisper. My father begins throwing russet bombs at the popsicle Marriott. My mother shrieks, batting them away and threatening the divorce she's already had for five years. Taylor reaches out and takes the test form out of my hand.

"You can't be here," she says.

"I can't?"

"No."

"Why not?"

"Because you're dead."

"I'm not dead," I protest. "I'm right here. I'm literally standing right..."

Taylor lowers the test and tries to lay it flat on the table, but she can't because the gun is in the way. I don't even know it's there, an old-timey, western six-shooter thing, until she picks it up and hands it to me.

I stick it in the waistband of my skirt like it's no big deal, like, of course she's handing me a gun; what else is she supposed to do when she confiscates a test? But the gun is heavy and now my skirt not only rides up from the bottom but also sags down from the waist and I feel like I'm this close to not wearing anything at all.

Taylor places the test flat on the table and extends her hand toward me again. Her hands and nails belong in a manicurist advertisement. Her ring finger sports a pink diamond. She reaches for me. I see it coming and do nothing to stop her.

She cups my right breast. Then, with a firm squeeze, she opens it away from my chest like she might open a medicine cabinet or a mini-fridge. All I can do is stare in shock. I'd never known they were on hinges.

She reaches inside and starts removing things. First a can of shaving cream. Then a pregnancy test stick. She piles thing after thing on the table in front of her. A shot glass. A ceramic Santa. A blooming hibiscus with a long green stem. A snow globe with a little wooden schoolhouse or a church or whatever inside. She shakes it and holds it in her hand for a second, peering inside like she's waiting to see if someone will open the little door and step outside into the snow.

The Slinky is the last thing I remember before I wake up. You know what I mean by a Slinky, one of those vintage aluminum coils that stretches from three inches to about four or five feet. The Slinky is a useless thing. It has no purpose. Sure, you can put it on the top step and get it going and watch it go all the way to the bottom. But I can do that with a rock or an old tire.

Anyway, Taylor reaches inside my chest and pulls out one end of a Slinky. And she keeps pulling and pulling, hand over perfect hand, as if removing a ropy internal organ, until there is easily twelve feet of silver coil on the table. It doesn't stack neatly, either. It forms an unruly pile over the other things. The Slinky shivers and rolls in the fluorescent light, threatening to flop off the edge of the table and onto the floor, which seems like it would be a bad thing because suddenly both of my parents are there next to me, making sure that does not happen, cooperating to keep the thing in the center of the table like they are trying to keep the midsection of a large python from slipping off the edge of a couch.

"Jesus, Cali," says my father. "You really are dead, kiddo."

"How can you advance to the next level if you're dead?" Asks Mom.

Taylor Boss just keeps pulling. Without breaking her rhythm, she cocks her head and looks at me with a quirky smile and I-told-you-so eyes. She opens her perfect mouth to say something and I can see just a little of the soft pink pillow of her tongue moving inside her fortress of blazing white teeth.

Then a small blue crab crawls out sideways onto her lower lip and down to her chin. It clicks one of its claws at me. *Snap.*

That's when I wake up. Every time. The snap of that little blue crab claw.

I'd tell you not to waste your time interpreting that dream. I'd tell you that I've already tried it. I'd tell you that you can't really know what any dream means, just like you can't really know another person. Or even yourself. Not really. We're all capable of anything.

But you'll do it anyway. You'll think that recurring dreams are somehow more important and that they need to be dissected for some coded meaning or whatever. You'll want to know the significance of the things Taylor Boss pulls out from behind my right boob. You'll go back to that lesbian idea. You'll wonder whether I'm extremely test-phobic. You'll insist on knowing about my relationship with my parents.

The thing that will really keep you busy is learning that Mr. McKenzie went to the science lab at least a couple of

Saturdays a month to do it – you know, IT – with one of his students.

But then, while you're still wrapping your brain around that one, you'll mention the dream to someone at Howell High, or at The Sandwich Deck, or maybe at the Ninety-Nine Cent Store, and the person you ask will tell you that one cold autumn morning Taylor Boss was found dead on the floor of a small, dilapidated duck shack on the edge of a marsh not far from St. Charles. I'm betting that the whole Mr. McKenzie thing will suddenly seem like small potatoes.

And then, when the dream still doesn't make any sense, you'll double-back and wonder if there is some sort of connection between Taylor Boss and Mr. McKenzie. And then you're going to really start thinking about that gun.

Maybe you already are.

But eventually you'll give it all up. You'll stop caring altogether and go on back to your own life. Good for you.

So, I won't waste my breath telling you not to try interpreting. Knock yourself out. If there's one thing my parents' divorce taught me, it's that people are going to do what they want to do and it's a waste of breath trying to talk them out of it. I'm no different. It applies as much to me as to anyone else.

* * *

I knew something bad was coming when Bill came downstairs and walked into my bedroom, shut the door and sat on the corner of my bed.

Bill. That's his name and so that's what I call him. I pretty much stopped calling my parents mom and dad after the divorce. I did it to hurt them. "You don't want to be a family anymore?" I said once. "Fine. You're Bill, and you're Karen, and I'm Cali, which is a stupid name and I hate it but I guess I'm stuck with it; and, by the way, it's now officially short for California and not Calico and if either of you tries to call me Calico again, I will set fire to the house and burn you alive in your sleep."

Bill took it all in stride, me using his actual name. Five years on, Karen still hated it. Even now, she wants to be mom again. Well, too bad.

Anyway, Bill came down and closed the door and took a seat. He'd never done that before. Just pushed aside my backpack and my phone and my history book and the pile of clothes that I rooted through every morning to get dressed and sat down. The bed sagged and groaned.

It was the closing of the door that tipped me off. He didn't need to close the door. He'd waited until Karen was at one of her stupid Dream Life meetings and Benji was at his best friend's house, obsessing over the latest release. Play Station or Xbox or whatever. So, Bill and I were totally alone in the house. He didn't need to close the door. But he did anyway.

"Cali," he said. His brow was deeply-furrowed and the rest of his face was scrunched up in a migraine, ice-pick-to-the-skull kind of expression, like he might be in actual physical pain. He grabbed my vintage AC/DC World Tour baseball hat and started tracing the letters with his thumb.

"It won't fit you, Dad," I said, collapsing down into my black beanbag. The air hissed out of it in a protracted wheeze of disappointment. In the movie version of that conversation, the soundtrack would be one of groaning metal bedsprings and a long beanbag wheeze of disappointment. "No one will believe you're an AC/DC fan anyway. I'd just stick with the Jethro Tull water bottle."

"I have something to tell you," he said to the hat, ignoring my attempt at humor.

"Divorce," I said.

He looked up. I was just being a wiseass, thinking that whatever he was there to tell me couldn't be all that bad. I thought maybe I could take the edge off things by casually tossing out a ridiculous scenario that we could laugh about before he told me whatever he was there to tell me.

I should have gone with cancer. Or a sex trafficking indictment.

Because when I saw his reaction, I could see that I happened to be right. I'm almost never right, about anything. Divorce. My parents were divorcing.

Sure, I'd feared it. What kid could not hear even a little yelling through the walls, or a fist pounding the dresser, and not fear divorce? A kid hears a bump in the night and comes up with monster. Every time.

But then the sun always comes up the next morning and the whole thing seems ridiculous. Fearing is not believing.

I hid my shock, locking down the panic in my heart and the howl of pain that was trying to force its way up my windpipe. I took Bill's surprise and ran with it.

"I'm not stupid, Dad," I said calmly, like I'd been waiting for him, like he'd just figured out divorce was coming but I'd known it for months. "But you're stupid if you go through with this."

"You knew? How did... Did she say something?"

"All you do is fight. You think I don't live here? That last one... Jesus."

"Does Benji know?"

"The only thing Benji knows is how to kill zombies."

"Benji," Bill whispered to himself. He closed his eyes. "How am I going to tell Benji?"

"How about you just not fucking do it at all, Dad?" He looked up. I wasn't a big cusser back then. My calm had started to crack. I wanted to stay all chill and unmoved but what I wanted more than that was to shriek and break things. "How about you guys act like fucking grownup adults? How about go get some counseling or whatever?"

"I can't do it anymore, pumpkin," he said. "I just can't. I've tried. *We've* tried. We've tried. Both of us. I don't want to leave your mother out of the effort. But mostly it's just been me who has tried. Karen hasn't tried at all. I shouldn't say that. But it's true. She hasn't tried one bit and I can't... I can't..."

Something terrible happens when a thirteen-year-old girl sees her father cry. She instantly stops being a child. She stops being a daughter. She becomes a consoler. She can't help it. Her, like, primeval nurturing instinct or whatever surges forward and she's more like a mother or a lover than a child daughter.

I was out of that beanbag before I knew what was happening, holding Bill's head in my arms as he clutched me around the shoulders, running my fingers through his moppy black hair, holding his hand through the strap of my AC/DC cap, rocking with him on the edge of my bed. I reached for a mostly clean Megadeth t-shirt and wiped his nose.

He grabbed my shoulders and held me out at arms length, looking at me with wet, red eyes.

"Let me tell you something, Cali. You can't count on any future in this life. Okay? You can't assume happiness or fulfillment is coming. You could get hit by a truck tomorrow

afternoon. Tomorrow. Your best friend could betray you.
You can go bankrupt or a tornado could suck up your
house, maybe the only house on the block, but it's your
house and up it goes. And then what do you have? Nothing.
Don't pin your dreams to the future. That's bullshit. The
dream is now. This is the dream. Okay? You have to live for
now. Understand? Be happy now. Be fulfilled now. Don't
hang around in a bad situation, hoping. There is no future.
There is only now. Karen doesn't understand that. Dream
Life has her eyes all glazed over. It's a cult. If there's one
thing cults are good at, its driving out the dissenters. So I'm
not waiting around anymore. I can't."

It was all Karen's fault. That's what I believed until
about two weeks after Bill moved out of the house. I raged
at her from behind a wall of silence, trying to burn holes in
her stupid divorce-causing face with my eyes. It was her
fault for not caring about Bill's feelings and for neglecting
the marriage and for pretending that Bill did not have
needs as a man. Yes, he actually said that to his thirteen-
year-old daughter and no, I did not really have any idea
what he was talking about when he said it except that it
sounded horrible and I hated Karen for it and my burning
hot eyes let her know it. How dare she ignore his needs as a
man just so she could spend most of her evenings at her
stupid Dream Life cult meetings and come home at ten
o'clock too tired to pay him any attention.

How. Dare. She.

After he had been gone a couple of weeks, Karen forced
a confrontation down in our laundry room that brought me
from coldly silent to shrieking and flailing in a matter of
seconds. Benji was up in his room, playing Zombie World
with his headphones on so we both just kind of laid into
each other at full volume until we were both sobbing.

I did not have the same instinct to comfort my mother
like I had my father, maybe because I was too much of a

wreck and full of anger. Or maybe the nurturing-comfort gene or whatever mostly works cross-gender. Like maybe Benji would have been more likely in that moment to instantly stop being a son and try to be Karen's comforting husband or lover.

I kind of felt sorry for her, not only because her husband had left her but because I had no desire to wrap her in my arms and stroke her hair and pull her head to my chest and whisper soothing things in her ear. I could see she was hurting. It seemed kind of unfair.

"His needs as a man?" Karen asked. We were both sitting on the floor by then. She had the washer. I had the dryer. To this day, the smell of lavender fabric softener triggers this memory. "He actually said that?"

All I had the energy to do was shrug and wipe my nose on my sleeve.

"Well, then, I hope he told you about satisfying those needs at the office."

"What?"

At the time, Bill worked as a budget analyst for the city of St. Louis. At thirteen, I did not have much of an idea of how, exactly, he made his living but I was pretty sure that satisfying his needs as a man was not part of it.

"Liar," I said, trying to hang onto my rage. I tore a fabric softener sheet into little squares and never looked at her.

"Okay. Fine. You believe whatever you want to believe, Cali. But let me tell you this: Bill is going nowhere good. Okay? I'm climbing. I'm always looking up for the next level. And I'm taking you and Benji up with me. Dream Life teaches you that you're either aspiring to get to the next level in life or you're falling. There is no being in the moment, or living in the now, or any of that Zen bullshit.

Okay? You're either climbing or falling. Bill is falling. The three of us?" Karen pointed to herself as though there were three of her. "Me and you and Benji? We're climbing."

"Whatever," I huffed with as much disgust as I could muster.

"You can hate me for it now if you want. I can't control that. But we will have money. And we will have leisure. We will travel the world in style. And you will one day have a doctorate and a professional practice and two beautiful children. And you will have a husband that supports you and that doesn't fuck his office assistant and that doesn't piss all over your efforts to better yourself and improve your life. And you will have all that because right now, while your dad is tending to his... his needs as a man, I have always insisted that we keep climbing for the next level."

That fight with Karen evened things out a little. I kind of hated them both about the same after that, and I kind of felt sorry for them both the same too. I decided that they were both crappy parents and that it was up to me to see Benji through the storm. I decided I was the best parent option in his life. I tried to step up and be the one to explain things and provide emotional support.

But if Benji was unsettled by the turmoil, he did not really show it. He found my sudden interest in his eleven-year-old world annoying. Every time I sat down to talk to him, it required that he pause his massacre of undead hordes and remove his headphones.

"It's not like they don't love us or anything," I said, not believing a single word. "They just want to be happy. That doesn't make them bad people. You do understand that, right?"

Benji shrugged. His eyes slid slowly sideways away from me to the screen and the closeup image of a gangrenous face, suspended in the process of exploding into wet, green, high-definition chunks.

"They only want what's best for us," I lied. "They'd, like, die for us, Benji."

"Okay."

Bill's sudden absence from our daily routine threw Karen into her predictable grim-faced crisis mode. She gets like Linda Hamilton's character in *The Terminator* movies, slinging around automatic weapons and survival gear, barking out commands like a drill sergeant as she tries to harden her kid to the reality of being hunted by a cyborg or whatever. Karen couldn't do a pushup if her life depended on it, and cigarette smoke makes her sick but you can bet that otherwise all that would be part of her crisis meltdown.

The other thing she does in crisis mode is dive deeper into Dream Life. Like when the hospital decided not to promote her from a Human Resources Assistant to a Human Resources Generalist. I never had any idea what that means. I still don't. Bill was just as clueless.

"Honey, you're good at what you do. There'll be another opportunity. The difference in pay is almost nothing anyway."

Karen had looked at him, stunned. She let the water run full blast in the kitchen sink behind her.

"You don't get it, do you? You don't even... It's the next step, Bill. It's the next level. Assistant, then Generalist, then Benefits Specialist, then Assistant Deputy HR Director, then Deputy HR Director, and then Director. How many times do I have to say it? Promises were made to me. I'm entitled to this. I'm getting a fucking lawyer and I'm going to fucking sue their fucking corporate health care asses."

She never did call a lawyer. What she did was throw herself deeper into Dream Life, attending meetings every single night after work for two months. Bill is worthless in the kitchen, so he took Benji and me through a sixty-day pizza-burrito-hoagie rotation that ruined my skin and got me addicted to Dr Pepper.

The crisis passed like all the others. Karen wore herself out on stress and lack of sleep, got sick, and then found a new perspective. She showered us all with the relentlessly optimistic blather she gets from her Dream Life handlers: things like you only get out of life what you put into it, and if you can dream it, you can be it, and share the dream to live the dream. Enough of that nonsense and we all started to appreciate how much we preferred the grimly determined, crisis-Karen to the relentlessly positive, cult-Karen.

Then, a year later, Bill sat on the corner of my bed and said the D-word and Karen went apeshit all over again. It took her three months to level off that time. I was deputized to look after Benji while she did "everything else."

She installed shelving in the right half of the garage, where Bill's 1976 black and red Ford Torino used to be. She stocked the shelves with enough of the Dream Life AAAA product line to supply the entire population of St. Charles.

The AAAA stood for Awakening ("one must awaken from one's self-defeating and stifling reality into the dream of possibility"), Ascension ("one must work diligently to climb from the lower levels of dream consciousness up to the pinnacle of self-perfection"), Actualization ("one must eliminate duality in one's life and actualize one's consciousness in the Dream Life one chooses to live") and Acceptance ("upon reaching ever-higher levels of dream consciousness, one must be willing to accept each of the three F's as an entitlement: fortune, freedom, and fabulosity").

A separate volume of Dream Life literature was devoted to explaining each of the four A's and each of the three F's. A much thicker volume explained the whole concept of Levels, and how to earn sponsorship credits from Up-Line Guides, and how to recruit Down-Line Dreamers. It all came with a lot of Dream Lifer gibberish: terms like hiving, and persuasion coding, and resister speak, and sub-pitching, and dream truing, and wealth visualization. I could go on.

Karen filled the garage with boxes of Dream Life booklets. She had way more Dream Life booklets than she had friends. The garage became the Dream Workshop. Not even Karen could sell the idea of calling our filthy, junk-packed garage the Dream Library. But she tried.

"I'm a Dream Recruiter, baby," she said once in her chipper, can-do voice when Benji asked her why his bike was barricaded behind a wall of boxes and cheap shelving. "Your mama is really getting the word out this time."

"Did you buy all those booklets?" I asked.

"At a Level 5 discount," she said, nodding.

"So now you can sell them for like a profit or whatever?"

"No, honey." She laughed a little as she hoisted a box up to start another row. The tower slanted a little with the additional weight. Benji yanked at his front tire. "I give them away to educate people about Dream Life."

"For free? But don't you just, like, lose money?"

"With a Dream Life quadruple-A product line?" She laughed and shook her head. "Not in the long run. These books are an investment. You only get out of life what you put into it. You have to share the dream to live the dream."

"Who are you sharing it with, exactly?"

372

"Anyone I can. Friends. Neighbors. New people I meet."

"That's not very many people," I said.

Karen repositioned the box and looked at me, hands on her hips.

"Cali, you need to broaden your perspective. Do you have any idea how many people come through that hospital in a day? In a month? Employees? Patients? Families? Vendors? I have access to a mammoth UDB. Absolutely mammoth."

"What's a UDB? Is that like a UTI?"

"No. UDB is my Unexplored Dreamer Base." She jabbed her arm into a box and handed me a booklet. "Page 55."

I was afraid she was planning to recruit me and Benji to start going door to door, waiting in line behind the Adventists or whatever. It never came to that. Most of the boxes stayed sealed, waiting for a demand that never seemed to come.

There were other boxes too. A lot of other boxes, smaller and flatter and filled with what the Dream Lifers called Dream Actualization Fuel or the DAF stock or the Dream Stock for short: lipstick, eyeshadow, perfume, shaving gel, nail polish, hair dyes, lash enhancers, moisturizers and skin serums, hair removal waxes and self-tanners. I could go on.

All these products and booklets were stamped with the Dream Life logo. I will see that logo in my sleep for the rest of my life. Capital D and capital L floating on a cloud above a palm tree on a sandy island. The palm tree bends out over the water. At the base of the tree is an open pirate's treasure chest, spilling gold coins. Doubloons or whatever. Like what good will gold coins do for you on a tiny, one-tree island? Or lash enhancers, for that matter.

If Karen could have personalized her license plate with that logo, she would have. She had to settle for DREAM, except it turned out that that actual spelling was already taken so she ended up with DREME, which she thought was maybe close enough.

"It's actually more effective," she said to me from the end of the driveway as she contemplated the rear of her almost-turquoise Hyundai compact SUV. "Because you read it and then you have to think about it and then read it again. And then it's like, oh, I get it! Dream! That's what life is all about, Cali. Climbing to a higher level of understanding. Well," she added importantly, "actualized understanding."

I looked at the license plate. DREME. I thought it might have been better to swap out the E's for A's but I kept my mouth shut.

I've never been much of a makeup person. Karen hates that about me. Up until the day I finally left Weldon Spring like a bat out of hell, she was always trying to slather me with Dream Stock.

"You could be so gorgeous, Cali. You could be a knockout. You just need to try a little harder. Get away from the rock band thing. Frill it up a little. You know? Here, let me show you what just a little Dream Blush will do for you."

My only friend back then was Stacey Moore. I had a couple of others but you get what I'm saying. Stacey was the only one I really talked to. She wasn't like beautiful or anything. She couldn't hold a candle to Taylor Boss. None of us could. But Stacey had okay lips, even though her mouth was too small for her teeth. She had good cheekbones and super-coarse black hair and full boobs with flashlight areolae. So she could get serious about making herself up when she wanted to.

Stacey came over sometimes to work on biology homework and we'd stay up in my room, getting nothing done except listening to deep cuts from the Ramones and Cheap Trick and The Clash and other bands that Karen hated. My room, my music.

Once when Stacey was over, Karen took advantage of the opportunity to make a pitch for a Dream Life makeover. It took forty minutes out of the evening. I left them sitting next to each other on the living room couch and went up to Benji's room where he was hunting zombies in an online gamer thing. The zombies were taking over all these landmarks around the world, like the Louvre and the Great Pyramid and Mount Rushmore.

I sat on his bed and watched as the gun on the screen endlessly redirected and then muzzle flashes lit up the darkened corners of the Lincoln Memorial.

"What's this one?" I asked.

"Apocalypse Dream." He didn't turn around.

"How do they kill you?"

He never answered.

The rules seemed simple enough. Kill all the zombies and advance to a new level. The new level was always harder. The scenery changed and the zombies came faster and in greater numbers.

The game itself bored me. Why would anyone want to get to the next level where everything was worse? I felt bad for whoever was responsible for mopping the green guts from Abe's face. I even felt kind of bad for what were basically just zombie tourists. They weren't actually hurting anyone. Looking disgusting and wanting to climb on the Eiffel Tower were not capital offenses.

And I didn't like how the game consumed Benji. He lost his cuteness when he played those games. His face went slack and he stopped blinking. Sometimes his mouth hung open. I could have set his bed on fire and he'd never have noticed.

But there was something about that gun.

It looked so real I could almost feel the weight of it in my hands. And the little feeling in my chest when that muzzle flash went off. Not that I have ever known one end of a gun from the other. But I kind of understood the appeal.

When I went back downstairs, Stacey was still perched on the edge of the couch. She looked like a vintage, discount-store mannequin. Her eyes had become giant blue oysters and her black hair seemed to foam out from the sides of her head. The Dream Life Lips Enhancer System had stained her teeth and made her mouth clownish. She looked up at me and smiled. It was terrifying.

"Beautiful," Karen gushed. She looked at me, standing over them. "See what a little touch here and there can do, Cali?"

I didn't answer. I couldn't.

"You know, girls, Dream Life is about more than looking fabulous. Dream Life is about being fabulous. It's about being the person you want to be and having everything in life that should be yours. I could sponsor you, Stacey, if you're interested."

"Me?" Stacey looked up, surprised.

"Sure!" Karen beamed. "Have a little confidence. Why not you?"

Why not her? Why not me? Karen had never offered to serve as my Dream Sponsor. Sure, she wanted me to look better, just like she wanted me to get a doctorate. Like that was ever going to happen. I asked her about college once when she was driving Benji and me around in the new Hyundai DREME machine, fresh off the lot.

"How are we paying for it?"

"They don't let you drive it off the lot without paying for it, hon."

"Not the car. College."

"I'm saving," she said.

"How much? Like, how much do you have saved so far?"

"I'd have more if your father paid what he's supposed to pay."

"How much, Karen?"

"Fifteen thousand. More or less. Bossy pants."

"Fifteen? That's not enough."

"Of course it's not enough. That's why it's invested. Silly."

"Invested."

"It will be, yes. Dream Life has its College Dreamer Plan. Investment of ten thousand or more gets you an extra one percent on Down-Liner sales above the minimum. I'm going to turn that fifteen thousand into one-hundred-and-fifty thousand. Wait and see, kiddo. God, I love these wipers. Look at that. So clear."

"And if there's not enough? By the time I graduate, I mean?"

"Not enough? First, you need a more positive attitude, Cali. Second, if you're so worried, I suggest you start working for a full scholarship."

I'll be lucky to get into some second-rate vocational school, learning to be a candy striper or whatever, not because I'm not smart, but because I'm not brilliant enough for a scholarship and because none of Karen's Dream Life money has ever gone into any kind of college fund. None of it.

But Karen didn't care about the facts. "If you can dream it, Cali, you can be it." I was still supposed to get that doctorate and have those two kids and buy that very large house right up the street from her own very large house she had not yet purchased on Dream Life Island and marry that man who needs me more than I need him.

All that. But she never seemed to consider me, like, part of her Dreamer Base or whatever. Not that I would ever want to be.

Karen sized up Stacey sitting on the edge of the couch and shifted into full Dream Pitch mode.

"The early levels are tough. I won't lie. They take commitment. You have to devote the time and you have to really work on seeding your dream. Visualizing each of those three F's: fortune, freedom and fabulosity. But the work really pays off. By Level 4, you have enough Down-Liners beneath you that you really start to take in some good money."

Stacey looked up at me. I rolled my eyes.

"So, like... what would I have to do to start?" she asked.

"Well, the initial Dream Seeding is two thousand dollars. That's not something I keep. That gets passed on to my Up-Liners. When I get to Level 6, I start getting a Dream Seeding Percentage. A DSP." Karen scrunched up her face as if she was Dream Pitching to a two-month-old infant in clown paint. "Just like you will when you get to Level 6. But you would start getting a percentage of product sales almost immediately."

"No way I can come up with two thousand dollars," said Stacey, standing.

"Maybe your parents can help you," Karen said, trying her best to sound indifferent. "Heck, maybe they'd like to join up and you could all do it as a family. Doesn't your father work in advertising?"

Stacey never became an official Dream Lifer. She did make a lot of unescorted trips out to the garage, the Dream Workshop, every time she came over to the house. I knew what she was doing. I didn't care.

At least, I didn't care until she started wearing the stuff at school. It wasn't that she looked horrible or anything. She actually found a way to tame it all down so she didn't look like she had when sitting on our couch. But about that time other things started to change too. She started dressing up and wearing perfume. Every so often she'd wear heels and anklets and she started spending more time with two other girls that she used to hate because they were all stuck up and bitchy but then, like suddenly, she decided they were not so bad.

On Saturday afternoons Stacey and I usually went to the Riverside Mall to just shop and eat and hangout or whatever. She had a car, but not me. Before Bill left and took his Torino with him, I always imagined getting my license and borrowing his car. I imagined that I'd be the one driving to the mall, or even driving the freeway out of St. Charles to Springfield or Kansas City, just to feel the world moving beneath me. Just to pretend that there was something more to my life.

But then Bill took a seat on the corner of my bed and out came the D-word and poof, there went the dream of borrowing his car. Even once I got my license, Karen never considered lending me her car unless she really needed me to run an errand. Whenever I mentioned wanting to borrow her butt-ugly Hyundai DREME machine for more than ten minutes, she'd offer to give me a lift or suggested I call Stacey. Like it was all about needing transportation and not about freedom.

"Freedom, Karen," I shouted at her. "It's one of your stupid three F's."

"That's a whole different level, hon," she said, flipping a pancake. She was determined not to understand.

I usually ended up calling Bill, hoping to exploit his guilt and his interest in being the better parent in the eyes of his children. He always made encouraging sounds and then took everything back because some strange quirk of timing made the idea impossible.

"So, Calico Kid wants to borrow the horse, is that it?"

"Don't call me that. But, yes. Just for a few hours. I promise I'll be careful."

"Sounds like a great idea to me."

"Awesome."

"Except..."

You can fill in the blank on your own. Either he needed the car for his own stupid life, or it was in the shop, or he'd already promised it to one of his own loser friends. It was always something. I'd made the mistake of reporting back to Karen. She'd managed to tap a fresh vein of anger and shook her head in disgust. She tossed a syrupy plate into the sink and gripped the kitchen counter with both hands.

"Your father."

Right.

380

The point is, Stacey always drove. She'd pick me up and we'd hang out at the mall and she'd drop me off at home. After the Dream Life makeover, she started acting and dressing differently and then she started not being available to do the Saturday-at-the-mall thing. I'd be stuck at home with Karen and Benji while Stacey would be all dolled up, cruising the mall with her other friends. I just kind of accepted that we were living different lives. It was like there was some chemical in the Dream Life makeover that convinced her she needed to start climbing up to a higher level.

It got to a point where we mostly saw each other at school and almost never on the weekend. She'd come over every so often to replenish her supply from the Dream Life workshop. She'd stay for an hour and then always had to get home for one reason or another.

Like I cared. Like I gave a shit.

Once I walked with her out to her car parked at the curb. She drove a used Mazda that her dad had bought her for her seventeenth birthday. The very next day, Stacey ran a red light and got herself t-boned by some kid in a Kia. The accident left a dent the size of a twenty-pound turkey. She complained to her dad that the passenger door no longer locked. She asked him if he would pay for the bodyshop work. He decided to make it a life lesson that she needed to learn for herself.

Stacey went on for days about how unfair life was. I tried to tell her that at least she has a car that works and that she doesn't have to beg her parents whenever she wanted to go someplace. She didn't have to ride the stupid bus to school.

"Or to the mall," I added. She accused me of not understanding her side of things. She didn't talk to me for two days after that.

I stood on the curb, tracing the dent with my finger as Stacey opened the driver's door. I asked if she wanted to hang out on Saturday and she gave me a bullshit excuse about helping her parents clean the garage.

"So then if I go to the mall there's, like, zero chance I'll see you there with Megan and Kylie."

She could tell I was mad. She told me to get in. I did.

"You have to promise not to tell anyone," she whispered. "And I mean not anyone, Cali. Not a fucking soul."

"What is it, already?" I asked, like I was only half-interested. She was leaning toward me in the front seat, her face close enough for me to kiss her.

Stop. It's not that.

I'm just saying it was the most genuine attention she'd given me in weeks.

"I'm not really cleaning our garage on Saturday," she said. "And I haven't been going to the mall."

You can guess the rest. The act of revealing her secret made her face glow. When she was done, she leaned back against the door and absorbed my reaction, which was, like, total disbelief. She reached across my lap and opened the glove compartment. She rummaged around and pulled out a cigarette and a blue lighter.

"And you're smoking now? Jesus, Stacey. Since when?"

"Since every so often," she said to a little serpent's tongue of fire. "Marcus thinks it's hot."

"Marcus? You call him Marcus?"

"Well, I don't fucking call him Mr. McKenzie."

"In the science room? Like, you mean..."

"The door locks. And there's totally no one there on Saturdays. We did it in his car a couple of times but it's too cramped and it's surprisingly hard to find a safe place to park."

"Stacey," I started, not really knowing where the sentence was going. "This is like a super bad idea. I mean he's, like, married and he's a teacher and you're a student and..."

"I knew that'd be your reaction," she said coolly, blowing smoke out the window. "One, he hates his bitch of a wife. Two, we're, like, so careful you wouldn't even believe it. Three, it feels so..." She broke off and closed her eyes and took another long drag, holding the smoke like she was savoring the experience, until she began to cough violently. "It feels so fucking good, Cali. I mean, oh my god is all I can say. He totally fills me."

"Eww." I made a face. "He's like a hundred."

"He's forty-one."

"Whatever, Stace. He's old."

"Hey, fuck you, Cali." Her face was instantly red. Her teeth bulged against the inside of her mouth like they wanted to bite me. "I should never have told you. And if you say anything, and I mean fucking anything, I will fucking kill you. Hear me, Cali?"

We stared at each other in silence. The smoke made me feel sick and lightheaded. All I could think about was getting out of that car.

"Marcus tells me all the time that when he dreams, he dreams of me. Me. Got that? And I'm starting to dream about him too. And you're just fucking jealous. You don't have anyone dreaming of you. You don't know what it's like to be in someone's dream. The only dream you have is of your mom's little pink vibrator. I hope you two'll be very happy."

We did not talk again for at least six weeks, not until two days after Taylor Boss' funeral. I'd see Stacey in the hallways, and she'd see me seeing her, but we'd both just keep walking. Like I even cared.

The news about Taylor Boss had ripped through the school like a tornado. Girls were openly sobbing in the hallways. Guys were unnaturally quiet, drifting from class to class with wide-eyed, somber expressions and, for once, uninterested in shouting something stupid in the halls so everyone could hear. Even the teachers were shaken and weepy.

Taylor Boss was one of those girls that everybody knew, even those who'd never met her. It was like when Princess Diana died; it kind of affected everybody, even people who hated her. Maybe no one hated Princess Diana; I don't really know. Before my time. But I think some people hated Taylor Boss. I was one of them.

Not that I had any reason to hate her. I didn't even really know her. I think Taylor was in such a different league that it felt better to dismiss her as someone not worth thinking about. And if you just couldn't help thinking about Taylor Boss – like when she passed you in the hall looking perfect and smelling perfect and acting perfect – then it was easier to roll your eyes and dismiss her as someone ridiculous. Someone that you didn't care about. But then it'd be impossible not to care because she'd be right there in front of you, being who she was and looking and acting the way she did and everyone all gaga over her, even the teachers and administrators who all, like, wanted to be her friend, and it would take hate, or something like it, to force yourself not to care.

384

Hating is like the last defense. It's the same reason we love to hate celebrities.

There's no denying that Taylor was beautiful. Soft, blond hair to the shoulders, clear blue eyes, the smile, the teeth, the perfectly proportioned face, the flawless skin, the womanly lips, the boobs, the legs. She had the whole package. It might have been easy to dismiss her as a slut or whatever except that she never really acted that way. She dressed expensively, and conservatively. Taylor Boss would never have been caught dead wearing anything out of my closet. I guess that's a weird thing to say, since she was caught dead.

I heard she wasn't wearing anything.

My point is that with everything Taylor could have had in the sex kitten department, she never seemed to use any of it. Her vibe was all, like, wholesome and innocent and goodhearted and so the biggest dig against her was that she was putting on a big act and that behind the scenes, she was, like, this depraved sex monkey who blew the entire football team after practice. Not that anyone ever believed those rumors but some people wanted to. I did.

But it was more than just her attractiveness, or that she came from money, which she did. Taylor was into everything and seemed to be good at all of it. Soccer. Acting. Choir. Cheerleading. Homecoming Queen, like, of course. She spoke fluent French. All her classes were Advanced Placement and she was a lock for some Ivy League college. Yale or whatever.

Taylor organized a community charity drive for the wife of our basketball coach. Coach Pete had burst into tears one afternoon after a pep rally. Word got around that his wife had just been diagnosed with cancer. Taylor Boss got busy and raised almost twenty thousand dollars. The local news came by the school one day and interviewed her

385

in the teachers' lounge. Some of the teachers and Coach Pete and Principal Warren were also interviewed. There was a lot of buzz about the interview the day before it aired. I watched it on the TV in our kitchen.

Not that I wanted to watch it. I even thought of changing the channel. I wanted to not care. I couldn't help it.

Karen was sitting at the kitchen table doing her Dream Tithing exercise. She counts out cash from all her sales the prior month, arranging it in tidy hundred-dollar stacks. You're supposed to hold each dollar with two hands and visualize what that dollar will eventually become – a mansion or a private jet or whatever – before placing it in a stack. You have to do the stacking three times. It was the end of the month so there had to be at least three thousand dollars on the table. It took forever. Benji and I were starving.

The news people had saved the charity-drive story for last, something nice to end things after the weather. My teachers talked about Taylor like she was some kind of supernatural force of goodness. Our history teacher, Mrs. Aiken, got all weepy. And they were all so proud. Like, not only was Taylor an angel on earth but that they were somehow responsible for making her and sharing her with the world. Karen looked up, a small stack of bills in each hand, just in time to see Taylor's school photo fill the screen.

"Now that kid is Dream Life material," she said, flapping one of the stacks of money at the TV. "She's going places. She's a natural."

Karen never said that I wasn't a natural. That I wasn't Dream Life material. That I wasn't going places without a whole lot of unnaturally hard work, like teaching an elephant to fly. She didn't have to. That was the thing about

Karen: It's what she didn't say that I always heard the loudest.

"Do you know that girl?" Karen asked.

I shrugged. "Everybody knows her. Especially the guys."

"And just what does that mean?"

"She's got a reputation." I didn't elaborate.

"A girl like that? Loose talk, I'll bet." Karen went back to gathering up the stacks of money. "If I were you, I'd hitch my wagon to her star. Get to know her. See if she'll be your friend. You can do much better than Stacey, honey. Stacey's a permanent Down-Liner if you ask me. You need to get up to the next level. Don't believe the idle gossip."

"I wonder if there was idle gossip about that woman in dad's office," I said. Then I walked out of the kitchen.

Taylor Boss did not have a mom. According to the news, her mom died of cancer when she was only ten. That was the reason she put so much energy into a charity drive for Coach Pete.

Taylor's father is a dentist. He's not like the picture of a dentist that you have in your head. Forget about your dentist. Dr. Boss is tall and broad-shouldered with thick, curly dark hair and his daughter's dreamy blue eyes. He used to be a football hero when he was at Penn State. Quarterback or whatever. Now he keeps just about everybody at Howell High cavity-free.

Dr. Boss. I don't know his first name. I don't think anybody knows. Who needs a first name when you can go by Dr. Boss? In our school, he was as popular as his daughter. Like he was some kind of honorary cool student. He was a big booster for our football team and hosted parties at his house, a giant three-story, glass-and-concrete monstrosity up on the hill. Everybody who was anybody went to those parties. I never went, of course.

But I heard a lot about them. Always lots of beer. "Dr. Boss has the best beer," the guys would say. And Dr. Boss has a bad ass stereo. And Dr. Boss played highlights of his Penn State games in his awesome home theater. And, "oh my god, Dr. Boss told the filthiest joke." And "Dr. Boss has the best pot." And, "we were so wasted that Dr. Boss let us crash in his living room and then he made everybody breakfast."

All the guys wanted to be Dr. Boss. All the girls wanted to make little baby Dr. Bosses. I mean, not really, but they talked like it. Even Stacey.

"I'm sitting in that dentist chair," she said once, "and he's got it, like, reclined all the way back and he's super close to my face and my mouth is open and his fingers are in there and all I want to do is suck on them and rip my blouse off and pull him to me and do it right there in front of his assistant. She totally wants him too; you can tell. That whore. Oh my god, he is so freaking handsome."

And he is handsome. Before I ditched Weldon Spring forever, Dr. Boss was my dentist too. But Stacey has decent teeth, a lot of them, and she can afford to fantasize about sex when she's in the chair. My trips to Dr. Boss were always about cavities and pain and bad news. Getting turned on was never really in the cards.

If you're suspecting that there was a darker side to Dr. Boss, then give yourself a gold star because you'd be right about that. If Taylor had a made-up reputation, then her dad had, like, an actual reputation. A drinking problem. A woman problem. An office assistant problem. Maybe a high school girl problem.

You'd never know it to look at him. I never smelled
booze on him or anything. He never groped me or
whatever. But all his hygienists and his receptionist are,
like, right out of a magazine and they all act like he's a god.
"Oh, Dr. Boss, you are so funny." And "Oh, you can't get up
just yet; I'll need to go see if Dr. Boss wants to come take a
look." And even, "Isn't Dr. Boss just the best?"

He treats all of them like daughters: too familiar and
indifferent at the same time. They'll do anything to be
noticed.

And then there was the little hesitation that people
sometimes had when they were talking about the latest big
party at Dr. Boss' place. Like it took some effort to steer
their words around ugly potholes in the story.

One of the stories that got around was the time when
Dr. Boss plowed his truck through the iron fence that
surrounds the Weldon Spring Cemetery where Taylor's
mom is buried. He called two guys on our football team in
the middle of the night and asked them to jump in their cars
and help pull him out before the cops got there. They found
him stinking drunk with one of his guns on the front seat.

Yeah. Guns again.

Dr. Boss has tons of them. He's a big hunter. He was
always taking guys in my school out hunting. Ducks and
deer and whatever. Guys at school were always gushing
about Dr. Boss' gun room. He collects them.

I kind of get collecting things. I collect music. I have
every album Aerosmith ever cut. Same with The Beatles
and early Eric Clapton, from The Yardbirds to the Blues
Breakers to Cream to Blind Faith. And all the metal that
came out of the seventies and eighties. I could go on
forever.

But why anyone would want to collect guns is beyond my understanding. I don't know anything about guns. So, I have no idea what kind of gun was on the seat of Dr. Boss' truck the night he crashed into the cemetery. Except that it was a pistol.

And I don't even know if any of that is true. I wasn't there and most of the gossip I heard in Howell High was bullshit.

But it sounded true.

It seemed like the whole city turned out for Taylor's funeral. It was held at the big Episcopal church on Medford Street and there was barely any room for standing. When I heard how many people were there, I was glad I didn't go.

I almost did go. Everybody else was going, whether they were actually friends with Taylor or not. There was a lot of pressure to show up. Stacey wouldn't stop insisting. It was like any of Dr. Boss' big parties. Everybody who was anybody was going. I wasn't anybody.

It made me wonder who'd show up at my funeral if I suddenly turned up dead. My family probably would. Bill would show up in his stubble, looking unemployed and smelling like pot. Karen would find some time between Dream Life meetings. They'd have to bribe Benji away from killing things online. But they'd all show and maybe even Stacey, if she wasn't busy with her other friends or screwing Mr. McKenzie in the science lab.

I'll need to make sure my funeral is not on a Saturday.

I remember thinking that Damien Alvarez might go to my funeral. At first, I thought he'd probably go and then I hoped he would choose not to go. I wouldn't want him having to sit in an empty church with Bill, Karen, Benji,

Stacey and the preacher or priest or whatever, looking at my coffin and my school picture up on a brass easel.

The photo would be of me in a shirt I hate, pretending to smile and having no idea at the time that I was posing for my funeral picture. They should have to tell you that before they take your official picture. They should give you a copy and ask if that is really the photo you want on the big brass easel looming over your coffin. I'd have worn my Judas Priest shirt and a different expression on my face, gotten rid of that stupid half-smile. I don't want to look phony at my own funeral.

Karen would probably want to know who Damien was. She'd turn and ask Stacey and Stacey would whisper that Damien was the school security guard who was fired for murdering Taylor Boss.

Not that he did murder Taylor. If Damien had had anything to do with Taylor Boss, he'd have been in jail, not just fired. But common sense is no match for gossip.

Stacey would probably repeat that gossip to Karen and then Karen would turn around and look at Damien again as the preacher or minister or whatever is struggling to talk about what a great person I was and how much I'll be missed and probably worrying that he'll go to hell for lying in church. I wouldn't want Damien to have to experience Karen's face, turning around every ten minutes to look at him sitting alone in the back of the church.

I know that's where Damien would sit – in the back – because that's exactly where I'd sit if I went to a funeral.

Not that I ever would go to a funeral. I'd probably stay home or go for a walk so I could really think about the person and really feel bad that they were gone. I wouldn't want other people turning and looking at me. I think that's what Damien would do if I ever turned up dead and had a funeral. He'd probably walk to the Ninety-Nine Cent Store on Brighten Avenue and feel bad that I was dead.

Mr. Goodnight might also go to my funeral, now that I really think about it. Not because he loved me or anything. But I think he'd probably care that I died. He'd probably be sorry he had not been able to stop me from dying. He'd probably worry about what other people thought about me suddenly being dead.

I'd love to see the look on Karen's face if that happened. She'd wonder what such a good-looking man was doing at my funeral. For a split second, she might wonder if Mr. Goodnight and I had been lovers. She'd be jealous that maybe I'd found true love or whatever and that I'd secretly been deliriously happy without ever having to climb Dream Life levels or get accepted into a good school or be on track to get a doctorate. She'd wonder how I'd skipped all the hard work and went straight to the handsome man part, even though I don't believe in marriage and don't ever want any kids. For a split second, Karen would forget that I was dead in my casket beneath my phony school photo and she would be impressed and envious.

So then she'd turn and ask Stacey and Stacey would whisper that Mr. Goodnight is a school counselor and that he talked to a lot of people in the weeks after Taylor's body was found. Karen would look back at him again and would see that he was sitting with his wife or girlfriend or whatever and then she would feel better that Mr. Goodnight and I were probably not lovers after all.

But Stacey would probably keep thinking about that. She'd be looking at my photo over my coffin but in her mind she'd have an image of Mr. Goodnight in her head and she'd start to wonder if I'd been secretly busy doing it with Mr. Goodnight while she was wasting her time underneath Marcus McKenzie on top of a science lab table. Mr.

McKenzie is not even a little bit handsome compared to Mr. Goodnight.

Mr. Goodnight always told me I could call him Alex if I wanted to but I always called him Mr. Goodnight. The one time I called him Alex, I started to blush. I hate it when I blush.

Two days after the big funeral, Stacey honked at me as I was waiting outside the school for my bus. There was a glare on the windshield that made it look like just another patch of gray Missouri sky, so I couldn't see inside the car. She had to get out and wave me over, flailing one of her arms. She seemed angry. I didn't really want to go over to her. I did anyway.

"He's a pig," she said when I climbed in and closed the door. Then she nearly screamed it, banging the steering wheel with her fist. "He's a fucking pig!"

I could see she was a mess. Her eyes were red and her cheeks had long drippy stains of Dream Life mascara. A little bubble of snot popped in and out of one nostril as she breathed.

"Who?" I asked. I knew who.

Stacey sped out of the school parking lot, screeching tires. She didn't say anything until we were sitting in the Dairy Queen parking lot. I watched Stacey staring into space, breathing in and out.

"What'd he do?" I asked finally. That popped the cork.

"He's ditching me like some... some whore! His stupid wife is pregnant because he's been fucking her while he's been fucking me and now he's decided," she made air quotes and squished up her face like she was eating a lemon, "we're not right for each other. He's all, it's

393

inappropriate, Stacey, and it's illegal, Stacey, and I could lose my job, Stacey, and I have to think about my family, Stacey. And I kind of lost my shit but then I reminded him that he dreams about me and that I dream about him and then he's all, they're just dreams, Stacey. They're not real. Who says that? Who says that your dreams aren't fucking real? Well, then fucking Marcus McKenzie isn't real. Marcus McKenzie must fucking die!" She broke into sobs. "I hate him. I hate him. I fucking hate him! He needs to fucking die."

There was so much I wanted to say. All of it would have only made her angrier. So I didn't say anything for awhile. I just watched her cry.

A guy on his cellphone was out on the sidewalk and kept looking in our direction and looking away again as he talked. He had no idea of the drama unfolding behind the quiet gray sky of Stacey's windshield.

"I'm sorry he hurt you," I said eventually, placing my hand on her arm and squeezing. It was like squeezing a wet sponge. She cried harder than ever.

She calmed down after awhile, although it seemed that was more because she was exhausted than because she'd found some kind of new perspective or whatever.

"I have to pee," she declared, sniffing. "Want anything?"

"No," I said. She wiped her face on her sleeve and opened the door.

"You're my only friend."

She'd said it without looking, not like she was grateful that I was her friend but more like she was angry that she didn't have any others, which I knew wasn't exactly true. I think I was just the only friend she'd told about doing it, and then not doing it, with Mr. McKenzie. She'd saved her other friends for happier things.

Stacey slammed the door and stomped off across the parking lot. I watched her disappear into the Dairy Queen. I opened the glove compartment, looking for her pack of cigarettes. I thought it might make her smile if she came back and I was smoking, like maybe that would mean we really were friends again. Like maybe I wasn't just the friend that takes out your garbage but a friend you had fun with. A friend you got lung cancer with.

If the cigarettes were there in the glove compartment, I couldn't see them. All I could see was the gun, smooth and flat and black, tucked beneath some papers. It looked heavy; like if I tried to pick it up, I wouldn't even be able to lift it.

I couldn't stop staring at it. I felt like it was looking back at me.

I closed the compartment door. The man on the cellphone was looking right at me. Or seemed to be. He looked away. I could feel my heart in my chest, trying to get out.

When Stacey came back, I pretended I hadn't seen anything. I didn't know what to think. I didn't know what it meant that she had a gun.

"So what're you going to do?" I asked as casually as I could.

Stacey pulled a cigarette out of her purse and lit it. She sucked on it like it was a straw and cracked the window and then blew a long, straight plume through the crack.

"The less you know, the better," she said. Then she drove me home.

I spent a lot of that afternoon and evening kind of panicked and confused. I wondered if I should call the police but then when I tried to imagine Stacey actually shooting Mr. McKenzie, it just seemed so ridiculous that I couldn't dial the phone.

Was just seeing a gun, like a 911 emergency, if I had no idea what it meant? Was I really going to poke three numbers and get my best friend arrested? Accuse her of intended-attempted murder or whatever? Maybe she was planning on just, like, wounding him. Didn't someone like Mr. McKenzie deserve to get shot in the foot? Didn't he deserve to have a mailbox with a bunch of holes in it? What if it wasn't even her gun? What if one of her other friends gave her a gun to hide?

I wanted to talk to someone before I did something like call the police and got my only friend arrested. Karen was not an option. She'd hound me for every last detail and then make sure I never saw Stacey again. The only person I could think of that might listen and care enough to give decent advice, but not care enough to get involved, was Bill.

When Karen came home from work, I told her I needed to borrow her car. I waited for her skeptical, *do you absolutely have to borrow my car or are you just looking for trouble* expression. Once I checked that box, I told her that Stacey needed me to pick her up at the auto bodyshop.

"Something's wrong with her car," I said. "They need to keep it overnight. Her parents are out at some function for her dad's work."

I watched her think about it, gears turning as she hung her purse on the hook just inside the front door. My excuse had torpedoed her usual followup, which was that maybe I should call Stacey for a ride, along with what would surely be the next layer of defense, which was that maybe Stacey's parents should pick her up. I was seventeen, almost eighteen. Playing those games made me feel like I was eleven.

"I don't know, hon," Karen said. "It's raining. Those roads are really, really slick. I've got to get some dinner going and I'd sure like some help. You don't know what it's like working all day and then coming home to deal with..."

"I'll pick up some chicken on the way back," I said. "You like the white meat platter, extra crispy, right? Twenty dollars should cover it."

I was close. I could feel her teetering. I gave her another push.

"Stacey said her folks are at one of those big advertising conventions. People from all over the country. She really doesn't want to call her dad. Man," I said, shaking my head in quiet amazement, "just think of the Unexplored Dreamer Base that Stacey's dad would have. The UDB or whatever."

"Well..." She slowly reached for her purse.

Karen was right that it was raining. But it was raining just regular water, not oil or banana peels and the roads were just like normal roads. Bill lived twenty-five minutes away in a weathered gray duplex. I wouldn't exactly say the neighborhood was in a sleazy area of town, which is what Karen likes to say when she's lecturing me about the risks of being a low-level Down-Liner all my life. "You need to keep climbing to a higher level, Cali. Don't be a Down-Liner like your father, living in a sleazy neighborhood as your life swirls down the drain."

The neighborhood was basically fine. But if I stood on the roof of one of the taller apartment buildings, I could probably hit the sleazy area of town with a rock.

When Bill pulled open his front door, his face froze in rigid surprise. The light above the stoop was out. I stood in the dark, getting wet and waited for his face to melt. Bill finally smiled and spread his arms wide and hammed it up like I was six.

"The Calico Kid! Out on a midnight ride!"

"It's six-thirty, Bill," I said. "Can I come in?"

Every time I set foot in my father's home, I was shocked at how small it is, basically, just one living room area, connected to a small hallway on one side and a tiny kitchen on the other. All the appliances are avocado green. They match the shag carpet perfectly.

Before the divorce, Bill worked as an assistant budget analyst for the city of St. Louis. The thing with his secretary put an end to that job, along with his marriage to Karen. So then he started his own company, which provided basic accounting services to small businesses. I don't know if you can call it a company because it was basically just Bill, but that's what he called it: Bill Watts and Associates, or just BWA, for short. He loved throwing that around, BWA this and BWA that. Eventually BWA provided mostly financial planning advice to startup businesses and people with bad credit. You know, because Bill is such an expert at life planning. Karen likes to use Bill as an example of what she calls Chronic Down-Liners, which are people who give regular Down-Liners a false sense of accomplishment.

Now Bill also has a part-time gig working for a friend who owns a greenhouse. In a separate room back behind the ferns, they have a secret grow operation. I'm not supposed to know that. If there's one thing that the people of Weldon Spring like to talk about the most, it's other people's secrets.

The room reeked of pot. A leggy, red-haired woman in cut-offs and a halter top was sprawled on the couch. She sat up straight when I stepped in and placed a photo book about the Grand Canyon on top of an ashtray.

"This is Hope," said Bill, palming the top of my head. "Hope, this is my daughter, Cali. Hope works with me out at the greenhouse."

"My, my," said Hope. "Calico Watts, in the flesh. Your dad talks so much about you, I feel like I already know you."

She had freckles and chipped green nail polish and long, rangy fingers and toes. I didn't like the shape of her eyes and I didn't like the way she said *flesh*. I wanted to grab the book about the Grand Canyon and hit her over the head and then ask her why, if she already knew so much about me, she thought it was okay to call me Calico Watts.

But I didn't. I smiled and nodded shyly and flicked the water droplets off my jacket and lied that it was nice to meet her.

Here's the thing about my stupid name. Bill likes to tell this story about the day his father, Fredrick Watts, my grandfather, died. Bill was only fifteen and he finds Fred on his back in the front yard, like, clutching his chest or whatever. This was when they were all still living in Trenton. Bill rushes across the yard and bends down and Fred whispers a single word in his ear: Calico. Bill did not need an explanation. To him, that word meant money. It meant wealth. It meant treasure.

Fred Watts liked to tell his kids, all seven of them, that even though they seemed very poor, which they were, the family was secretly wealthy. Fred spun this tale that his great-grandfather, Woodrow, had been a tycoon. Woodrow Watts was a Boston insurance salesman. One day, Woodrow disappeared from his family and his job. He just, like, vanished. It was years before people realized where he'd gone. Woodrow had dropped everything and headed west to this little town in California called Calico, where he'd heard that people were starting to mine for silver. Woodrow showed up in Calico and bought some land and started digging. According to Fred, Woodrow struck it rich. He married his second wife while the first one was still trying to figure out where he'd gone.

According to Bill, Fred always told him that Calico started raining silver in the late 1880s and it became this big boomtown. Fred told his kids that there was a mine out there with the Watts' name on it. Like it was just an open hole in the side of a mountain, waiting for them to show up with empty buckets. So Bill never forgets this story. And when he makes the mistake of marrying Karen, they have the brilliant idea to name their first born, Calico.

All my aunts and uncles heard the same stories about Woodrow. All my cousins are freaks with totally normal names. I suppose I should be glad that Woodrow Watts didn't strike it rich in Frankenstein, Missouri. One of my teachers is from Nothing, Arizona. I have a second cousin who lives in Oatmeal, Texas. I should be grateful.

I've always hated my name, anyway. Calico is either a kind of cat or a spotted rag from India or whatever. I came up with a list of a dozen other names that I thought were better just for being normal. Amanda. Christine. Lianne. Belinda.

When Bill and Karen refused to legally change my name, I insisted on being called California instead of Calico. At the time, I knew a girl named Dakota and another named Virginia. It seemed like my best option. Bill had smiled and wrote the words Watts, California on a piece of paper and told me to look it up.

We eventually agreed that they would refer to me as Cali. Bill likes to forget that agreement whenever possible. All my parents' friends call me Calico. Sometimes Karen warns them in advance. It never makes any difference.

I looked down at Hope sitting on the edge of Bill's couch, resting her freckled arms on her knobby knees and tried to imagine what her parents thought of their naming decision. Hope. I'll bet they're still hoping.

"So, what's up, kiddo?" Bill asked and then couldn't stop talking. "Take your jacket off. Have a seat. Want something to drink? Nasty weather out there."

"I can't stay," I said. "I wanted to get your advice about something."

Bill looked shocked. His eyes were little computer screens, scrolling probability data on all the worst-case scenarios. I was pregnant. I couldn't tell Karen. Should I keep the baby? Then he seemed to remember Hope. He tried to act as if this was normal. Like I was always coming around seeking his wisdom.

"Okay, shoot."

An interesting command, given the subject. He lowered himself into a chair.

I wanted to say that I needed to speak to him in private but I didn't want to seem rude. I should've just called him on the phone but I hate talking to Bill on the phone. I needed a face-to-face. I tried to tell him my concern without really telling him. Everything I said came out in a kind of code, as if we had a history of speaking a secret language. Ubbi dubbi or whatever.

"If you had a friend that you thought was, like, maybe involved in a bad situation, and was going to do something bad that could, if it even happened at all, which maybe it wouldn't happen but maybe it might happen, and if it did happen, it could get this person in super bad trouble, like, you know, prison trouble, would you call the police and get the person in trouble, first to prevent the person from getting in even worse trouble later, or would you just, like, stay out of it?"

Bill looked at me like he had an ice cream headache.

"What?" he asked. "Cali, I don't..."

"Okay. Pretend you have a friend that you think might commit a crime. And you really don't want to lose this friend because even though the friend is kind of a jerk and has walked out on you, the friend is still a friend and you don't want the friend to go to prison. You know that talking to the friend won't do any good because the friend will just tell you you're crazy and pretend nothing criminal is going on. Would you call the police and get your friend in trouble and, like totally end any chance that this person will ever talk to you again, or would you just stay out of it?"

Bill looked at Hope and back at me. A thin finger of smoke snaked up out from beneath the Grand Canyon book and drifted over the table.

"What kind of criminal act?" he asked, clearing his throat. I shrugged.

"Let's just say murder. And I could be totally wrong, like maybe the friend isn't doing anything illegal at all. But let's just say murder."

"Murder? If it's murder, then screw the friendship and call the police. No question. Murder is everybody's business. But listen, Cali." He broke off and pointed to the futon love seat. "Have a seat for a minute."

I perched myself on the edge of the futon. It used to be cream. Now it's gray with a purplish stain that looks like Rhode Island. Who buys a cream futon love seat? I was already wishing I had never come.

"Some things," he said, "are technically against the law but really don't hurt anyone, okay? Not murder, obviously, but other things that maybe are illegal in some states but not in other states. And usually those sorts of crimes really don't involve serious consequences, even if you're caught. It's a slap-on-the-wrist sort of thing. Some people just need to live in the now and not follow the common social blueprint or worry what society thinks of their choices. And in those sorts of situations, it's best to just let the person live his or her own life and learn their own lessons and have their own peace. Understand, pumpkin?"

Hope's gigantic, Great Plains freckled forehead wrinkled. She smiled at me sympathetically, like she was silently urging me to understand something basic. *Sometimes mommies and daddies say mean things to each other but they still love you.* My brain suddenly felt the gun pulsing inside the glove compartment of Stacey's car. Like it was alive. Like it had telepathic powers.

I knew where Bill was headed. He was concerned about himself, as usual. At that point I knew the visit was pointless. I just wanted out.

Maybe my response was mean. It felt necessary at the time.

"But what if the crime involves, like, lots of other people in the community and people are starting to talk about it and word will eventually get around that the person is making money by totally breaking the law? Wouldn't it be better if I put a stop to it sooner rather than later? Would the police keep me anonymous, or..."

When I left, Bill and Hope were both standing, hands on their hips, staring at the same dingy spot on the avocado carpet where I had been standing when I told them that I needed to really think about what to do next.

Bill had made one last play, encouraging me not to judge others too harshly and to think independently of people who seemed to live for any opportunity to judge others harshly.

"Like your mother, for example," he said. "She's a really good person, Cali. The best. Seriously, the best. But she likes to believe every little thing she hears and then pass it on as if it's true just so she can bring people down and destroy their lives. She lives for a future that is never coming. You know that. You've seen that. So that means Karen's jealous of people who are free enough to throw caution to the wind and truly live in the moment. Do you understand what I'm saying?"

I understood he was shitting his pants about that greenhouse.

"Don't tell Karen I was here," I said, as I stepped out into the rain and was closing the door. Then I stopped and turned and stuck my head through the opening. Bill and Hope were looking at each other. "Hey. It'd be great if I could borrow your car sometime. You know, just to feel free for awhile. Karen doesn't understand that like you do. Dad."

I drove to the nearest Henny Penny's and rolled down my window. I spoke into the orange metal rooster beak and inched forward. There was a blue Toyota in front of me, idling at the pay window. It had a broken rearview mirror on the passenger side. It hung limply against the side of the car, dangling from a cable like an eyeball that had popped out of its socket. My spine lit up like a bolt of lightning.

It was pouring as I drove into Stacey's neighborhood. The sound of fat raindrops hitting the roof of Karen's Hyundai was like driving beneath a waterfall. Karen called and wanted to know what was taking so long. She and Benji were hungry. She didn't mention the rain or the streets that used to be so dangerously slippery. I told her I was almost home.

When I reached Stacey's house, I parked at the corner and cut the headlights. Her car was in the driveway, like always. Her parents had the garage privileges. I zipped up my jacket and stepped out into the rain.

It was all so ridiculously easy. It was like I was expected. The broken passenger door opened. The glove compartment opened. I lifted up the papers with two fingers. The gun metal gleamed in the dim glow. Like the thing was glad to see me. Like it had been waiting.

I put the gun in my jacket pocket. It felt heavy and cold, like a dense slab of ice. I quietly closed everything up and ran back to the idling Hyundai. The whole thing took thirty seconds and I was gone.

On the way home, the windows steamed so much that I could barely see and I had to blast the air conditioner. I imagined getting in an accident and some police officer finding the gun and wanting me to explain it. I had no idea what I would say.

The very possibility freaked me out and I had this, like, quiet little panic attack as I drove home. I wanted to pull over at the nearest dumpster and throw the thing away. That would have served my purpose, which was just to keep Stacey from giving Mr. McKenzie a third nostril. Throwing the thing away would do that.

But I was already under its influence. I was like Frodo with a chance to drop the ring into the fires of Mount Doom. The gun didn't want to be thrown away. It sat heavily in the dampness of my pocket, nestled up against my thigh. The gun and I were already in a relationship. I didn't really have any other friends.

Easily the most dangerous part of this plan was getting a firearm into the house, past Karen, and safely into my room. That was why Stacey kept it in her car. I didn't have my own car.

It took some doing. I had to create a diversion by dumping a pint of coleslaw and a Dr Pepper on the kitchen floor. I bolted upstairs and jammed the gun under my mattress while Karen was cursing on her hands and knees. I was back with a handful of rags from the laundry room without her having any idea I had left.

Benji had looked at me quietly from the kitchen table. He was like a houseplant that you just stopped seeing after awhile, taking in carbon dioxide and expelling oxygen. Processing everything. Watching.

Stacey was noticeably upset the next day at school. I asked what was wrong. She claimed she was having her period. A rough one. I knew she was lying. Stacey's period always makes her better, not worse. I figured the truth was that I had screwed up her murder plot and she was now freaking out about who had been snooping around in her car and why.

"Better than not having a period," I said. I shouldn't have. I thought her distress was all about the mysteriously missing gun.

Stacey stared at me, mouth agape. The feeling was all too familiar. I remembered the look on Bill's face when I accidentally guessed the divorce. Stacey looked away. I realized I'd done it again. No period.

"No way!"

I said it with too much enthusiasm. Not, like, happy enthusiasm or anything but more like shock or whatever that someone could have such an epically bad week.

Stacey turned and stormed off through the crowded hall. People could tell something was wrong. They slowed down and looked, watching her go, and then went on, not caring.

I felt sorry for her. I almost chased after her but I knew she'd just push me away until she was ready to talk. I knew she'd curl up someplace, probably her car, and cry her eyes out and beat her steering wheel and scream. I remember thinking for the first time as I watched her stomp away that maybe the gun had never been intended for Mr. McKenzie in the first place.

That thought felt heavy and cold in my gut. Like I'd swallowed a frozen rock. Then it felt like I was the frozen rock, tumbling end over end, sinking through dark water where no one could possibly see. I stood by my open locker and stared at nothing.

That day stands out not just because of Stacey, but because that was the day Damien Alvarez was fired. I was in North Hall on my way to biology just when Principal Warren and a different security guard and Damien were leaving Admin and headed for the main doors. Damien was in the middle, head down.

I stopped and watched. Damien looked up just as they were making the turn. Our eyes met. He didn't, like, do anything to show that he'd seen me. But I could tell he did. He looked right at me. Like he usually did, only more serious and without that little smile or nod. He had some blood on his face and caked in his nose.

Principal Warren opened the main doors and followed the others outside. Coach Pete and Nurse Katherine were standing in the Admin doorway, watching. Once the main door had closed behind Principal Warren, they looked at each other and went back inside the office.

The fight had happened out behind the cafeteria, by the dumpsters. Damien came up behind Mike Mills and Rick Faber and everybody had started punching. People said that Mike and Rick were just headed out to the back lot and that Damien followed them and started hassling them. They were both on the football team and everyone knew that Rick was a favorite of Dr. Boss. Rick had been saying pretty openly that Damien had killed Taylor. That was the talk of the school after they found her. After she turned up.

Not like people were cool with Damien before Taylor died. He was a security guard, well, a safety officer is what they call them because they don't want it sounding like we're in prison. There were three of them at Howell High that rotated on a schedule. Most of the students called them screws. Their whole purpose was to catch us doing something wrong. Like we were already guilty, whether we knew it or not. They had nothing to do with safety.

Damien Alvarez had always been kind of a target just for being a screw and for the way he looked. Taylor's body in that duck shack just sort of sharpened the attention on him.

Not everybody who was talking about Damien as a murderer actually believed it. But some did. Not me, but others did, mostly because everybody saw Damien drive off with Taylor that last day. I don't think that proves anything. Just like when the police came to Damien's place and put him in handcuffs and stuffed him in a squad car. He lives right down the block from a school bus stop. The timing couldn't have been more perfect. People were really talking then.

I still don't think it really proves anything. Stacey went on and on about how on the inside, people aren't who you think they are. She said that any of us is capable of anything, even murder.

"You could murder someone," she said, "Or I could."

I said Damien did not seem like the type. Then she called me naïve. It was that day when I got into her car after Taylor's funeral. The day I first saw that gun.

"You are so naïve, Cali. You just like him because he keeps looking at you. He makes you feel special. Maybe that's how he got Taylor into his car."

"Taylor Boss?" I kind of snorted at the idea. "Seriously? She didn't need anyone to make her feel special."

We were still parked outside the Dairy Queen, watching the man on his cellphone. Stacey blew a long, white thread of smoke out the window. It curled and lingered for a second before the breeze plowed through it like a fat tire through a puddle. Stacey spoke to her cigarette, like I wasn't even part of the conversation.

"Well, she's dead, okay? And if you had a boyfriend, you wouldn't give a shit about a murdering high school screw."

The fact was, at that point, neither of us had a boyfriend. Not like I'd ever had one. At least Stacey went to a prom. I wouldn't be caught dead at a prom, having to blow some guy I secretly hated in the backseat of his car. I'd sooner go to a funeral.

I didn't say anything. I was still too freaked out about the gun and I knew Stacey was upset about Mr. McKenzie and I didn't want to argue. So I let the whole Damien thing go.

But it's not like I was under his spell or anything. It's not like I was in love or infatuated or whatever. I didn't even know Damien Alvarez. We'd never spoken a single word to each other. Not one.

But we did have this thing about looking at each other. It just sort of happened. I don't know when it started. Not like really staring at each other or anything. We'd just kind of recognize each other in the hallways. It was a glance and sometimes a nod. He waved once but mostly it was a glance and a nod and a little half smile before he looked away.

At first it was just kind of no big deal but then it became this, like, thing. Seeing each other, recognizing each other with our eyes, became something that sort of stood out in the moment. It became something I'd sort of anticipate. Not like I'd pine for it or whatever, but when it didn't happen, when I went a day without that silent exchange of glances, that stood out too.

I didn't care that Damien was Mexican or whatever. Howell High has plenty of Latinos and that's like no big deal to anyone until someone gets murdered, then somehow Mexico becomes part of the explanation.

I also didn't care much that Damien was not especially attractive. He was big, not just tall and broad, but also in a pudgy kind of way. His face was a bit pockmarked with old acne scars and his hair was dark and curly and sometimes looked like it needed washing. He shuffled the halls like he was supposed to do, looking for kids doing something wrong. Breaking up fights and telling people to stop running. Checking the restrooms.

Howell High safety officers communicated by radio. Damien wore his radio on a belt holster, like it was a gun. It was always turned on too loud. He didn't look much older than some of the seniors. Except for his size, the radio and the black uniform were the only things that really set him apart.

I saw Damien once at the Ninety-Nine Cent Store not far from the school. Sometimes I walked there during lunch period just so I could get away from everybody. I was kind of addicted to these neon sugar-frosted super-sour candies they sold and that I could never find anywhere else. But once I was there, I usually just browsed up and down every aisle, wasting time.

The shelves of the Ninety-Nine Cent Store were full of products you'd find in a regular store, except in miniature, little tiny shampoos and little tiny boxes of cereal and little tiny screwdrivers and hammers. They had lots of regular-sized stuff too but it was all made in China and Vietnam or wherever, probably by some poor kid who got to take two cents home to his family of eight where he had to sit at the table and eat his bowl of rice or whatever and listen to his mom go on about how he needed to work harder so he could get himself a doctorate.

But none of the stuff at the Ninety-Nine Cent Store was absolutely worthless. It all had maybe just a little value to someone. A miniature-sized value. It all had a place on the shelf. It all had a chance of being chosen. That might be why I liked that place. It might be why I stole so much.

I didn't steal, like, tons of stuff or anything. Just, maybe, one thing every couple of visits. There was never any rhyme or reason to it. Always something small and always from the center shelf, because I could just flick it off with a finger right into my open purse without even slowing down.

Stupid things. A tiny little Scotch Tape. A pack of pink paper straws. A little ceramic Santa Christmas ornament sprinkled in silver glitter. A bag of red hair scrunchies. A pregnancy test stick. Pens. A tiny can of shaving cream. A plastic shot glass with an image of a hula girl.

I'd usually keep whatever it was in my purse for a couple of days and then eventually I'd leave it sitting on a desk or a chair, someplace I could conveniently check on. And when I did check, the thing would always be gone. Like I'd busted it out of jail or something. Like I'd helped it escape from an orphanage of almost worthless things.

Once I was in the Ninety-Nine Cent Store and I'd flicked a pack of sticky notes into my purse. They were flower-shaped and made to look like hibiscus. I kept moving, head down, to the end of the aisle. I didn't see Damien Alvarez. I nearly ran into him. And I mean, like, literally almost ran into him. Another inch and my nose would have smashed into his shoulder. I couldn't tell if he was just coming around the corner or if he'd been standing there the whole time, watching me. He was wearing his black uniform and his radio was on his belt. He had large feet and I remember that one of his big, black shoes was untied.

I looked up, startled, and our eyes met for just a tiny fraction of a second. I quickly looked back down and kept moving. I should have apologized. Or he should have. Neither of us said anything.

I kind of freaked out inside, that maybe the school security guard had just seen me stealing some hibiscus sticky notes. I went up the snack aisle and put the pack of notes next to the donuts, swapping it for a bag of chips. I paid for the chips and left the store without making any effort to see where Damien was or what he was doing. I left the chips on a bench outside the school.

That was on a Friday. By the next Tuesday, I had basically relaxed about the whole thing. I'd seen Damien twice in the hall. We did our glance and nod and smile thing like nothing had happened. Like the near collision at the Ninety-Nine Cent Store had happened between two other people that neither of us knew.

But then on Wednesday, I came to school to find a hibiscus sticky note on my locker. Just that once. It never happened again.

I panicked that maybe he was toying with me. Or warning me. But even after the panic subsided – after all, I hadn't actually stolen anything that time – I didn't really know what to think about it. I never breathed a word to anybody. Certainly not to Stacey. Not even to Mr. Goodnight, which is saying something because I ended up telling Mr. Goodnight more than I'd ever told anybody in my life.

Mr. Goodnight was my first real sexual crush on a man. I'm not including celebrities, which is not even close to the same thing. I had a kind-of crush on more metal musicians that you can shake a stick at. Never the front man. It was always some guy in the background. The serious keyboard guy. The rubber-necked bass player. Usually longish hair and a wiry frame but never trying to hog the spotlight for attention. But those crushes were never real. They were fantasies to waste time.

Mr. Goodnight was a real crush. He was truly handsome or I thought he was, anyway. I never really heard anyone else say so. He was kind of tall and thin, like me, and he had light brown hair that reminded me of a beach. His eyes were a quiet blue-gray with little flecks of gold that were like tiny leaves floating on the surface of a pond.

Everything about him was calm and comforting. He wore pleated slacks and soft blue dress shirts. His cologne or aftershave or whatever smelled like what I imagine a deep forest smells like on a warm summer night. His watch was round with a clean, white face rimmed in gold and with a simple leather band.

He crossed his legs when we talked, interlacing his fingers over his lap. They were long and smooth and precise in the way they moved, helping him shape his words, like he was sewing ideas to the sounds with invisible thread. The pads of his fingers were rosy and full, like they were made to touch delicate things.

He always moved his chair off to the side so there was never a desk between us. It wasn't his office. He was just borrowing it. It always felt like we were meeting someplace that neither of us owned. Two strangers visiting. I imagined we were in a hotel room suite, just talking before anything else happened.

I didn't always want to have sex with Mr. Goodnight. At first, I didn't want anything to do with him at all. After Taylor turned up dead, the school staff kind of went bonkers, making all of us aware that the school district was providing an onsite counselor to talk to people. People were upset but I don't know if Mr. Goodnight had many takers. For awhile, almost every interaction with a teacher or the school staff worked its way down to a question about whether we wanted to sit down and talk with someone about our feelings.

They never mentioned Taylor's name. It was always just about our feelings. Like it was our feelings that had been found dead inside a duck shack on the edge of a marsh.

Which is good in a way, because if someone had asked whether I wanted to talk about Taylor Boss, I'd have said no. When Mr. McKenzie asked if maybe I wanted to sit down with someone to talk about my feelings, I almost said yeah, sure, I'd like to talk about the embryo in Stacey's belly. I'd like to talk about how I probably saved your stupid life by stealing her gun. I'd like to talk about prison.

But I didn't. He could tell I was brooding over something. I couldn't tell you what that was. Life in general, probably. I was sitting alone in the back of the science lab after the class had emptied out, off in my own little world, doodling or whatever.

It irritates Karen when I brood. She likes to do that turn-that-frown-upside-down thing. Got to fake it till you make it, honey. She says brooding slumps my shoulders and completely destroys my face. Not registers on my face. Completely destroys.

Anyway, I wasn't even really aware of Mr. McKenzie until he was standing right next to my stool, looking down at me. He placed his hand on my arm and I flinched.

"Everything okay, Ms. Watts?"

I flinched and covered up whatever I was doodling and then pulled at my skirt. I said something stupid I don't remember, then got up and headed for the door. That's when he asked if I wanted to talk about my feelings and I didn't say what I really wanted to say and stuffed the anger back down into my throat to the bottom of my gut where I kept the gun. Well, not actually kept the gun. The gun was actually under my mattress. But that's where I kept the idea of that gun. Down in the wet dark of my gut.

We almost never see emotion on our own faces. I don't know what my face looked like. I only know what Mr. McKenzie looked like. He looked worried. He looked like a man who didn't know what was going to happen next. I figured that meant he was looking at the face of rage and hate and that the worry on his own face was for himself. His future. His job and family.

Turns out the worry was for me. Two days later, I felt a hand on my shoulder while I was alone at my locker. I turned to look at this guy I'd never seen before.

"My name is Mr. Goodnight."

Altogether, we met four times: that first one and then the followup meeting and then the two others. Each meeting lasted about an hour. He was easy to talk to. I liked the sound of his voice. It was, like, so perfect and polished and smooth. His words were like river rocks. And his eyes were like little bits of sea glass that kept disappearing behind the wave of his eyelids.

I'd rather have just been quiet. Just watch him look at me. Listen to him say words to me.

But I couldn't, of course. Keeping the meeting going meant that I had to talk. I had to share things that held his interest. I couldn't tell him about Mr. McKenzie. Or about Stacey. She'd hate me. Her life would get even worse and Mr. McKenzie would fail me out of two classes.

Mr. Goodnight wanted to talk about Taylor Boss. It was like every time her name came up, Mr. Goodnight wanted to spend more time paying attention to me in our own little hotel suite. I may be a loser but I'm no dummy.

So we talked about Taylor and my feelings. I told him I felt sad. I told him that if something like that could happen to someone like Taylor Boss, then what did that mean for someone like me? I told him nothing meant anything to me anymore. I told him that my life felt mostly empty and that sometimes it was a relief to feel sad and angry just because it was something. It was something to feel.

He asked if had experienced the death of a family member or a good friend before Taylor. I said no. I almost told him that I never really knew Taylor Boss but then I liked the idea that maybe Taylor and I had been so close that her death had nearly destroyed my life. I wanted to be that close to another person. So close that their suddenly being gone nearly kills you, or your being gone almost kills them.

I liked the idea that Mr. Goodnight would be impressed at how well I was holding up under the circumstances. I imagined him talking to a colleague after I left the office. A strong young woman, that one.

Mr. Goodnight asked if I spent a lot of time thinking about death. I told him that I spent a lot of time trying not to think about death, which was the same thing in my book. He laughed. I laughed at him laughing.

It felt good to say those things. He was a good listener. He started to make wrapping up sounds, like he was satisfied and ready put an end to our meeting. I didn't want it to end. I wasn't going to tell him about the dream. Why encourage him to think I'm a freak. But then I figured it might make him want to keep talking.

"What kind of dream?" he asked.

"The kind that keeps happening. Not like every night or whatever but, like I've had the same dream two or three times since they found her."

I kept it simple. Just the part about trying to take the test without a working pencil and then going up to the front of the room and handing it to Taylor, who places it on top of the old-timey gun. I told him I wake up every time the little blue crab crawls out of her mouth and snaps his claw at me.

He sat very still and just looked at me. I didn't want that to end. I wanted to close my eyes and for that to go on forever. Feeling him look at me. Feeling him seeing me.

"What do you think that means?" He asked eventually. "The crab snapping his claw at you."

I shrugged.

"I don't know. That she's dead. Or like the crab thinks I killed her. Like it's my fault. Or it's like it's this warning that I'm next."

I kind of playfully snapped my hand at him like it was a little blue claw. I thought it might make him laugh. It didn't.

He asked if I'd like to arrange a time to talk some more and I said okay. I tried to say it in a way that made it sound like I was indifferent. We made an appointment for the next afternoon.

That night I fantasized that he was in bed with me. We weren't doing it or anything. He was just there under the covers with me. I would talk and Mr. Goodnight would listen. His sea-glass eyes would disappear and reappear. My naked skin would press against his naked skin, like I was talking with my entire body and he was listening with his entire body, and when he did talk, his fingers would shape his words on my naked back, like it was a kind of chalkboard and the tips of his fingers were writing words in the chalk dust.

That night I dreamt of him and in the dream, we did do it. Over and over. It was like floating in the ocean and being at the mercy of currents pushing up against my body. My eyes snapped open in the dark and my body kept rocking in a tide that was no longer there. I was so disappointed to wake up. I tried desperately to go back asleep and to find him again.

Morning came and I lay in bed, listening to Karen yelling for Benji to get up and get ready for school. I remembered what Stacey had told me about not knowing what it was like to be in another person's dreams. That made me imagine that maybe Mr. Goodnight had also dreamt about me.

It was the thought of meeting with him again that got me out of bed. I felt like I wanted to tell him everything. Not about Taylor or Stacey or Mr. McKenzie. I wanted to tell him more about me.

When Mr. Goodnight opened the door, he was smiling in that soft, quiet way of his. He smelled like forest. He thanked me for coming, like I was doing him some huge favor. I mumbled and blushed. He said I could call him Alex.

I tried. Just the once.

He asked me to describe my future. I went way too long without an answer. I honestly didn't know what to say. I knew the words we're all supposed to say – college and career options and making a family and whatever – but I couldn't even make up that kind of bullshit. His eyes wouldn't let me. I had to tell him the truth. But the truth was that there was no future. Not for me.

He asked me about my family and I kind of gave him the basics. Then he asked me to share the first memory that came into my head about each of my parents.

"My parents? Really?"

"Sure. Something that helps me understand who they are to you. But only if you want to, Cali. I don't want to pressure you. You can walk out that door any time you want."

That was the very last thing I wanted.

I almost went into Karen's Dream Life obsession, because that pretty much sums up Karen. But then I had a flash-fear that his eyes would grow wide and he'd tell me that he was also involved in Dream Life, or that he was actually married or had a girlfriend and that she was big-time into Dream Life, and then the race would be on to kill myself before I could die of disappointment.

Instead, I told him about the time in the fifth grade when we were all supposed to make something out of popsicle sticks and then bring it in for show and tell. I wanted to make a boat, a Noah's Ark kind of thing. Karen insisted a boat would be too hard and would end up looking terrible. She wanted me to make a house. We fought about it until I refused to make anything. Karen made the house by herself. She even made a little chimney and found a little mailbox at a craft store. The mailbox had a working pop-up flag. She gave it to me to turn in. I threw it in the dumpster at school. I lied to the entire class that I had made a boat that my mom accidentally sat on. Everybody laughed.

Mr. Goodnight did not laugh. He just smiled a little and nodded.

"What about your dad?"

The memory about Bill was harder to choose. There were several. One was that whole divorce conversation in my bedroom. Another was the fight Karen and Bill had this one time while they were making Thanksgiving dinner. A bunch of their friends were coming over and Karen was freaking out over god knows what. Bill wanted to be outside washing his Torino so he could show it off, but Karen was putting him to work. His job was to make the mashed potatoes and they fought with each other the whole time he was at the sink, peeling. He didn't boil them long enough and they were too hard to mash. Bill started smashing them with a meat tenderizer. Bits of potatoes flew everywhere. Karen screamed at him that he was ruining Thanksgiving. Benji and I went upstairs. It did ruin Thanksgiving.

A third memory that came to mind about Bill was actually after the divorce. I was fifteen. Bill was in that phase when he was feeling bad about not being more present in the lives of his own kids. Karen liked to harp about that until every so often, Bill would try to spend time with us. Then she'd resist, one excuse after the other, just like she does when I ask to borrow the car.

Bill had to go to Kansas City to pick up a custom gearshift for the Torino and he convinced Karen to let him take me along. He seemed so sad and depressed and so grateful that I had agreed to go with him. I fell for it, of course. I threw myself into the role of saving him, bucking him up. I made up silly road games and he eventually started laughing and telling jokes and clowning around and I felt really good that I had made that happen.

I felt kind of powerful for a change. It felt good to be away from the house. I liked having a relationship with Karen's ex-husband. She had divorced him and so she could no longer share in my relationship with Bill.

After we picked up the gearshift, Bill took me to a department store. He needed a new tie and I set myself to finding the right one. We went through dozens. I draped each one of them around his neck and then stepped back to judge and compare, cocking my head this way and that, like I was some men's fashion expert or whatever. After that, he said he'd buy me whatever I wanted. I pulled him by the hand over to Women's Wear.

I was in my first and only, like, real girly phase. It lasted for, like, five minutes. I'd soaked in too much Dream Life babble from Karen. I'd become secretly convinced that makeup and girl clothes would change everything about my life. At the very least, I thought that a girly wardrobe was a good first step toward getting a boyfriend.

Not that I'd have known what to do with a boyfriend. But I knew what it took to catch one. I knew what I was supposed to do for a boyfriend. I couldn't go shopping with Karen because that was exactly what she was always pushing for. I didn't want her to think she was right.

I picked out a dress and tried it on in the changing room. It was a ridiculous thing for me to wear. Pale blue, hip-hugging Lycra or whatever down to my knees with shoulder cutouts and a teardrop-shaped opening that stretched so far down the back, I could almost see my own ass crack. I posed and turned and imagined myself in heels and made up like a Dream Life model. The awkward, gangly creature in the mirror looked alien, as if I was staring through a window at someone else gawking back at me. Judging me. Not someone I liked. Someone I'd roll my eyes at.

Bill's eyes popped when I came out of the dressing room.

"Wow! You look..." He never finished.

The saleslady said I looked great. She herself looked perfect. Petite and plastic and just-so with stiff auburn hair. She smelled like chemicals.

"There is not a boy in this city who would not drop to his knees in an instant," she said. "You are full-on gorgeous, honey."

I wanted to believe, of course. But I was also kind of freaked out at the idea that any pimply faced punk with a hard-on would get a good view of my ass crack.

"Okay," I said, looking at Bill. I gave him a long, final chance. "I guess we'll take it?"

He shrugged in a your-decision kind of way. I looked back at him as I walked to the dressing room. He gave me two thumbs up.

I changed back into my jeans and my Def Leppard World Tour t-shirt. I walked out with the dress dangling from a finger, no heavier than a washcloth. I handed it to the saleslady. She got busy.

"It's sure... a slinky little number," Bill said, as he handed her his credit card. "Maybe too slinky?"

I did my best to look offended. We ganged up on him. It was all a big joke. He handed me the bag as we were walking to the car.

"You know your mother will confiscate that dress as soon as she sees it," he said, looking at me sideways.

"Yeah. Probably."

I imagined Karen not knowing what to say. Like, after all her effort to get me into a dress, that was the dress I had picked out? And I'd picked it out with Bill? And I'd be all, oh so you want to dress me up as a Dream Life girl? Well, how do you like me now? I know how fucked up that is. But I kind of liked the idea.

"If you want, I can store it at my place," Bill said. "Just let me know when you need it."

I was fifteen, but I wasn't stupid. Bill wanted cool-parent credit for buying me the dress but he didn't want to have to take shit from Karen for buying me a slutty, ass-crack outfit.

Bill was always all about Bill. Just like Karen was always all about Karen.

"I'll keep it," I said. "Leave Karen to me."

I held the bag in my lap the whole ride home, trying to imagine just when or where I would ever put it on and just what every guy I knew would think when they saw me. I imagined what they'd want from me. When I got home, I stuffed the bag under my mattress, almost exactly where I would eventually, roughly two years later, hide Stacey's gun. I never wore it. Eventually, I snuck it out to the trash.

Bill found opportunities to call me slinky for, like, a month after that trip. Well, well. If it isn't slinky.

I protested, but it was better than the Calico Kid. It was our private little joke in our private little relationship. I think I liked that it excluded Karen. And I liked to imagine that I could be a totally different person if I wanted to. Even if that person was skanky and gross, and showed her ass crack to anyone who wanted to see it. I was free to be whoever I wanted to be. All I had to do was put on that dress.

"Does he still call you slinky?" Mr. Goodnight asked.

"Not much. Every once in awhile, usually when Karen is around. So he can exclude her."

"Are you angry at your father... at Bill... for buying the dress?"

"I asked him to."

"I know you did." Mr. Goodnight leaned back in his chair and waited.

"I, like, insisted on it."

"I understand."

There was a PA announcement about a pep rally. I pretended to be distracted. Mr. Goodnight was still waiting, his perfect fingers interlaced like something woven. I wanted to touch his mouth. I wanted him to kiss me. I wanted to strip off all my clothes and fling them across the room so that I could feel the cool tile beneath my bare feet and watch him looking at me. I wanted him to see all of me. I wanted him to stand up and hold me. He didn't twitch.

"I was, yeah. Angry. I guess. Not anymore."

"Why not?"

"Because it was, like, totally my idea. And because it was years ago."

We were both silent. There was a hole between us. He wanted me to fill it.

"I even don't care enough to be angry. Not anymore. I don't care about, like, anything anymore. Bill is Bill. Karen is Karen. Nothing matters. Living in the shitty now like some Zen master or whatever, or dying on a hamster wheel for some... some... freaking... make-believe future that isn't even mine. It doesn't matter. The whole planet is dying and no one even cares. All the bees are dying and the glaciers are melting and the sea levels are rising and it just keeps getting hotter. And the freaking Amazon is on fire and it doesn't even matter. Fuck your teacher? Have his baby? Kill his baby? It doesn't matter. Die in a stupid duck shack out in... in freaking nowheresville? It doesn't matter. Ditch your friend. Save a life. Steal shit and throw it away. Go to college or don't. Kill someone or don't. Get arrested or don't. Maybe you're guilty; maybe you aren't. None of it matters. I don't care about anything. I don't care about anyone. I don't care. I don't care. I don't even freaking care anymore."

I never wanted to cry. I was surprised that happened. I couldn't stop. It just kept coming. Mr. Goodnight never moved. He just watched me go at it. I wiped snot on my sleeve. I felt humiliated and stood up quickly, wiping my eyes. Mr. Goodnight stood up too.

"Are you leaving?" he asked.

"Yes."

"Would it be okay if we talked some more, Cali?"

"No." I meant it.

I opened the door and walked out. I felt his eyes on my back all the way up North Hall. Even after I turned the corner and there was no way he could see me. I felt those beautiful eyes.

That was a Friday.

Saturday was like a prison. I kept to my room and pretended I had lots of homework. I just didn't have the energy to deal with Karen. Screams and gunfire blared from Benji's room.

I made the mistake of coming downstairs for a bowl of cereal. She was at the table in her robe, doing her Dream Tithing thing. She looked at me over the twenty-dollar bill she was holding. She closed her eyes and finished her silent little manifesting prayer or whatever and placed the bill carefully in the nearest stack of money.

"You look awful," she said.

"Thanks."

"I didn't mean it in a bad way, Cali. Don't be such a grump. Maybe you should turn that frown upside-down. Benji and I are going shopping. Why don't you come."

"I don't want to go shopping. I have homework to do."

"Come on. We'll have fun. I have a Dream Life meeting that'll just take an hour or so. I think I've got a lock on some new recruits. You guys can wait in the car and then we'll get some lunch and go into town."

"Homework," I said. I didn't have the energy for more syllables. I poured milk over the mound of Cheerios and then decided I hated the name.

Cheerios. Turn that frown upside down.

I poured the whole thing into the sink and headed for the door. Karen was squaring up the tiny stacks of cash with two painted fingernails. Dream Life Super Gloss No-Chip Ruby. She didn't look up.

"Suit yourself. We both know you're not doing homework. You need to think about what kind of person you want to be, Cali. What kind of life you want. Moping for god knows why up in that room is not ever going to get you up to the next level in life. At some point, you're just going to have to try."

I waited until they left. I watched Karen's Hyundai back out of the driveway and then took off my headphones. I sat on the corner of my bed and listened to the sound of the empty house around me. It felt like a coffin. I unplugged the headphones from the stereo and listened to AC/DC and Led Zeppelin and Van Halen as loud as I could take it. So loud the vocals lost their shape and the bones rattled in my chest. I felt nothing.

I turned off the music and got dressed. I left the house and walked to the bus stop and waited for the Number 15, which would eventually stop at the mall. It was good to feel the cold air in my lungs. The sky was a happy blue and the sun was so bright, it seemed to rattle the last yellow and orange leaves still hanging on for dear life.

As I walked, I caught myself wondering what Mr. Goodnight was doing. Wondering if he was someplace raking leaves, pausing and leaning against the rake as his beautiful wife or girlfriend or whatever brought him a cup of hot cocoa. I could see his soft smile and his quiet eyes, and his beautiful hands wrapped around the rake handle until one of them lets go and reaches for the steaming mug.

I shook my head and forced myself to think of something else. Anything else.

Damien Alvarez, his face, bruised and bloody as he stepped into North Hall. His eyes locking on mine as Principal Warren turned Damien's large, doughy body for the doors.

Taylor Boss. Not in the dream but naked on the floor of that duck shack. Then that little blue crab. Snap.

I sat down heavily by the window and the bus doors hissed closed. It gave me a strange comfort to feel the weight of the gun in my purse, pushing against my lap. I could never take the gun anywhere during the week. I could take it out from its place under the mattress but it had to stay in the room. The weekends were the only times that I did not have to encounter a metal detector.

It's not like I had planned to use it. I just sort of carried it around in my purse. I liked having the secret. I was the only one who knew it was in there. There was a special kind of thrill when I'd be, like, out with Karen at the grocery store or whatever and she'd be doing her thing, having no idea that her daughter was packing a firearm. Just knowing it was there was enough. I felt something. I had a pulse.

The mall was boring as always. I didn't buy anything. I just kind of went up one side and down the other on every level. I went in a few stores, almost at random, not because

I saw anything I really liked. No one asked if I needed any help. I was invisible. I looked for things to take.

Not like I really would. I'd never steal at the mall. Too risky, for one. But also too expensive. It's not like I really want the stuff I swipe. It has to be crap. It has to be almost worthless. Plus, to get caught and then they find a gun in your purse? Going to prison for armed robbery of a Lucky Brand belt? Best Buy headphones? An Old Navy t-shirt?

Maybe I was a loser, but I wasn't a stupid loser.

I went to the food court and ordered a thing of onion rings and a Dr Pepper. I sat at a table and just watched people living their lives. They flowed all around me, as if I was a chunk of rock poking out of a river. All of it together made a roaring sound in my ears. It was like the sound of all that water dumping on top of Karen's Hyundai the night I stole the gun from Stacey's car. Like a waterfall.

Stacey never saw me. She was with Megan and Kylie. All had boobs out to here, heels, hair, the whole thing. Something was so funny, they could barely stand up straight.

I thought of the last time I'd seen Stacey, storming away down North Hall because I had guessed her secret. I wondered if Megan and Kylie had any idea. I wondered about the life inside her. Whether she would keep it. I wondered if all the laughing and carrying on was, like, above where Stacey had been the last time I saw her, as if she'd gotten better, or if she'd drilled even further down into her misery and found some new little pocket of hilarity. Something that'd be good for about ten minutes.

I followed them. I kept my distance so they'd never see me. They went in all the girly stores. They bought cheap rings and bracelets and makeup. Everything was funny. Everything was amazing. I couldn't hear them but I didn't have to. Every guy was either so hot they couldn't stand it or so disgusting they couldn't stand it.

They're all the very best of friends.

They passed right by the Little Miracles maternity store without even a sideways look. Not even Stacey. I tried to decide what that meant. Probably that Megan and Kylie had no idea. Probably that the littlest McKenzie was not long for the world.

Then I decided it probably didn't mean anything. Nothing meant anything anymore. Everything was meaningless. If Stacey didn't care, then I didn't care.

They disappeared into Victoria's Secret. I pretended to shop for sunglasses across the hallway, my purse knocking heavily against my leg. After twenty minutes, I gave up.

Karen called just as the bus was pulling out of the parking lot.

"I thought you had homework."

"I finished."

"Where are you?"

"At the mall with some friends."

"What friends?"

"Stacey and Megan and Kylie. Do you need something, Karen?"

"I need you to come home. It's getting late."

"I don't have a car. Remember? I'm kind of at Stacey's mercy. Unless you want to come pick me up."

I got off the bus early. I didn't know why. I told myself that the bus stank of BO, which it did, and that a walk would do me good.

I didn't realize what I had actually been thinking until I cut across the South View Mini-Mall parking lot and turned onto Clendon Street. As I walked, I brushed my fingers along the tall, white wooden fence that ran the length of the Sundown Trailer Court. Every now and then, a missing plank opened a narrow view to a row of dingy double-wides. I saw a brown dog and a rusty swing set and a purplish car up on blocks. Someone was watching the game. Someone was playing a live cut of Iron Butterfly's "In-A-Gadda-Da-Vida." Copenhagen. 1971.

I looked that title up once. "In-A-Gadda-Da-Vida." I was sure it was Italian or something. Like something beautiful or divine or whatever. But it's supposed to be how a drunk would say "in the Garden of Eden."

Maybe that is beautiful.

Clendon Street abutted North Sequoia, which was on the school bus route. Damien Alvarez's place sat five houses from the corner. It was nothing to write home about without cop cars everywhere. Kind of a light brown with a carport and a blue tarp on one side of the roof, held in place with rows of cinderblocks. The front door was a dirty white. Brown curtains were drawn behind a double window that faced the street. Damien's car was nosed in under the carport against the house. A green Toyota with one black door. That was the door Taylor Boss had opened and closed on the last day anybody had seen her alive.

I passed the house without slowing or looking. I had the feeling of eyes on my back, just like I had when I walked out of my meeting with Mr. Goodnight. I could feel the hair on my skin. I stopped two houses later and turned back.

Don't ask me why. I didn't know why. I still don't.

430

I stood in front of the house, remembering the electricity that buzzed through the school on the Friday that police cars had been in Damien's driveway and in the road. He hadn't been in school that Friday, which added instant credibility to the story. But he had been back to work the next Monday, like nothing had ever happened. Like he had just been out sick or on vacation or whatever.

I tried to imagine him in handcuffs, like people had seen that day. Police bending him into the backseat of a black-and-white. The only picture in my head was of Damien weeks later, on his last day of work, when he looked up at me in North Hall as Principal Warren was escorting him out. Blood on his face.

I kept my eyes on the brown curtain. I looked for movement. I wondered if he was there, bottle in his hand, gun in his hand, knife in his hand, rope in his hand, looking at me just standing there on the sidewalk, not moving. Waiting for him.

I felt something.

I felt my own heart. Urgent. Terrified. Pumping blood into my ears.

It felt good to feel. It was something, at least. It was something.

I wanted more.

I stepped into the driveway, trying not to think. Time fell away. Suddenly I was at the door, standing on the little concrete stoop, with no memory of actually getting there. Just like in a dream.

The stoop was in the sun but cold, like a square of frozen butter. There was no traffic on the street behind me. It reminded me of that book by Stephen King, where all the streets and highways were quiet and still because everybody was dead.

I didn't knock. It was like I was just waiting for it to open on its own so I could step inside. I had no idea what I'd say to him. I had no idea what he would do when he saw me.

I placed my hand on the knob and left it there. It felt frozen. An icy stone. In my head, a zombie crawled over the back of Abraham Lincoln, "In-A-Gadda-Da-Vida" soaring in the background. The world was dangerous and unpredictable. I had something to lose. I wanted more.

Beside me, I felt that maybe that curtain moved. Just a little.

I let go of the knob and unzipped my purse. I pushed against the gun with the back of my hand, just enough. I pulled out the folded, hibiscus sticky note. I'd almost thrown it away a hundred times. I stuck it in the crack of the door and stared at it for a few long seconds. Then I turned and walked away.

I had to force myself not to run.

I kept to myself that night and most of the day on Sunday. Karen was working Dream Life for all it was worth, on a high for having recruited three new Down-Liners to deepen her Dreamer Fuel Base or whatever.

"I can see that house, Cali. I can just see it. Cute little private beach right out the back. And a little dock with a sailboat. Not a sailboat, a cataman. Cataman? Is that what they're called? Catamans? A boat. And nothing but the deep, blue sea out there. Seagulls. Little, fluffy white clouds. A few more days like today and my Up-Liners will be pulling me up to Level 6 for sure. I am moving up! Tonight's a milkshake night."

I escaped to Benji's room and sat on his bed. He was at his desk, headphones on, microphone rotated down over

432

his mouth. On the computer screen in front of him, crosshairs inside a pale green circle passed over a crowd of people milling around a foreign marketplace. Everyone wore white robes. All the women wore those things. Hijabs.

"What's the game?" I asked, not really caring. He didn't hear me.

A bearded man in a black robe crossed the street and worked his way through the crowd. He stuck out like a black wolf in a flock of white sheep. His face magnified to fill the screen. The crosshairs found his temple.

"Wait for it," said Benji, calmly into his mic. "Not yet. At the fountain. Repeat, at the fountain. Dead man walking." He waited, frozen in concentration. "Do it now."

The man in black lost his face in a red explosion. His body crumpled over the lip of a stone fountain and down into the water as pigeons burst up into the air and people fled in all directions, screaming.

"Jesus," I said. "That's, like, so... effing real."

"Roger that, Camel One," said Benji, ignoring me. "That was my sister. Negative. She has a Class 5 visitor clearance. Roger that. Stand by, Camel One."

He took his headphones off and looked at me.

"You have to go," he said. "This is about to get serious."

"Oh," I said. I stood up. "Karen's talking milkshakes."

"Strawberry. Hold the whip."

I fell into Monday like a dead man into a fountain. There was nothing I wanted. Nothing to anticipate except the end of it. My purse felt light and pointless against my leg without the gun, like a sheet of paper hanging from my shoulder on a piece of string.

433

I shuffled through the halls in a world of my own. I looked up in time to see Stacey, who was already turning away. I just kept on walking.

Mr. McKenzie was all about oxidants and reductants. Free radicals were freak show enemies of the natural order.

"Normally electrons are paired up." He cupped two white plastic balls in his hand and held them up. Someone snickered. "Nature loves the buddy system." He placed one of the balls on the front table and held up the other one between two fingers. "Every now and then, you encounter that lone electron. No friends. No bonds. Orbiting all alone. Maybe because of a normal metabolic process or maybe because of a hostile environment. X-rays. Ozone. Pollutants. Industrial chemicals. Whatever the cause, free radicals are unstable and highly reactive. They scavenge the body, looking for that bond. And the longer they go on without a bond, the more damage they cause to cells, proteins and DNA. Not to be trusted, these loners."

Everyone laughed.

I laid my head on the table.

After class, I stopped in the middle of the hall. People had to steer around me. We knocked shoulders as they passed. I didn't apologize and neither did they. I didn't care.

All I cared about was Mr. Goodnight, standing at my locker, his beautiful hands slipped comfortably into his pleated pockets. Like they were shy in public.

"I'd like to talk," he said, although more as if he had used telepathy than his mouth. "If you don't mind."

I looked around to see who was watching. No one. We were invisible.

"Now?" I asked.

"This is your free period, right?"

I followed him to the same office, our romantic little hotel suite. It didn't feel that way at first. It felt like I was in trouble. Like the hotel suite was all fake, an interrogation room disguised like an office made to feel like a hotel suite just to get me to talk. But when he closed the door and crossed the room and pulled his chair out from behind the desk so that there was nothing between us, all the old feelings began flooding back into my body. I felt like crying, like right where I'd left off the previous week, even before he started speaking.

"I'm concerned about you," he said quietly.

"You don't care," I said. "Not really. No one does. Not even me."

"You're wrong. I do care. Others care. You care."

"I really don't effing care. I don't feel anything anymore."

In my head I was naked. His long, pale fingers raked my hair. He kissed my temples. He traced my eyebrows with his thumbs.

"I'd like to ask you a few questions, Cali. And I'd like you to answer honestly. You don't have to tell me anything if you don't want to. But I'd like you to trust me. I'd like to know the truth."

I looked down at my hands. I nodded.

"Have you ever tried to hurt yourself?"

"No. Like, you mean..."

"Physically hurt yourself. In any way."

"No. Like offing myself or whatever? No."

"In any way. Cutting. Burning."

"No."

I held out my forearms like he might not believe me.

"Have you ever thought of doing something like that?"

"No. Maybe. Yes. I mean, like, I've thought about it. But not really. Not for real."

"Okay. That's good to know. Last time we talked, you said some things."

I glanced up, but not for long.

"You said some things about... well, about having sex with a teacher. Has that..."

"No." I flushed and wiped my face with my hands. "God, no. I was just... it was just, like, an example. Not me. Jesus."

"Okay. Okay. Anyone you know?"

I faltered. He saw it.

"Be honest."

"No," I lied. "It was just... it was stupid. I shouldn't have said that. I was upset. I was... no."

He looked at me for a long time. I held my ground. I don't know why. Who was I protecting? Why did I even care? I couldn't take the silence.

"What... I was just upset. Okay?"

He nodded.

"Okay. You also mentioned stealing. Do you steal things?"

I didn't speak. He waited. I shrugged.

"I'm not a cop," he said. "I won't tell a soul. It's your business, not mine. It's not for me to stop you. But if you are, Cali – if you are stealing – I'd sure like to know why."

I could hear the dull roar of students pushing through the hall. Someone laughed. Someone slammed a locker.

"I don't know why," I tried to say. The words tangled and stuck in my throat like dry sticks. "It's just stupid stuff. Little, like, worthless…" I looked up at him. My eyes were starting to burn. "I don't know why. I don't think about it. It just comes over me. I don't do it a lot. Just sometimes. I'm sorry."

"You don't need to apologize to me. You haven't done anything to me. Are you afraid, Cali?"

"Of what?"

"Of being hurt. Killed. Are you afraid of ending up like Taylor Boss? Does that worry you?"

"No. I don't know. Probably not." Words came out that were not mine, arranging themselves into thoughts I didn't recognize, like someone else was using my mouth. "Sometimes I like being afraid."

I had no idea what that even meant. I only knew, suddenly and for the first time, that it was true. Mr. Goodnight nodded his head a little, as if he was answering a question for himself.

"Why do you think that is?"

I shrugged and picked at my fingers. They seemed like red, raw, ragged little bones compared to his.

"Better than feeling nothing," I said. "Better than feeling dead."

I didn't look up. I could not see his expression. I felt him nod.

"You're right," he said. "It is better. Sometimes we have to shock ourselves, just to… just to feel a pulse. To feel alive."

"I guess. Yeah."

"But there are other ways, Cali. There are better ways to prove we're not the walking dead."

I thought of Benji killing zombies.

"Like?"

"Well, like we can shock ourselves with kindness. With compassion. With love for someone or something outside of ourselves."

He waited. It was suddenly so quiet. Everybody was in class and the halls beyond the closed door had been abandoned. Mr. Goodnight leaned forward, placing his elbows on his knees so that his hands, patiently clasped, drifted into my field of vision. They were like two sea creatures, octopi or whatever, suspended in invisible water, embracing.

"And if it's fear you want, Cali, well, there's no fear quite like the fear that guards the door to confession. The fear that guards our feelings. If you really want to feel alive, try sharing your feelings. Try letting something out. That takes a lot more courage than pulling a blade over your arm or shoplifting. Find something terrible inside yourself. Or something wonderful. Make an offering of it to the gods. Free yourself of what you're holding inside."

Silence. I imagined him staring at the top of my bowed head. I felt a tear sliding its way slowly along the ridge of my nose. It hung there, trembling like a woman on a bridge. I watched it fall and splat against the tile.

"Try telling me the truth about something, Cali. Something you don't want to let out into the world. Shock yourself with a bit of courage you didn't realize you had. Open the door just a little. Make an offering."

I looked up. I found his quiet, complicated eyes. I leapt.

I think of that week as the beginning of the end.

I felt overwhelmed after that meeting. My head was full of shouting voices. I lived in my headphones. I lived in metal. In punk. In riot. In grunge. I tried to beat the chaos into submission with more chaos. Metallica. The Beastie Boys. AC/DC. The Clash. The Ramones. Iron Butterfly. "In-A-Gadda-Da-Vida" on a loop. I didn't care as long as it was old and loud. Old because the things I felt were not new and shiny and popular. They were zombie feelings, up from the shallow grave. Ragged and angry. Loud because that was the only way to distract myself from the thing that was suddenly loose and pacing in my head.

I saw Stacey every day in the hall and every day she turned away, always a split second before our eyes might have made contact, usually shouting out to someone else or making a show of laughing and having the best time ever.

At home, Karen was gone almost every night at her Dream Life meetings. When she was home, she spent her time hunched over her laptop at the dining room table, building out her Dream Life social media platform to cast a wider net for new recruits. She used the photo of herself in a bikini and sporting sun-bleached hair. She's in mid-cartwheel on a beach in Pensacola. The photo is over twenty years old. She borrowed her motto for the caption: If you can dream it, you can live it!

Benji and I stayed out of her way. We ordered pizza and watched bloodbath TV with the lights off.

"You sure?" He kept asking.

"Bring it," I said. "Turn it up."

On Friday night, Karen busied, cleaning everything up for a Dream Life meeting she was hosting at our house the next day. The meeting was for orienting her new Down-

Liner recruits and selling them their first Dream Life inventory.

Everything had to be perfect. Every surface had to be scoured. Benji got window duty. He hung a bottle of Windex from his belt loop like a weapon. I was assigned the vacuum. Karen wanted me to do every room in the house, even those no one would ever see.

"No one is coming in my room, Karen." I said this to her back as we were standing in the kitchen.

"Doesn't matter, Cali. One day, when you have your own house, you can keep it as filthy and looking as unsuccessful as you want."

"My room's not filthy."

Karen turned, holding a sudsy rag and looked at me. Behind her, the sink water hissed down into the drain. Her grim "Linda Hamilton" was showing. All she needed was a cigarette and machine gun.

"Just do it."

I did my part and then secluded myself in my newly vacuumed room. I collapsed into my beanbag and played Led Zeppelin on my headphones with the lights off. I listened to "Stairway to Heaven" five times before taking the headphones off. Karen was still bumping around downstairs, giving Benji orders like he was the young John Connor whose job it would be to save the world from his own future. I watched the green level meters on my stereo, pulsing like a heartbeat, until I fell asleep.

Karen would have preferred me out of the house before her new money-maker recruits arrived. The last thing she wanted was to have unsuccessful-looking loser-spawn scurrying like rats around her clean house. I made a point of waiting until the doorbell had rung five times and strange voices filled our house before emerging from my room. I walked down the hall and paused at Benji's closed door.

"On my mark." His voice was tense and muffled. "Keep your cover."

I moved on, descending the stairs to the living room below. The gun in my purse banged against my leg.

There were six of them huddled around the coffee table, sitting in chairs that had been stolen from other rooms. From above, it looked like a kind of séance. Karen was pulling one product after another from the boxes at her feet and passing them around the circle. Every now and then she'd lapse into a sermon about how joining Dream Life could change everything for them. She explained that it was important for them to begin assessing their friends and colleagues for people who would benefit from joining the Dream Life family.

"How is this different than a pyramid scheme?" one of them asked. Karen laughed and gave them her best reassuring smile.

"Book one, Chapter three," she said, digging into another box. "Pyramid schemes are illegal. Dream Life is not. Dream Life only guarantees success and personal fulfillment, not wealth. The amount of money you make through Dream Life is entirely up to you and how committed you are, just like any other job." Karen paused and looked around the table. "Although Dream Life is like a job that gives you a new raise and a promotion every time you make a new friend."

Karen laughed. Then everyone laughed.

Karen looked up as I reached the bottom of the staircase. She took in the AC/DC shirt and the old jeans. Her eyes told me to keep walking, through the kitchen and out the door and far, far away. I pretended not to understand.

"Can I borrow the car?" I asked as I walked into the living room. Everyone turned around. Karen's jaw was set and her eyes unblinking.

"Oh, honey, I don't want to make everyone move their cars. I'm going to need it after the meeting anyway. You might want to call Stacey. Just this once."

"Okay, Mother," I said sweetly as if in some foreign language. "Just this once."

I left, grabbing my coat off the hook by the door. I didn't mean to let the door slam, but I also didn't mind.

The world outside was cold and gray and just starting to spit snow. It was the first snow of the season. It was early. Some people live in places where it snows so much that it's like no big deal and if you ask them when the first snow of the season was, they wouldn't be able to tell you. It was always a big deal to me. The first snow of the season was on that day. It was the last snowfall I'd ever see.

It collected in small, whitish clumps on the grass and on the hoods of the cars that filled our driveway and lined the curb. I wondered what the neighbors thought about all those cars. Birthday. Football. Funeral.

There was a breeze on the walk to the bus stop that made me wish I'd grabbed a heavier coat. I stuffed my hands deep into my pockets and hunched my shoulders and bowed my head into the wind.

I imagined that in that same moment, Mr. Goodnight was in his front yard, raking leaves in the sunshine as if he lived in a completely different area of the country. He was holding the rake like a flagpole and drinking the hot cocoa that someone had made for him. Someone he loved. I imagined walking up the sidewalk to his house, wherever it was. I imagined the look on his face when he saw me standing on his lawn. It would take a couple of seconds for him to recognize me out of context. Then would come the look of surprise. Maybe happy surprise.

But then he would remember.

"Try telling me the truth about something, Cali. Something you don't want to let out into the world. Shock yourself with a bit of courage you didn't realize you had. Open the door just a little. Make an offering."

"I dream about you. I dream about us, like, together. I love you. I want you to love me. I want to be touched. I want to be held. I want to feel you naked against me. I want you to tell me something secret."

And then Mr. Goodnight's face would do again what it had done in that little, make believe hotel suite. It would cloud over, like an octopus disappearing behind a cloud of ink. His throat would dry up and fear would seal his lips. He'd cross his arms again, only this time letting the rake and the cocoa fall to the ground, hiding his beautiful, pure fingers in his armpits.

The bus was mostly empty and quiet. I sat in the back and huddled up against the window. Outside, the mighty Missouri River slid past St. Charles in a cold, wet hiss that I couldn't hear but I could imagine. Something escaping. Something leaving.

There were five people in front of me. Four of them kept their heads bent to their phones, oblivious to the world. The other one drove the bus.

The Riverside Mall was a blender of color and sound. Horrible pop music from all directions, shrieking children and clumps of teenagers perched on benches and in doorways, raking the shoppers with savage, desperate eyes. Kiosk vendors marked their prey and made their come-ons, pretending every stranger was special and in need of special attention. "You have such amazing eyes. Can I ask you a question?"

I wandered my usual route, from one end of the mall to the other and back again several times. I was a ghost, invisible to all of them. Even the kiosk vendors seemed to look right through me to the next person. Anytime I left the crowded hall and stepped into a shop, it was like I became suddenly visible to other people. The clerks bared their teeth in greeting and warned me with their eyes not to waste their time or steal anything.

I recognized several people from school. No one recognized me. Or maybe if they did recognize me, they pretended not to.

Mr. McKenzie strolled right past me, a daughter on one side and a son on the other. I watched them go. He was holding his daughter's hand.

I realized that Mr. McKenzie could have been Bill, with me on one side and Benji on the other, before Bill had come down to my room and sat on the corner of the bed and said the D-word and started crying. Before Karen found out that his assistant was better at meeting his needs as a man.

I wondered if Mr. McKenzie's wife was also in the mall. I wondered what she'd say if she knew that, at least for awhile, Stacey Moore had tended to her husband's man-needs. I imagined pulling out the gun, gathering the entire McKenzie family in the back of some store, Victoria's Secret maybe, and forcing Marcus McKenzie to his knees and telling him that if he wanted to live to see another day, then he had to admit what he had done. I imagined him crying and begging for mercy, pleading with me as his family looked on, horrified but waiting for the truth. Mall security show up, shouting and pointing, and wishing they carried guns but then eventually they too grow quiet and wait to hear what Mr. McKenzie had to confess.

In my head, he was shaking and crying. I pushed the gun right into the soft skin of his temple. I gave him the count of three.

Mr. McKenzie slowed and looked backward in my direction. His daughter tugged him forward but he resisted. As if maybe through some ESP or whatever, he knew I was watching him. But even though he seemed to look right at me, he never saw me. He turned around and kept walking until he was gone.

I sat in the food court and ate things I didn't want, keeping an eye out for Stacey and her friends. There were so many people, it was hard to imagine that she would not show up at some point. Not that I wanted to talk to her or that she would have anything to do with me. But it was something. It was a purpose.

I removed my purse and set it down on the table in front of me. It clunked heavily. The thing inside stretched the leather just below the zipper. If I stared at the purse long enough, it started to look kind of like a facial expression. Not like a whole face or whatever, but just the bulge of a nose and part of a smile. Like there was someone inside trying to get my attention. ?You have such amazing eyes. Can I ask you a question?"

I killed time. I watched people.

I watched time. I followed people.

I wandered to the theater and looked at posters and bought a ticket. It didn't matter what movie. I don't even remember it. A big tycoon-type is married to a serial killer and doesn't know it. He's too involved with his money to notice until it's too late. People in his life start dying. He's next.

I sat in the back row and watched people in cozy groups of two and three push their heads together in the dark and say things to each other and laugh. I dozed off and on until it was over.

I left the theater through a side door that dumped me into the parking lot. It was cold and snowing. The failing afternoon light reminded me of gray water absorbed into piles of dingy cotton rags. It was calmer and quieter than inside the mall. I zipped up my coat and threaded the cars like metal bales of hay in a concrete field.

The movie people don't coordinate with the bus people. I saw the Number 15 bus pulling off from the curb while I was still too far away to do anything about it. I stopped in the middle of the parking lot and watched it go.

I looked back at the theater through a steam cloud of my own breath and wondered if I should go back and wait inside. The cold and damp were uncomfortable, but it was the idea of going back into the mall that made me shiver.

I turned and kept walking.

I stood alone at the snow-dusted bench, trying to read the bus schedule mounted on a pole. The sheet of numbers was behind a clear plastic plate that had been defaced with black grease marker. I couldn't read the departure times for the Number 15 bus because someone had decided that a penis and testicles were more important.

I could have looked up the schedule on my phone, but I suddenly didn't really care to know. The bus would come whenever the bus came. I brushed the snow off the bench, sat down beneath the big black penis and waited, watching the tops of my shoes disappear one flake at a time.

I did not recognize the car the first time it passed. I just had a sense of it approaching and then moving on. Something was wrong with the muffler, which was hanging too low, and the engine sounded wet and congested like a car with a cold. Then it was gone in a cloud of snow and what did I care?

But when it returned a minute later and pulled up next to the bus stop, there was no mistaking the green Toyota with a black passenger door. That black door opened right in front of me. It groaned like metal does when it's cold. I imagined it was the same way that same door had opened for Taylor Boss.

Damien Alvarez didn't say anything. He just looked at me, kind of like he'd always looked at me in the hallway. Like he looked at me that last time as they were escorting him out of the school, dried blood on his face.

I stared back at him, the snow falling softly, swaying between us like a lace curtain in a breeze. There was no steam from my mouth because I was not breathing. My hand gripped my purse. I felt the hardness inside.

I guess that's where the courage came from. If you want to call it that.

I stood up, crossed the sidewalk and climbed inside. I closed the car door with a groaning slam. The air was warm and smelled of cigarettes and pine air freshener. I closed my eyes at the relief of being out of the cold. Damien watched me and waited. When I opened my eyes, I saw the hibiscus sticky note stuck to the dash in front of me.

I glanced over at him. Damien had always looked large. Not super tall or fat or whatever, just kind of big all over. But packed inside that car, he seemed like a giant to me. His brown hands were plump and doughy, folded around a little toy steering wheel. The driver's seat was partly broken and sagged back on the side that was closest to me. He was in jeans and a stained blue t-shirt that partly covered a skull tattoo on his bicep. I could only see the bony mouth and part of the nose socket.

It was the first time I'd ever seen Damien when he was not wearing his security uniform. His right eye still showed a purplish bruise and swelling from the fight with Mike Mills and Rick Faber.

I extended a finger and lifted the sleeve of his shirt to see the rest of the skull. The tip of my finger pushed along the smooth skin of his arm. The eyes of the skeleton were emerald green. A flat mariachi hat with a red rose in the center slanted down over the top of the skull.

"Nice," I said.

Damien looked down, as if to see precisely where I had touched. Then he looked at me.

"Where do you live?" he asked. I swallowed.

"I don't want to go home."

He was quiet. We looked at each other.

"Where then?"

"I don't care. Anywhere. Not home."

The car accelerated away from the bus stop. The wipers smeared the snow over the windshield, which began to fog. Damien turned on the blower. When the freeway rose into view, I realized that I had been wrong. I realized that I did care. Even if I didn't know why.

"Take me where you took her," I said. "That's where I want to go."

I didn't look at him when I said that but I felt him turn and look at me. I smoothed the hibiscus against the dash, pressing my thumb against the fold mark from when it had been in the bottom of my purse.

"Why?"

"I don't know."

We rode mostly in silence as he worked his way through St. Charles. Traffic was slow in the city. Everyone was hesitant because of the snow. The streets were slippery, or at least it looked as if they could be slippery, and everyone suddenly seemed too scared to drive.

"What's your name?" he asked, when we'd finally cleared the city and headed north on Highway 79. Traffic was much lighter. No turning or stopping. Just a straight line into curtains of snow.

"Cali," I said.

"Cali. That's short for something, huh?"

I didn't answer. I felt my phone buzz in my purse. I kept my eyes on the wall of trees that seemed to float past my window.

The snow was mesmerizing. It made everything look like nothing was real. Like none of what was happening was actually happening. Like this was a dream. Like I would wake up back at the movie theater and see that everyone had left and that the credits were still rolling and that I was alone. I'd sit up and think about needing to catch the Number 15, but before I could stand, I'd remember this weird dream about getting in a car with Damien Alvarez and telling him to take me to the last place that Taylor Boss was alive. I'd remember the skull tattoo and touching his arm with my finger and the little paper pine tree swinging from the knob of his radio.

"Haven't seen you at school," I said, which was stupid because I knew he'd been fired, and he knew I knew.

"Working at the theater," he said.

"Riverside Mall?"

"Yeah. And Highland. Depends on the day."

"You like that?"

He looked at me sideways and waited, like he was giving me time to take back the question. Which I probably should have. His expression soured, probably suspicious I was rubbing it in his face that he'd been fired and was now picking up after people.

"You mean do I like taking out the trash and cleaning bathrooms?"

"Maybe you do," I said, keeping my eyes on the floating trees. I don't know why it came out snotty. I guess I was trying to sound tough and unafraid. I was neither. "I don't know."

"Hmm. Well, maybe you like stealing other people's shit."

I whipped my head around and glowered at him. He had a little smirk on his face. Maybe he thought he was being funny. I didn't.

"Yeah, maybe I do. And maybe you like killing people. Girls."

The smirk drained away. I couldn't read the residue it left behind.

"Yeah, maybe I do," he said.

"Maybe you'll try to kill me."

"Maybe I will."

It was nearly dark by the time he slowed the car and turned onto a small road that wound off through the trees. As we turned, the car behind us hissed away up Highway

450

79. It was suddenly darker without those headlights through the back window. We were in the only car I could see. Snow was falling hard. It was collecting on the shoulders of the road. A thin, white blanket covered the darkening ground beneath the floating trees.

The road connected to Old Highway 79. Damien headed north again, and I was glad to see some other cars, even if it was only a few. But that didn't last long.

Damien turned off the road again so that we were headed east down a series of ever smaller roads that twisted and turned through trees and tall bushes. Our headlights revealed only a few feet of road through the static of snow before the road changed direction.

I've never been a whiz at directions, but even with all the turning, I could tell we were getting closer and closer to the Mississippi River. Not that I could see anything. I couldn't see anything except trees and snow and road and that little paper pine tree deodorizer swinging from the radio. But I could feel that river nearby. Like I had ESP or whatever. I felt a billion flakes of snow landing on the surface of the water as it flowed past my life and carried them all the way to the Gulf of Mexico. Like the river was a train and every snowflake was a passenger feeling lucky to be aboard. Escaping. Leaving.

The road made a sharp turn out of the bushes into a kind of wide, half-circle opening. At first, all I could see was snow coming down in giant fat flakes in front of the headlights. Then as my eyes adjusted to the extra space, I could see the snow falling all around us.

It reminded me of the snow globe in my dream, and of Taylor Boss looking at the little church or schoolhouse or whatever inside, holding it in her hand like she was some kind of god looking at the world she had made, before setting it on the table next to the hula shot glass and the ceramic Santa and then starting to pull on that Slinky.

It was so beautiful, all that snow. Tons and tons of it falling all around, but so gently and without a sound. It was beautiful in a slow, sad way. In a way of understanding and apology. In a way that makes you wish the world beyond the snow was different. I remember wanting to get out of the car. I wanted to stand in the dark and feel the flakes kiss my upturned face. I wanted to feel them accumulate at my feet, combine and rise up my legs and hips, swallowing the tip of each finger, then my arms and shoulders.

I wanted to be buried in it.

Damien stopped the car with a jolt. As if he'd read my mind. As if he was going to let me out. I was wrong.

"Someone's here," he said.

He was peering intensely forward through the snow. I looked where he was looking. At the far end of a clearing was a small cabin-like structure made of gray wood. It had a brown door and a pitched, red metal roof with a stubby black chimney. Beyond the cabin was water. A marsh extended behind the trees and shrubs on either side. A pale, white mist hugged the surface, wafting slowly among the reeds.

In the front of the shack was a black pickup. The lights were off. A thin trail of exhaust rose up through the falling snow.

"I'm not going any closer," he said. "This is the place. This is where she wanted to go. Satisfied?"

I studied it for a minute.

"What's it like? Inside, I mean."

It took a minute for him to answer. I waited.

"Not much to it. Just one room. Two bunks. Table. Chairs. Wood stove. I wasn't really… I didn't really notice much."

"Why?"

"Because all I could see was her."

"Why?"

Damien looked at me. I could see his irritation. His discomfort. I kept the question on my face. I didn't look away.

He turned off the headlights, then inched the car off the road into the snowy grass until it was up against a group of large, droopy willows. He turned off the engine. The sudden silence weighed a billion tons. We watched the idling truck.

"'Cause she was always nice to me," he said. "She said my name. You know, like she knew me. Even though she didn't. Not really, I mean. She squeezed my arm whenever she saw me. Looked up into my face. Like she was happy to see me. I imagined…"

He didn't finish. We stared out at the snow. I thought of Mr. Goodnight. His quiet, complicated eyes. His fine, beach-colored hair. His long, elegant fingers.

"You imagined she liked you," I said. "You imagined being with her."

Damien didn't look at me. He didn't act surprised that somehow I knew his mind. But he nodded. Just once.

"She was naked?"

He nodded. Just once.

"Did she take her clothes off for you? Did you take them off?"

Silence. Just the snow. For a long time.

"She asked if I could give her a ride. She needed a favor because her car was... she didn't really say. Her car was dead. She needed a ride."

"Here?"

Damien nodded.

"I picked her up after school and took her to her house. She ran inside and came back with two fudgsicles. Off we went. She was just like always. She didn't talk about herself. She wanted to talk about me. Like she was really interested in my life. Interested in me. She told me I needed to move back to New Mexico. We talked a lot about Gabriella. She said every daughter needs a father."

"You have a daughter?"

I hate how I blurted the question. I don't know why it seemed so surprising that he was a father. I guess he seemed too young. I tried to imagine him in the role. Doing father-like things. I tried to imagine the moment when he stopped being a guy like all the guys in school and turned into a man.

I couldn't imagine no longer thinking of myself as a girl, suddenly being a woman. I wondered if maybe that was never meant to happen. Like I'd never make it to that part.

Damien scratched a small gash in the steering wheel with a fingernail, picking at a wound.

"She's nine. Very pretty. She's got long black hair and big brown eyes. She likes painting things." He pointed at the hibiscus. "She paints tropical flowers. And she's big into math. And bugs. And outer space. She wants to be a scientist."

I nodded. I traced the hibiscus with my finger. I waited for more.

"I used to paint houses. We had a good crew. Decent money. Then *el Jefe* got busted for dealing. We all got laid off. I spent a lot of time looking for work. My wife had a good job that came with decent healthcare. It also came with a boyfriend on the staff. He had money for a lawyer. All I had was a lot of anger. Boyfriend tried to keep me out of my own house. I messed him up. So, then I had a lot of anger and a restraining order."

I nodded. I waited.

"I also had a cousin selling enchiladas out of a strip mall in St. Charles. So I just left. It killed me but it felt like the right thing." He shook his head. "Not the right thing. It felt like the only thing. Now Gabby's nine, my cousin moved his enchiladas to Pasadena, and I'm on my hands and knees scraping gum off the floor of the cineplex. Landlord wants to evict my broke Mexican ass. I hate this place."

I watched the exhaust from the black pickup waft up into the snow. It disappeared into the air like the tip of a candle flame disappears. Or like where being a child disappears. There's no way to pinpoint exactly where it stops. It's there and then it's gone. The silence began to hurt. I looked at the little shack and then at him.

"What happened in there, Damien?"

It was awhile before he said anything. I thought he might not answer. He fiddled with the keys hanging from the ignition and I thought he was going to start the car and drive off.

"My tank was near empty," he said. "Like always, I guess. She insisted on paying for gas. We pulled over at the Chevron on 79 and she started digging through her purse for her card. I was outside taking off the gas cap and I looked inside the window. I could see inside her purse. She opened the door and I looked away. I didn't want her to know that I'd seen the gun. I don't know why. Maybe because I figured it was a secret. Maybe because I didn't know what to think about it. I guess I figured it was for protection. A girl like her. Probably lots of men after her. It was like, oh, shit, she carries a gun. Of course she does. I probably would too if I looked like her."

It was hard to ignore the coincidence.

It was harder to ignore the comparison. I was not a girl like Taylor Boss. I did not have any men after me. I did not need a gun for protection. I could walk naked through the streets of St. Charles after dark and not have to worry about that kind of attention. But I had a gun anyway. Just like Taylor. It wasn't really my gun and it didn't have my initials on it or whatever like hers probably did, but I thought of it as mine. I wondered what Damien would think if he happened to see its gray glint inside my purse. I wondered just how quickly he would have ruled out personal protection from men as the reason I was carrying.

My purse vibrated, like my gun wanted a say in things. It vibrated again. Karen's irritation found my knee and travelled the length of my leg. I wanted to pull out my phone and throw it in the snow. I didn't. I kept still.

"When we got out here, I drove her up to the front door. I asked her what this place was and why she was here. I thought we were coming out to, like, an actual house. She said it was her dad's duck shack. She said this is where he came to get away when she was a kid. I asked her if she was a duck hunter and she made a face and said she hated guns and killing animals. I wanted to ask her about what she was carrying around in her purse. I wanted to ask her what the hell she was doing out here; I should have. I should have asked her. I didn't. I asked her if she was okay out here alone. She could tell I was worried. She said she was meeting someone."

Damien gave a sharp little half-laugh, half-cough.

456

"Meeting someone. Right. I figured then that she wasn't so goody, two-shoes as she liked people to believe. I figured her car was just fine and that she just didn't want people to know she was gone. She had a ride back. She was going to meet some guy out here and they would drink and take off their clothes and do things and listen to music and probably get stoned and I was just her dumb Mexican driver that she was pretending to like. I was just her fucking servant wrapped around her fucking little finger all because she squeezed my arm and smiled."

"Damien," I repeated. I looked at him. "What happened in there?"

He wasn't listening.

"I didn't know what to think. I can get real, like…"

"What."

"Jealous. Angry. Always gets me in trouble. I can kind of lose control. I had no reason to think she … you know… that she was interested. But I think I kind of hoped it for a second. I think I kind of hoped it."

"Damien."

"She opened the door and got out. It was so sunny that day. Geese were flying overhead and ducks were making a racket in the water. Light was reflecting off the marsh behind her. The air was so bright all around her body. Like the light was coming from her. She was so beautiful. Then she turned back and leaned in and put her knees on the seat." He nodded at me. "Right where you are now. And she leaned over and kissed me. Like… a full on-the-mouth kiss. She held my fat ugly face in her hands and looked at me. I didn't know what to say. She got out again. She told me that daughters need their fathers. That I needed to be a good man and to be near Gabriella. She thanked me for the ride. Then she closed the door and went inside."

I looked at him as he stared out into the snow. The windshield was fogged along the bottom like a little misty mountain range rising out of the dashboard.

"I wanted to follow her. My blood was just, like, you know... racing. It was like she'd never stopped kissing me. Like I could still feel her lips. I wanted to tell her what I was feeling. I knew the door wasn't locked. I wanted to just push my way inside and..."

He broke off. Like he knew that telling me what he wanted, sharing his heart, was a dead-end road. I know what that feels like. So I didn't push. I just waited. I watched the last of the light drain away down beneath the tall grasses and into the marsh.

"I didn't go in," he said. "I just backed up the car and left. I made it all the way to the Chevron on 79 before I had a thought that kind of changed everything. I pulled over and turned around and headed back. I was just, like... I was shaking all the way back here."

"I don't understand," I said. "What thought?"

Damien sighed. The weight of it was still heavier than the air in his lungs.

"I'd picked her up right after school. Right outside the school."

"So?"

"Metal detectors."

That's all he needed to say. A chill crawled up my spine like a frozen spider. Taylor's initials weren't on that gun. It wasn't her gun. She hated guns. She didn't carry a gun around with her for protection. That was daddy's gun.

"She didn't have it when you picked her up," I whispered. "That's why she had you take her to her house first."

458

Damien made a sound.

"I thought she wanted a fudgsicle."

I touched his arm.

"Damien..."

"I didn't know what to expect. I'd kind of hoped I was just crazy. That I'd find another car outside. That I'd hear music or laughing or... But I couldn't stop shaking."

Damien started to cry. His whole body shook in a gentle rolling tremor. He pressed his head against the steering wheel. I reached over and rubbed his back. His voice came as a choking wet whisper.

"It was terrible. Oh god, it was so terrible. She was sitting under the window. She was looking at me. Like, right at me. Like always. It was so sunny. The ducks were out there, making noise. And she was... she was so still. Her clothes were in this perfect little stack on the table. And the... I shouldn't have touched it. I wanted to get it away from her. I should have kicked it away."

Damien straightened and sniffed. He looked at his right hand. He made a peace sign.

"I got blood on these two fingers. It burned for days. As if I'd touched a stove. I drove back to the Chevron and called 911. I borrowed a phone from this guy. I didn't want to use my cell. I didn't give my name. I just gave directions and cut the call. I knew it made me seem guilty. But I felt guilty. I was guilty. I could have asked about the gun. I could have taken it. I could have asked about her life instead of going on about mine. I could have stopped her. I was guilty. I was running from that. I still am."

"The police..."

He nodded.

"Yeah. Well." Damien swallowed. "I came to my senses. I called them two days later. Told them what happened. They came to my house and picked me up."

I touched his arm. I squeezed it. Maybe just like she had squeezed it. He looked at me. His eyes were red and trembling.

"Damien. It wasn't your fault. You weren't in her head. You couldn't have known. Who could have had any idea? Her of all people?"

"I could have known. We don't pay enough attention to each other. She was always paying attention to everyone else. Who was paying attention to her?"

"Everyone," I said. "She got all kinds of attention."

"All kinds except maybe the right kind. What if no one ever really saw her? What if no one ever really looked? I mean really looked. I could've known. And then I did know. Part of me knew. That's why I was shaking. Like the things we know try to get our attention. But then it was too late."

We sat for a long time. The snow made shadows on the other side of the steamy windshield. The willow branch outside my window had turned almost completely white.

"What's it short for?"

His voice surprised me.

"What?"

"Cali. What's it short for?"

"Calico." I wanted to say California. I would have. I wasn't thinking.

"Calico," he repeated. "Calico. Man. I love that." He kept saying it. "Calico. Calico. Calico." Like some kind of incantation or whatever. "That's like... that's the coolest name. Where did..."

460

"Family name," I said. "Long story."

"What's your last name?"

"Watts."

"Calico Watts." He smiled a little and wiped his eyes with the backs of his hands and sniffed. "Damn, girl. That's a name."

"That's a name," I said and laughed a little.

I was cold and uncomfortable at the attention. I started clearing the windshield in front of me with my hand. I wanted him to start the car and turn on the heat. But I also liked the quiet. I liked that nothing was moving. Just our voices. Just the two of us inside a car that was inside a snow globe. I liked the intimacy of it. I liked the size and warmth of Damien next to me. I didn't really want that to end. I liked that no one knew where I was.

I kept clearing the steam away in circles. The hood of the car was completely white. At the edge of the marsh, the little gray shack was cold and still. The truck was still out front. Still idling.

"That's not right," I said.

"What?"

"The truck. It's just, like, sitting there. No one's come or gone. It's just sitting there. Wasting gas."

Damien cleared his side of the windshield. We watched it.

"Let's pull up and just take a look," I said. Damien stared at me with wide, frightened eyes. He shook his head.

"No, no, no."

"We'll just say we're lost, or..."

"No. I can't go back there. If I'm caught back here... it'll look... I shouldn't be here. I'm sure it's fine."

"What if it's not fine?" I asked. I hate that word. *Fine.* Everyone always says they're fine. No one is fine. Nothing is ever really fine. That's the thing people say when the opposite is true. I stared at him. "You said we need to pay closer attention to each other."

Damien looked away. I opened the car door. The sudden light was jarring.

"I'm afraid," he said. "I know it's stupid. But I am."

"Me too," I said.

"Then why?"

"Because fear is better than nothing. Don't worry. I'm sure I'll be fine."

I stepped out beneath the willow branch. My shoe sunk through the snow and down into the soft marsh grass.

"Cali..."

I closed the door and stood for a moment, just looking and listening. It was perfectly silent. In all directions, snow fell against the darkness in giant doilies of frozen lace.

The marsh, so nearby, was invisible. Somewhere close were families of sleeping ducks, floating under snow-dusted sprays of grass, beaks tucked under their wings, the downy edge of single feathers moving in the warm current of duck breath. And somewhere beyond that, the mighty Mississippi, passing through in the night. Leaving everything behind.

It was too cold for what I was wearing. I started shivering. I couldn't tell how much of it was fear. I unzipped my purse and held it close to my body. I started walking.

I moved slowly, picking my path sideways as best as I could in the darkness, stepping around small bushes and clumps of tall, wet grass, until I found the hard trail that led to the shack. I imagined Damien back in the car, trying to clear the windshield and watching me. Wrestling with himself. He'd want to turn on the headlights so I could see but he also wouldn't want to attract attention. He'd want to come with me but the nightmares were already more than he could bear.

The idling truck made a low purring sound. I stopped maybe fifty feet away and just watched it for a minute, hoping for something. I didn't know what that might be. Something. Anything. Like maybe the silhouettes of two people talking. Just like Damien and I had been talking. Parked in the snow and talking and crying about a girl I didn't know, a girl that maybe nobody really knew, clearing the windshield and looking through the dark at the last place she'd been alive.

But the only things moving were two streams of white exhaust. One from the truck and the other from me.

I put one foot in front of the other and just kept moving. Ten more steps and I was close enough to read the back plate: DRBOSS.

I stood behind the tailgate. The bed was empty. I could see through the back window, clear through the front windshield to the front wall of the duck shack in front of the truck. It was empty.

I walked to the front door of the shack. I listened. I knocked. I put my right hand into my purse. I waited.

No one came. I knocked again. I waited. I grabbed the knob. It felt like a frozen stone. It felt like the frozen thing in my gut when I first realized that Stacey's gun might never have been meant for Mr. McKenzie. I heard Damien's car start. It seemed a long way away. I turned the knob and pushed at the door.

The smell was first, before the door was open even an inch. Old and wet. Mildew and rot. It was dark inside but my eyes adjusted and I could make out the basics: a single room, square and sparse with simple stick furniture. A table and some chairs. Two bunk beds. A black iron wood stove in the corner. A window. The wood of the walls and floor was old and gray.

The place was empty except for the cold, which was as dense as water. It felt much colder inside than outside. I could feel it pushing up against my face as I stood in the doorway.

My own white breath entered the space and spread out in front of me. I followed, stepping inside. I let the door swing closed behind me.

I tried to see what she had seen. The empty room of simple furniture. Afternoon sunlight streaming in. I tried to hear what she had heard. The ducks on the water outside. The sound of Damien's car. Pulling away. Leaving her. I tried to feel what she had felt. The expanse of marsh. The Mississippi leaving. The heaviness of her purse at the end of its strap. The thing in her head and her heart that no one knew about and would never know about. The thing, whatever it was, that had brought her here.

There was only one window, directly opposite the door. It pulled me forward, like windows do, into the center of the room. There was nothing to see through that window. Just a flat square of darkness between me and the marsh. Fat, ghostly snowflakes appeared at the top and floated down until they disappeared at the bottom.

Beneath the window, the wood was darkly stained. The stain was a single shape that started narrow and expanded.

It bent where the wall met the floor and stretched out toward my wet shoes.

It looked like a shadow. Like I was blocking some light source behind me.

I kind of freaked inside. I felt my heart surge and sweat on my skin. I stepped backward in a straight line until I felt the door against my shoulders. I could hear a car engine. It sounded faint and far away. I couldn't tell whether it was coming or going. I reached behind me blindly for the doorknob, still staring at the dark shape in the wood. It felt like it was staring back at me. I couldn't look away. I turned the knob and pushed my back against the door. I hadn't turned the knob all the way. It took three tries. The last one was hard and I panicked. I stumbled backward outside, almost falling. I let go of the door and it closed in front of me with a heavy slap.

I sensed light. I sensed movement. I turned.

Damien's car was behind the pickup. The headlights were on. Damien was standing on the far side of the truck, staring into the passenger-side window. His black hair was speckled with snow. He looked up at me. His face should have looked brown. It didn't. I thought of Benji's walking dead. Damien pointed.

Only half of Dr. Boss was on the front seat. His upper half had slipped down beneath the steering wheel. I couldn't see anything past his shoulders. Most of one leg was still up on the seat. He was missing a shoe.

"He's fucking dead," Damien whispered.

I pulled at the driver's door handle. The door sprung open and Dr. Boss's right arm flopped out into the air. A bottle of vodka clinked off the frame of the truck and dropped into the snow at my feet.

I grabbed his wrist and tried to find a pulse with my thumb. I honestly couldn't tell. All I could feel was my own pulse hammering away in my head. Damien opened the passenger door and we looked at each other over the seat.

"What do we do?" I asked.

"I'm not touching him," he said. "Call the police."

I fumbled for my purse.

A cough came from beneath the steering wheel.

It took Damien's strength to pull Dr. Boss out of the truck. All I could really do was keep his head from smashing against the doorframe as Damien muscled him out from beneath the steering wheel and dragged him by the armpits out into the snow.

Damien slipped and fell backward, pulling Dr. Boss on top of him. Damien scrambled to his feet and brushed himself off and we just kind of stared down at my dentist.

It was hard to see him that way. As my dentist. Our positions were reversed. Nobody ever looks down at their dentist. They look different that way. His square, handsome face was unshaven. His eyelids were crusted. Dried vomit covered part of his jaw, neck and shoulder. His mouth was hanging open. He had nice teeth.

He was breathing. I said his name and nudged him with my foot.

"Dr. Boss? Dr. Boss!"

His eyes fluttered and then half opened. We knelt down over him. His breath stank. We shouted questions at him as if he was deaf. He just looked up at us. I knew his eyes were green. They didn't look green. He closed them and passed out.

It took both of us working together to get him into the back of Damien's car. Damien took the shoulders and I took the feet. We sat him up but he fell sideways and knocked his head hard against the passenger window before we could catch him. Damien went around the other side to lean him back up. I went to the pickup to find his shoe.

I found it wedged between the door and the seat. On the floor was another empty vodka bottle. And a gun.

I straightened. All I could do was stand and stare. The bottle had a square, white label that was like a patch of light in the shadows on the floor of the truck. The gun was even brighter. Sleek and silver. I wondered if it was the one she'd used. I wondered if she'd been carrying it around with her on the weekends, like me, or if she'd waited until that one, last day as Damien sat in his car outside her house, first to the gun case and then to the freezer for two fudgsicles.

I wondered which one Dr. Boss had to identify first.

I wondered what they'd said when they gave the gun back to him.

I felt Damien behind me.

"Oh, shit," he said. He was only in a t-shirt. He had to be freezing.

He moved me aside and reached down and pulled the gun out with one finger. We looked at it in silence. It was so clean. The snow disappeared against the metal.

I thought about my dream, about the old-timey pistol that Taylor Boss had handed to me and that I'd stuck into my waistband. I remembered the pink diamond on her finger. I wondered if Damien had dreamed about her too.

"Is it the same one?" I asked.

Damien nodded. He turned and trudged past the car and outside the spray of headlights into the darkness that bordered the side of the duck shack.

"Where are you going?"

He didn't answer. I followed in his large footsteps.

He stopped maybe twenty or thirty feet past the duck shack. He dropped his shoulder and stretched back his arm and hurled the gun up into the air with more than a grunt. It was closer to a scream. Sounds of panicked rustling and splashing came through the dark on all sides. Then a distant, heavy splash.

Damien sniffed. He spoke to the marsh.

"Wish I'd done that before. Might've done some fucking good."

He turned and looked down at me. His face was big and wet. His hair covered in snow. I saw the boy inside the man. He was so alone. He was so trapped in that aloneness. I watched him cry.

I took my purse off my shoulder. I held it open to him. Like an offering.

* * *

Leaving St. Charles was one of the easiest things I've ever done. The hard part was figuring out that staying put was unnatural. That I was the mighty Mississippi pretending to be a puddle in the gutter. After I figured that out, it all kind of came unstuck.

I came unstuck.

Not that it didn't take some planning. And this is the part where you start to wonder if I was just made for a life of crime. But I didn't think of this as stealing. Not really, because the money was mine. Or it was supposed to be. Karen said she and Bill had saved fifteen thousand for my college fund. She said she'd invested it in Dream Life. Or she said she was going to invest it.

So that's all I took. Fifteen thousand. She had more than that in the little portable safe on the floor of her closet. Bill had bought the safe six months before they divorced. The combination is their anniversary date in case you ever need some extra cash. It's in a banker's box marked Self Help Material.

Because she's so dang smart.

Anyway, I followed the instructions on the box and helped myself. I left Karen something to count and to hold in her hands for her little Dream Tithing thing. I'm sure that ritual went a little faster after I left.

So, it wasn't really stealing. Not really.

Same with Karen's car. I didn't steal it. I borrowed it. I took the extra key she keeps in the kitchen drawer and walked to the bus stop. Not the school bus stop, the other one. I took the Number 8 bus to the hospital where she works and roamed around the parking lot until I spotted the almost-turquoise Hyundai DREME machine between two normal cars. Like I'd ever steal that thing.

I drove straight over to Bill's place. The snow along the sides of the streets had lost its purity and had turned to a dingy gray slop that splattered everywhere.

But I felt better than I could ever remember. Not happy or whatever. Just better. Unstuck. Moving. Thinking. Feeling. I pounded on the door and got Bill out of bed. He was surprised to see me.

"Slinky," he said, rubbing his eyes and yawning.

"Morning, Bill."

He held the door open.

"Come on in."

"No, I'm not staying."

I could hear Hope's voice from another room, asking who it was. Bill's confusion asserted itself.

"What'r... what..."

I handed him the key to the Hyundai.

"I need to borrow the Torino. Karen says you can use her car today as long as you pick her up after work. She said don't call her till after three-thirty because she's in meetings or whatever."

He rubbed his stubbled face again. He reached out and took the key like it was a dirty Kleenex.

"What?"

"I have a date. I need your car. I can't date in a turquoise Hyundai, now can I?"

He looked at his watch.

"You have a date at nine-thirty in the morning?"

"No, I have a date after school. I won't have time to come get your car."

"Shouldn't you be in school right now?" That's when the real implausibility hit him. "Wait. You have a boyfriend?"

"Ha. Ha. Ha. That's what Karen said. You should both feel relieved that he doesn't have his own car and that he's not, like, involved in some totally illegal pot racket. Not that

I said that to Karen. You know how she is about drugs. She'd freak. Cops everywhere."

I could see him preparing to defend himself. He was ready to tell me everything that Karen and her type didn't understand about marijuana's bad rap. He probably worried about what I thought of him and wanted to correct the record. He wanted to test my knowledge of the greenhouse. I didn't give him a chance.

"Oh, I'm supposed to ask you about last month's child support. There, I asked you. But you know that'll be first on her list of things to talk about when you pick her up. You might want to think about that." I lowered my voice to just above a whisper. "I wouldn't tell her about your little thing on the side. Dope, I mean. Not Hope."

Bill stared down at me. His morning breath made little white steam clouds. I just stood there on the stoop and waited for him to work through his options. Eventually, he fumbled around behind the door and produced the car key on its familiar leather fob just as Hope appeared, wrapped in a quilt, orange hair everywhere. Her big white flipper feet paddled through the shag.

"Hey..." she struggled with a yawn. "Cali."

I reached for the key. Bill held on to it.

"Be. Careful." He was fully awake then. The thing he really cared about was suddenly in harm's way. He widened his bloodshot eyes so that I'd pay attention. "Park away from other cars. Watch your speed. That thing'll get away from you in a hurry. Pay attention. Keep the radio off. No texting and driving. The streets are slick. And..."

I yanked. The key came free.

I drove to school. The halls were mostly empty. I was ready for someone to ask me why I wasn't in class. That never happened. Not that administrators didn't see me. They did. Even the new screw saw me. He was bald and wiry, and his uniform pants were too long. Nothing like Damien. He looked at me and then looked away. I think that maybe for the first time, I'd looked like someone who knew what in the hell she was doing.

Mr. Goodnight was sitting at his desk, writing on a notepad. I got to watch him for a few seconds before he looked up. His hand moved smoothly back and forth across the pad but the rest of him was so still, as if he was quietly watching some pale, tentacled creature explore a square of yellow sunlight with a stick.

He stood when he saw me in the doorway. He smiled. His lips parted a little, but he said nothing.

"I'm sorry," I said. "About last time. I didn't mean..."

"Don't apologize." He winced a little. Like remembering my confession caused him a kind of dull pain. "I asked for that. I'm glad you were honest. How are you, Cali?"

"Better," I said. "I think I'm better."

I wasn't there to talk. I knew if we started talking, I'd never want to leave.

And I was all about leaving.

I stepped forward before he could start in on something. I handed him the folded piece of paper I was prepared to leave on his desk in case he was not around. He took it and opened it. I watched those beautiful eyes read the single sentence and then the name: Stacey Moore.

He folded up the paper and slipped it into his pocket. We looked at each other for a long second or two. He nodded.

472

In my memory, Mr. Goodnight reached out and pulled me into him. To this day, whenever I want to, I can feel myself flattening my cheek against his chest. Closing my eyes. Hearing his heart. Breathing him in. A forest at night. His beautiful, pale hands pressing against my shoulder blades. Our bodies expanding and contracting together. Like we were a single person.

I'm not delusional or whatever. It's more like a dream than an actual memory. But it's probably one of the most real things I took with me from St. Charles. That memory of what could have happened. That and the words he gave to me before I left.

"When I was fifteen?" I turned at the door and looked back at him, waiting for him to finish. "I stole lawn ornaments. It was a thing in our neighborhood to decorate your lawn. Little ceramic gnomes. A family of plastic deer. Owls. A flamingo. A couple strands of lights. I put them in the woods behind our house. I never knew why. People replaced them. I stole the replacements."

I just looked at him across the room. I wasn't sure what to say.

"You asked for a secret.," he said. "No one knows that about me, Cali. Just you."

I drove west. I knew exactly where I was going even if I didn't know exactly why. The signs call Calico, California a ghost town, but all the tourists seemed real enough. There were no buckets full of silver sitting around with my name on them. Not that I was expecting any.

There was a restaurant, though. I ordered a burger and watched people and thought about my great- great-grandfather, Woodrow Watts. I wondered what it was that finally snapped inside him and put him on the road. I wondered if my parents hated me as much as Woodrow's wife and kids must have hated him. I imagined Bill picking Karen up at the hospital in the DREME machine. The two of them sitting in the parking lot, lost and fighting.

My cellphone buzzed almost nonstop since Colorado Springs. I decided nothing good would come of answering. But I did text selfies every so often just to calm them down. That was way more than Woodrow Watts ever did. I sent Bill a shot of the Torino idling in front of the Calico Ghost Town sign. Then I moved on.

I first met Jimi outside a grocery store in San Diego. I'd been in town all of ten minutes. He'd locked himself out of his car. I gave him my cellphone so he could call a friend. He's tall and lanky with dirty-blond, shoulder-length hair and a long, simple face. He has a nice mouth and complicated eyes: bluish green with gold flecks.

Jimi was working as a sound technician and playing small gigs with a local band at night. Electric bass. His dad is a long-time construction foreman but was once a roadie for Aerosmith. Jimi's real name is Osbourne. His parents still call him Ozzy. He hates that name. He tolerates Oz. I'm the only one who calls him Jimi. His last name is Hendrix.

After he got back into his car, Jimi invited me to his next gig. His band covered a lot of classics. Zeppelin. Stones. Creedence Clearwater. Joplin. Grateful Dead. Jimi stood in the back shadows behind the drums, his bass slung over his shoulders down to his hips. He didn't move much below the neck. Just, like, his fingers on the strings and his head working the groove.

You'd hardly even know he was there.

That was nearly two years ago. Jimi and I have been together ever since. We live in a tiny house with a tiny

backyard and a little tiny garden. I'm working as an
assistant sound engineer at a recording studio. The walls in
the lobby are decorated with autographed guitars. My boss
is a hardcore music geek named Eric. Eric's sister is
married to one of Eddie Van Halen's oldest friends.
Between Eric and Mr. Hendrix, I'm hearing lots of old
stories and I'm learning tons about the business side of
music. Jimi wants me to enroll at the community college for
a music engineering degree. So it's probably back to school,
once I've saved enough for the tuition.

I haven't had the dream about Taylor Boss since I left
Missouri. Can't say that I'm particularly sad about that.
Nothing about that time seems real to me now. Sometimes
it's good for a shiver and then I just move on.

I did have a dream just last week about Gabriella
Alvarez. Damien was with her. She was showing him how to
look through a telescope that for some reason had been
mounted to the hood of his car. They were both propped up
against the windshield. It was summertime on a warm,
clear night. Gabriella had a high, giggly laugh. I couldn't
figure why they didn't just put the tripod or whatever on
the ground. Then I realized the car was more like a boat.
They were floating through the marsh. Well, it was a marsh,
maybe not the marsh. I didn't see any duck shacks. You
know how dreams are.

I could see through the telescope.

The stars were so dense, they looked like snow.

I never saw Damien again after the night we dropped
off Dr. Boss at the hospital. I'm sure it all looked very
suspicious, dragging him out of the backseat the way we
did. He was out cold. They searched his pockets and found

some pills. I'm pretty sure they had to pump his stomach but it's not like they told me anything.

They asked us what happened. I did the talking. I left out the gun. Guns. They asked us to wait, so we did. We sat in these super uncomfortable chairs in the waiting room. People were hacking and crying and carrying on. Damien and I just sat and watched and waited. We didn't talk.

He reached over and held my hand. I let him. It was about the only thing in that moment that felt right. Someone paged a Dr. Taylor and I felt Damien's hand jolt. He was still out on that marsh. We both were.

The police split us up and asked us questions separately. By the time my interview was over, Damien was gone. The officer drove me home in his squad car. I never saw him again.

Damien's house was the last place I went before I pointed Bill's Torino toward the Missouri border. I pulled into the driveway and sat there for a minute. I thought about going to the door and knocking but decided against it. I didn't know what to say. Not that there wasn't anything to say. There was too much.

I was leaving and there was too much to say.

I got out and walked up to his car. The door was unlocked. I opened it and stretched over to the passenger seat and peeled the hibiscus sticky note off the dash. I opened my purse and pulled out the envelope. I stuck the flower to the front of the envelope and wedged it behind the gearshift where he would be sure to find it.

I made sure to lock the door before I closed it. Telescopes are expensive and ten thousand dollars is still a lot of money.

Shock yourself, Mr. Goodnight had said.

Every now and then I hold down the fort while my boss is off at some meeting. All I really have to do is answer the phone if it rings. I like to turn off the studio lights and queue up Pink Floyd or the Live from Copenhagen cut of Iron Butterfly's "In-A-Gadda-Da-Vida." I flick on all six soundboards and watch the lights pulse across the panels.

I've never had an EKG or whatever. But I imagine that's what my heart looks like on a screen.

I gave Bill a tour when he and Hope finally made the road trip to San Diego to pick up his car. He was relieved to see that it was still in good shape. He made a slow inspection tour all the way around, brushing it with his fingertips like he'd found a long-lost child. Hope went to their motel for a nap and left us to talk. I showed him the studio, then we walked across the street and met Jimi for pizza and beer.

Bill sat across the table and looked at us. We were all talking but between the words, Bill was looking at us, looking at me as if he was trying to figure me out. As if he was trying to recognize me and couldn't.

"So, Karen's finally an HR Director," I said. "Guess that's good news."

Bill narrowed his eyes. He was trying to see if I was being a smart ass.

"For Triple-A Septic? Not what she had in mind, I think."

"It's something," I shrugged. "Still can't really believe she's got a record."

"Lucky she didn't go to jail," said Bill. "She's got Benji to thank for that, I think. A boy needs his mother."

I shook my head.

"Got to be at a higher level than Karen to get jail time. That's strictly Up-Liner stuff."

Bill moved his empty glass around his napkin.

"She wants me to convince you to come back. She thinks you're throwing your life away. She says she has big plans for you. Big dreams. Nothing she hasn't already told you herself. She's frustrated that you're not listening. She thinks you'll listen to me."

Bill took a long look, as if he was working through something. I waited.

"But I'm going to tell her that you seem good, Cali. You seem okay. I think we need to get out of your way and leave you to it. Live your life. That's just my take. I'll tell her anything you want me to."

I found Jimi's hand under the table and squeezed it. In my head I saw colored lights pulsing to the sound of my heart. I saw stars glinting in the dark water beneath tall marsh grasses. I felt the stretch of small, downy wings. I felt a life unfolding. I looked at Bill.

"Tell her this is the dream. Right here. This is the dream."

For Your Consideration

Independent writers and publishers, deprived of the reach and resources of their gold-plated, establishment relations (by a difference that requires astronomical telescopes and laser technology to calculate), live and die by the reviews of their readers, or the lack of such reviews. The same astronomical tools and laser technology is necessary to measure the depth of gratitude the author feels for those who, having now finished this book of stories, are willing to leave a review on Amazon to either encourage other readers or warn them away. It takes just a moment, and you will have made a tremendous, even if incremental, difference in the lives of those who read independently published books and those who write them. Also, Heaven. You'll go to Heaven. Eventually. Thank you.

Reviews at: https://amzn.to/3gPdOeT

Visit Owen Thomas at his author website for information on upcoming books, photos, videos, excerpts, interviews, purchase links and to register for updates: www.OwenThomasLiterary.com.

ABOUT THE AUTHOR

Owen Thomas is a life-long Alaskan and avid reader. He has written five books: *The Lion Trees* (which has garnered over sixteen international book awards, including the Amazon Kindle Book Award, the Eric Hoffer Book Award, the Book and Author Book of the Year, the Beverly Hills International Book Award and, most recently, a finalist in the 2020 Book Excellence Awards); *Mother Blues*, (a novel of music and mystery set in post-Hurricane Harvey Texas); *Message in a Bullet: A Raymond Mackey Mystery*, (the first in a series of detective novels); *Signs of Passing* (a book of interconnected short stories, and winner of fourteen book awards, including the 2014 Pacific Book Awards for Short Fiction, also named one of the 100 Most Notable Books of 2015 by Shelf Unbound Magazine); and *This is the Dream*, (a collection of stories and novellas that explore that perplexing liminal distance between who we are and what we want). Owen divides his time between Alaska, Arizona and Hawaii and maintains an active fiction and photography blog on Facebook, Tumblr and on his author website at www.owenthomasliterary.com.